MAN AND WIFE

Tony Parsons

HARPER

This novel is entirely a work of fiction. The names, characters and incidents portrayed in it are the work of the author's imagination. Any resemblance to actual persons, living or dead, events or localities is entirely coincidental.

Harper
An imprint of HarperCollins*Publishers*
77–85 Fulham Palace Road,
Hammersmith, London W6 8JB

www.harpercollins.co.uk

This paperback edition 2003
1

First published in Great Britain by
HarperCollins*Publishers* 2002

ISBN 978-0-00-785590-2

Extract from *Les Misérables* by Alain Boublil and Claude-Michel Schönberg, English lyrics by Herbert Kretzmer. With kind permission of Alain Boublil Overseas Limited.

Typeset in Garamond 3 by Palimpsest Book Production Limited, Grangemouth, Stirlingshire

Printed in Great Britain by
Clays Ltd, St Ives plc

BY THE SAME AUTHOR

Man and Boy

One For My Baby

The Family Way

Stories We Could Tell

My Favourite Wife

MAN AND WIFE

Tony Parsons is the author of *Man and Boy*, winner of the Book of the Year Prize, and translated into 38 languages. His subsequent novels – *One For My Baby*, *The Family Way*, *Stories We Could Tell* and *My Favourite Wife* – were all bestsellers. He lives in London.

Visit www.AuthorTracker.co.uk for exclusive information on Tony Parsons.

Praise for Tony Parsons

'Memorable and poignant – nobody squeezes more genuine emotion from a scene than Tony Parsons' *Spectator*

'Unashamedly touching . . . funny and well-written'
Telegraph magazine

'Any parent in a similar situation would probably learn more about dealing with extended families by reading this than going to a therapist' *Sunday Express*

'As ever [Tony Parsons] is in impressively depth-charging, straight-talking form. A broadsheet mind with a tabloid tongue, he remains one of the few male writers prepared to look beyond his own navel in search of answers' *GQ*

'Entertaining. Hugely so. Parsons has the skill to grip you by the collar and drag you into the heart of the story'
Manchester Evening News

'As witty and sharp as you would expect from Parsons but it is not at all bitter – rather profoundly moving. It will strike chords with many readers' *Yorkshire Post*

For my father

part one: *the man of her dreams*

The Most Beautiful Girl in the World

My son comes to my wedding.

He's my best man. That's what I tell him. 'You're my best man, Pat.' He looks pleased. He has never been a best man before. Not that he makes a smirking speech about what I got up to with sheep during my wild youth, or tries to get off with the bridesmaid, or even gets to look after the rings. He's only six years old.

So Pat's best man duties are largely ceremonial. But I mean it when I tell him that he is my best man.

He's the best of me, my son, and this special day would feel hollow if he wasn't here.

In a few days' time, when the wedding cake has gone and the new married life has begun, and the world starts getting back to normal, some teacher will ask Pat what he did at the weekend.

'I went to my dad's wedding,' he will say.

And although he doesn't tell me any more than that, I can guess at the knowing laughter that unguarded, innocent remark, endlessly replayed, will cause in the staff room. How they will chuckle. How they will sigh. A sign of the times, my son's teachers will think. Children spending the weekend watching one of their parents get spliced. What a world, eh?

I know that my father would have felt the same way, although the old man wouldn't have found it remotely funny.

Even in his last years, when he was finally becoming resigned to what modern men and women do to their lives, and to the lives of their children, I know that my dad really wouldn't have wanted his grandson to spend his Saturday afternoon watching me get married.

A nice kickabout in the park would have been all the excitement he needed.

But I think they are all wrong – my son's teachers, my father, anyone who thinks that the first time should be considered more special than the last time.

Placing no other above thee . . .

What can be bad about placing no other above thee? How can another try at getting it right ever be wrong? Unless you're Elizabeth Taylor.

As the years pass, and I start to see more of my father staring at me from the mirror, I find myself more often than not in agreement with his views on the lousy modern world.

But you were wrong about this one, Dad.

We all deserve a second chance to find the love we crave, we all warrant another go at our happy ending, one final attempt to turn our life into something from one of those songs you loved so much.

You know.

One of the old songs.

It's a small wedding. Tiny, even. Just a few close friends, what's left of our families – our mothers, our children, her sisters, my dad's brothers, my mum's brothers – and the two of us.

Me, and the most beautiful girl in the world.

And I can't stop looking at her.

Can't take my eyes off that fabulous face.

Can't get over how wonderful she looks today, smiling in the back of our black cab, making our way to that little room on Rosebery Avenue where we are to be married.

I feel like I am seeing Cyd for the very first time. Does every man feel this way? Even grooms with plain brides? Does every man feel that his bride is the most beautiful girl in the world? Probably.

With all my heart, I want the best for her. I want this day to be perfect, and it chews me up because I know that it can never be perfect.

There's no father to stand by her side, and no father to welcome her into a new family.

Our dads were both working men from the old school, strong and gentle and unsentimental, and those tough men from that tough generation had hearts and lungs that proved surprisingly fragile.

Our fathers went years before their time, and I know that we will miss them today, today more than ever.

And there are other reasons why there will be a few clouds hanging over this perfect day.

There will be no church bells for us, no hymns, no doting vicar to join us together, and tell us when we are allowed to kiss. Because no church would have us. Too many miles on the clock, you see. Too much life lived.

I thought that I would regret that too. The lack of the sanctified. I thought that would be a definite damper on the proceedings.

But when she takes my hand, somehow it doesn't matter any more, because I can sense something sacred in the small, secular room with the women in their hats, the men in their suits, the children in what my mum would call their Sunday best.

Everybody smiling, happy for us, white lilies everywhere, their scent filling the air.

There's no place more sacred than this place.

And if anyone is blessed, then we are blessed.

A small wedding. It's what we both wanted. Making official what we have known from very near the start – that we are building a life together.

And to tell the world – the best is yet to come. What could be more hopeful than that? What could be more right? More sacred?

If I am honest, there's a large chunk of me that is relieved to be avoiding the traditional wedding.

I am glad to be skipping so much of it – from the dearly beloved pieties of the church to the mildewed graveyard waiting just beyond the shower of confetti to the multi-generational disco where drunken uncles wave their arms in the air to 'Wake Me Up Before You Go-Go'.

Goodbye to all that.

Just a simple ceremony joining together two complicated lives.

Lives that are not just beginning, lives that already have a history. And you can see the happiest part of those lives, those histories, in the two small children who stand with their grandmothers in the front row of what passes for the congregation.

A solemn little girl in a long yellow dress, primly clutching a bouquet of white flowers to her chest, a child with her mother's wide-set eyes, dark hair and lovely face.

And a slightly younger boy in a bow tie and frilly dress shirt, no jacket – what's he done with his jacket? He was wearing it the last time I looked – who can't match the girl's show of unsmiling formality, can't even get close to it, so he grins shyly and shuffles inside his brand-new shoes, looking as though this is his very first time out of trainers.

Peggy and Pat.

Her daughter and my son.

My beautiful boy.

Pat is holding my mother's hand. And as the registrar asks about the rings, I notice that my boy's face is changing.

The smooth, sweet roundness of the baby and the toddler he once was is dissolving to be replaced by sharper, more angular lines. Time is moving on, slipping by when I wasn't looking, and my boy is starting to look handsome rather than pretty. Growing up, every day.

Cyd smiles at me as though we are the last lovers left alive. And I think – no buts. I have absolutely no reservations about this woman. She's the one. In sorrow and in joy, from this day forward. *She's the one.*

And my spirit lifts because today I feel brand new, as though the good old days are about to finally start. Although there are many things behind us, some of them wretched and sad and painful, there's also so much ahead of us, so much to look forward to, so much yet to come.

I am certain about this woman. I want to spend the rest of my life with her. In sickness and in health. For richer, for poorer. Forsaking all others. *Fine by me. I want her face to be the last thing I see at night and the first thing I see in the morning. I want to watch that face as it changes through the years. I want to know every birthmark on her body, to commit every freckle to memory.* To have and to hold. Until death do us part. *Count me in. Good. Great. Where do I sign up?*

There's just one tiny, tiny pang of doubt . . .

And I force it from my mind, refuse to acknowledge its existence. It doesn't go away. It's a small and distant misgiving, lurking in some secret part of my heart, but I can't deny it's there.

Not so much a cloud over this perfect day, more of a distant rumbling of thunder.

You see, I know that I am in this room for two reasons. Because I love her, certainly. I love my bride. I love my Cyd. But also – how can I put it? – because I want to rebuild my family.

It's not just the husband bit that I want to get right this second time around.

It's also being a father.

To her daughter. To any children we may have together. And to my boy. I want a family for him, too, as well as myself. A family for my boy. For both of us.

A family once more.

I am here for this incredible woman. But I am also here for my son.

Is that okay? Is it forgivable to be here for two reasons? For two people? Is it all right that our love story isn't the full story?

Someone is talking to us so I try to ignore that sound of faraway thunder. The registrar is asking the bride if she promises to love and to cherish.

'I do,' says my wife.

I draw a deeper breath.

And I do, too.

one

My son has a new father.

He doesn't actually call the guy *dad* – come on, he wouldn't do that to me – but I can't kid myself. This guy – Richard, bloody *Richard* – has replaced me in all the ways that matter.

Richard is there when my son eats his breakfast (Coco Pops, right? See, Pat, I still remember the Coco Pops). Richard is there when my boy plays quietly with his Star Wars toys (playing quietly because Richard is more of a Harry Potter man, not so big on light sabres and Death Stars and Jedi Knights).

And Richard is there at night sharing a bed with the mother of my son.

Let's not forget that bit.

'So how's it going?'

I asked my son the same question every Sunday as we took our places in the burger bar, our Happy Meals between us, among all the dads and little boys and girls just like us. You know. The weekend families.

'Good,' he said.

That was all. Good? Just good? And it's funny, and a little bit sad, because when he was smaller, you couldn't stop him talking, he was full of questions.

How do I know when to wake up? Where do I go when I am asleep? How do I grow up? Why doesn't the sky stop? *You're* not going to die, are you? Obviously *we're* not going to die, right? And is a Death Star bigger than the moon?

You couldn't shut him up in the old days.

'School's okay? You get on with everyone in your class? You're feeling all right about things, darling?'

I never asked him about Richard.

'Good,' he repeated, poker-faced, drawing an impenetrable veil over his life with one little word. He picked up his burger in both hands, like a baby squirrel with a taste for junk food. And I watched him, realising that he was wearing clothes that I had never seen before. What family day out were they from? Why hadn't I noticed them before? So many questions that I couldn't even bring myself to ask him.

'You like your teacher?'

He nodded, biting off more Happy Meal than he could possibly chew, and making further comment impossible. We went through this routine every weekend. We had been doing it for two years, ever since he went to live with his mother.

I asked him about school, friends and home.

He gave me his name, rank and serial number.

He was still recognisably the sweet-natured child with dirty-blond hair who once rode a bike called Bluebell. The same boy who was so cute at two years of age that people stopped to stare at him in the street, who insisted his name was Luke Skywalker when he was three, who tried to be very brave when his mother left me when he was four and everything began to fall apart.

Still my Pat.

But he didn't open his heart to me any more – what frightened him, the things that made him happy, the stuff of his dreams, the parts of the world that puzzled him – why *doesn't* the sky stop? – in the same way he did when he was small.

So much changes when they start school. Everything, in fact. You lose them then and you never really get them back. But it was more than school.

There was a distance between us that I couldn't seem to bridge, no matter how hard I tried. There were walls dividing us, and they were the walls of his new home. Not so new now. Another few years and he would have spent most of his life living away from me.

'What's your Happy Meal taste like, Pat?'

He rolled his eyes. 'You ever have a Happy Meal?'

'I've got one right here.'

'Well, that's exactly what it tastes like.'

My son at seven years old. Sometimes I got on his nerves. I could tell.

We still had a good time together. When I gave up my inept interrogations, we had fun. The way we always had. Pat was a pleasure to be around – easy-going, sunny-natured, game for a laugh. But it was different now that our time together was rationed. This time together had a sheen of desperation because I couldn't stand to see him disappointed or sad. Any minor unhappiness, no matter how temporary, gnawed at me in a way that it really hadn't when we still shared a home.

These Sundays were the high point of my week. Although things were going well for me at work now, nothing was as good as this day, this whole glorious day, that I got to spend with my boy.

We didn't do anything special, just the same things we had always done, bouncing merrily between food and football, park and pictures, games arcade and shopping mall. Happily frittering away the hours.

But it felt different from when we lived together because now, at the end of all these ordinary, perfect days, we had to say goodbye.

The clock was always running.

There was a time in our lives, in that brief period when I was looking after him alone, when his mother was in Japan, trying to reclaim the life she had given up for me, when I felt Pat and I were unique.

I stood at the gates of his primary school, separate from all the mothers waiting for their children, and I felt that there was nobody like us in the world. I couldn't feel like that any more. The world was full of people like us. Even McDonald's was full of people like us.

On Sundays the burger bar was always packed with one-day dads making stilted small talk with their children, these wary kids who came in all sizes, from lovely little nippers to pierced, surly teens, all those fathers making the best of it, looking from their child or children to their watch, trying to make up for all the lost time and never quite succeeding.

We avoided eye contact, me and all the other one-day dads. But there was a kind of shy fraternity that existed between us. When there were unpleasant scenes – tears or raised voices, the Egg McMuffin abruptly and angrily abandoned, an overwrought demand to get Mummy on the mobile phone immediately – we felt for each other, me and all the other Sunday dads.

As Pat and I lapsed into silence, I noticed that there was one of them at the next table being tortured by his daughter, a saucer-eyed ten-year-old in an Alice band.

'*Je suis végétarienne*,' said the little girl, pushing away her untouched Big Mac.

Her father's mouth dropped open.

'How can you possibly be vegetarian, Louise? You weren't a vegetarian last week. You had that hot dog before *The Lion King*, remember?'

'*Je ne mange pas de viande*,' insisted the little girl. '*Je ne mange pas de boeuf*.'

'I don't believe it,' said her father. 'Why didn't you tell me you've turned vegetarian? Why didn't your mother?'

Poor bastard, I thought, and I saw the man's love life flash before my eyes.

Probably a corporate romance, the woman in from the Paris office, trailing clouds of charm, Chanel and an accent that would make any grown man melt. Then a whirlwind courtship, seeing the sights of two cities, the time of moonlight and Interflora, an early pregnancy, probably unplanned, and then the woman buying a one-way ticket back to the old country when the sex wore off.

'*Je suis allergique aux Happy Meals*,' said the girl.

Pat had stopped eating. His mouth hung open with wonder. He was clearly impressed by the girl at the next table. Everything bigger children said or did impressed him. But this was something new. This was possibly the first time he had seen a bigger child speaking a foreign language outside the movies or TV.

'Japanese?' he whispered to me. He assumed all foreign languages were Japanese. His mother was fluent.

'French,' I whispered back.

He smiled at the little girl in the Alice band. She stared straight through him.

'Why is she talking French then?' he asked me, suddenly perking up. And it was just like the old days – Pat bringing me one of life's little puzzles to unravel. I leapt upon it with gratitude.

'That little girl is French,' I said, keeping my voice down. I looked at the poor bastard who was her father. 'Half French.'

Pat widened his eyes. 'That's a long way to come. French is a long way.'

'France, you mean. France is not as far as you think, darling.'

'It is, though. You're wrong. France is as far as I think. Maybe even further.'

'No, it's not. France – well, Paris – is just three hours in the train from London.'

'What train?'

'A special train. A very fast train that runs from London to Paris. The Eurostar. It does the journey in just three hours. It goes through a tunnel under the sea.'

My son pulled a doubtful face. '*Under* the sea?'

'That's right.'

'No, I don't think so. Bernie Cooper went to French in the summer.' Bernie Cooper – always addressed by his full name – was Pat's best friend. The first best friend of his life. The best friend he would remember forever. Pat always quoted Bernie with all the fervour of a Red Guard citing the thoughts of Chairman Mao at the height of the Cultural Revolution. 'Bernie Cooper went to the seaside in French. *France*. They got a Jumbo. So you can't get a train to France. Bernie Cooper said.'

'Bernie and his family must have gone to the south of France. Paris is a lot closer. I promise you, darling. You can get there from London in three hours. We'll go there one day. You and me. Paris is a beautiful city.'

'When will we go?'

'When you're a big boy.'

He looked at me shrewdly. 'But I'm a big boy now.'

And I thought to myself – that's right. You're a big boy now. That baby I held in my arms has gone and I will never get him back.

I glanced at my watch. It was still early. They were still serving McBreakfasts in here.

'Come on,' I said. 'Let me help you with your coat. We're going. Don't forget your football and your mittens.'

He looked out the window at the rain-lashed streets of north London.

'Are we going to the park?'

'We're going to Paris.'

We could make it. I had worked it out. You don't think I would just rush off to Paris with him, do you? No, we could do it. Not comfortably, but just about. Three hours to Paris on Eurostar, an afternoon wandering around the sights, and then – whoosh – back home for bedtime. Pat's bedtime not mine.

Nobody would know we had gone to Paris – that is, his mother would not know – until we were safely back in London. All we needed were our passports.

Luck was with us. At my place, Cyd and Peggy were not around. At Pat's place, the only sign of life was Uli, the dreamy German au pair. So I didn't have to explain to my wife why I needed my passport for a kickabout on Primrose Hill and I didn't have to explain to my ex-wife why I needed Pat's passport to play Sega Rally in Funland.

It was a quick run down to Waterloo and soon Pat had his face pressed against the glass as the Eurostar pulled out of the station, his breath making mist on the glass.

He looked at me slyly.

'We're having an adventure, aren't we? This is an adventure, isn't it?'

'A big adventure.'

'What a laugh,' smiled my son.

Three little words, and I will never forget them. And when he said those three little words, it was worth it. Whatever happened next, it was all worth it. Paris for the day. Just the two of us.

What a laugh.

My son lived in one of those new kind of families. What do they call them?

A blended family.

As though people can be endlessly mixed and matched. Ground up and seamless. A blended family. Just like coffee beans. But it's not so easy with men and women and children.

They only lived a mile or so away from us, but there were things about their life together that were forever hidden from me.

I could guess at what happened between Gina and our son – I could see her still, washing his hair, reading him *Where the Wild Things Are*, placing a bowl of green pasta before him, hugging him so fiercely that you couldn't tell where she ended and where he began.

But I had no real idea what went on between Richard and Pat, this man in his middle thirties who I didn't know at all, and this seven-year-old child whose skin, whose voice, whose face were more familiar to me than my own.

Did Richard kiss my son good night? I didn't ask. Because I really didn't know what would hurt me more. The warmth, the closeness, the caring that a good-night kiss would indicate. Or the cold distance implicit in the absence of a kiss.

Richard was not a bad guy. Even I could see that. My ex-wife wouldn't be married to him if he was any kind of child-hater. I knew, even in my bleakest moments, that there were worse step-parents than Richard. Not that anyone says step-parent any more. Too loaded with meaning.

Pat and I had both learned to call Richard a *partner* – as though he were involved in an exciting business venture with the mother of my son, or possibly a game of bridge.

The thing that drove me nuts about Richard, that had me raising my voice on the phone to my ex-wife – something I would really have preferred to avoid – was that Richard just didn't seem to understand that my son was one in a million, ten million, a billion.

Richard thought Pat needed improving. And my son didn't need improving. He was special already.

Richard wanted my son to love Harry Potter, wooden toys and tofu. Or was it lentils? But my son loved Star Wars, plastic light sabres and pizza. My son stubbornly remained true to the cause of mindless violence and carbohydrates with extra cheese.

At first Richard was happy to play along, back in the days when he was still trying to gain entry into Gina's pants. Before he was finally granted a multiple-entry visa into those pants, before he married my ex-wife, my son's mum, Richard used to love pretending to be Han Solo to my son's Luke Skywalker. Loved it. Or at least acted like he did.

And quite frankly my son would warm to Saddam Hussein if he pretended to be Han Solo for five minutes.

Now Richard was no longer trying, or he was trying in a different way. He didn't want to be my son's friend any more. He wanted to be more like a parent. Improving my boy.

As though improving someone is any kind of substitute for loving them.

You make all those promises to your spouse and then one day you get some lawyer to prove that they no longer mean a thing. Gina was part of my past now. But you don't get divorced from your children. And you can never break free of your vows to them.

That's what Paris was all about.

I was trying to keep my unspoken promises to my son. To still matter to him. To always matter. I was trying to convince him, or perhaps myself, that nothing fundamental had changed between us. Because I missed my boy.

When he was not there, that's when I really knew how much I loved him. Loved him so much that it physically hurt, loved him so much that I was afraid some nameless harm would come to him, and afraid that he was going to forget me, that I would drift to the very edge of his life, and my love and the missing would all count for nothing.

I was terrified that I might turn up for one of my access visits and he wouldn't be able to quite place me. Ridiculous? Maybe. But we spent most of the week apart. Most of the weekends, too, even with our legally approved trysts. I was never there to tuck him in, to read him a story, to dry his eyes when he cried, to calm his fears, to just be the man who came home to him at night. The way my old man was there for me.

Can you be a proper dad in days like these? Can you be a real father to your child if you are never around?

Already, just two years after he went to live with his mother, I was on the fast track to becoming a distant figure. Not a real dad at all. A weekend dad, at the very best. As much of a pretend dad as Richard. That was not the kind of father I wanted to be. I needed my son to be a part of my life.

My new life.

Cyd and I had been married for just over a year.

It had been a great year. The best year ever. She had become my closest friend and she hadn't stopped being my lover. We were at that stage when you feel both familiarity and excitement, when things are getting better and nothing has worn off, that happy period when you divide your time between building a home and fucking each other's brains out. Shopping at Habitat and Heal's followed by wild, athletic sex. You can't beat it.

Cyd was the nicest person I knew, and she also drove me crazy. The only reason I went to the gym was because I didn't want her to stop fancying me. My sit-ups were all for her. I hoped it would always be that way. But if you have been badly burned once, you can never be totally sure. After you have taken a spin through the divorce courts, forever seems like a very long time. And maybe that's a positive thing. Maybe that stops you from treating the love of your life like a piece of self-assembly furniture.

It wasn't like that with my son. I planned to stay with Cyd

until we were both old and grey. But you never know, do you? In my experience, relationships come and go but being a parent lasts a lifetime. What's the expression?

Till death do us part.

There were lots of things we were planning to do in Paris.

Pat wanted to go up the Eiffel Tower, but the queues were dauntingly long, so we decided to save it for some other time. I contemplated taking him to the Louvre, but I decided he was too small and the museum was too big.

So what we did was take a bateau-mouche down the Seine and then grabbed a couple of croque-monsieurs in a little café in the Marais.

'French cheese on toast,' Pat said, tucking in. 'This is really delicious.'

After that we went for a kickabout in the Jardin du Luxembourg, booting his plastic football around under the chestnut trees while young couples necked on park benches and pampered dogs sauntered around with their noses in the air and everybody smoked as though it was the fifties.

Apart from the boat trip down the river, and the fancy cheese on toast, it wasn't so different from our usual Sundays. But it felt special, and I think our hearts were lighter than they ever were in London. It was one of those days that you feel like putting in a bottle, so you can keep it for the rest of your life and nobody can ever take it away from you.

It all went well until we got back to the Gare du Nord. As soon as we went up to the departure gates on the station's first floor, you could see something was wrong. There were people everywhere. Backpackers, businessmen, groups of tourists. All stranded because there was something on the line. Leaves or refugees? Nobody knew.

But there were no trains coming in or leaving.

That's when I knew we were in trouble.

I was glad that my own father was not alive to see all of this. The shock would have killed him, I swear to God it would.

But I knew in my heart that I didn't spend endless hours with my own dad. My old man never took me to Paris for the day.

I may have grown up with my dad under the same roof, but he worked six days a week, long hours, and then he came home speechless with exhaustion, sitting there eating his cooked dinner in front of the TV, reflecting silently on the latest dance routine from Pan's People.

My old man was separated from me by the need for work and money. I was separated from Pat by divorce and residency orders. Was it really so different? Yes, it was different.

Even if I rarely saw my father – and perhaps I am kidding myself, but even now I believe I can recall every kickabout I ever had with my old man, every football match we went to together, every trip to the cinema – my father was never afraid that someone would steal me away, that I might start calling some other man *dad*.

He went through a lot in his life, from a dirt-poor childhood to world war to terminal cancer. But he never had to go through that.

Wait until your father gets home, I was told by my mum, again and again.

And so I did. I spent my childhood waiting for my father to come home. And perhaps Pat waited too. But he knew in his heart that his father was never coming home. Not any more.

My old man thought that the worst thing in this world you can be is a bad parent to your child. But there's something almost as bad as that, Dad.

You can be a stranger.

And of course I wanted my son to have a happy life. I wanted him to be a good boy for his mother, and to get on okay with her new husband, and to do well at school, and to realise how lucky he was to have found a friend like Bernie Cooper.

But I also wanted my son to love me the way he used to love me.

Let's not forget that bit.

two

By the time the black cab finally crawled into the street where he lived, Pat was fast asleep.

I rarely saw my son sleeping these days, and I was surprised how it seemed to wipe away the years. Awake, his sweet face seemed permanently on guard, glazed with the heart-tugging vigilance of a child who has had to find a place between his divorced parents. Awake, he was sharp-eyed and wary, constantly negotiating the minefield between a mother and father who at some point in his short life had grown sick of living under the same roof. But, asleep, he was round-faced and defenceless again, his flimsy shields all gone. Not a care in the world.

The lights in his home were blazing. And they were all out on the little pathway, lit up by the security light, waiting for our return.

Gina, my ex-wife, that face I had once fallen in love with now pinched with fury.

And Richard, her Clark Kent lookalike, gym-toned and bespectacled, every inch the smug second husband, offering comfort and support.

Even Uli the au pair was standing watch, her arms folded across her chest like a junior fishwife.

Only the enormous policeman who was with them looked vaguely sympathetic. Perhaps he was a Sunday dad, too.

Gina marched down the path to meet us as I paid the driver. I pushed open the cab door and gently scooped my son up in my arms. He was getting heavier by the week. Then

Gina was taking him away, looking at me as though we had never met.

'Are you clinically insane?'

'The train –'

'Are you completely mad? Or do you do these things to hurt me?'

'I called as soon as I knew we weren't going to make it home by bedtime.'

It was true. I had called them on a borrowed mobile from the Gare du Nord. Gina had been a bit hysterical to discover we were stranded in a foreign country. Lucky I had to cut it short.

'Paris. Bloody Paris. Without even asking me. Without even thinking.'

'Sorry, Gina. I really am.'

'"Sorry, Gina,"' she parroted. '"So sorry, Gina."'

I might have guessed she was going to start the parrot routine. If you have been married to someone, then you know exactly how they argue. It's like two boxers who have fought each other before. Ali and Frazier. Duran and Sugar Ray. Me and Gina. You know each other too well.

She did this when our marriage was starting to fall apart – repeating my words, holding them up and finding them wanting, throwing them back at me, along with any household items that were lying around. Making my apologies, alibis and excuses all seem empty and feeble. Below the belt, I always thought.

We actually didn't fight all that often. It wasn't that kind of marriage. Not until the very end. Although you would never guess that now.

'We were worried sick. You were meant to be taking him to the park, not dragging him halfway round Europe.'

Halfway round Europe? That was a bit rich. But then wanton exaggeration was another feature of Gina's fighting style.

I couldn't help remembering that this was a woman who had travelled to Japan alone when she was a teenager and lived there for a year. Now that's halfway round the world. And she loved it. And she would have gone back.

If she hadn't met me.

If she hadn't got pregnant.

If she hadn't given up Japan for her boys.

For Pat and me. We used to be her boys. Both of us. It was a long time ago.

'It was only Paris, Gina,' I said, knowing it would infuriate her, and unable to restrain myself. We knew each other far too well to argue in a civilised manner. 'It's just like going down the road. Paris is practically next door.'

'Only Paris? He's seven years old. He has to go to school in the morning. And you say it's only Paris? We phoned the police. I was ringing round the hospitals.'

'I called you, didn't I?'

'In the end. When you had no choice. When you knew you weren't going to get away with it.' She hefted Pat in her arms. 'What were you thinking of, Harry? What goes on in your head? Is there anything in there at all?'

How could she possibly understand what went on in my head? She had him every day. And I had him for one lousy day a week.

She was carrying Pat up the garden path now. I trailed behind her, avoiding eye contact with her husband and the au pair and the enormous cop. And what was that cop doing here anyway? It was almost as if someone had reported a possible kidnapping. What kind of nut job would do a thing like that?

'Look, Gina, I really am sorry you were so worried.' And it was true. I felt terrible that she had been phoning the hospitals, the police, thinking the worst. I could imagine how that felt. 'It won't happen again. Next Sunday I'll –'

'I'll have to think about next Sunday.'

That stopped me in my tracks.

'What does that mean? I can still see him next Sunday, can't I?'

She didn't answer. She was finished with me. Totally finished with me.

Tracked by her husband and the hired help, Gina carried our

son across the threshold of her home, into that place where I could never follow.

Pat yawned, stretched, almost woke up. In a voice so soft and gentle that it did something to my insides, Gina told him to go back to sleep. Then Richard was between us, giving me an oh-how-could-you? look. Slowly shaking his head, and with this maddening little smile, he closed the door in my face.

I reached for the door bell.

I just had to get this straight about Sunday.

And that's when I felt the cop's hand on my shoulder.

Once I was the man of her dreams.

Not just the man who looked after her kid on Sundays. The man of her dreams, back in the years when all Gina's dreams were of family.

Gina yearned for family life, ached for it, in the way that is unique to those who come from what were once called broken homes.

Her father had walked out just before Gina started school. He was a musician, a pretty good guitarist, who would never quite make it. Failure was waiting for him, in both the music business and the smashed families that he left in his wake. Glenn – he was Glenn to everyone and dad to no one, especially not his children – gave rock and roll the best years of his life. He gave the women and children he left behind nothing but heartache and sporadic maintenance payments.

Gina and her mother, who had given up a modestly successful modelling career for her spectacularly unsuccessful husband, were just the first of many. There would be more abandoned families like them – women who had been celebrated beauties in the sixties and seventies, and the children who were left bewildered by separation before they could ride a bike.

From her mother Gina got her looks, a perfect symmetry of features that she was always dismissive of, the way only the truly beautiful can be. From Glenn her inheritance was a hunger for a stable family life. A family of her own that nobody could ever take away. She thought she would find it with me because that was exactly where I came from. She thought I was some kind of expert on the traditional set-up of father, mother and child living in a suburban home, untouched by divorce statistics, unshakably nuclear. Until I met Gina, I always thought that my family was embarrassingly ordinary. Gina made us feel exotic – and that was true of my mum and dad, as well as me. This smiling blonde vision came into our world and up our garden path and into our living room, telling us we were special. *Us*.

Our friends all thought that Gina and I were too young for marriage. Gina was a student of Japanese, looking for a way to live her life in Tokyo or Yokohama or Osaka. I was a radio producer, looking for a way into television. And our friends all reckoned it was much too soon for wedding vows and a baby, monogamy and a mortgage. Ten years too soon.

They – the language students who thought the world was waiting for them, and the slightly older cynics at my radio station who thought they had seen it all before – believed that there were planes to catch, lovers to meet, drugs to be taken, music to be heard, adventures to be had, foreign flats to be rented, beaches to be danced on at dawn. And they were right. All of those things were waiting. For them. But we gave them up for each other. Then our son came along. And he was the best thing of all.

Pat was a good, sweet-natured baby, smiling for most of the day and sleeping for most of the night, as beautiful as his mother, ridiculously easy to love. But our life – already married, already parents, and still with a large chunk of our twenties to go – wasn't perfect. Far from it.

It wasn't just a job. Gina had given up a whole other life in Japan for her boys, and sometimes – when the money was tight, when I came home from work too tired to talk, when Pat's brand-new teeth were painfully pushing through his shining pink gums and he could no longer sleep all night – she must have wondered what she was missing. But we had no real regrets. For years it was fine. For years it was what we had been waiting for. Both of us.

A family to replace the one that I had grown up with.

And a family to replace the one that my wife had never known.

Then I spent one night with a colleague from work. One of those pale Irish beauties who seemed a little bit smarter, and a little bit softer, than most of the women I worked with.

And it was madness. Just madness.

Because after Gina found out, we all had to start again.

I sent money every month.

The money was never late. I wanted to send it. I wanted to help bring up my son in any way I could. That was only right and proper. But sometimes I wondered about the money. Was it all being spent on Pat? Really? Every penny? How could I know that none of it was being blown on the guy my ex-wife married? Bloody Richard.

I didn't know. I couldn't know.

And even that was okay, but I felt like the money should give me certain basic human rights. Such as, I should be able to call my son whenever I needed to talk to him. It shouldn't be a problem. It should be normal. And how I missed *normal*. A few days of normality, full board – what a welcome mini-break that would be.

But when I picked up the phone I always found I couldn't dial the number. What if Richard – strange the way I called him by his first name, as if we were actually friends – answered? What then? Small talk? Small talk seemed inadequate for our situation. So words failed me, I replaced the receiver, and I didn't make the call. I stuck to the schedule worked out in advance with Gina, and my only child and I might as well have been on different planets.

But I still felt like the monthly money – which my current wife, I mean my second wife, I mean *my wife* thought was a tad too generous, by the way, what with us wanting to move to a bigger place in a better area – should mean something.

It wasn't as though I was some wayward bastard who didn't want to know, who had already moved on to his new family, who was quite keen to forget all that went before. I was not like one of those scumbags. I was not like Gina's old man. But what can you do?

I'm only his father.

My wife understood me.

My wife. That's how I thought of her. Second wife always sounded plain awful. Like second home – something you get away to at the weekend and during the longer school holidays. Or second car – as if she was a rusty VW Beetle.

Second wife sounded like second-hand, second choice, second best – and Cyd deserved far better than all of that. All that second business wasn't good enough for Cyd, didn't describe her at all. And new wife – that was no good either.

Too much like trophy wife, too much like so-many-years-my-junior wife, too many images of dirty old men running off with their secretaries.

No – my wife. That's her. That's my Cyd.

Like Cyd Charisse. The dancer. The girl in *Singin' in the Rain* who danced with Gene Kelly and never said a word. Because she didn't have to. She had those legs, that face, that flame of pure fire. Gene Kelly looked at Cyd Charisse, and words were not necessary. I knew the feeling.

Cyd understood me. She would even understand about Sunday afternoon in Paris.

Cyd was my wife. That was it. That was all. And this life I was returning to now, it was not new, and it was second to nothing.

This was my marriage.

Before I went into our bedroom I checked on Peggy.

She was out for the count but she had kicked off her duvet and was clutching a nine-inch moulded-plastic doll to her brushed-cotton pyjamas. Peggy was a pale-faced, pretty child with an air of solemnity about her, even when she was what my mum would call *soundo*, meaning fast asleep.

The doll in her tiny fist was a strange-looking creature, cocoa-coloured but with long blonde hair and blue, blue eyes.

Lucy Doll. Marketing slogan – *I Love Lucy Doll*. Made in Japan but aimed at the global market place. I was becoming an expert on this stuff.

There was nothing WASPy about Lucy Doll, nothing remotely Barbie about her. She looked a little like the blonde one in Destiny's Child, or one of those new kind of singers, Anastacia and Alicia Keys and a few more I can't name, who are so racially indeterminate that they look like they could come from anywhere in the world. Lucy Doll. She had fully poseable arms and legs. Peggy was crazy about her. I covered them both up with an official Lucy Doll duvet.

Peggy was Cyd's child from her previous marriage to a handsome waste of space called Jim. This good-looking loser who did one right thing in his life when he helped to make little Peggy. Jim with his weakness for Asian girls. Jim with his weakness for big motorbikes that he kept crashing. He came round to our house now and then to see his daughter, although he was not on a fixed schedule like me with Pat. Peggy's dad turned up more or less when he felt like it.

And his daughter was crazy about him.

The bastard.

I had met Peggy before I met Cyd. Back then Peggy was just the little girl who looked after my son, in those awful months when he was still fragile and frightened after I had split up with his mother. Peggy looked after Pat in his early days at school, spent so much time with him that they sometimes seemed like brother and sister. That bond was fading now that their lives were increasingly separate, now that Pat had Bernie Cooper and Peggy had a best friend of her own sex who also loved Lucy Doll, but Peggy still felt like more than my stepdaughter. It felt like I had watched her grow up.

I left Peggy clutching Lucy Doll and went quietly into our bedroom. Cyd was sleeping on her half of the bed, the sleep of a married woman.

As I got undressed she stirred, came half-awake and sleepily listened to my story about Pat and Paris and broken trains. She took my hands in hers and nodded encouragement. She got it immediately.

'You poor guys. You and Pat will be fine. I promise you, okay? Gina will calm down. She'll see you didn't mean it. So how's the weather in Paris?'

'It was sort of cloudy. And Gina says she has to think about next Sunday.'

'Give her a few days. She's got a right to be mad. But you've got a right to take your boy to Paris. Jump in bed. Come on.'

I slipped between the sheets, feeling an enormous surge of gratitude. What Gina saw as an unthinking, reckless act of neglect Cyd saw as a good idea that went badly wrong. An act of love that missed the train home. She was biased, of course. But I said a prayer of thanks that I was married to this woman.

And I knew it wasn't the wedding band that made her my wife, or the certificate they gave us in that sacred place, or even the promises we had made. It was the fact that she was on my side, that her love and support were there for me, and would always be there.

I talked on in the darkness, feeling the warmth of my wife next to me, trying to reassure myself that this mess could be fixed.

I would call Gina in the morning, I said. I had to get it straight about next Sunday and if I should pick Pat up at the usual time. And I had to apologise for worrying her sick. I hadn't meant to cause all this trouble. We only went to Paris because I didn't want Pat to be like the other kids with their part-time dads. The half-French girl who had turned vegetarian, and the countless millions like her. I wanted Pat to feel he had a real father, who did special things with him, adventures that he would remember forever. Like my dad did with me.

My wife kissed me to cheer me up, and no doubt to shut me up, and then she kissed me some more.

It soon became a different kind of kissing. It became the kind of kissing that has nothing to do with soothing and cuddles and reassurance. The kind of kissing that had started everything.

I'll say this for our marriage – it hadn't changed the quality of the kissing.

Then she was waiting for me, her black hair fanning out across the pillow, her face lit only by the glow of a streetlamp coming through the slats of the blinds. This woman I was still mad about. My wife.

I moved towards her without reaching for the little wooden box in the bedside drawer that contained our family planning.

Then I heard her sigh in the darkness.

'Don't make me go through this every time, Harry. Please, darling. Come on. You already have a kid. Didn't we agree on all that?'

I had been reading a lot about baby hunger recently. It was regularly featured in the 'You and Yours' pages of our Sunday paper. Women desperate to give birth. It was supposed to be all the rage. But my wife didn't have baby hunger. She acted like she had already eaten.

We had discussed having a child of our own, of course. I wanted it now, because it would make us a family. Cyd wanted it one day, because there were other things she had to do first. Work things. Business things. We both had a vision of a happy life. But no matter how much I loved my wife's adorable bum, I couldn't kid myself that they were the same vision.

So I reached for the little box of condoms, wondering what she meant about already having a kid. Did she mean Pat? Or Peggy? Or whichever one I happened to be with at the time?

That was the trouble with being a guy like me. It got complicated. All these parts of your life that never seemed to fit together. Sometimes you couldn't even recognise your own family.

But after we made love I slept facing the same way as my wife, our bodies tucked tight together, my right arm lightly curled around her waist.

And for all those sweet hours that we slept like that, making spoons and dreaming, she was the only one for me, and it wasn't complicated at all.

three

'You can't make an omelette by keeping your dick in your trousers,' Marty Mann told me. 'That's the trouble with you, Harry. You're a born romantic. You're going to get your foolish heart broken. You're going to get butt-fucked by fate. What other way can it end?'

We were sitting in his well-appointed office at Mad Mann Productions, talking about work. Only work. But Marty was one of those go-getting, self-made businessmen who always made work sound like something else. Like the rougher end of jailhouse sex, in fact.

Marty was always promising male, middle-aged commissioning editors that he would 'make you my bitch'. He didn't get merely excited about the TV programmes he produced, he 'got a boner'. He was never let down in a business deal, he was 'humped and dumped'. He didn't just work hard, he 'fucked like a rattlesnake'.

It made me wonder what his married life was like. After a couple of drinks on a Saturday night, I could imagine him asking his wife if she would consider a co-production deal.

I had known Marty a very long time. Siobhan, his wife of about two years, had once been my kind of girlfriend, of about two hours. Just before my first marriage broke up.

Marty and I had started out together, on late-night talk radio, working the nut shift. I produced, and Marty made sad, lonely people sound wildly entertaining. Then we went into TV together and I thought that our partnership was my meal ticket for life. Right up until the lunch where he sacked me.

We eventually made it up. Because I bounced back with a younger, hotter talk-show host, while Marty lost his bounce altogether. When he had been suitably humbled by the grim realities of zero-rated daytime television, trying to sell jewellery that would make your skin turn green, we found that we could be friends again.

These days we were on the same side of the camera. Mad Mann Productions no longer produced shows featuring the dyed-blonde shock jock who caused so much controversy back in the nineties. Now Marty was a programme maker. He was always on my case because my production company made just one show, *Fish on Friday*. You might have seen it. The one with Eamon Fish, that young Irish comic? Eamon was famous for dating weather girls. It was said he knew more about warm fronts than any man in the country. Marty would never put his faith in one young stand-up comic pretending to be a talk-show host. Marty had a whole raft of programmes.

'*Six Pissed Students in a Flat*,' he said, hitting a button on the remote. One wall of his office was covered with TV screens and every one of them switched to his latest concept. Beautiful young people in minimal clothing raising their voices in rented accommodation. 'It's got the lot – sex, youth, drama, low overheads, pierced nipples. *Six Pissed Students in a Flat*, Harry. The advertisers are weeping with gratitude.'

He hit another button. The screens switched to a weird-angle black-and-white shot of two young men struggling with the owner of a convenience store. 'Ah, this bit is great,' Marty chuckled as the man behind the counter produced a baseball bat and began wildly lashing out. One of the young men pulled out a gun.

'*You've Been Robbed!*' Marty said. 'Hilarious – and sometimes tragic – real-life footage of violent robbery. A, er, savage indictment of, you know, our violent society.' Another button. Footage of Vietnam villages exploding into orange flames, hippies fornicating in the mud at Woodstock, students confronting the National Guard, all given a coating of melancholy by the Kinks singing 'Waterloo Sunset'. '*All Your Yesteryears*. Making the past funky. One for the baby boomers – and their children. Show the spoilt little bastards what they missed.'

Our production companies couldn't have been more different. I worked out of a back room in Soho with a couple of part-timers, Marty had a big office full of staff. I had Eamon Fish on the midnight shift, Marty had *Six Pissed Students in a Flat* on prime time.

'You can't have just one show,' Marty insisted. 'It's no good having all of your eggs in one chicken. And Eamon's not going to be hot forever.'

'But I like working with just one production. That means I can really focus on Eamon. Get the most out of him.'

'What if it all goes wrong? What happens then? You know what TV programmes are like, don't you?'

'Women?'

He slapped his desk. 'Exactly. TV programmes are just like women. You've got to have your chicken in a number of pies. Diversify, dude. You've got to spread your seed.'

Marty had a wife at home who was expecting their second child. Siobhan was a former programme maker who had made the switch to homemaker. She was a smart, beautiful Irish redhead who I sometimes saw at launch parties and screenings but I had no idea if she was happy or not. I couldn't help noticing that Mad Mann contained a greater proportion of attractive young women than you would expect in a production company of this size.

But I listened to Marty. He knew his stuff. And I listened to him because work was increasingly important to me. Not just because I was self-employed now. Not just because the number of bills I had to pay seemed to be growing every year. The real reason I worked so hard was because I was good at it. This was what I did best.

Dealing with commissioning editors, production co-ordinators, and the talent. I could talk to these people, I could get them to do what needed to be done. Tearful make-up girls, surly floor managers, drunken lighting technicians. I had seen it all before. Guests with stage fright, guests who turned up drunk, guests who froze when the red light above the camera came on. That was nothing new. This was my world, and I spent time here because there was nowhere else that I felt so comfortable.

Even if you have just the one show, television demands that you work long days. Early mornings and late nights, script meetings and full rehearsals, too much coffee and not enough daylight. Sometimes I lost sight of why I worked so hard. And then I remembered.

I worked hard for Pat, of course. For Cyd and Peggy too. Also for my mum, now that my dad had gone. And whatever my wife said, I couldn't stop myself feeling that I was also working for my child. Not the little boy who lived with his mother, or the little girl who lived with me. My other child. The one who hadn't been born yet.

A young woman came into Marty's office without knocking. She was one of several slim young redheads who worked at Mad Mann, women who looked a lot like Siobhan did when she was single. This one bent over Marty's CEO-sized desk, rummaging in one of his drawers.

'What's the matter, darling?' Marty smiled. 'Lost your stapler?'

'I need the pilot of *Six Pissed Students in a Flat*. For your Hungarians.'

Marty pulled out a battered-looking VHS and gave it to her.

'We're selling the concept all over,' he told me. 'There's going to be *Six Pissed Chinese Students in a Flat, Six Pissed Polish Students in a Flat*. The world is sporting a stiff one.'

We watched the redhead go.

'We're going for a couple of drinks at the Merry Leper,' Marty said. 'Want to come, Harry? She's got a friend.'

'I've got to get home. There's a bit of a party.'

'Sounds good.'

'Well, it's a party for seven-year-old girls.'

'Some other time then.' Marty saw me to the door of his office.

'Don't forget what I said about keeping your eggs in more than one chicken.'

'I'll remember.'

He embraced me.

'You know the trouble with you, Harry?'

'What's that?'

'You believe in true love.' My old friend smiled sadly. 'That stuff always ends in tears.'

It should have been a happy moment.

The four of us were eating cake. Cyd and me and Peggy and Pat. Our newly blended family, enjoying their pudding. But when Pat had finished wolfing down his cake, my son – at an age when he was highly amused by all bodily functions – accidentally let out a surprisingly resonant belch.

'Ha!' he said, grinning sheepishly. 'Now *that's* funny!'

Peggy daintily dabbed her lips with a napkin. 'No, actually, it's not remotely funny, Pat. It's just disgusting. Isn't it, Mummy?'

Cyd smiled at the pair of them. 'It's just – well, it's not very nice. But I'm sure Pat's not going to do it again.'

'Well, *I* don't find it funny,' said Peggy, who for a little girl could already do a convincing impersonation of minor royalty.

'And I'm sure a big boy like Pat doesn't find it funny,' said Cyd, 'not when he thinks about it.'

My son was devastated.

I knew that the belch had just slipped out, and that he had only drawn attention to it because he was certain it would be a source of general hilarity and rejoicing. And for the first time, but not the last, I was torn. Torn between loyalty to my son and loyalty to my wife.

To be honest, I didn't particularly want him burping and farting and belching around me either – he could save the gas-orientated gags for his leering little friends at school, who would no doubt reward every windy emission with a standing ovation, and tears of helpless mirth, and much thigh-slapping. But when I saw his cheeks burning with humiliation and his eyes filling up with tears, I could feel my blood rising.

He didn't deserve to be shamed. Not for one lousy burp.

'He's only a kid,' I said to Cyd. 'What do you expect? Oscar Wilde? Let him eat his cake in peace, will you?'

Peggy and Cyd stared at me. My wife said nothing, just sort of widened her beautiful eyes in surprise. But her daughter smirked knowingly.

'Well, goodness me, *somebody* got out of sleep the wrong side today. May I please have some more cake, Mummy, please?'

Cyd reached for the cake. It had a little bride and groom on top. Because this was at our wedding reception. We had been married for just under two hours. And although I didn't realise it yet, the honeymoon was over.

When my wife was still my girlfriend, she was wonderful with my son.

Cyd would talk to him about school, ask his expert opinion on how *The Phantom Menace* compared with the first three Star Wars films, wonder if he would like some more ice cream.

He grinned shyly at this tall stranger with the Texan accent, and I could tell he shared his old man's feelings for this woman. He was nuts about her.

Cyd acted like she had known him all his life, this little boy who she didn't actually meet until he was ready to start school. She didn't try to be his mother, because he already had a mother, and she didn't try to be his best friend, because he soon had Bernie Cooper. She didn't force her relationship with Pat – and that's why it worked. It all seemed to come naturally to her. There was genuine warmth and real affection between them, and it was more than I could have hoped for.

Cyd was as easy with Pat as she was with her own daughter, caring and sweet but not afraid to administer some gentle discipline when he got out of hand. Getting out of hand didn't happen very often – Pat was an engaging, even-tempered boy of four when Cyd met him, and any infringements were mostly because he was overexcited about some Star Wars-related game. Bouncing on a sofa while wearing muddy trainers and brandishing his plastic light sabre. These were his most heinous crimes.

And when she talked to my son, this girlfriend who would become my wife, when I heard the fondness in her voice, the warm, casual familiarity that she bestowed on him, I felt almost giddy with happiness and gratitude.

But after we were married, I needed more than that. I knew it wasn't fair, it wasn't fair at all, but this need came from some secret chamber in my heart, and I just couldn't deny it.

From the moment we were pronounced man and wife, I needed her to love him.

I came home to loud music, wild dancing and a house full of three-foot-high females in their party clothes.

Peggy was eight years old today.

The walls of her bedroom were covered in the moody images of the latest hunky, hairless boy bands, papering over the *Pocahontas* posters of a few years ago, and many of her games featured Brucie Doll – Lucy Doll's official, moulded-plastic constant companion.

But at all of Peggy's social gatherings, the sexes were now separated by a strict apartheid. A couple of years ago Pat would have been invited to this party. Not any more.

I picked my way across a living room full of little girls trying to move like Kylie Minogue in her latest video. There was a wrapped present from Hamleys under my arm. Peggy's eyes widened with theatrical glee as I handed it over.

'Happy birthday, darling.'

She tore off the wrapper and gasped with wonder.

'Lucy Doll Ballerina!' she read, hungrily devouring the words on the pink cardboard box. *'You'll love her! Marvel at her elegance! Not suitable for children under three years of age! Small parts may pose a choking hazard! All rights reserved!'* Peggy threw her arms around my neck. 'Thank you, Harry!' She handed the doll back to me. 'Make her dance! Make Lucy Doll dance to Kylie!'

So I jigged around with Lucy Doll Ballerina for a bit. You

couldn't do much with her arms, they either stayed stiffly at her side or had to be raised into a vaguely Fascist salute, but she could do the splits with alarming ease, her plastic pelvis as flexible as any porn star's.

Peggy snatched her back from me to show to one of her little friends.

'Look at this, Agnes,' she said. 'Lucy Doll Ballerina. Small parts may cause choking! *Fantastic*.'

Cyd was in the kitchen with the mothers. I don't know what had happened to the fathers, but they were all somewhere else. My wife was covering a tray of tapas with clingfilm. She ran her own catering business, so our house was always full of food that someone else was going to eat. She came over and kissed me on the mouth. 'Did you get her Ibiza DJ Brucie Doll?'

'Sold out. No more Ibiza DJ Brucie Dolls until next week. So I got her Lucy Doll Ballerina instead.'

'They've *never* got any of the Brucie Doll merchandise in stock,' said one of the mothers. 'It gets right on my tits.'

'Maybe we shouldn't be encouraging the Lucy Doll thing,' I said.

The mothers all stared at me in silence. Most of them were a good few years older than Cyd. My wife became a parent when she was in her middle twenties. Like me. A lot of these mothers had left it until the biological clock was nearing midnight.

'Why on *earth* not?' one of them demanded in the tone of voice that had once frozen an entire boardroom of middle-aged male executives with bollock-shrivelling fear.

'Well,' I said, looking nervously at their disapproving faces. 'Doesn't the whole Lucy–Brucie thing reinforce unhealthy sexual stereotypes?'

'I think Lucy Doll is a great role model,' one of the mothers said.

'Me too,' said another mother. 'She's in a long-term relationship with Brucie Doll.'

'She works,' said yet another. 'She has *fun*. She *travels*. She has lots of *friends*.'

'She's a *musician*, a *dancer*, a *princess*.'

'She lives a very well-rounded and fulfilled life,' said my wife. 'I wish I could be Lucy Doll.'

'But-but,' I stammered, 'doesn't she dress like a bimbo? Just to please men? Isn't she a bit of a tart?'

The silence before the storm.

'A bit of a *tart?*'

'*Lucy Doll?*'

'She's in touch with her sexuality!' they all said at once.

I made my excuses and retreated to my study at the top of the house.

There was something about the mothers that baffled me. They were all well-educated, intelligent women who had grown up reading their Germaine Greer and Naomi Wolf, women who had gone out into the world and made serious money from high-powered careers, often raising their children alone.

But inside their Lucy Doll Playhouses, their little girls pretended to be women who were nothing like them. They cooked, cleaned and fretted about when Ibiza DJ Brucie Doll might deign to come home.

Peggy and her friends, all these children born in the nineties, were confident, self-possessed little girls who spent what felt like every waking hour parodying old-fashioned female virtues. They loved fashion, adored dressing up, knew all about the singers and supermodels of the moment. They had an obsession with shoes that would have shamed Imelda Marcos. For hours on end, they preened, they posed, got lost in the mirror. They constantly practised putting on make-up – seven, eight years old and they were addicted to cosmetics, two years at school and already they put cheap creams and potions on their brand-new, perfect skin. They aspired to be all that their mothers had fled from. They dreamed of being fifties housewives. Perhaps that was why the mothers often seemed on the verge of losing their temper.

My wife had the balance right. She was a great mother, but she also had this business that was really starting to take off. She could make money, make a home, and make it all seem like the most natural thing in the world.

I was so proud of her.

When I ventured back downstairs the mothers had all gone, and their children with them. Cyd and Peggy were plucking party streamers from the carpet.

'Poor Harry,' my wife laughed. 'Did they give you a rough time?'

Peggy looked up and smiled. 'What's wrong with Harry?'

'He's just not used to a world run by women,' my wife said.

It was true. For the first thirty years of my life I had lived in homes where males outnumbered females by two to one. First with my dad, my mum and me, then later with Gina and Pat. Now I was in the minority.

Cyd held out hands that were covered in multi-coloured paper streamers.

'Come on, handsome, dance with your two girls.'

Sometimes my world felt like one of those warnings on a box – the bit about small parts causing choking.

But when Cyd and Peggy and I danced to Kylie Minogue in the remains of the party, burst balloons and coloured streamers underfoot, bits of birthday cake trodden into the parquet floor, then we laughed out loud, laughed with pure, undiluted joy, laughed so much that we could hardly sing along to 'Can't Get You Out of My Head'.

And for once my life seemed as well-rounded and fulfilled as the one lived by Lucy Doll herself.

four

My mother still slept with the lights on.

In the house where she had spent most of her married life, where she was a young wife and mother, the house that had been her home for so long, she attempted to sleep at night with all the bedroom lights blazing.

'I can't seem to nod off, Harry. I lie there with my *Hello!* and Radio 2 on low – next door have got a new baby, did I tell you? She's a little smasher – and as soon as I drop off, I wake up again. Funny, isn't it? Isn't it strange?'

'It's not strange at all, Mum. The reason you can't sleep is because you've got a hundred-watt bulb burning right above your head. It's a sleep deprivation technique. A form of torture.'

'Oh, I don't know about that, love.'

'Of course you can't sleep. You can't sleep because you don't turn your light off. Can't you try sleeping with the light off? Can't you try it just once, Mum? Please?'

'Oh, I couldn't do that,' she said, smoothing my son's golden bell of hair as he sat on the floor between us, consulting the TV listings in the *Radio Times*. 'I couldn't lie there all night in the dark. Not without your dad.'

My father had been dead for two years.

It was already two years since my father lay in that hospital bed, his brain fogged by pain and the killers of pain, the sickness overwhelming him. And I thought that the old man's lung cancer would surely kill both of them. I didn't think that my mother could live without my father. But they were tougher than they looked, women like my mum, those forever wives, the dutiful homemakers whose one act of rebellion was wearing miniskirts for a brief period as the sixties became the seventies. Women like my mum were built to survive anything. Even their hard man husbands. She couldn't sleep without leaving the lights on, it was true. But she could live without him. She had proved that by now.

My parents had seemed like one living organism for so long – Paddy and Elizabeth, who made the long journey from teenage sweethearts to doting grandparents, the grand tour that so few married couples still get to make – and I could never imagine one of them without the other.

I knew that my father couldn't live without my mother. Her going first would have killed him, it would have robbed him of his main reason for living. And I always assumed that she could not survive without him.

I was wrong.

My mother was from the last generation of women who expected to be taken care of by the men they married. She saw nothing strange in letting my dad do the driving, make the money, sit in the big chair, coming back from work and scoffing his dinner – his 'tea' – like a tribal chieftain home from the wars.

But in old age, in widowhood, it turned out that my mum's generation of women had an independent streak that they were never given credit for. All those housewives from the fifties and sixties, all those brides of austerity, the last generation of women who made clothes for their children – inside their sensible pastel-coloured cardigans, they were made of steel.

My mum didn't die. My dad's death didn't kill her. She refused to let his death be her death too.

She saw her friends for coffee and cake, exchanged gossip with a floating social forum known simply as 'the girls on the bus', she knitted chunky jumpers for the neighbour's baby, the little smasher next door – my mum thought that all babies were little smashers – she played Dolly Parton at full volume on her Sony mini stereo system.

'Lovely voice,' she said of Dolly Parton. 'Lovely figure.'

She called her pack of brothers every day – it was almost impossible to reach her on the phone, she was always engaged – she fretted about their jobs, their children, their health.

My mum was living without my father, the man she built her world around. She was living her life without him. That seemed incredible to me. And, I suspected, to her too.

My dad's death had left her maddened with grief. She cried in supermarkets, on the bus, at all the wrong times. She couldn't help herself. She cried until the tears were all gone. But she coped. More than that, she learned to engage with life, to fend for herself, to laugh again.

'I'm not dead yet,' she was fond of pointing out.

Apart from the lights burning all night long – what did she think would happen to her in the darkness? – my mum carried on. Not as normal, because normal was gone now, but in a world that had changed, a world without her beloved Paddy. And she did it because my mother was a woman who didn't just love my father. She loved people. All kinds of people.

The young neighbours and their new baby. The old woman on the other side, my Auntie Ethel, who wasn't really my auntie at all, who was a young wife and mother with my mum, more than half a lifetime ago.

She loved those old friends who met her in the new Starbucks in the high street of the suburban town where she had made a life. And her family. All her brothers, their numbers only now starting to dwindle. The women they married. Their grown-up children, now with children of their own. And then there was me, her only child.

But above and beyond all the rest of us, my mum loved her grandson. Her Pat. My son was the best reason she had for carrying on with my old man gone.

'He's the love of my life, aren't you, gorgeous? He's my little darling.'

My son smiled patiently, reaching for the remote.

There was a kind of genius about my mother, and it was a genius for making you feel loved. Not just because her conversation was peppered with terms of endearment, all these *sweethearts, loves, darlings, beautifuls* and *angels* that seemed second nature to her and to women of her background and generation. She had a way of making you feel as though you were more important than anything else in her world, even if she was only making you a cup of tea, or smoothing your hair, or knitting you something that you would only wear when you saw her.

She was not exactly a merry widow – she spent too many days at the graveyard, and I feared that she would sleep with the lights on forever – but my mum had learned to go on living. My father's clothes were still in the wardrobe, still not ready for the charity shops, but his spirit did not haunt this house.

My mum had finally filled it with her own spirit.

The smell of Old Holborn and Old Spice was gone. There was no longer brown ale sitting on top of the fridge and a bottle of Irish whiskey standing on top of a little chest of drawers that was known as the drinks cabinet. And the music had changed. That was what I noticed most of all. That was how I really knew that my father's ghost had flown.

I walked into the house where I was a boy and I no longer heard Sinatra and Dean Martin and Nat King Cole. There were none of the old songs playing – Sammy Davis Junior moaning 'What Kind of Fool Am I?', Frank during the Capitol years, Tony Bennett's *16 Most Requested Songs*, soundtrack albums that spanned the years between *Oklahoma!* and *West Side Story*.

My mum gave all of my dad's music to me. She had her own records to play.

My mother loved country and western. Songs with stories and tunes, songs that let you know exactly where they stood. Happy songs. Sad songs. Songs for dancing, drinking, mourning the man you had lost. She was wild for all that twangy, tear-stained stuff, although I had no idea if she had always loved it or if Dolly Parton, Tammy Wynette and Patsy Cline were new tastes. It was my old man who was the DJ in this house. MC Paddy Silver and his swinging vinyl. Not any more.

My mother had been dealt two terrible blows in recent years. She lost my father, the man she had loved ever since he came back to her East End home with one of her brothers after they had sparred together at the local boxing club. She lost the man she spent a lifetime loving, that roaring boy, that strong man who learned to be gentle. Lost him to lung cancer, lost him to time.

And although I could hardly stand to admit it to myself, let alone to her, in some crucial way she had also lost her grandson.

It was just not so easy now I was divorced. Now that Pat was living with his mother, and I was not living with either of them, it was not so easy for my son to spend endless hours with his grandmother.

With all my heart, I wished it were different. I wished it was as simple as the old days, when I was still with Gina and my mum saw Pat all the time, or even later, when Gina was trying her luck in Japan, attempting to get her life back, and I was looking after Pat alone, that time when my mum was like a mother to both of us. I wished it was as straightforward as it used to be, because I knew that Pat was the centre of my mum's universe. But it would never be like that again. The centre of the universe had shifted.

That's who gets forgotten in a divorce. The grandparents. These old people who worship the little boys and girls who are produced by their own grown-up, messed-up children, the fallible somehow begetting the perfect. Divorce makes grandparents feel as though all that unconditional love they have to give is suddenly surplus to requirements.

So I made an effort. I did everything to pretend that the centre of the universe was where it had always been. Half of my time with Pat was time spent with my mum. We jumped in my car and drove out to Essex, on roads that I had known all my life.

I remembered those roads when I was a child coming back from my nan's house in the East End, asleep on the back seat of my old man's Morris Minor. And I knew those roads as a teenager, zipping around in my Escort trying to impress the big-haired girl by my side. And later still, on those roads as a young husband and father, driving my little family out to see my proud parents. And much later, driving on those roads in my little two-seater sports car, Pat by my side, struggling against sleep, missing his mother, not wanting to talk about it.

I knew those roads. I remembered driving on them to see my dad getting sicker, my dad dying, the day of his funeral. All those car rides from London to Essex, from the edge of the city to the edge of the sea, measuring out my life, never imagining what would be coming next, never dreaming.

Now once more it was Pat and me driving out on those Essex roads to see my mum in the house where she slept with the lights on.

Gina gone. My old man gone. Cyd and Peggy not really a part of these rides out to Essex, to this old established part of our lives. My new wife and her child had their lives in London, and we left them there without even having to discuss it.

Growing up, growing old. You expect all of that. But my little family was growing smaller and more fragile. And you are never ready for that.

Pat was comfortable in the house where I grew up. Something wound tight inside him seemed to relax out here. He spent the best part of his childhood in the old house. No parents fighting, crying, going their separate ways. No great upheavals or infidelities or thrown mobile phones out here in the sprawl where the town finally gives way to the countryside. Just Star Wars videos and cups of tea, and going to the fridge without having to ask anyone's permission. Sweet, simple hours spent sitting on the floor listening to familiar voices singing old songs in the back garden. And every moment of those easy days filled with an uncomplicated, unconditional love. First from both of my parents, and now from just my mother. The love remained.

'He's the man of my dreams. Aren't you, gorgeous?'

My son smiled patiently, and wandered off to rummage around upstairs. His oldest toys were out here, many of them too young for him now. A collection of Star Wars videos of course, and plenty of stuff he would no longer watch, wrestling tapes and cartoons from Disney, gathering dust, marking the years. He had a bedroom here, stacks of clothes, and a life. He could have followed the path from television to fridge and back again with his eyes closed.

Everything was easy out here. The stilted conversations we often had over our Sunday Happy Meals were not needed. We slumped in front of the TV, my son and I, while my mum made lunch, which she called dinner, or dinner, which she called tea, or a cup of tea, which she called a nice cup of tea.

She refused our help with used cups, cutlery and dishes. Pat and I had been well trained by the women in our lives, and we did our bit around the houses we lived in without even thinking about it, without being asked.

But my mum would not hear of it. In her own home, she laid down the rules and one rule said that she did the lot. She was the boss who served. Her word was law, her way of doing things was not negotiable. Sometimes I watched her through the little serving hatch, singing a Dolly Parton song, clanging about in the kitchen, and I wanted to hug her in that fierce, unembarrassed way that my son sometimes hugged her.

We loved her, and we loved it out here because we did not have to think about anything. What a relief – to just switch off brains that had been taught to negotiate the marshland of divorce, remarriage and blended families. Can he have a Coke? Can he watch a video? Can he leave the table and does he really have to eat all of those lentils? How good it is to not have to think about what is good for you. But it never lasts.

After our star-crossed trip to Paris, my timekeeping became meticulous. Getting back to London, getting Pat back to his mother, I always allowed for road works on the A127, pile-ups on the M25, Sunday afternoon football in north London. We just couldn't be late again.

'Time to go home, darling,' I told my son. And he gave me a look that you should never see on the face of a seven-year-old. More than anywhere, said the look on my son's face, this place feels like my home.

So what's that other place?

We left my mum just as it was getting dark, and I knew that soon the lights would be on and would stay on all night long, while my mum lay in bed humming Dolly Parton songs to keep her spirits up, and my father's old suits waited in the wardrobe, far too precious to be given away to Oxfam.

five

Gina was waiting for me in the school car park.

She must have come straight from the office because she was in a two-piece business suit, wearing heels and carrying a battered old briefcase. She looked great, like some fashion editor's idea of a working woman, although thinner than I ever remembered her being. My ex-wife was still beautiful, still a woman who turned heads in the street. But she looked more serious than she ever did in her twenties.

'Sorry I'm late, Gina.'

'It's okay. We're both early.' She gave me a peck on the cheek, squeezing my arm. She had forgiven me for Paris, I guess. 'Let's go and see teacher, shall we?'

We went into the main school building and walked down corridors that seemed unchanged from the ones I remembered from all those years ago. Children's paintings on the wall, the aroma of institutional cooking, distant shouts of physical exercise. Echoes and laughter, the smell of disinfectant and dirt. We made our way to the office of the headmistress without having to ask for directions. This was not the first time we had been summoned to our son's school.

Pat's headmistress, Miss Wilkins, was a pale-faced young woman with a white-blonde crop. With her Eminem haircut and funky trainers, she didn't look old enough for the top job, she just about looked old enough to be out of school herself. But promotion came fast around here. Pat's school was ringed by tough estates, and many teachers just couldn't stand the pace.

'Mr and Mrs Silver. Come in.'

'Actually it's Mr Silver and Mrs McRae,' Gina said. 'Thank you.'

Miss Wilkins softened us up with the usual comforting preamble – our son was a lovely boy, such a sweet nature, adored by teachers and children alike. And then came the reason why we were here.

He was completely and totally out of control.

'Pat is never rude or violent,' said Miss Wilkins. 'He's not like some of them. He does everything with a smile.'

'He sounds like Mr Popularity,' I said. I could never stop myself defending him. I always felt the need to put in a good word.

'He would be. If only he could stay in his seat for an entire lesson.'

'He goes walkabout,' Gina said, nervously biting her thumbnail, and for a second it was as if she had been brought here because of her own misbehaviour. 'That's it, isn't it? He just wanders around the class. Chatting to other children. Chatting away while they are trying to do their work.' She looked at me. 'We've been here before. More than once.'

'May I ask you a personal question?' Miss Wilkins said. She may have had a different kind of haircut, but she still sounded like every teacher I ever knew.

'Of course,' said Gina.

A beat.

'Was it a very stressful divorce?'

'Aren't they all?' I said.

We followed Miss Wilkins down the corridor. There was a small square pane of glass in the thick slab of every classroom door. Like the spyhole in a prison cell. The albino head of Miss Wilkins bobbed in front of one of them for a moment and then she stood back, smiling grimly, raising an index finger to her lips. Gina and I peered through the window into our son's classroom.

I spotted him immediately. Even surrounded by thirty other six- and seven-year-olds, some of them with the same shaggy mop top, all of them in the same green sweater that passed for a uniform in these parts, I couldn't miss him.

Pat was in the middle of the class, bent over a drawing, just like all the other children. And I thought about how shiny his hair always looked, like something from a conditioner commercial, even when it needed what my mum would call a good old wash.

On the blackboard the teacher had sketched a cartoon of planet earth, a chalky globe lost in all that black space, the blurry lines of the continents just about recognisable. She was writing something above it. *Our World*, it said.

The children were all drawing intently. Even Pat. And for a moment I could kid myself that everything was all right. There was something moving about the scene. Because of course these inner-city children came from every ethnic group on the planet. But the trouble was the drawing my son was bent over belonged to someone else. He was helping a little girl to colour it in.

'Pat?' the teacher said, turning from the blackboard. 'Excuse me. I've asked you before to stay at your own desk, haven't I?'

He ignored her. Still radiating that rakish charm, peering out shyly from under that golden fringe, he eased between the desks, peering over the shoulders of his classmates, flashing smiles and muttering comments to children who were all concentrating on planet earth.

'Yes,' Gina said, and I didn't need to look at her to know that she was holding back the tears. 'In answer to your question. It was a very stressful divorce.'

We did these things together.

There was no question that only one of us would go to the school, get lectured to by the surprisingly prim punk headmistress, and have to fret about our son all alone.

We were both his parents, no matter where he lived, and nothing could ever change that fact. That was our attitude.

Gina was miles better at all of this stuff than me – not feeling the need to be defensive about Pat, always communicating with the staff, opening up about our personal problems, giving anyone who was vaguely curious a guided tour of our dirty laundry, which was surely getting a bit threadbare and old by now. And I took it to heart a lot more than she did. Or at least I let it depress me more. Because deep down, I also blamed the divorce for Pat's problems at school.

'Cheer up, Harry, he'll grow out of it,' Gina told me over coffee. This is what we did. After being dragged along to the school every few weeks or so we went to a small café on Upper Street. We used to come here in the old days, before we had Pat. Now these mid-morning cappuccinos were the extent of our social life together. 'He's a good kid. Everybody likes him, he's smart. He just has difficulty settling. He finds it hard to settle to things. It's not attention deficiency syndrome, or whatever they call it. It's just a problem settling.'

'Miss Wilkins thinks it's our fault. She thinks we've messed him up. And maybe she's right, Gina.'

'It doesn't matter what Miss bloody Wilkins thinks. Pat's happiness – that's all that matters.'

'But he's not happy, Gina.'

'What do you mean?'

'He hasn't been happy since – you know. Since we split up.'

'Change the record, Harry.'

'I mean it. He's lost that glow he had. Remember that beautiful glow? Listen, I'm not blaming you or Richard.'

'Richard's a very good stepfather.' She always got touchy if I suggested that perhaps divorce had not been an unalloyed blessing in our child's life. 'Pat's lucky to have a stepfather like Richard who cares about his education, who doesn't want him to spend all his time with a light sabre and a football, who wants him to take an interest in museums.'

'And Harry Potter.'

'What's wrong with Harry Potter? Harry Potter's great. All children love Harry Potter.'

'But he has to fit in, the poor little bastard. Pat, I mean. Not Harry Potter. He has to fit in everywhere he goes. Can't you see that? When he's with you and Richard. When he's with me and Cyd. He always has to tread carefully. You can admit that, can't you?'

'I don't know what you're talking about.'

'The only time he's relaxed is with my mum. Children shouldn't have to fit in. Our little drama has given Pat a walk-on part in his own childhood. No child deserves that.'

She didn't want to hear it. I didn't blame her. I would like to have thought that our son's trouble at school was nothing to do with us, and everything to do with the fact that he was a lazy git. But I just couldn't believe it. The reason he had ants in his pants at school was because he wanted to be liked, he needed to be loved. And I knew that had something to do with me and my ex-wife. Maybe it had everything to do with us. How could I not wonder what it would have been like if we had stayed together?

'Do you ever think about the past?'

'How do you mean?'

'Do you ever miss us?' I said, crossing the line between what was acceptable and what was not. 'Just now and again? Just a tiny bit?'

She smiled wearily at me over her abandoned cappuccino. There was no warmth left in either the coffee or her smile.

'Miss us? You mean staying home alone while you were playing the big shot out in the glamorous world of television?'

'No, that wasn't really –'

'You mean going to your launches, and your parties, and your functions and being treated like the invisible woman because I looked after our son, instead of presenting some crappy little TV show?'

'Well, what I was actually –'

'People thinking I was second-rate because I was bringing up a child – when what I was doing was the most important job in the world. Telling people I was a homemaker and some of them actually *smiling*, Harry, some of them actually thinking it was *funny*, that it was a *joke*.'

Not all this again.

'I'll get the bill, shall I?'

'When what was really funny was that I had the kind of degree that these career morons could only dream about. When what was funny was that I was bilingual while most of those cretins hadn't quite mastered English. Miss any of that? No, not really, Harry, not now you come to mention it. And I don't miss sleeping in our bed with our little boy sleeping in the next room while you were out banging one of the office juniors.'

'You know what I mean. Just the lack of complication. That's all. There's no need to drag up all that old –'

'No, I can't say I miss it. And you shouldn't either. You shouldn't miss that old life, because it was built on a lie. I like it now, if you really want to know. That's the difference between you and me. *I like it now.* I like my life with Richard. To me, these are the good old days. And you should be grateful, Harry.'

'Why's that?'

'Because Pat has a stepfather who cares about him deeply. Some step-parents are abusive. Some are violent. Many of them are indifferent.'

'I should be grateful that my son is not being abused? Give me a break, Gina.'

'You should be grateful that Richard is a wonderful, caring man who wants what's best for Pat.'

'Richard tries to change him. He doesn't need changing. He's fine the way he is now.'

'Pat's not perfect, Harry.'

'Me neither.'

'Oh, Harry. We all know that.'

We glared at each other for a few moments and then Gina called for the bill. I knew her well enough not to try to pay it.

We always did this – supported each other, tried to be friends, and then for an encore drove each other nuts. We couldn't seem to stop ourselves. In the end we maddened each other by picking at old wounds, we turned the closeness between us into an infuriating claustrophobia.

I knew that I had angered her today. And that's why the

news she told me as we were walking back to our cars sounded like an act of supreme cruelty and spite.

'None of this matters,' she said. 'The trouble at school. All that tired old crap we keep dragging around the block. None of it matters any more, Harry.'

'What are you talking about?'

'We're going to America.'

I just stared at her.

'I've been meaning to tell you. But it wasn't definite. Not until this week.'

I thought about it for a while. But I didn't understand. Not yet.

'How long would you be gone? I'm not saying taking Pat out of school for a couple of weeks is a bad idea. Might do him some good. A break might be what he needs. It's not as though he's learning very much right now.'

My ex-wife shook her head. She couldn't believe that I could be so slow.

'Come on, Harry.'

And as we stood in that deserted school car park, I finally started to get it. I finally started to understand that my ex-wife could do whatever she liked. What a sucker I had been.

'Hold on. Tell me you mean a vacation, Gina. Tell me you're talking about Disneyland and Florida?'

'I'm talking about leaving London, Harry. And leaving the country. I'm talking about us moving there for good. To live, Harry. Richard and me and Pat. Richard's contract is ending, and he's never really settled here –'

'Richard hasn't settled here? Richard? What about Pat? What about Pat being allowed to fucking settle?'

'Would you like to watch your language? He's seven years old. Children are very adaptable. They get used to anything.'

'But his school is here. And his grandmother is here. And Bernie Cooper is here.'

'Who the hell is – oh, little Bernie. God, Harry, he can make some new friends. It's a work thing, okay? Richard can get a better position in the States.'

'But your job is here. Look at you, Gina. You finally got your life back. Why would you throw that away?'

'My job's not quite what I wanted. I don't even get to use my Japanese. What's the point in working for a Japanese company if I don't even get to use my Japanese? Don't worry, we're not talking about a place in the city. From Connecticut the train into Manhattan only takes –'

'Don't worry? But when would I see him? What about his grandmother?'

'You would see him all the time. The school holidays go on for ages. You could come over. London to New York is nothing. What is it? Six hours?'

'Have you talked to Pat about this? Does he know it's not going to be a quick tour round Minnie Mouse and then back home?'

'Not yet.'

I shook my head, trying to get my breathing under control.

'I can't believe you're thinking of dragging him to the other side of the world,' I said, although that really wasn't true. I could believe it very easily. I began to see that she had always had this thing inside her, this belief that life would be better at the other end of a long-haul flight.

For years Gina had felt this way – when she was single, after we split up. And she still did. In the past Japan was the Promised Land. Now it was America. It was completely in character, this desire to start again on the other side of the world. Oh, I could believe it too easily.

'What's wrong with London? This is where he belongs. His family and friends – Gina, he's *happy* here.'

She lifted her hands, palms raised to the heavens, taking it all in – Miss Wilkins, the trouble at school, the impossibility of our son sitting still for an entire lesson, Paris and the broken Eurostar, life in north London.

'Well, obviously not. It will be a better life over there. For all of us. I don't want Pat's childhood to be like mine – always different homes, always different people around. I want his childhood to be like yours, Harry.' She placed her hand on my arm. 'You have to trust me. I only want what's best for the boy.'

I angrily shook her off.

'You don't want what's best for the boy. You don't even want what's best for yourself. Or that loser dickhead you married.'

'Why don't you watch your mouth?'

'You just want revenge.'

'Believe what you want, Harry. It really doesn't matter to me what you think.'

'You can't do this to me, Gina.'

She was suddenly furious. And I saw again that we could never recreate what had once existed between us. We could be polite, affectionate even, concerned about Pat, but the love we had lost was impossible to duplicate now. Because it was all used up. What do they say? Married for years, divorced forever. That was us. Gina and I were divorced forever.

'You broke the promises – not me, Harry. You fucked around – not me. You were the one who got bored with the marital bed, Harry. Not me.'

She shook her head and laughed. I looked at the face of this familiar stranger. From his mother my son got his Tiffany-blue eyes, his dirty-blond hair, those slightly gappy teeth. She was definitely his mother, and I no longer recognised her.

'And now *you* tell *me* what I can and can't do, Harry? You've got some nerve. I am taking my son out of the country. Start living with it.'

Then she pressed her car key, and the double flash of lights as the central locking came off seemed to glint on her wedding ring.

Not the one she had when she was with me.

The new one.

six

Richard was one of those pumped-up business types that were starting to show up all over town. The bespectacled hunk. The six-pack nerd.

Ten years ago a man like Richard – who does things with other people's money – would have been all spindly legs and narrow shoulders. But you have to be tough to live in the city these days, or look like you are. I didn't know what he was doing – a lot of weights, some cardiovascular stuff, maybe a few boxercise classes – but when I barged into the restaurant where he was having lunch with some business colleagues, for once he looked more like Superman than his mild-mannered alter ego.

Richard was the last one to look up at me. The other three saw me coming. Maybe it was my clothes – the kind of jacket that my mum would call a car coat, old chinos and boots. Pretty much standard uniform for a TV producer, although those clothes stood out in a swanky restaurant where they served hearty Tuscan peasant food for executives on six figures a year.

Richard's companions saw me all right – the young Armani hotshot, the older, silvery geezer and the fat guy – but they were not quite sure what to make of me. I swear that one of them – the fat guy – was about to ask me for another bottle of sparkling mineral water. But when I opened my mouth, he realised I wasn't there to pour the Perrier.

'You're not taking Pat away from me, you bastard,' I said. 'Don't you even think about taking Pat out of the country.'

His dining companions stared from Richard to me and back again, uncertain what to make of this scene. A cuckolded husband? A homosexual love spat? I could see that they didn't know Richard well enough to get it immediately. So he spelled it out for them, never taking his eyes off me.

'This gentleman is the father of my stepson,' Richard explained. 'The poor little bastard.'

And that's when I lost it, lurching across the table, scattering bread rolls and little silver dishes of olive oil, which I am almost certain the peasants don't have in their Tuscan farmhouses. Richard's dining companions recoiled, half rising from their chairs, shrinking from the trouble, but two waiters were on me before I could reach him. They started pulling me away, one of them trapping my arms to my side in a bear hug, the other trying to get a grip on the collar of my car coat.

'You leave us alone,' I said, digging my heels into the sawdust-strewn floorboards, managing to reach out and grab a fistful of linen tablecloth, despite my pinned arms. 'You just leave my son alone, Richard.'

The waiters were too strong for me. Unlike Richard, I hadn't spent hours pumping iron and running on the treadmill. I felt all the strength go out of me as they easily pulled me away. But because I still had hold of the tablecloth, I took it with me, and it all came crashing down: the glasses, the plates of robust pasta dishes, the rough-hewn chunks of bread, the little silver dishes of olive oil.

On to the floor and into their laps.

And Richard was on his feet, angry at last, ready to try out his new biceps and eager to punch my lights out, seafood linguini dripping down the front of his trousers.

'You're not taking my son away just because you can't cut it in this city, Richard.'

'That's for Gina and me to decide.'

'I'm his father, you bastard. And I'll always be his father. You can't change that.'

'One question, Harry.'

'What's that, dickhead?'

I watched him wipe a prawn from his tomato-stained flies.

'What the hell did she ever see in you?'

It was Eamon Fish who first told me about the blended family. Which is ironic, because Eamon was the most single man I knew. The sap was still rising in Eamon, but it hadn't quite reached his head yet.

Although he was a modern boy about town, Eamon was painfully old-fashioned when it came to love, marriage and all of that. Blame it on his Kilcarney background. He had a single man's view of wedlock, simultaneously wary and romantic. But I'll say this for Eamon – he was the only one who warned me about what I was walking into.

'Harry, good man you are,' he called to me across my wedding reception. 'I want a word with you.'

I watched him weave his way through the crowd, nodding and smiling as he went, polite and friendly to people who recognised him, grateful to the ones who didn't. He was holding his champagne flute aloft to prevent spillage, looking even more dishevelled than usual, all shirt tails and floppy fringe and droopy eyelids, but he had those dark Irish good looks that belonged to a young Jack Kennedy, so even in his cups he resembled a rake rather than a slob. He put his arm around me, clinked our glasses.

'Here's to you. And your lovely bride. And your – what do they call it? – blended family.'

'My what?' I was still laughing.

'Your blended family. You know. Your blended family.'

'What's a blended family?'

'You know. It's like *The Brady Bunch*. When a man and a woman put their old families together to make a new family. You know, Harry. A man living with kids that are not his own. A woman becoming a mammy to children she didn't give birth to. A blended family. Like *The Brady Bunch*. And you, Harry. You and *The Brady Bunch*. God bless you, one and all.' He put his face next to mine, and pulled me close. 'Good on you, pal. Here, let's sit for a minute.'

We found a quiet table in the corner and Eamon immediately produced a small cellophane bag from out of a jacket that was still sporting a beat-up carnation. This was new. The Charles was new. When I first met him, he had never taken anything stronger than draught Guinness and a packet of pork scratchings.

I looked anxiously around the room as Eamon carefully tipped a mound of white powder on to the back of our wedding invitation and began chopping out chunky white lines with his black Am Ex.

'Jesus, Eamon. Not in here. You can't take this stuff when there are kids around. At least take it to the toilets. This is not the time or the place.' Then I came out with one of my father's lines, almost as though the old man was speaking through me. 'Moderation in all things, Eamon.'

That gave him a chuckle. He started rolling up a ten-pound note.

'Moderation? You're – what? Thirty-three now? Thirty-two? You're already on your second marriage. You've got a son who doesn't live with you and a stepdaughter who does. So don't lecture me about moderation, Harry. There's nothing moderate about you.'

'There are children around. And my mum. And my Auntie Ethel.'

'Your Auntie Ethel doesn't mind, Harry.' The chopped white lines were deftly hoovered up his nose. 'She was the one who sold it to me.' He held out the rolled-up, slightly damp tenner to me. I shook my head and he put his drugs away. 'Anyway – congratulations to you, mate.'

'Thank you.'

'Just don't ruin it this time.'

'What does that mean?'

'Keep your head out of the clouds and your dick in your trousers.'

'Oh yes, that's one of the traditional wedding vows, isn't it? Church of England, I believe.'

'I mean it. Don't get restless when the fever wears off. Don't start thinking about the grass being greener next door, because it's not. Remember that your knob is attached to you, rather than the other way round.'

We watched Cyd coming towards us across the crowded room. She was smiling, and I don't think I'd ever seen her looking lovelier than at that moment.

'And don't forget how you feel today,' Eamon said. 'That above all. I know what you are like, because all men are the same. We forget what's in our hearts.'

But I wasn't listening to him any more. I thought that the day I needed marital advice from a coked-up comedian would be a black day indeed. I got up to talk to my wife.

'You look happy,' she said.

'I'm better than happy.'

'Wow. Better than happy. Then I hope I don't disappoint you.'

'You could never disappoint me. As long as you do one thing.'

'What's that?'

'Dance with me.'

'You're easy to please.'

So I took her in my arms, feeling that long, slim body in her wedding dress, and as Ella Fitzgerald sang 'Every Time We Say Goodbye' we moved in perfect harmony and, although there were friends and family all around, for as long as the music played my wife's face was all I could see.

The police finally let me go.

Richard and the restaurant both decided not to press charges. So I drove home, thinking about all the things that Cyd and I had talked about before we were married. We had spent hours discussing all the big stuff. It was what our relationship was built on. That and our desire to fuck the arse off each other, of course.

We talked about our parents, those old-fashioned husbands and wives who married young, stayed together all their lives and were parted by death too soon. We talked about our parents, not simply because we loved them, but because that was the kind of marriage we intended to have.

And we talked about our own wrecked relationships – hers worn down by Jim's constant tom-catting, mine blown up by a stupid one-night stand that crawled into the daylight. And we talked about our children, the lives we wanted for them, and our fears that the divorces would leave scars that lasted for a lifetime.

We talked about how my son would fit into our new family, how we would make him feel like a full member, even though he lived with his mother, even if he was only visiting. And we talked about my relationship with Peggy, how I was going to be some kind of father to her, even though she had a dad of her own. When we looked at our lives it sometimes all seemed convoluted and scary, but we thought that being crazy about each other would be enough to get us through. And it was, for a while. Because we loved each other. Because we could talk about anything. Almost anything.

The only thing we kind of edged around was having a child of our own. The baby subject – the biggest subject of all – was put on hold. We blamed work. What else does anyone ever blame?

'I just want to get Food Glorious Food up and running before we start trying for a baby,' Cyd had said. 'It's really important to me, Harry. Please try to understand.'

Cyd's company was named after the Lionel Bart song from *Oliver!* Serving sushi, baked ziti, spring rolls, chicken satay and mini-pizzas all over the West End and the City.

'But you never know with a baby,' I said. 'Sometimes people try for a baby and it takes time. My parents waited years for me.'

'And you were worth waiting for. And our baby will be worth waiting for. She'll be a beautiful baby.'

'Might be another boy.'

'Then he will be a beautiful baby. But this isn't the time. Look, I want a child as much as you do.'

I wondered if that was true.

'Just not now. Just let me get this thing off the ground. One day, okay? Definitely one day. There are things I want to happen first.'

Food Glorious Food was good, and growing really fast. Launches, openings and promotions were all asking Food Glorious Food to feed the faces of their partygoers. It took up a lot of Cyd's time, but this was something she had always dreamed of doing. Her own business. So she rushed from fashionable new hotel to first night, while I queued for condoms in Boots like a teenager from the dawn of time. Anything else, sir? Well, yes – I'd quite like a baby, now you come to mention it. Got any in stock?

'I want to build something of my own,' she said. 'I've never done that in my life. I've always worked for other people in little jobs that didn't mean a thing to me. For most of Peggy's life I've been a waitress. But I've got this thing I'm good at, Harry. This thing I can do really well. I can cook anything, and I'm not afraid of hard work, and I'm smart enough to understand what my clients want. I'm not useless. I've got skills.'

'I know you do, I know you do.'

'I want to make something of my own, make some money, make you and Peggy proud of me.'

'I'm proud of you already.'

'But you understand? Please try to understand. I want this marriage to work. And of course children are one of the things that marriage is all about. But so is understanding each other.'

'I understand.'

And I smiled when I said it, to show her it was true. I understood. At least, I think I did. I wanted her business to do well. I knew it was important to her. I could see Cyd wasn't like the mothers of Peggy's friends who had retired from high-octane careers to have children. My wife was doing it the other way around. And she was at least as smart as those other mothers. Why shouldn't she have it all, too?

But I guessed it wasn't just her catering business that was staving off baby hunger. She had been worn out by Jim, and maybe she just wanted to give our marriage time to grow before adding any more complications to the mix. And in my heart I suspected that there was some other reason, a reason that could never be spoken, that Cyd wanted to defer pregnancy.

I had a hunch that my wife didn't completely believe that I could keep all those wedding vows, that in the end I would turn out to be nothing special. Just another Jim. She didn't want a baby with someone who wouldn't stay with her. Not a second time. And I could understand that. Because I felt the same way.

But as I drove home from the restaurant, I saw that having a baby wouldn't make things more complicated for us. It would make everything a lot simpler. A baby of our own was just what we needed. To hold it all together. To create a home that would find room for all of us. Including Pat.

As I felt the muscles in my upper arms throb, still sore from the grappling techniques of the waiters, I realised we needed a baby to make our blended family into a proper family.

I needed to be a real father again. To Peggy. To the baby that Cyd and I would have together.

And to the boy they wanted to take away.

'Can you give me a hand with this stuff, honey?'

Cyd was getting ready to go out to a gig. The kitchen was full of silver trays covered in clingfilm. Tonight it was antipasti – fat tomatoes stuffed with rice, prosciutto served with figs, thick slices of mozzarella decorated with sprigs of basil, pane alle olive, and tiny pizza marinara the size of compact discs.

So I helped my wife to carry it all out to the car, while she told me about the event. The business was still new enough for her to be excited.

'First night. Off-Shaftesbury Avenue. Some Hollywood star who wants to do theatre. Ibsen, I think. I don't know. Something Scandinavian. We're catering for 200 at the after-show party.'

When her station wagon was loaded with Italian delicacies she slammed it shut and looked at me. And that's when she knew that something was wrong.

'What is it?'

'Gina. And that loser she married. They want to leave the country. Taking Pat with them.'

'For good?'

I nodded. 'Bastards, the pair of them.'

'What's caused all this?'

'Richard. London hasn't worked out for him. He wants to try his luck in New York. As if his little career is the only thing that matters. As if Pat hasn't got any rights.'

She put her arms around me. She knew what this meant.

'How would you feel about Pat coming to live with us?' I said.

'Gina wouldn't agree to it, would she?'

'What if she did? Would it be okay with you?'

'Whatever makes you happy, babe.'

'Thanks.'

I felt a stab of sadness. Because she didn't say that having Pat come to live with us would make *her* equally happy. Of course she didn't say that. How could she? She said that she wouldn't object – and I knew that my wife was a kind-hearted, generous woman, and that she loved me, and that she meant it.

So why wasn't that enough?

Because I wanted him to matter as much to her as he did to me. Even though marriage had changed everything, and being the wife of Pat's dad was very different from being the girlfriend of Pat's dad. But I wanted her to see him with my eyes – how unique he was, how special, how beautiful. I wanted Cyd to look at Pat with the eyes of a parent. But only blood can make you feel like that. And with the best will in the world, you can't fake blood.

'Jesus,' she said, looking at her watch. 'I've got to run. Can we talk about this when I get home?'

'Sure.'

She squeezed my hand, kissed my cheek.

'It'll all work out, babe, I promise you. Got to run now. Don't forget that Jim's picking up Peg.'

How could I forget?

Jim's sporadic outings to see his daughter had taken on the importance of a state visit. Excitement mounted in our house days before the event. I should have been sympathetic to Jim – another part-time dad, separated from his flesh and blood. But I was resentful, bitter and jealous. For all the usual reasons –

that my wife loved him first (definitely) and best (probably). And there were reasons that had nothing to do with my jealous heart.

Jim turned up when he felt like it. He stayed away when it suited him. This should have reduced his stock in our house, but somehow it didn't. He got away with murder. No matter what he did, Peggy was mad about him, was delirious with excitement when he came to call on his Norton.

And from Jim and Peggy I learned that children want to love their parents, want to love them with all their heart.

Even when they don't deserve it.

Jim was late. Very late.

Peggy was perched on the back of a chair by the window, her face pressed against the glass, waiting for the appearance of her father's motorbike.

But Jim wasn't coming. I could sense it, because it had happened before. There would be no night out with Peggy's old man. Not this time.

The phone rang and Peggy rushed to get it. I knelt on the floor, picking up the accessories of Air Pilot Lucy Doll and her high-flying friends. It's so easy for a kid to lose these fiddly bits, and then they go crazy because they can't find them. I carefully replaced a male flight attendant's drinks tray.

Peggy came back into the room with the phone, trying to be brave, sucking in her bottom lip to stop it shaking.

'It's Daddy. He wants to talk to you.'

I took the phone. 'Jim?'

In the background I could hear the music. '*Baby, pull my love pump/ Baby, pull my love pump/ Baby, pull my love pump/ But not so hard next time.*'

'I'm at the dentist,' Jim said, raising his voice above the music. 'I can't make it this time. Bloody shame. Try to explain it to her, will you, Harry? I feel really bad, but I've found something that urgently needs filling.'

I hung up the phone.

Peggy had disappeared.

I found her in her bedroom, hiding under her duvet. On the walls were posters of boy bands and Lucy Doll in all her incarnations, their fixed grins and perfect worlds shining down on one sad little girl.

I stroked her head. 'Your dad will see you next time, darling. You know he loves you.'

'He's got a bad tooth.'

'I know.'

'And it hurts him.'

She sat up and I dried her eyes with an official Lucy Doll tissue, thinking what a great kid she was, and how she deserved better than her feckless father. But then every child in the world deserved a better father than Jim.

'Tell a story, Harry. Not from a book. Tell a story from your head. A real one.'

'A real one?'

'Um.'

'Okay, Peg.' I thought about it for a minute. 'Once upon a time, there was an old man called Geppetto.'

'That's a funny name.'

'And Geppetto found a magical piece of wood that – guess what? – could laugh and cry.'

She gave me a dubious smile.

'Really?'

'Honestly.'

'You're making this up, Harry,' she said, her smile growing.

'I'm not, Peg,' I said, smiling back at her. 'Every single word is true. And from that piece of magic wood – guess what? – Geppetto made Pinocchio.'

'Who was Pinocchio?'

'He was a puppet, Peg. Just this piece of wood that could act like a human. He could laugh and cry and everything. But what he wanted, more than anything in the world, was to be a real dad.'

Did I say dad?

I meant boy.

Pinocchio wanted to be a real boy.

seven

'Only twice in your life do they pronounce you anything,' Eamon said. 'The first is man and wife. The second is dead.'

There was always work. Even when my mother was sleeping with the lights on, and my wife was directing me to the condoms and my son was packing for a new life on the other side of the ocean, there was always work.

Work is far easier than family. It is easier to feel like you are some kind of successful human being at work. Whatever you do, don't try that at home.

'I come from one of those huge Irish families,' Eamon said, moving across a TV studio floor that was set and lit to look like one of those clubs where he honed his stand-up routine. 'Ten kids.'

Whistles from the audience, who were encouraged to act as though they were in some intimate Soho basement, rather than an antiseptic television studio in White City.

'Yeah, I know. Can you believe it? Ten of us. But after the tenth my parents had this great method of contraception. Never failed. Every night before they went to bed, they would spend a couple of hours with me and my brothers and sisters.'

Even when my ex-wife was accusing me of harassing her husband, and talking about restraining orders, when there was really no need because soon I would be restrained by the Atlantic Ocean, there was still work. And when every hour with my son felt like another hour gone – that's what the absent dad feels most acutely, not the *being with*, but the countdown to the *being apart* – there was still work, with its cold crumbs of comfort, with its quick fix of fulfilment, and Eamon and his brilliant career.

'One day my dad came home early and found me mam in bed with the milkman,' Eamon said. 'She was naturally horrified. "Oh God!" she says. "Don't tell the postman!"'

Eamon Fish had come a long way since he first showed up at my door two years ago, dark-eyed and good-looking and scared, fresh off the stand-up circuit, wondering if TV was going to make him famous or swallow him alive. Now he had all the trappings of success – a show that was in its fourth series, three National Television Awards, two undecorated flats in fashionable neighbourhoods (Temple Bar, Dublin and Docklands, London) and – oh yes – a £200-a-day cocaine habit.

Despite coming so far from the green fields of Kilcarney, and despite making such a splash in London, Eamon still enjoyed playing the wide-eyed Irish boy, fresh off the farm and the early Aer Lingus flight from Cork. He clung to the myths of his past life like a drowning man with a wonky lifebelt.

I had produced Eamon's late-night talk show from the start. *Fish on Friday* worked because we played to Eamon's strengths. Despite those two years on the box, he was still a stand-up at heart. He could talk to the guests, banter with all the bit players of the showbiz whirl, but he was never so good as when he was talking to himself.

'Most of the babies in Kilcarney are very beautiful. It's true, I tell you.' The little nervous cough he used for punctuation. Stolen from his hero, Woody Allen, although Eamon had made that cough his own. 'But I was so ugly when I was born that the midwife said, "He's not done yet," and shoved me back in. I don't know. It's so different over here – all the gynaecologists are *men*. What's that about? That's like getting a mechanic who has never owned a car.'

His monologues about the men and women back in his home town of Kilcarney were always the best segments, with the biggest laughs, and when he was most at ease. And he was young enough to still be getting better. After two years in front of the cameras, Eamon had a confidence that wasn't there before. These days Eamon wasn't quite so desperate to be liked, he could relax into his material, knowing that he still had control over his audience. Like other people I had worked with in television, his audience was the one thing in his life that he could actually control.

'I'm thinking of getting back together with my girlfriend. Mem. She's Thai. A dancer. Well, not really a dancer.' Cough. 'More of a stripper.' Cackles all round. The studio audience were eating out of his hand. They laughed even when he wasn't joking. 'Great, great girl. And I look at all these photographs of when we were together – on holiday in Koh Samui, at Christmas in Kilcarney, the lap dance she gave me for my birthday – and it just feels like we should be together. But those photographs are a warped record of our relationship. I know that. Where are all the bad times? We didn't take photos of those. And I wonder why we only take pictures of the good times. Why didn't I take a photograph of Mem when she had cystitis? Her PMT – where's that in the photo album?' Rueful laughter. Mocking catcalls from the girls. 'We broke up because we disagreed about marriage. Single men actually know more about marriage than married men. If we didn't, we would be married too. Personally I think that marriage consists of overestimating the difference between one woman and all the other women. And my ex-girlfriend thinks – oh, Jesus, Jesus.'

Suddenly there was blood everywhere. The blood was over Eamon's hands and face, splashing on the microphone. So much blood that you couldn't see where it was coming from.

The floor manager stared at me, as Eamon reeled backwards, covering his face with his hands, and the audience gasped – shocked, appalled, but laughing a little, wondering if this was all part of the act. I was making *cut-it, cut-it, cut-it* gestures across my throat to the director up in the gallery when it dawned on me that the blood was coming from Eamon's nose.

There was always work. No matter how bad things got at home, there was always that.

Then Eamon's nose almost fell off on live television.

And then there wasn't even work.

Pat didn't talk about moving.

I knew Gina had discussed it with him, had tried to explain why it was happening and what it would mean. She had spoken of Richard's job in Manhattan, the family home in Connecticut – names that were as remote to Pat as Mars and Venus. She had attempted to reassure him that although he wouldn't see me every Sunday, like now, there would be long, long holidays where he could stay with me and see his grandmother and Bernie Cooper and all the things he loved in London. She had told our son that he would be happy.

All that old bullshit.

And in the end – I could imagine his pale face staring at her, giving nothing away, not even his fear – she played her trump card.

When they left London and moved to their new home in Connecticut, surrounded by all those fresh green pastures on the far side of the hill, she would buy him the one thing that he had always wanted.

A dog.

That's what my ex-wife promised her son, that was his compensation for giving up London, his grandmother, his father, his best friend, his life. When he moved to another country, she would buy him a dog. A magical mutt who would make everything all right.

I cursed Gina, and the way her decisions, her choices, could still tear my world apart. After all this time I still wasn't free of her. Fragments of Gina were embedded in every part of my life, like a grenade that had exploded long ago, like the black shards of shrapnel that wormed their way out of my father's body for fifty years. The past never setting you free, long gone and there forever. I would never be free, because she had my son. And now she was planning to take him away.

Only the lawyers could stop her.

When I raised the subject of moving – always with a

breeziness I did not feel – that little face I loved so much seemed to turn into a mask.

'You going to send me a postcard, Pat? You going to send your dad a postcard as soon as you get to America?'

'I'll text you. Or email. Or phone on the telephone, maybe.'

'You don't want to send me a postcard? I like getting postcards. Postcards are great.'

'But I don't know how.'

'Mummy will show you.'

'Will she? Then I might post a card to you. I *might*.'

'The important thing is – come home soon. Come and stay with me. In your holiday. That's what matters. Okay, darling?'

'Okay.'

'And Pat?'

'What?'

'I'll miss you.'

'Miss you too,' he said, and I got down on my knees and held him in my arms, my face buried in his dirty-blond hair, smelling the hot chocolate on his breath, and choked with love for him.

'America will be lovely,' my mum said, and I felt she was trying to cheer up both her grandson and her son. 'New York, New York – my word! So good they named it twice! What a lucky boy.'

'It's over the water,' Pat said, tilting his face to her. 'Like France. In Paris. Only a bit further. You can't get a train, you know. You have to go on the plane.'

'You'll have a lovely time in America, sweetheart.'

And the funny thing about my mum is that she probably meant it. She loved her grandson so much, and with such a purity of love, that what she cared about most was his happiness.

And if she thought that it was barking madness – Gina dragging him around the globe, leaving his friends and school, abandoning his father, and his grandmother, and a life that was finally starting to settle into some kind of routine – then my mum said nothing.

We were at my father's grave.

Both my mother and my son considered a trip to the cemetery to be an ideal way to spend a Sunday afternoon. They were both big grave visitors. I was less keen. I had seen my dad's body in the back room of the funeral director's office, and I had no doubt that the spark that had made him the man he was had flown. I didn't believe that we would find him in the graveyard of the old church on the hill, that church that looked down on the fields where I had roamed with my air rifle as a boy. My father was somewhere else now. But coming to this place didn't make me sad any more.

I can't remember when visiting my father's grave stopped being sad. It was after the first year or so, when we were all starting to be grateful for his life, rather than shattered by his death. Now the visits didn't really feel like acts of mourning. They were more practical in nature – to change the flowers, to wipe the headstone clean, to remove the odd cigarette butt or beer can left by some local punk who was trying to be a man.

These visits were also ceremonial. We came here to remember my dad, to state that he still mattered, that he was still loved. We came to this place because otherwise there was nowhere else to go. Only into memory, and into dreams, and all the photos that were starting to fade.

And there was something else.

With the packing for America already begun, I felt the need to bring my boy to his grandfather's grave today, just as – against all advice – I had felt the need to bring him to see his granddad when the old man was dying in hospital. They worshipped each other, that hard old soldier and that sweet-faced child, and then, as now, I believed I owed it to them both to give them a chance to say goodbye.

Later we went back to my mum's place and she put on her carpet slippers to kick a ball around with Pat in the back garden.

She seemed to be in high spirits, blasting a plastic football in the rose bush, singing snatches of Dolly Parton, claiming against all the evidence that she was Pele, and it was only when her grandson got bored and mooched off to watch a video that the mask slipped.

'He's in a right old pickle,' she said, shaking her head, furiously cleaning her gleaming sink. 'My darling boy is in a right old pickle.'

She was right. And her words made me think about how momentous this move would be, how unimaginably huge in my son's life. Pat leaving London. Pat leaving one half of his parents, his best friend Bernie Cooper, his school, his home, the only life he had ever known. I still couldn't begin to comprehend how all this could happen.

My mum was right. Pat was in a right old pickle. Her boy was in a right old pickle.

It took me quite a while longer to realise that my mother was talking about me.

We sat in my car outside Gina's house, both of us reluctant to go inside.

We sat there for ages – Pat fiddling with the radio, trying to find some Kylie Minogue, and me just staring at him – his uncombed hair, his grass-stained clothes, and all his careless beauty.

Eamon reckoned that I would get him back when he grew up. But I knew by then my son would be someone else, and the child I loved so much would be gone forever. So we sat in the car, silenced by all that was about to be lost. Then lights started coming on in Gina's house, and I knew it was time to go inside.

Usually Pat was handed over like a Cold War hostage at Checkpoint Charlie. I escorted him to the gate, Gina waited at her front door. And the pair of us watched him cross no-man's-land – the garden path – that marked the gap between one world and another.

Tonight was different. Tonight Gina came out and approached the car. I lowered the window, expecting to get an earful for assaulting her husband or getting back late or ruining her life or something. But she smiled at me with what looked a little like the old warmth.

'Come inside for a bit, Harry. Don't look like that. It's okay. Richard's playing golf.'

Pat was suddenly excited, Kylie forgotten. 'Yeah, come inside, Daddy, and you can see my room where I live!'

I had never been inside their home before. Ironic that I should be shown around now that there was a For Sale sign outside. I made half-hearted attempts to cry off, but they both insisted. I admit I was curious. So with my son taking my hand and my ex-wife following me, I was escorted into a real metropolitan home, a temple to urban affluence, lots of light and glass and open space, all polished floors and Asian knick-knacks and tasteful black-and-white photos on the walls.

'Nice place, Gina.'

'The mortgage is a killer. That's one of the reasons . . .'

Her words trailed off. She knew I wasn't interested in their financial woes.

You would never guess that a child lived in this house. Where were the toys, the mess, the clutter? Pat took my hand and dragged me up a flight of stairs. Gina followed us, her arms folded across her chest, still smiling.

Pat's room was the one thing that looked familiar. There were ancient Star Wars toys everywhere – a couple of plastic light sabres, lots of eight-inch action figures, the grubby grey wrecks of the Millennium Falcon and X-Wing fighters that he had played with a few years ago. And there were the books I knew from bedtimes past, books that I had read until he was sleeping – *Where the Wild Things Are*, *The Tiger Who Came to Tea*, *The Snowman*, *The Lion, the Witch and the Wardrobe*, and of course all the Star Wars movie tie-ins and picture books. And there were really old toys – a cracked Speak and Spell, a battered stuffed simian who went by the name of George the Monkey, Pat's one excursion into the comforting world of cuddly toys. There was some new stuff too – a *Phantom Menace* duvet and pillowcases, books from school, Harry Potter paperbacks on his little desk.

It was a bigger room than he had slept in when we were living together, and it was also a lot tidier. Either he had changed his laid-back ways or he was living in a far more disciplined household.

'What do you think of my room, Daddy?'

'I think it's fantastic, darling. I can see that you've got all your stuff here.'

'That's right. I do.'

Gina touched his hair. 'Pat, why don't you go downstairs and watch a video for a bit?'

Our boy looked stunned. 'Can I? Isn't it bedtime yet?'

'This is a special night. Why don't you go and watch the first film?' When Gina talked to Pat about the first film, she meant the first Star Wars film. 'Not all of it – just until the 'droids get taken prisoner, okay?' That was the old deal, wasn't it? That was what she always used to say – *just until the 'droids get taken prisoner*. I had heard that one before. I had even used that one myself. 'Then brush your teeth and put your pyjamas on. I want to talk to your daddy.'

Pat rushed downstairs, not believing his luck, and Gina smiled at me in our son's bedroom.

'Harry,' she said.

'Gina,' I said. She was so thin and pretty. My ex-wife.

'I just wanted to say something to you.'

'Go ahead.'

'I don't know how to put it into words. I guess I just want to tell you – I'm not trying to steal him away from you.'

'That's good.'

'Whatever happens – wherever we are – you'll always be his father. And nothing will ever change that.'

I said nothing. I didn't tell her that I was seeing a lawyer in the morning. I didn't tell her that Pat would be making his way to the departure gate over my dead body. I knew she was trying to be kind. But she wasn't telling me anything that I didn't know already.

'Life can't always be about the past, Harry. We're only thinking of the future, Richard and me. The future of our family. That's what the move is about. I want you to try to understand. We're just thinking about the future. That's what a family does, Harry.' Then she laughed. 'Can I show you something?' Suddenly she looked all anxious, as though we were newly introduced strangers, paralysed by politeness. 'Are you okay for time?'

'I've got all the time in the world, Gina.'

So I followed her from Pat's bedroom to a room one flight up. It was some kind of small study. There was a blue iMac, filing cabinets, a bookcase. A photo of Pat on the desk, two years old, naked and grinning in a paddling pool. Gina's room.

She opened a large flat cardboard box and took out a sheaf of photographs. They were all of Pat. There must have been two dozen of them. Eight by ten, black and white, professional quality.

And they were beautiful.

They must have been taken a couple of months ago, when the summer was holding on, because Pat's hair was still long and shaggy, before he had it cut, and his skin had a light tan. He was bare-chested, happy, glowing with life. He was laughing in most of the photographs, smiling with a shy kind of amusement in the others. They had all been taken on the same sunny afternoon. He was fooling around for the camera in a garden I didn't recognise. Probably Gina's garden. The garden of this house.

And these black-and-white pictures of my son took my breath away. Because the photographer had captured him to perfection.

In the pictures Pat kicked up a glistening sheet of water in a paddling pool, he slid across wet grass, almost exploding with delight, he smashed a plastic football into the garden fence, he rocked with laughter. His eyes, his face, his shy limbs – the photographer hadn't missed a thing. I was stunned that anyone could catch him so absolutely.

'You take these?'

Gina shook her head. 'Only this one,' she said.

And she showed me another picture. Clearly taken on the same day, with the same camera, but not by the same photographer. In the picture Pat was standing still, smiling bashfully at the camera. With him was a young woman – exotic, smiling, one arm draped around my son's bare shoulders. She looked beautiful. And sexy. And nice. All the things that anyone could ever want.

'You never met my friend Kazumi, did you?' Gina said. 'We shared a flat in Tokyo for a year. She's in London now. Trying to make it as a photographer. She fell in love with Pat. As you can see.'

And all at once I wanted to meet her. This photographer who looked at my son and saw with total clarity his gentle, laughing spirit. This stranger who saw through the careful, unsmiling mask he had learned to wear. This woman who could see my son with exactly the same eyes as me.

It was suddenly alive in my head, the thought that was the very beginning of betrayal, the most dangerous thought that a married man could ever have.

She is out there. She exists.

I just haven't met her yet.

eight

I had thought that my lawyer would help me to keep my son. I had assumed he would tell me Gina was planning to break some inviolable law of nature, and that justice wouldn't allow her to get away with it.

And I was dead wrong.

'But parents have certain rights. Don't they?'

'Depends what you mean by parent,' said Nigel Batty. 'There are all kinds of parents, aren't there? Married parents. Unmarried parents. Adoptive parents, step-parents, foster parents. Define parent, Mr Silver.'

'You know what I mean, Nigel. Love-and-marriage parent. Sperm-and-egg parent. A birds-and-bees parent. A biological parent. The old-fashioned kind.'

'Oh, the old-fashioned kind. *That* kind of parent.'

Nigel Batty was a small, pugnacious man with a reputation for fighting for the rights of husbands and fathers who were being shafted in the divorce courts.

When I had first met him, when he had acted for me during my divorce from Gina, and our subsequent scrap over where Pat would live, Nigel's beady eyes had been hidden behind milk-bottle glasses. Laser vision had corrected his myopia and dispensed with the spectacles. But he still squinted out at the world from force of habit, and it made him seem distrustful and wary and hostile, looking for trouble.

I had never really let him off the leash with Gina. He had wanted to make her look like the Whore of Babylon, destroy her in court, and I just didn't have the heart for it. Whatever had happened between us, Gina didn't deserve that kind of fight. And neither did my son.

I had thrown in the towel in the fight for custody, believing that it was the best thing for Pat. I had tried to do the decent thing. And now I felt like the biggest sucker of all time.

Batty had his own reasons for being fanatical about the rights of men. In his past there was an international marriage, twin daughters and a messy divorce. I knew that he never saw his daughters. But for some reason I imagined that he could make it all work out differently for me.

'My wife can't do this, can she? She can't just take my son to live in another country. I mean – *can* she?'

'Is the residential parent preventing contact?'

'Speak English, Nigel, will you?'

He sighed.

'If this move takes place, will your ex-wife stop you from seeing your child?'

'It's the Atlantic Ocean that will stop me seeing my son.'

'But your ex-wife is not intending to deny you access to your child?'

'She's denying me access by moving to another country.'

'I see.'

'Look – what can we do? How can we stop her? I don't care what it takes, Nigel. I don't care what you have to say or do. It's all fine.'

'I hate to say I told you so. But you were the one who wanted to play by Marquess of Queensberry rules.'

'Bottom line, Nigel – can she just take my boy out of the country?'

'Bottom line? Not without your consent.'

'My consent?'

He nodded. 'If she takes your son out of the country without your consent, then she is doing something very naughty.' He smiled nastily. 'We call it abduction.'

'She needs my okay?'

'Exactly.'

'But that's great news! Isn't it? That's terrific news, Nigel. And what can she do if I don't give my consent?'

'She would have to make an application to court for leave to remove the child permanently from jurisdiction.'

'So just by withholding consent, I can't be sure I'd stop her?'

'If you wanted to deny consent, and she wanted to fight, then the court would decide. That's what it comes down to. Would it be difficult for you to visit your child if the move went ahead?'

'Well, it's Connecticut. I can't nip round on a Sunday afternoon, can I?'

'No, but her side would no doubt argue that there are plenty of cheap flights from London to the East Coast. And you're in gainful employment, as I recall.' He glanced at his notes. 'Television producer. Of course. That must be interesting. Anything that I might have seen?'

'I started out on *The Marty Mann Show*. Now I do *Fish on Friday*.'

'Ah, excellent. *Why do Kilcarney girls close their eyes during sex?*' Little Woody Allen cough. He did it very well. '*Because they hate to see a man enjoying himself*. Most amusing.'

Which reminded me that Barry Twist, the show's commissioning editor, had been leaving messages for me to call him all week. The station was suddenly worried about Eamon just as I had other things to worry about. But for the first time it really dawned on me what Marty meant about not keeping all your eggs in one chicken. If Eamon went down, I would go with him.

'If this move to America goes ahead, is your ex-wife denying you reasonable access?'

'How do you mean?'

'Would you ever see your son again?'

'Well, she says I could come over. And see him in the holidays. Or he could come back here. But it's not the same, is it? It's not the same as being in London together. It's not the same as having a life together.' I shook my head. 'I can feel him . . . slipping away.'

'I know the feeling.'

'I don't know how we can explain it to him. Moving to America, I mean.'

'Oh, you can sell a seven-year-old anything. The question is – why should you? Listen, Mr Silver. We can make her seek permission to take the child out of the country. Convince the court that your child would be at risk in some way if the move goes ahead. Letting it go to court would be time-consuming, traumatic and expensive though. I have to warn you – it would also be unpredictable.'

I made an effort not to look at the photograph of two smiling small girls on his desk. Because I knew that Nigel Batty had fought exactly this same fight and lost.

'What happened to me wouldn't necessarily happen to you,' he said, reading my mind. 'Your wife would need to give details of the proposed arrangements for your child. Accommodation, education, health, maintenance, childcare, contact. Then the court would decide if it needed to exercise any of its powers.'

'What are the chances?'

I could hear him breathing in the silence.

'Not good. There's something called the maternal preference factor. Do you understand that term?'

'No.'

'It means that, ninety-nine times out of a hundred, the father gets fucked.'

'But that's not fair.'

'Post-divorce parenting is almost always the prerogative of the mother. The law is meant to care about the welfare of the child. In reality, the law cares about the wishes of the mother. Spot the difference? Not the welfare of the child, but the wishes of the mother. If your ex-wife can convince the court that she has no intention of denying you contact, and that your child's wellbeing would not suffer because of the change of residence, then she can pretty much take your child where she wants. And if I may get personal for a moment – that is exactly what happened to me.'

He picked up the photograph on his desk, studied it for a

moment, and then placed it down again, now facing me. I saw two smiling children, lost forever to their father.

'Then there's no hope.'

'There's always hope, Mr Silver. You can withhold consent. We can apply for a contact order. At the very least, that would slow her down. Make her go to the airport the long way round. Who knows? It might even stop her leaving the country.'

'And the order would say that I must be allowed to see my boy? She couldn't stop me seeing Pat?'

'Well, not exactly. You would have contact as the named person in the contact order.'

The named person. Once I was a father. Now I was a named person.

'We hear a lot about absent fathers in our society, Mr Silver. We don't hear so much about decent fathers who are denied contact with their children because of the whim of a judge. I have seen men destroyed by losing contact with their children. And I mean quite literally destroyed. Nervous breakdowns. Suicides. Alcoholics. Heart attacks. Blood pressure so high that a stroke was inevitable. Men killed by the loss of their children. Men who had done nothing wrong.'

'But I did.'

'What?'

'I did something wrong. I'm not like those other men. My first marriage. The break-up. It was all my fault.'

'What was your fault?'

'Our divorce. The break-up of our marriage. It was my fault. I slept with someone else.'

My lawyer laughed out loud. 'Mr Silver. Harry. That's completely irrelevant. You don't have to be true to your wife. Goodness me, that's what this country is all about.' His face became serious again. 'There's something else you have to consider, Mr Silver, and it's the most important thing of all.'

'What's that?'

'You have to ask yourself what happens if you win.'

'That's all good, isn't it? That's nothing but good. If I win, then Pat stays in the country and Gina has no choice. That's just what we want to happen, isn't it?'

'Well – how's your ex-wife going to feel if you stop her moving to America?'

'I guess . . . she will start to hate me. Really and truly hate my guts.'

Not for the first time, I remembered Gina's dream of living in Japan that I stole on our wedding day. Now I would be stealing her dream of living in America. I would have denied her two shots at happiness.

'That's right, Mr Silver. You will be preventing her from living her life where she chooses to live it. And that is highly likely to have some impact on your son. In fact, you can count on it. Frankly, if you stopped her leaving, then she could poison him against you. Make it harder to visit. Make it harder all round. That's what usually happens.'

'So you think I should give her my consent to take Pat out of the country?'

'I didn't say that. But you have to understand something about family law, Mr Silver. We don't get involved. The lawyers, I mean. As long as the parents agree, we leave you to it. If you can't agree, then we come in. And it can be very hard to get rid of us.'

I thought of what my life would be like with Pat in America. How empty it would feel. And I thought about what my life with Cyd and Peggy would be like with Pat gone. The three of us had had some great times together, and we would do again. I remembered mostly silly things like dancing to Kylie, mucking about with Lucy Doll, and all of those still, quiet moments when we closed the door on the world and didn't even feel the need to talk. But with Pat in another time zone, there would always be a shadow hanging over even the best of times. I looked forward to watching Peggy grow up. Yet at the same time I wondered how well you could bring up someone else's kid when you couldn't even bring up your own. And I thought of my life if Gina and Pat stayed. I could see her loathing me, resenting me for her husband's stalled career, blaming me for everything that was wrong in her life. I tried to think about what was best for my son – I really did – but I was consumed by the knowledge of how much I was going to miss him.

'Whatever I do, I lose him,' I said. 'I can't win, can I? Because if I give my consent or withhold it, the same thing happens. I lose him for a second time.'

Nigel Batty watched me carefully.

'Make the most of your family,' said Nigel Batty. 'That's my advice. Not as a lawyer, but as a man. Count your blessings, Mr Silver. Love your family. Not the family you once had. But the family that you have now.'

nine

At the entrance to the supermarket, Peggy and I had our way barred by a fat young mother stooping to shout at a small, grizzling boy of about five.

'And I'm telling you, Ronan, for the last time – *bloody no!*'

'But I want,' sobbed Ronan, snot and tears all over his trembling chin. 'But I want, Mum. I want, I want, I want.'

'You can't *have* any more, Ronan. You might *want* but you can't *have*, okay? You've had enough, all right? You'll be sick if you have any more today. You can have some more tomorrow, if you're a good boy and eat up all your dinner.'

'But I want now, Mum, I want right now.'

'You're not getting any more and that's final. So shut it, Ronan.'

'Want, want, want!'

'This is what you want, Ronan,' said the woman, suddenly losing it, and she grabbed Ronan's arm, spun him around and slapped him hard across the top of his legs. Once, twice, three times. And I realised the woman wasn't fat at all. She was pregnant.

Ronan was silent for a split second, his eyes widening with shock, and then the real howling began. The pregnant young woman dragged him away, his screams echoing all the way from cooked meats to household goods.

Peggy and I exchanged a knowing look.

She was sitting in the supermarket trolley, facing me, her legs dangling, and I could tell that we were thinking the same thing.

Thank God we are not like that.

The pair of us often felt a bit superior in the supermarket. We looked in mute horror at all those frazzled, frequently pregnant young mums dragging their sobbing brats past another sugar counter, and all those ominously silent, red-faced fathers ready to explode at the first wrong word from their sulking, surly children, and we thought – we are better than that.

I think Peggy thought that it was just a question of good manners. For an eight-year-old child, she had a sense of decorum worthy of Nancy Mitford. These dreadful people clearly didn't know how to act in a supermarket. Common as muck, most of them. But for me it was about more than correct supermarket etiquette.

When Cyd was working, out catering for a conference in the City or a launch party in the West End, and Peggy and I did the supermarket run alone, I often looked at those real mums and dads shopping with their real sons and daughters, and I thought – what's to envy?

When you looked at the bickering reality of genuine parents and their genuine children, what was so great about it? In a crowded supermarket near closing time, it was easy to believe that the real thing wasn't all that it was cracked up to be.

Peggy and I had fun. Perhaps it was because going to the supermarket together was still a rare enough event to feel like a minor adventure, although it was happening more and more now that Food Glorious Food was taking off, but we always zipped happily up and down the aisles, Peggy holding our list in her snug trolley chair, laughing appreciatively as I casually disregarded the aisle speed limit. And although to the world we must have looked like just another dad out with his daughter, there was none of the petty squabbling that we saw among many of the real parents and their real children.

We were better than that.

Peggy and I always had a laugh in the supermarket.

At least we did until today.

It was Tony the Tiger's fault. If Peggy hadn't had a hopeless three-bowls-a-day addiction to Frosties, then this trip to the supermarket would have been just as painless and uneventful as all the rest.

But Tony the Tiger spoilt everything.

'Bread,' Peggy said, frowning as she read her mother's shopping list.

'Got it,' I said.

'Milk?'

I held up a plastic pint of semi-skinned. 'Da-da!'

Peggy laughed, then scrunched up her eyes. 'To . . . to-i . . . er.'

'Toilet rolls. Check! That's it, Peg. We got the lot. Let's rock and roll.'

'Just my breakfast then.' We were in the aisle next to all the cereals. The brightly coloured boxes and leering cartoon characters were all around. 'Frosties. They're grrreat!'

'Don't need any, Peg. There's lots of cereal at home.'

'Not Frosties, Harry. Not Tony the Tiger. They're grrreat!'

Peggy liked her Frosties. Or perhaps she just liked Tony the Tiger and his catch phrase. But I had seen her have this exact confrontation with her mother a few times before.

Peggy liked Frosties, but Cyd always bought multi-packs of cereal. And the unwritten rule in our house clearly stated that Peggy had to eat the lot – including Coco Pops, Wheaties and the dreaded Special K – before we bought another multi-pack. We couldn't get another multi-pack just because she had noshed all the Frosties.

When the Frosties controversy had arisen in the past, Cyd simply moved on down the aisle, and the subject was dropped. But with me, Peggy sensed that victory and extra Frosties were in her grasp.

'Mummy said, Harry.' She reached out and pulled a jumbo pack of Frosties from the shelf. Tony the Tiger grinned at me. He kept grinning even when I took the box from her and put it back on the shelf. 'Oh, *Harry*. You disappoint me, you really do.'

'No, Peg. Listen, we'll get some more Frosties when you've eaten all the other stuff. I promise, okay?'

A dark cloud passed over her face. 'We will get some now. This very minute. I mean it, Harry. I'm not kidding.'

'No, Peg.'

She started climbing out of the supermarket trolley. She was getting a bit too big to ride in there, and suddenly the trolley lurched to one side and I had to catch her.

'Jesus Christ, Peg, you'll split your head open.'

'Don't swear, Harry. It's very vulgar.' She pulled a pack of Frosties from the shelf. I took them from her and threw them back. People were starting to stare. The way we stared when Ronan was getting smacked for his whining and his wanting.

'Now stop making a fuss, Peg, and let's go home.'

I went to pick her up and place her back in the trolley, but she wriggled and shook. 'Don't touch me, Harry. You're not my father.'

'What did you say?'

'You heard me, I believe.'

I went to pick her up again but she took two steps backwards and raised her voice.

'I want my mummy. You are not my daddy. Stop acting like you are.'

An old lady with a basket containing two tins of cat food and a packet of Maltesers stopped to investigate.

'Are you all right, dear?'

'She's fine,' I said.

'Excuse me,' said the cat lady. 'I'm not talking to you. I'm talking to the little girl.'

'He acts like he's my daddy but he's not,' Peggy said, her eyes suddenly filling with self-pity. 'He's really not. He's just pretending.'

'Oh, here we go,' I said. 'Here come the tears.'

'What an awful man you are,' said the old girl.

The young pregnant mother and Ronan happened to be passing. Ronan had cheered up considerably. He was just finishing off a bag of California Roll-flavour crisps. 'Are you all right, darling?' said his mum.

'She's upset,' said the old cat lady. 'She wants her mummy.'

'Who's he when he's at home?' said the young mum, indicating me.

'I don't think he's anyone,' said the old girl. 'Are you anyone? Are you her daddy?'

'Well, not exactly.'

'No, he's certainly *not*,' said Peggy, hugging the leg of Ronan's mum. 'My daddy has a motorbike.'

The old lady smoothed her hair. Ronan stared at me with wary curiosity. Flakes of crisps were all around his mouth. Saving them for later, my mum would have said.

Then suddenly there was a store detective, all brown shirt and shaven head and biceps. 'What's going on here then?'

'This is ridiculous,' I said. 'We're going home now.'

I made to pick up Peggy, but she recoiled as if I was approaching her with a bloodstained chainsaw in my hands.

'Don't let him touch me!'

'He'll never get you,' said the old lady.

'I'd like to see him try it,' said Ronan's mum.

'Mum?' said Ronan, starting to cry. You could see the masticated chunks of crisps in his mouth.

'I'll sort this out,' said the store detective.

Then he was in my face, this crop-haired white boy with a sprinkling of acne running down his thick pink neck. His meaty hands pressed lightly against my chest. Over his shoulder I could see the old lady and the young mum with their arms around Peggy, all of them glowering at me.

'I need to have a word with you, sir,' said the detective, taking my arm. 'In the supervisor's office. Then we'll see if the police need to be involved.'

I furiously shook him off. 'The police? This is nuts.'

'Are you this child's father?'

'I'm her mother's husband.'

'We'll see about that.'

'I'm not going anywhere with you. We're going home right now.'

The thin veil of politeness slipped from his eyes. I got the impression he was glad to let it go.

'You're coming with me, pal,' he said, his voice a little lower now but somehow more convincing. 'We can do it nicely or the other way, but you're coming with me.'

'Crazy,' I said. 'It's plain crazy.'

But I let the store detective lead me away, leaving Peggy with her new protectors.

'Mum,' I heard Ronan say. 'Can I have –'

'No, you fucking well can't,' said his mum.

I spent two hours in a little room set aside for shoplifters, the perpetrators of trolley rage and other assorted crazies. Just me and the spotty detective. In the end, they didn't call the police. They called my wife.

I heard them before I could see them as their footsteps echoed through the warren of storerooms and offices in the bowels of the supermarket. The door opened and there they were, my wife and my stepdaughter, escorted by some sort of white-coated manager.

'Hello, Harry,' Peggy said. 'What's this room then?'

'Madam?' said the man in the white coat. 'Is that him?'

'That's him,' Cyd said. 'That's my husband.'

She didn't sound too happy about it.

'Try to have a good time,' Cyd said, as our black cab crawled through the early-evening traffic of the West End. 'I know you're not in the mood for going out. Not after being arrested.'

'I wasn't arrested.'

'No?'

'I was only taken in for questioning.'

'Oh.'

'There's a difference.'

'Of course. But please try to have a good time. For me.'

'I will,' I said. 'For you.'

And I meant it. I knew that this was a big night for her.

Cyd was always accompanying me to work-related functions. Start-of-series dinners, end-of-series dinners, award ceremonies galore, and all the other compulsory fun that we had to endure as part of my working life as the producer of *Fish on Friday*. She never complained.

Unlike Gina, who usually came home from these things in tears of rage after someone had treated her like a moron because she was a homemaker. Unlike Gina, Cyd actually seemed to have a good time at these things. Or at least pretended she did, for my sake.

And tonight it was my turn to stand by Cyd. We were going to a dinner organised by the Caterers Guild. It was the first year that the chief executive of Food Glorious Food had been invited. I was her plus one.

'Are you sure I shouldn't have put on a tie?' I said. I was still in the sweatshirt and chinos that I had been apprehended in. 'They're not all going to be in suits and ties, are they?'

Cyd stared at me doubtfully. She had been so wrapped up in what she was going to wear – in the end she slid into this little black number that showed off those legs that I loved so much, dancer's legs, legs that could have belonged to Cyd Charisse herself – that she hadn't taken a lot of notice of me.

'Well, what do you wear at one of your dinners? You know, the ones we have to go to when *Fish on Friday* comes to the end of a series?'

'You come as you are. You wear what you like. But that's TV.'

'Oh, you'll be fine. I was told it's only an informal thing.'

The do was in a restaurant called Deng's that I had been to with Eamon and a couple of executives from the station. A great big barn of a place that served Modern Asian – which meant immaculately presented variations of what you would get in the restaurants of Soho and Chinatown, but served under ironic Andy Warhol-style pictures of Deng Xiaoping, and in much smaller portions. The waiters at Deng's wore beautiful Mao suits from Shanghai Tang. The clientele usually wore the expensive-casual that we sported in my game.

But not tonight.

As our taxi pulled up, my stomach lurched when I saw that tonight the men were all in black tie.

Apart from me, of course.

'Oh, Christ,' said Cyd. 'I'm so sorry, Harry.'

'Whoops.'

'Do you want to go home?'

'I'll butch it out.'

'You don't have to, babe. This is my fault.'

'I want to support you tonight. What's the worst that can happen?'

'You'll feel like a complete dickhead?'

'Exactly.'

We went inside. I moved through the black-tie crowd like a nun in a knocking shop, conscious of stares and sniggers, but ignoring them all.

I wasn't going to let a bunch of chicken satay merchants stop me accompanying my wife on her big night. Sally, Cyd's assistant, waved like mad from the other side of the room, and started forcing her way over to us. Sally was a kind of relation – Gina's half-sister, and my former babysitter. She was wearing some kind of elaborate ball gown, silky and strapless, like something Lucy Doll would sport on a big date with Brucie Doll. It was the first time I had ever seen her looking like a grown-up woman. She was very excited, but calmed down when she saw me.

'What's wrong with Harry?'

'He didn't know,' said Cyd.

'Luke Moore wants to meet you,' Sally said, taking Cyd's arm.

'Luke Moore? He's here?'

'And he wants to meet you.' Sally was babbling now. 'He told me he's heard lots of good things about Food Glorious Food and might put some business our way.'

'Who's Luke Moore?' I said.

'He's only, like, the biggest thing in the world,' Sally said. 'He runs Cakehole, Inc.'

'Luke Moore does most of the blue-chip catering in the financial district,' Cyd said. 'If you put something in your gob in the City, chances are Luke Moore and Cakehole, Inc. did the catering.'

'Come *on*,' Sally said, dragging my wife away. I followed close behind.

Luke Moore was a big man. Tall, stocky, built like a former athlete who was only just starting to pile on the pounds. His hair was a little too long for someone who wasn't Rod Stewart. About forty, I guessed, but looking good in that tuxedo.

I disliked him immediately.

He was surrounded by chortling sycophants who were hanging on to his every word.

'Apparently scientists have discovered a food that reduces the female sex drive by ninety-nine per cent,' he said. 'It's called wedding cake.'

While his flunkies howled with laughter and wiped away their tears of mirth, Luke Moore saw Sally, who was pushing Cyd forward.

And then he saw Cyd. Then he saw my wife.

'You must be the woman behind the best little catering firm in town,' he said, taking her hand and not letting it go.

'And you must be a smooth-talking devil.' Cyd smiled.

'It's true – I have heard so many good things about your company. We must get together. See if we can't help each other.'

'Sounds good,' said Cyd, and I noticed that she wasn't exactly breaking her arm trying to free her hand from this old rake. 'This is my husband.'

Luke Moore looked at me for the first time. 'I thought he was your janitor.'

The sycophants started splitting their sides. But, as my cheeks burned, my wife stuck up for me.

'Actually my husband is a very important man, Mr Moore. He's the TV producer, Harry Silver.'

'Of course,' said Luke Moore, who had clearly never heard of me. 'I am an enormous fan of your work.'

'Right.'

'Marty Mann was really something special when you were working together. Rather sad, what's happened to him, don't you think? All these dreary little programmes with low overheads and high impact. *Six Pissed Students* and all the rest. I've nothing against making money. Far from it. But I am so glad you're working with Eamon Fish now.'

I was impressed. And flattered.

'Eamon Fish,' said one of the sycophants. 'He's bloody good.'

'Yes,' said Luke Moore. 'He has a sort of B-list style about him.'

I smiled, biting my tongue. Why is it the only people who talk about the B-list are people on the C, D and E-lists?

'Plus,' said Luke Moore, 'junkies always have a certain appeal, don't they? You always wonder what's going to happen next.'

'He's not a junkie,' I said. 'He's suffering from exhaustion.'

But Luke Moore had finished with me. He bowed forward slightly, lifted Cyd's hand and – right there in front of everyone – gave it a kiss.

I nearly puked.

'I always need good people,' he said. 'My business needs a woman like you, Cyd. We really must try to do something together.'

'I'd like that,' said my wife. Then they exchanged cards, and I knew it wasn't just trying to be polite.

These two would see each other again.

'Maybe you should get Luke Moore to go to the supermarket with Peggy,' I said in the cab going home. It had been a rotten evening, and I was drunk and jealous and tired of people looking at me as if I should have used the tradesmen's entrance. 'Maybe Luke bloody Moore could explain to her why she can't have Frosties every time she wants them. Maybe Luke Moore could explain to Peggy why her useless bastard father only turns up when he feels like it. Maybe good old Luke Moore –'

'Harry,' Cyd said, taking my hand. 'Calm down, babe. Luke Moore doesn't want to marry me. He doesn't want to care for me and read to Peggy and help us to cook Christmas dinner.' She stroked my face with all of the old tenderness. 'He just wants to fuck me.'

'Oh,' I said, starting to sober up.

'Do you know how many times a day a woman sees that look?'

'Once or twice?'

She chuckled. 'Maybe even more. But I'm a married woman. So shut up and kiss me, stupid.'

So I kissed her, feeling stupid, but also feeling grateful, and lucky, and as much in love as I had ever been. There was no way I was going to lose this incredible woman. Not to Luke Moore or anyone else. Not unless I did something crazy.

And why would I ever do a thing like that?

ten

Emblazoned diagonally across the For Sale sign outside Gina's home – SOLD. When she came to the door, I could see packing crates stretching the length of the hall. It was really happening.

I wanted to do something different with Pat. The usual Sunday trinity of pictures, park and pizza didn't seem like quite enough. I wanted him to have a great time. I wanted to see his face lit up with joy. I wanted him to remember today.

So we drove down to Somerset House on the Strand. It's a grand old building but we weren't going inside. We were here for the fountains.

They gave us coloured umbrellas to cover ourselves and we began racing through the forest of fountains in the courtyard, my son's face screwed up with delight as the water bounced off his brolly.

Gene Kelly, I thought. *Singin' in the Rain.* Just singing and dancing in the rain.

The courtyard was crowded when we arrived, but after a while the other children and their parents wandered off for drier, more sedate entertainment. But Pat couldn't get enough of the mini-fountains that some genius had installed in the courtyard of that beautiful old building. So we stayed at Somerset House all afternoon, running through the water with our umbrellas above our heads. Soaked to the skin, our hearts pumping, and almost bursting with happiness.

Then as it started to get dark, we drove out to my mum's place and went to the old park. Just the three of us. My mother and my son and me, walking by the lake in the dusk of a November afternoon. The park was empty. Everyone gone. Last year's leaves underfoot, and that winter smell in the air, fireworks and mist and another year slipping away.

And it reminded me of another day in this same park. The day we took the stabilisers off Bluebell, Pat's bike.

I remembered my old man, the cancer already growing inside him, although we didn't know it yet, running behind Bluebell, always losing ground, but saying those three words again and again.

I've got you.

I've got you.

I've got you.

Then, when it was dark, I took Pat home to his mother. I walked him to the door, and knelt in front of him, so that we were the same height.

Kissed him, told him to be a good boy, and squeezed him like I would never let him go.

And the next morning Pat, and his mother, and her new husband, all caught the plane to their new life in another country.

There was still no sign of Eamon.

The warm-up man had come and gone and the studio audience were getting restless. Their mood was darkening by the minute. They were here to have a good time and, as my mum would have put it, would laugh to see a pudding roll. But waiting for the star to show up was starting to feel too much like hard work. The cameramen looked bored. The autocue lady sat behind her monitor and did her knitting. The floor manager pressed his headphones and muttered something to the director up in the gallery. He looked over at me and shrugged.

'I'll get him,' I said.

The dressing-room door was locked. I banged on it and called Eamon's name. No reply. I banged harder this time, called him a little gobshite, and told him to open up. Silence. And then, finally, the patter of classic trainers.

Eamon unlocked the door and as I went inside he sank to his knees and began searching for something under his dressing table. I cursed him, assuming he was looking for a few misplaced grains of cocaine. But it wasn't that.

'She's here somewhere,' he said. 'I know she is – ah!'

He got up, a few grubby scraps of paper in his hand. He began spreading them on his dressing table, and putting them together like a jigsaw puzzle for the under-fives. It was a photograph of a girl. An East Asian woman. Dark. Lovely. Someone I had met.

'Mem,' he said. 'My beautiful Mem. Oh, how could you be so cruel? I loved you so much, you dirty little bitch.'

I watched him assemble the photograph he had torn to pieces. It was a Polaroid, one of those pictures taken for lovers at tourist spots. A man and a woman on a summer's day, squinting into the camera in front of Notre Dame. Eamon and his Mem in Paris.

'What happened, Eamon?'

'She's married. Turns out she's fucking *married*.'

'Mem's married?' I remembered Mem pulling off her dress in the table-dancing club where she worked. She didn't look married. 'But she always seemed so . . . single.'

'Got a husband and a kid back in Bangkok. A little boy. Pat's age. Turns out she's been sending money to them all this time.'

'Jesus.' I put my arm around him. 'I'm sorry, Eamon.'

'We met up. To talk about getting back together. She seemed keen. Missing me. And I had bought her a ring. An engagement ring from Tiffany. A real one. Isn't that a laugh? When she went to do whatever it is they do in the toilet, I tried to hide it in her wallet. Thought it would be a surprise. And that's when I found the picture of her and the husband and the little kid. Bitch. I thought she meant it when she said she wanted to come back to me, Harry. But I was just a fucking cash-point machine.'

We both stared at the destroyed picture he was trying to put back together.

'Do you think if I sellotaped it up it would look okay, Harry? What do you reckon? Or should I try superglue?'

'Listen, Eamon. You have to worry about that later. There's a few hundred people out there waiting for you to do *Fish on Friday*.'

'The show? How can I think about the show when Mem's got a husband and kid?'

'You have to. That's what it's all about. Going on when you don't feel like it. Doing a great show when you're down. This is the life you chose. You can't take a night off because your heart got kicked around.'

'Kicked around? It's been mashed and mangled. The girl I wanted to be my wife can't marry me because her husband wouldn't like it. I need a line, Harry. It's in my coat. I've been saving it for an emergency. And here it is. Chop a couple out, would you?'

Now it was my turn to be angry. I took the small packet of cocaine from his coat and flung it in his face.

'Is she the reason you're falling to pieces? Some girl? She's got a husband and kid back in Thailand so you reach for the magic dust? Are you nuts? You're going to throw it all away for one girl?'

'Not one girl – *the* girl. Don't you understand anything about love, you miserable bastard, Harry?'

'Plenty, pal. Look, I know Mem's a lovely-looking woman. But there are plenty more fish in the sea.'

'And all of them so slippery, Harry.'

He picked up the cocaine and stuffed it in his pocket, followed by the scraps of torn-up photograph. Then he brushed past me, pausing at the dressing-room door.

'Ah, but how could you ever understand, Harry? Sure, you're a married man. What would you know about romance?'

The Sundays were the worst.

With Pat gone, the day of rest was never-ending.

I wandered around the house feeling lost, unable to recognise my life, while in the kitchen Peggy was helping Cyd to make her special recipe for dumplings.

I could tell that the dumplings were for Food Glorious Food

rather than our dinner because there must have been about six hundred of them. They were on silver trays all over the kitchen, these little packets of dough that my wife and her daughter were carefully stuffing with meat, chopped garlic and herbs, getting them ready for grilling.

'Texan dumplings,' Cyd said.

'Like the cowgirls eat,' Peggy said.

I stood in the doorway, watching the pair of them working. They were both bare-armed, wearing matching aprons, their black hair pulled back off their lovely faces. They looked as though they were having a great time.

'Lonesome without him, huh?' Cyd said.

I nodded, and she rubbed my arm. I didn't have to explain how I felt on Sundays. She loved me enough to understand.

'Need any help?' I said.

'What – from *you*?' Peggy said.

Cyd smiled. 'Sure.'

Peggy showed me what to do.

You had to get a circle of dough, put some meat in the middle, sprinkle on the herbs and garlic, and then fold it shut, pinching the top together so that you got this pattern of indentations.

Surprisingly enough, I was completely crap at it. My over-stuffed dumpling fell apart before it could even be placed on one of the silver trays. At first it was highly amusing to all three of us that my dumplings were rubbish. But after a while, as they continued to collapse, the joke wore thin.

'Not like *that*, Harry,' Peggy sighed. 'You're putting too much *stuff* inside.'

She showed me how to do it with her nimble fingers and soon my technique improved. I could tell that Peggy got a kick out of being the teacher, and for a while we were all working in happy dumpling-making harmony. Then from somewhere, I felt a kind of restlessness.

'You know what?' I said. 'Maybe I'll go and see my mum.'

'Why don't you?' Cyd said. 'She'd like that.'

'Think you can manage here without me?'

They were both far too kind to answer such a silly question.

I wasn't the only one who was missing Pat. There was a small boy outside our house. A good-looking, dirty-faced kid whose beat-up old bike was slightly too big for him.

'Where's Patrick then?' he said.

'Pat? Pat's gone. He went last week. To America.'

The boy nodded.

'I knew he was going. But I didn't know if he was goned yet.'

'Yes, he's goned. Gone, I mean. Were you at school with him?'

But the kid had gone. Pedalling off on that bike that looked as though it had belonged to an older brother or sister. That small boy, wondering how he was going to fill his day without my son.

Bernie Cooper. Pat's first best friend.

When I was a boy there were lots of people I could go to visit without warning.

All those friends whose doorsteps I could just turn up on, and know I would receive a warm welcome. Now the friends were all grown, and I was a man, and the only person in the world I could visit unannounced was my mum.

'Harry,' she said, letting me in. 'Hello, love. I was just about to go out.'

I was dumbfounded.

'On a Sunday? You're going out on a Sunday?'

'I'm going to the Union Hall with your Auntie Ethel. We're going line dancing.'

'Line dancing? What, that cowboy dancing? But I thought we could watch a bit of telly.'

'Oh, Harry,' laughed my mum. 'I can watch telly when I'm dead.'

The door bell rang and a seventy-year-old cowgirl came inside. Instead of her usual sensible cardigan, floral skirt and chunky

Scholl sandals, Auntie Ethel from next door, who wasn't really my auntie at all, was wearing a stetson, a fringed, spangly jacket and cowboy boots.

'Hello, Harry love. Coming line dancing with us?'

'You look great, Ethel,' said my mum. 'Annie get your gun.'

'Granny get your gun, more like,' said Auntie Ethel, and they both laughed like overflowing drains.

'Ethel's been before. She's already a bit of an expert. Aren't you, Ethel?'

Auntie Ethel smiled modestly. 'I can do the Sleazy Slide, the Hardwood Stomp and the Crazy Legs. I'm still having problems with my Dime A Dance Cha Cha and my Shamrock Shuffle.' She began to jerk stiffly around the living room, almost colliding with a lime-green pouffe. 'Step forward on left, stomping weight on to it – hitch right knee slightly whilst swinging foot side to side – hitch right knee a little higher.'

'Is that your Dime A Dance Cha Cha, Ethel?'

'No, love, that's my Shamrock Shuffle. And I'll tell you what – it's doing wonders for my lumbago.'

I looked at Auntie Ethel and then at my mum.

'You're not going out dressed like that,' I told her.

But I needn't have worried. My mum was going to see if she liked it before she bought any of the cowboy kit. I saw them off. And it was only when my mum was waiting for Auntie Ethel to edge her Nissan Micra out of the drive that she turned to me.

'You'll get him back, love. Don't worry. We'll get him back.'

'Will we? I'm not so sure, Mum.'

'Children need their dads.'

'Dads don't matter the way they used to in your day.'

'Every kid needs both of its parents, love. They do. It takes two to tango.'

I didn't have the heart to point out to my mum that nobody did the tango any more.

Not even her.

Auntie Ethel beeped her horn and rolled down the window of her Nissan.

'Wagons roll,' she said.

It was after midnight when I got home.

The bed was full. Peggy was sleeping in her mother's arms, sucking methodically on her thumb, her dark hair plastered to her bulging baby's forehead, as if she was fighting a fever.

'Bad dream,' Cyd whispered. 'Something about her dad falling off his motorbike. I'll make sure she's off and then take her back to her room.'

'It's okay. Keep her here.'

'Do you mind, babe?'

'No problem.'

So I kissed my wife and went to sleep on the sofa. And I truly didn't mind. Peggy needed her mum tonight. And alone on the sofa I didn't have to worry about Peggy waking up, or Cyd feeling too tired for sex, or if I was taking up too much of the duvet. There was nobody to cuddle downstairs, but also nobody to spoil my sleep.

That's the thing about sleeping on sofas. You get used to it.

'You need to get some romance back in your life,' Eamon told me. He pushed some pasta from one side of the plate to the other. He wasn't eating much these days. 'Some excitement, Harry. Some passion. Nights when you don't go to sleep because you can't bear to be apart. You must remember all that. Think back, think hard.'

'You think I should get my wife some flowers?'

He rolled his eyes. 'I think you should get yourself a mistress.'

'I love my wife.'

'So what? Romance is a basic human right. Like food, water and shelter.'

'You don't mean romance. You mean getting your end away. You're thinking about your nasty little knob. As usual.'

'Call it what you will, Harry,' eyeing up one of the waitresses as she took his uneaten food away. 'But if you got a bit on the side, you wouldn't be harming your marriage. You would be keeping it together.'

'Try explaining that to my wife.'

'Ah, your wife wouldn't know.'

'But I would. You don't understand. I don't want a new woman. I just want my wife back. The way we were.'

'You married men make me laugh,' Eamon chuckled. 'You complain about a lack of excitement under the old marital duvet. But you don't have the nerve to go out and look for some. You know exactly what you want, but you don't have the guts to get it.'

'That's what being married is all about.'

'What – frustration? Disappointment? Disillusion? Sleeping with someone you don't fancy? Sounds fucking great, Harry. Sounds terrific. Remind me to stay single.'

'I still fancy Cyd,' I said, and I meant it.

Sometimes I watched her face when she didn't know I was looking and I was shocked at how lovely she was, shocked at the emotion she could stir in me without doing a thing.

'And I think she still fancies me. When she remembers to, that is.'

Eamon had a laugh at that.

'What I mean is – a marriage can't end just because the honeymoon is over,' I said.

'But the honeymoon is *the best bit*.'

'Don't worry about our sex life – it's fine. When we can work up the energy. It's just – I don't know. The spark seems to have gone out. She's always busy with work. Or she comes home tired. Or the boiler has burst. It never used to be this way.'

'Women change, Harry,' Eamon said, leaning back, getting expansive. 'What you have to understand is that at different times in her life, a woman is like the world.'

'How's that?'

'Well, from thirteen to eighteen, she's like Africa – virgin territory. From eighteen to thirty, she's like Asia – hot and exotic. From thirty to forty-five, she's like America – fully explored but generous with her resources. From forty-five to fifty-five, she's like Europe – a bit exhausted, a bit knackered, but still with many places of interest. And from fifty-five onwards, she's like Australia – everybody knows it's down there somewhere, but very few will make the effort to find it.'

'You're going to need some better material than that when you come back.'

'Yeah,' Eamon said dryly. 'When I come back. Excuse me.'

He went off to the bathroom. We had agreed with the station that Eamon would take a sabbatical for however long it took to pull himself together. I knew he was depressed about taking a break from the show. But the station was demanding that he cleaned up his habit before he went back on air. That's why we were having this lunch. So I could convince Eamon that he needed professional help.

Eamon came back to the table, his eyes glazed and watery, his skin parchment pale. Not again, I thought. I tapped my nose and he dabbed his linen napkin at a flake of white powder by his nostril.

'Whoops,' he giggled.

'Listen, there's a doctor in Harley Street. She treats . . . exhaustion. The station wants you to see her. I'll come with you.'

'Oh, great big hairy bollocks. What am I? A kid? I don't need any help.'

'Listen to me, Eamon. You've got an enormous talent and right now you're in danger of pissing it away.'

'I don't need help, Harry.'

'If you don't see this doctor, you will eventually lose your show.'

'I'm fine.'

'You will certainly ruin your health.'

'That's my business.'

'You will probably get in trouble with the police.'

'Fuck 'em.'

'You will definitely put all your hard-earned money right up your nose and straight down the toilet.'

'I can do what I like with it.'

'And you will also shrink your penis.'

'What?'

'You heard me.'

He stared at me for a moment. 'What's this doctor's name then?'

His mobile phone began to vibrate. Not ring, just convulse. He picked it up and started talking, even though phones were not allowed in here. It was his ex-girlfriend. It was Mem. He was immediately on the verge of tears, running agonised fingers through his floppy black hair.

'I'm not harassing you . . . was it twenty messages? Surely not quite that many? Anyway, I just want to see you, my little lemon-flavoured Popsicle . . . Why? Just to talk to you, to explain . . . Mem, we can have it all again . . . I want to be the only man you lap-dance for . . . please, baby . . .'

Two businessmen at the next table stared at him with contempt.

'Who's the comedian with the mobile?' one said. 'There are supposed to be no phones in here.'

'Duh,' said the other, impersonating a dumb mobile phone user. 'I'm on the train . . .'

Eamon wheeled on the pair of them.

'It didn't ring, did it?' he demanded. 'I've got it on vibrating alert and no ring, right? So there's no fucking difference between me talking into this fucking phone and you two dickheads talking to each other about the financial markets or Tiger Woods or whatever floats your pathetic boats, is there?'

Good point, I thought, indicating that we would like our bill. He should incorporate that into the act, too. But Jesus – he was ready to explode.

And as they threatened to punch our lights out, I thought about what Eamon had said about a woman being like the world. If his theory was correct, then that made my wife America. But after a year and a bit of marriage, she still didn't feel fully explored.

Sometimes I felt I didn't know her at all.

* * *

I don't know why I started driving by Gina's place. I knew there was nobody home. The new people weren't moving in for a while, and even the dreamy au pair had buggered off back to Bavaria. But I found it – I don't know – soothing.

Even though it was not my house, and it was no longer Pat's home, and I had no warm memories of the place. Driving past my son's old place, thinking of how only last week his things were waiting for him up in his room – his clothes in the wardrobe, some of them too small for him now, his bed, his *Phantom Menace* duvet cover, the pillow that he slept on – somehow made me feel a little less lonely.

So I circled the house like an old lover, filled with longing, worn down by time.

And that's when I saw Pat's bike.

It had been left in their front garden. He was always doing that – parking his bike on the little front lawn after returning from the park and then just forgetting it, or trusting that the entire world was as innocent as him.

The only reason nobody had nicked it already was because it was almost completely hidden behind a scrubby bush. I parked my car, climbed over the token garden wall and picked up the bike. I would take care of it until my son came home. Or maybe they would want me to send it over.

'Is she in?'

I looked up. He was a very thin young man with dyed yellow hair. Asian. One of those fashionable young Japanese men that you sometimes see in the artier parts of London, haunting galleries and specialist record shops. This one looked as though he had been crying. I stared at him over the small garden wall.

'Who are you talking about? Do you mean Gina?'

He looked up at the house. 'Kazumi.'

The name rang no bells. 'Wrong house, mate. Try next door.'

'No. This is the place she's staying.' His English was good. 'I'm sure of it.' He scanned the street, shaking his head. 'I know this is the place. There she is!'

A young Asian woman was slowly coming down the street on a bicycle. She had that glossy, swinging Japanese hair, but it seemed just a shade lighter than normal. She stopped in front of Gina's house and pushed the hair out of her eyes. I saw her face. Pale, serious, slightly older than I had first thought. Not a girl, but a woman. Maybe around the same age as me.

And she was the most attractive woman I had seen for a long time. Since – well, since I first saw my wife.

She looked at the young man. Not pleased to see him. The hair swung back in front of her strikingly special face. She left it there, a veil between her and the world.

'Kazu-chan,' he said, and I suddenly thought – of course.

Gina's friend from Japan.

The one who looked at Pat through her camera and really saw him.

Kazumi.

He spoke to her in soft, urgent Japanese, his head slightly bowed, the dyed blond hair masking his grief.

She shook her head, telling him no, wheeling her bike up the garden path. The young man sat on my ex-wife's garden wall and began to sob, burying his face in his hands.

She shook her head again, this time with a kind of exasperated disbelief, and struggled with a big set of keys to open the front door. She was having trouble finding the right two. Then she finally opened it up and the burglar alarm began to sound its warning.

Just before she closed the front door, she glanced at me for the first time – standing in the middle of the little lawn, holding my son's abandoned bike, watching her tap in the code to the alarm.

I caught the expression on her face, saw how she was looking at me.

As if I was just another lovesick madman.

eleven

A postcard from New York.

On the front, a shot of Central Park with the seasons changing. Silvery skyscrapers peek over a thousand trees of rust, green and gold. Fluffy white clouds in a bright-blue sky.

On the back, a message from my son, each letter meticulously printed.

DEAR DADDY

WE WENT TO THIS PARK. THEY GOT DUCK. I LOVE YOU. LOVE YOUR SON.

PAT xxx

'Drunk goes into a confession booth in Kilcarney,' Eamon said. 'The priest goes, "What do you need, my son?" Drunk goes, "You got any paper on your side, mate?"'

We were in a waiting room in Harley Street. There were deep sofas, an elderly lady at a small reception desk and real-estate brochures on lacquered tables. Money and ill health filled the air. Eamon's fingernails were chewed down and bloody.

'You'll be okay,' I told him.

'School bus in Kilcarney. There's this old drunk – swallowing his tongue, singing rebel songs, puking up. Completely out of it. The little kids have to help him off. Then one of them says, "Fuck, now who's going to drive?"'

'She's a really good doctor. She has seen models, musicians, everybody.'

'Man walks into a Kilcarney bar. "Give me a fucking drink." Bartender goes, "First perform three tasks. Knock out the bouncer. Pull a loose tooth out of the guard dog. And give the local whore the shag of her life." Guy knocks out the bouncer with a sweet left hook. Guy goes into the backroom and soon the guard dog starts barking and yelping. Guy walks back into the bar, doing up his flies. "Right," he says. "Where's the dog with the loose tooth?"'

'Try to relax.'

'This is bollocks. I don't need any help. Those bastards at the station.'

'Mr Fish?' the receptionist said. 'Dr Baggio will see you now.'

Eamon was shaking. I put my arm around him as we stood up. And that's when the room seemed to blur at the edges. That's when my legs suddenly felt as if there was no strength in them, and as my vision slipped and smeared, my legs went to nothing and I saw the deep, lush Harley Street carpet rushing towards my face.

When I awoke I was on Dr Baggio's couch and Eamon was sitting by my side, his face creased with concern. Dr Baggio had wrapped something around my arm.

I realised she was taking my blood pressure.

'Did your father suffer from hypertension?'

My dad's face swam before my eyes. 'What?'

'Your blood pressure is 195 over 100.'

'Fuck me, Harry,' said Eamon. 'You're the sick one, not me.'

'Do you understand what that means?' asked Dr Baggio. 'It's very serious. The first number is the systolic pressure – the pressure in the arteries when your blood is pumping – and the second number is the diastolic pressure – when the heart is resting, filling with blood before its next contraction. Your blood pressure is dangerously high. You could have a stroke. Did your father have high blood pressure, Mr Silver?'

I shook my head, trying to take it all in.

'I don't know,' I said. 'He didn't even tell us when he had lung cancer.'

I knocked on Gina's door, even though I knew she wasn't home. And I wondered what I was doing here. I knew it was for something that I couldn't find at home. But I didn't know what. Not yet.

Kazumi's almond-eyed face appeared above the safety latch. She pushed back that torrent of swinging black hair. 'Yes?'

'Is Gina around?'

'Gina is gone.' I was surprised how little accent her English had. Just a soft burr that sounded almost Scottish. 'Gina not here any more.'

'Ah, of course.' I looked up and down the street, shaking my head, as if suddenly remembering something. Then I looked back at Kazumi and smiled. 'I'm Harry.'

'Harry? Not – Gina-san's Harry?'

Gina-san. Honourable, respected Gina. I hadn't learned a lot of Japanese in five years of marriage to a Nihon-obsessed wife, but I knew this much.

'That's me.'

For the first time I saw her smile. It was like some magic light coming on in the world.

'I've heard about you. Of course. Gina-san's former – I mean, Pat's father, yes?'

'The very same.'

'Sakamoto Kazumi,' she said. Wherever she learned to speak English with a Scottish accent, she was still Japanese enough to give me her family name first. 'Staying here. Until the new people move in. Keeping eye on the place. And very convenient for me. Very lucky.'

'Kazumi? Did you take those pictures of my son?'

She smiled again. I couldn't take my eyes off her. 'The very same,' she said. Funny, too.

'I loved them. I mean it. Incredible. You really caught him.'

'No, no. Just taken quickly in the garden.' Japanese modesty, despite the Scottish accent and good English. She nodded briefly, emphatically, a gesture that seemed so Japanese to me. 'He's a beautiful boy,' she said, and I knew she wasn't being polite. She meant it. You could see it in those photographs.

This stranger thought my son was beautiful.

'But you must know that Gina-san is in America with her – with Richard. And with Pat-kun.'

Pat-kun. The affectionate honorific touched my heart. Dear, sweet, little Pat, she was saying. My first wife had taught me more than I realised.

'I forgot,' I said. 'Sometimes I forget things.'

That was a lie, of course. But everything else was true, all that stuff about the brilliance of her photographs. And it was also true that she had a way of making me forget things.

Like where I was meant to be, and who I was meant to call, and the fact that I was married.

Kazumi took me in and gave me tea. She didn't have to do any of that, but she said she felt like she knew me already.

Kazumi had been Gina's best friend in Japan. They had shared a tiny flat in Tokyo for a year. Gina was planning to return to Japan, to make the move permanent. And then she met me. Kazumi knew all about that. If she also knew about the reasons we didn't live happily ever after, and she must have done, she was far too polite to mention it.

'Her boys,' Kazumi said. 'That's what she always called you and Pat. Her boys.'

Not any more, I thought. But I felt a rush of gratitude that we could sit in Richard and Gina's house, sipping green tea, and Kazumi could say out loud that once upon a time I had mattered to her friend.

And she told me her story. Not all of it. But enough for me to know that she had been an interior designer in Japan who had always dreamed of being a photographer. Western photography obsessed her. Weber, Newton, Cartier-Bresson, Avedon, Bailey. For as long as she could remember, that was what she wanted to do with her life, to look at the world and record what she saw. And then something happened in Tokyo – she didn't say what, but I guessed it had something to do with a man – so she caught a plane to Heathrow, left the old life behind.

It turned out that the Scottish accent came from three years at university in Edinburgh when she was in her late teens and early twenties, not long after sharing noodles, an apartment and a life in Tokyo with Gina for a year.

'Always wanted to study in Edinburgh,' Kazumi said. 'Ever since I was little children size.' The perfect English had only tiny fault lines in the language, making it sound impossibly charming. 'Very beautiful. Very ancient.'

Her stay there must have overlapped with the early years of my marriage to Gina, and I expressed surprise that we hadn't met back then.

'Gina-san was very busy in those days. Very busy with her two boys.'

But I knew it was more than that. In the early part of our relationship, Gina and I thought that we were completely self-sufficient. We honestly believed that we didn't need anyone else. Not even our oldest and dearest friends. We let everyone drift away. It was only when everything fell apart that we saw how wrong we had been.

'Who was that man, Kazumi? The man in the garden? The one who was crying?'

I knew I was pushing it. But I was curious about this beautiful, self-contained woman who could inspire nervous breakdowns on her garden path.

'Ah. Crying man? That was my husband.' She thought about it. 'Ex-husband.'

Then she was on her feet. She had told me enough. Too much, perhaps.

'You want to see more photo of Pat? Just had contact sheet develop.'

We went up to Gina's old study. The house was almost empty now. The only things that were here belonged to Kazumi.

She spread a sheaf of eight by tens out on the floor. She was technically brilliant. Composition, clarity, her choices all seemed sublime to my layman's eyes. The monochrome images of my son goofing around in the garden perfectly captured the fleeting moments of his childhood. And although the photos were all black and white, they were infused with real warmth. I felt again that she liked my son.

'Why did you leave Tokyo?'

Strangely, I want to know more. I want to know why she is so far from home, a story that I suspect has nothing much to do with Henri Cartier-Bresson or Robert Capa.

'I was like Gina.'

'How's that?'

'*Shufu*.'

I had picked up scraps of Japanese over the years. But not enough. I was guessing now.

'A . . . mother?'

'No, no. That's *oka-san. Shufu* means literally Mrs Interior.'

'Mrs Interior?'

'Housewife, they say England. Homemaker, they say America. In Japan – *shufu*. But Gina wanted to be *shufu*. No?'

'Yes, I guess. For a while.'

Until she decided she wanted her life back.

'My husband wants me to be *shufu*. I don't want it so much!'

She seemed to find it highly amusing. But I didn't know if it was the very idea of her being a housewife that tickled her funny bone, or if it was the job description of Mrs Interior. Or perhaps she was just covering her embarrassment.

'And it didn't work out?'

Obviously it didn't work out, Harry, you bloody idiot. Otherwise she wouldn't be here with her husband crying in her front garden and other strange men knocking on her door and lying through their teeth.

But she had told me enough for one day.

'Married,' she said, and I didn't immediately realise that she was talking about me now.

She was looking at the thick gold ring wrapped around the third finger of my left hand. 'Married again. Married now. To some other lady. Not Gina-san.'

I looked at my wedding ring, as if noticing it for the first time, as if it had been planted there. I hadn't contemplated removing it before I came to see Kazumi. It hadn't even occurred to me.

Because I couldn't get it off these days. Something had happened to that ring. It got stuck.

'Didn't work out,' Kazumi said to herself, as if this was a new phrase that she would quite like to take for a test drive. 'It just didn't work out.'

Gina sent me a photograph.

And I saw that my son had a new smile.

It was gappy and gummy and pulled at my heart. Two teeth were gone. On the top, right in the middle. The missing teeth gave him a ludicrously jaunty air – he looked like a drunken sailor returning from shore leave, or a raffish prize fighter out on the town.

In the picture he was all dressed up, kitted out for the camera, head to toe in official New York Yankees merchandise. Baseball cap, sweats, and what my mum would call an anorak. All dark blue, all carrying that white Yankees logo. Under that anorak, he was wearing a stripy blue-and-white Yankees shirt that was a few sizes too big.

He looked like a little American. I phoned him immediately, not reading the letter from Gina, not caring what else was in the envelope.

Gina picked up but went to get him immediately.

'What happened to your teeth?' I asked him.

'They falled out.'

He sounded surprisingly calm.

'Did it hurt?'

'No.'

'You'll get new ones, Pat. You'll get grown-up teeth to replace the ones you've lost.'

'Meat teeth for my milk teeth. I know. Mummy told me.'

Those two front teeth had been wobbling for ages. For some reason, I had assumed that I would be around when they fell out. Now they were gone, and they reminded me of all I was missing.

I realised there was a matchbox in the envelope. It said: Il Fornaio – 132a Mulberry Street – between Hester and Grand.

'You having a good time in America?'

'New York is very big. Bigger than London, even. And the taxis, right? They're yellow, and not black at all. But where we live, they got fields. It's not the city, where we live.'

'You go to this restaurant with Mummy and Richard? You like Il Fornaio, darling?'

'They got pizza. Did you look inside?'

Inside the matchbox were two jagged pearls. My son's missing front teeth.

'Are these for me? Can I keep them?'

'You can sell 'em to the Tooth Fairy.'

'Maybe I'll just keep them for myself. Maybe I'll just keep them. How does that sound?'

'That sounds okay.'

'You okay, darling?'

'I'm very busy.'

'I bet you are.'

'Still unpacking.'

'Is there much left to unpack?'

'I don't know. I'm only seven.'

'That's right. I forgot. Well, no more of our Sundays for a while.'

'I know. Connecky – connacky –'

'Connecticut.'

'Yes. Connecticut is too far for you to come. On a Sunday.'

'But we can talk all the time on the phone. And I'll come out to see you. And you can come back here and stay with me during the holidays. Soon. Very soon.'

'But where will I stay?'

'I'll find you somewhere good. In my house.'

'What about my stuff? Where will all my stuff go?'

'We'll make sure there's room for your stuff. Plenty of room.'

'That's all right then.'

'America's going to be great. You'll love it. Where you're living, there's lots of space.'

'I can have a dog. Mummy said. We're going to get a dog as soon as the unpacking is done and we're not quite so busy.'

'A dog? That's great. What are you going to call him?'

'I don't know yet. Because he might be a girl dog. So it's different.'

'And Pat?'

'What?'

'Don't forget me, okay? Don't forget your old dad who loves you so much.'

'I don't never forget you.'

Then Gina was on the line, wanting to talk. I didn't want to ask her how it was going. As long as Pat was all right, I didn't want to know. I didn't care. But she wanted to tell me all about it.

'We're staying with Richard's family in Connecticut. He's been catching the train into Manhattan every day, looking for a job in the city.'

'Wait a minute. I thought he had a job to go to. I thought it was all arranged.'

'He did, but he quit.'

'He quit already? You've only just got there. How could he have quit already?'

'It wasn't what he expected. He thought he could walk into something better, but the economy's rough all over. Not many jobs around for someone like Richard. And accommodation is a nightmare. Do you want to commute for three hours every day? Or walk to work and live in a shoebox? That's the choice.'

'So it's not what you expected?'

'Overqualified. That's what they're calling Richard. How can somebody be overqualified? How can you be too smart for a job?'

'Beats me. I guess that's the price of genius. But Pat's okay?'

'I think he loves it, Harry. Richard's family make a big

fuss of him. Treat him – I don't know. Like one of their own.'

Decent of them, I thought. But I said nothing.

'Richard's sister has got a little boy a year younger than Pat. They hit it off. Spent a lot of time together. They're out in Connecticut too. All of his family.'

'But it's not what you expected?'

'There's no Promised Land, is there? I am starting to realise that now.'

'So when are you coming home?'

She sighed. 'This is home now, Harry. Richard's been offered another job, at Bridle-Worthington.'

'What's that? I don't know what you're talking about.'

'They're brokers, Harry. Bridle-Worthington are brokers on Wall Street.'

'I thought he was overqualified.'

'It's not exactly what he was looking for. A lot less money. But they've offered Richard a job. As I say, not the salary he would have liked, but for now –'

'I thought you either commuted for hours or lived in a shoebox. I thought that's what you said.'

'Nowhere's perfect. But Connecticut is beautiful. An hour on the train to New York, maybe a little more. We're looking at schools in Hartford and New Haven. They are a million times better than what he would be in if we were still in London. London is finished.'

'Not for me, Gina. London's not finished for me. Look, why are you telling me all this?'

'Because I want you to know it's not about taking Pat away from you, Harry. It's about getting a better life. For our family.'

'What about me?'

'You've got your own family.'

'Not since you stole my son.'

She was silent for a moment. I could hear her seething, across all those thousands of miles.

'What a relief to be away from you, Harry. How great it will be to have you out of my life. That's what I'm looking forward to most of all. Making you a stranger.'

Then she was gone.

And in one hand I had the dead phone, and in the other, those two priceless little pearls.

twelve

Some nights we put Peggy to bed and one of us would read to her until she was sleeping and then we would watch TV and make love on the sofa and our little family seemed to be thriving.

Some other nights Peggy stayed over at her dad's place, and things were never as good. Jim Mason had a new girlfriend, and the woman was clearly making every effort to show how wonderful she was – making space in their relationship for Peggy, lavishing her with attention and presents, acting as if it would be like this forever. It was on these nights when Peggy was absent that Cyd always seemed to work late.

Everything took a little longer when Peggy wasn't around. The launch parties in the West End, the conferences in the City – maybe it was just a coincidence, but there were no early nights for Cyd when there was no Peggy to come home to. Yes, maybe it was just coincidence. That's what I thought. Until I started to recognise his car.

I waited by the window until I saw the Porsche 911 come into view. It was always late by now, the early hours, and the familiar 911 came down our street with the menacing grace of a shark moving through shallow water.

The 911 parked. I could see their shadows. I could watch the silhouettes of my wife and Luke Moore as she sat in his Porsche, just talking. That's all. Just talking.

But by the time I heard her key in the lock I was in bed, lying very still on my side, eyes closed, my breathing even.

My wife tiptoed into our bedroom and began taking off her clothes as quietly as she could.

Pretending to be coming home late from work, while her husband lay there in the darkness, pretending to be asleep.

There was some old man sitting in my father's chair.

It made me feel like I had come to the wrong place. None of us ever sat in my dad's chair – not my mum, not Pat, not me. The old armchair by the fireplace was not the best seat in the house – it faced the TV at an awkward angle, and its soft cushions were sunken with the ages – but it was always my dad's chair, a suburban throne in his pebble-dash palace, and although he had been dead for two years now, it was still my dad's chair. So who was this old man?

'Howdy, pardner,' he said to me.

Howdy, pardner?

What was he going on about?

The old man was practically the exact physical opposite of my father. Where my dad was gleaming, chrome-smooth bald, this geezer had a luxuriant head of silvery hair, elaborately brushed back. Where my father was stocky, thickset and muscular, this character was as wasp-waisted as an elderly gigolo. And at home my old man always wore his Marks & Spencer mufti – carpet slippers, baggy gardening trousers, and cardigans in any colour, as long as it was forgettable. A real suburban dad, despite the horrific war wounds that I knew were hidden under his sensible sweaters.

This impostor was dressed like a cowboy.

A fringed shirt. Pointy-toed, stack-heeled boots. Tight, skinny Levi's with a big buckled belt. You could almost see the bulge of his ageing meat and two veg. Glen Campbell's granddad.

'Howdy, pardner,' he repeated, slowly getting up out of my dad's chair. Taking his time about it. 'Tex is the name. You must be Harry. Mighty pleased to meet you, stranger. Elizabeth has told me all about you.'

Nanci Griffith was singing 'Lone Star State of Mind'. My

mum came into the living room carrying a tray of tea and biscuits, humming to herself.

'I see you've met Graham, dear,' she said.

'Graham? I thought –'

'Tex is my line-dancing name,' he said, without a trace of shame. 'Graham – I don't know. It just doesn't sound right when you're doing the Walkin' Wazi, does it?'

'Ooh, you should see Graham – I mean Tex – doing the Walkin' Wazi,' my mum chuckled, passing around the ginger nuts. 'He really kicks his old legs in the air.'

A line-dancing friend. So that was it. Perfectly innocent. Nothing suspicious. Two sprightly OAPs having a bit of a boogie in the autumn of their years. Completely natural. But I couldn't help it. I was still stunned by the presence of Tex.

My mother – who had six brothers, who had no daughters or sisters, who had spent her entire life surrounded by men – had always been strictly homosexual in her friendships. Every friend she ever had was a woman. Apart from my dad. He was her best friend of all.

'Met your mother when we were doing the Four-Star Boogie,' he said, as if reading my mind. 'Gave her a few tips. Her and – Elsie?'

'Ethel,' my mum said. 'The Four-Star Boogie.' She tutted at the memory. 'That's such a tough one. All that turning.'

'Pivoting,' Tex gently corrected her. 'The Four-Star Boogie is a four-wall line dance,' he informed me, as if I gave a toss. 'As opposed to something like the Wild, Wild West, which of course, as you probably know, is only a two-wall line dance.'

'You from round these parts, Tex?'

'Southend. Straight down the A127, take a right at the old Fortune of War.'

'Graham was an insurance salesman,' my mum said. 'Retired now, of course.'

Tex poured the tea. 'One lump or two?' he asked me. 'I'm sweet enough already.'

My mum guffawed at this as though it was Noël Coward at his pithy best. When she went back into the kitchen for the milk chocolate digestives, I excused myself to Tex and followed her.

'I thought you went line dancing with Auntie Ethel?'

'Ethel's dropped out. It's her arthritis, Harry. All that stomping gives her gyp. Poor old thing.'

'What's John Wayne doing in our front room? What's he doing in Dad's chair?'

'He's all right, old Graham. Don't worry about him. He's harmless. He gives me a lift home in his car. He's a bit full of himself, I grant you. All the old girls have got a soft spot for him.'

'What about you?'

'Me?' My mum laughed with genuine amusement. 'Don't worry, Harry, I'm past all that. When I ask a man in for tea and biscuits, that's exactly what I mean. All he's being offered is a custard cream.'

'Does Tex know that?' I thought of the obscene rise in the old gent's Levi's. Although my mum was in her seventies, I could see how she might catch the eye of some randy old git. She was still a lovely-looking woman. 'He's not going to start reaching for his six-gun, is he?'

I said it with a grin, to pretend that I already knew the answer.

But my mum wasn't smiling now.

'I had a husband,' she said. 'That'll do me for one lifetime.'

'Your mother needs to express her sexuality,' my wife said. 'She's still a woman.'

'She's a little old lady! She should be expressing – I don't know – her knitting.'

We were getting undressed for bed. Something we had done perhaps one thousand times before. It still excited me to see my wife taking off her clothes. The long limbs, casually revealing themselves. I don't think she felt quite the same way about watching me put on my stripy pyjamas.

'I think it's great she's got a male friend, Harry. You know how much she misses your father. You don't want her to sleep with the light on for the rest of her life, do you?'

'She was with my old man forever. She's bound to miss him. And it's right she misses him.'

'Am I supposed to be faithful to you when you're dead?'

I snorted. 'I'll be happy if you're faithful to me when I'm alive.'

She froze inside the T-shirt she was pulling over her head. Then her face appeared, her eyes narrowing. 'What does that mean?'

'Nothing.'

'Come on.'

'You just seem a bit too friendly with that guy.'

'Luke?'

'Is that his name?'

'Jesus Christ, Harry. I'm not interested in Luke. Not that way.'

'You said he wants –'

'I don't care what he wants. Wanting is not the same as getting. He's smart enough to see what I'm doing with the company. He knows I can help his business. I think he can help mine. I admire him, okay?'

'You admire a sandwich merchant?'

'He's a brilliant businessman. He's worked hard for everything he's got. I know he's a bit flash. I know you didn't like what he said about Eamon. I didn't like it either, okay? But this is strictly business. Do you honestly believe I would think about him in that way? I don't go around shagging anything that moves, Harry. I'm not a man. I'm not you.'

'So how does it work? You and old Luke? I'm just curious about your relationship.'

'His company has more work than it can handle. If something comes up and they're fully stretched, he calls me.'

'No – I mean how does it work with you and him? On that other level. Does he know you're not interested in him that way? Is he cool about that? Or is still hoping to get his hands on your canapés? Don't tell me, because I know the answer.'

I knew I should have shut up by now but I couldn't stop myself. I was afraid that I was losing her. Which was kind of ironic, as I was the one who went knocking on Gina's door when I knew she wasn't home.

'Shall I tell you what makes me sad, Harry? You think he's only interested in me for one thing. Maybe – just maybe – he's interested in me for two or three reasons. Did that ever cross your mind? Why do you find it so hard to believe that someone could like me for what I can do? Not for what I look like? Why is that so hard?'

Because I am still crazy about you, I thought. Because I can't imagine any man looking at you and not feeling exactly what I feel. But I said nothing.

'I don't even want to talk to you.' She turned on her side, angrily killing the light. I turned on my side, reached for the light.

We lay in the darkness for a while and when she spoke there were no tears in her voice, no anger. Just a kind of bewilderment.

'Harry?'

'What?'

'Why do you find it so hard to believe that you're loved?'

She had me there.

Kazumi had told me she took a photography class in Soho every morning. After a couple of practice runs, I found that if I timed it just right, I could catch her on the short walk from Gina's home to the tube station. I couldn't believe that I was doing this thing. But I did it just the same.

I pulled up to the kerb beside her, sounding my horn, the stalled rush-hour traffic howling with protest behind me. I tried to look surprised.

'Kazumi. I thought it was you. Listen, do you want a lift into town? It's not out of my way or anything.'

She got in, a little reluctantly, not as pleased to see me as I'd hoped she would be. She was struggling with a large cardboard box with 'Ilford photographic paper' written on the front. She had a couple of cameras with her. But she didn't look anything like a tourist.

I asked her how she liked London, what techniques she was studying right now, if she missed Japan. I talked too much, babbling mindlessly, my cheeks burning, too excited to see her. Eventually she managed to get a word in.

'Harry,' she said.

Not Harry-san? Not honourable, respected Harry? I admit I was a little disappointed.

'You're married, Harry. With a beautiful wife. A wife you love very much.' It was all true. She stared out at the paralysed, angry traffic, shaking her head. 'Or am I missing something?'

No, I thought. It's me. It's me who's missing something. And suddenly I knew exactly what it was.

The smell of Cajun cooking.

Cyd was in the kitchen experimenting with red beans, rice and what was probably a catfish when I dumped the pile of glossy brochures on her chopping board.

'What's that?'

I picked one up at random, showed her the palm trees, blue seas and white sand, like a street trader showing off his wares. 'Barbados, darling.' I began flicking through the brochures. 'Antigua. St Lucia. The Cayman Islands.'

'Are you crazy? We can't go to the Caribbean. Not now.'

'Then what about the Maldives? The Red Sea? Koh Samui?'

'I'm not going to Thailand, Harry. I have to work.'

I took her hands in mine. 'Run away with me.'

'Don't touch me. I smell all fishy.'

'I don't care. You're the love of my life. I want to take you to some tropical paradise.'

'What about Peggy?'

'Peg comes too. The Indian Ocean. Florida. Anywhere in the world. For a couple of weeks. For a week. She can snorkel. Get a tan. Ride the banana boats. She'll love it.'

'I can't take her out of school.'

'Gina took Pat out of school.'

'I'm not Gina. And we can't go away for two weeks.'

There were other brochures. Skinny ones, with glittering urban landscapes on the cover instead of sun-drenched beaches.

'Then what about a mini-break? Just for a few days? Prague. Venice. Or Paris – Pat loved Paris.'

'I'm too busy at the moment, Harry. Work's really taking off. Sally and I can hardly handle it. We're thinking of taking someone else on.'

'Barcelona? Madrid? Stockholm?'

'Sorry.'

I sighed. 'Do you want to see a movie? Maybe we could get something to eat in Chinatown. Sally can babysit.'

'When did you have in mind? Sundays are good for me.'

So my wife and I took out our diaries and, surrounded by her experimental Cajun cooking, we tried to find a window for romance.

part two: *your heart is a small miracle*

thirteen

My wife.

I could always spot her across a crowded room. Something about the curve of her face, the tilt of her head, the way she pushed her hair out of her eyes. Just a glimpse was all it took. I couldn't mistake my wife for anyone else. Even when I wasn't expecting to see her.

It was a party at the station to launch the new season of programmes. Wine and canapés, gossip and flattery, a speech from Barry Twist about forthcoming attractions. An evening of compulsory fun. There was a lot of that in my game. And even though Eamon was officially resting and there was no *Fish on Friday* in the spring schedule, I thought I should be there. Marty Mann's advice had been nagging at me more than I cared to admit. Maybe I should be searching around for new talent, looking to diversify. Maybe only a fool pinned all of their hopes on just one person. But right now I couldn't think about any of that because my wife was here. I pushed my way through the crowd. Cyd was not surprised to see me.

'Harry. What are you up to?'

'Working.' If you could call it working, these few hours of small talk and Chardonnay. My old man would have considered it a big night out. For me it was another day toiling at the coalface. 'How about you?' Although of course I had guessed by now.

'Working, too.' For the first time I noticed she was holding a silver tray by her side, empty apart from a few crumbs of fish cakes or satay. 'Sally's babysitting for me. I mean – *us*. I got a call this afternoon. Luke and his people usually cater for this do, but they're snowed under right now. It's a good job for me to get.'

Luke. Wanker.

We smiled at each other. I was so glad to see her. I was feeling party-lonesome until her face was suddenly there. Cyd had been to quite a few of these evenings with me, although not recently. And although she never ducked these dos, this wasn't really her thing at all – too much smoke, too much alcohol, and too much meaningless chitchat with people she would never see again, people who were always looking over your shoulder for someone more famous. Too much like hard work. But she had been with me in this room before, so it didn't seem that strange to see her here. Even with a silver tray in her hands.

I touched her arm. 'Can I get you a drink?'

She laughed. 'Got to work, babe. I'll see you later, okay? We can go home together, if you can stick around until I've cleared up.'

She gave me a peck on the cheek and went back to the kitchen to load up with more satay and fish cakes, while I wandered around the party trying to avoid people who would want to talk about Eamon and his nervous exhaustion. There was a bank of TV sets in the middle of the room, repeating a loop of trailers for the new season's shows. A lot of Marty Mann shows. *Six Pissed Students in a Flat* was coming back, so was the CCTV programme, *You've Been Robbed!* I stood there nursing my beer, watching the tasters for irreverent game shows, irreverent talk shows and irreverent dramas.

Tired old irreverence, I thought. It's killing television.

A couple of suited and booted business types appeared by my side, tossing peanuts into their mouths and gawping at the screens as though they had never seen a television before. They couldn't be from the TV station or any of the production companies that made the shows, because they were far too formally dressed. We had a strict dress code at the station – you had to be fashionably scruffy at all times. Maybe they were advertisers, invited to give them a taste of cut-price glamour.

Cyd brushed past me carrying two silver trays piled high with sashimi. She gave me a wink, and bent to place one of the trays on a table. The men turned away from the bank of screens, their jaws working furiously on their peanuts.

'Look at the legs on that,' one of them said.

'They go all the way up to her neck,' said the other.

'No arse, though.'

'Flat as a pancake.'

'And no tits.'

'You don't get tits with legs like that.'

'You need a nice arse though.'

'I'll give you that.'

'You need either tits or arse, right, even with legs like that. Because you need something to hold on to when you start your ascent.'

'Great legs, though.'

'Get those wrapped around your neck, mate, you'll never want to come up for air.'

They chortled in perfect harmony, watching my wife walk away.

I stared at the pair of them, my face burning. I kept staring, wanting them to notice me.

They didn't notice me.

Then all the peanuts were gone and, after rifling in the salty bowls for a bit, they sloped off, looking for more tasty snacks. I went looking for my wife. When I caught up with her she was handing out her sashimi to a bunch of women I vaguely recognised. They were helping themselves to raw fish while simultaneously managing to ignore Cyd completely. These bloody people. Who did they think she was? Nobody?

Cyd smiled at me. She had a lovely face. She was always going to have a lovely face, no matter how many years went by. But I couldn't smile back at her.

'Get your coat. We're leaving.'

'Leaving? I can't leave. Not yet, babe. What's wrong? You look all –'

'I want to go.'

'But I've got to work. You know that.'

The women were starting to stare at us. They were holding slivers of salmon and tuna in their podgy fingers. I took Cyd's arm and pulled her aside. Her silver tray banged into someone's back. The sashimi wobbled precariously.

'I mean it, Cyd. I'm going home. Right now. And I want you to come with me. Please?'

She wasn't smiling any more.

'You might be going home, Harry, but I'm working. What happened? Come on. Tell me. Did someone say something about Eamon? Is that why you're upset? Forget about Eamon. Marty's right – get something new going for yourself.'

I wanted to tell her – don't waste your time here. I know exactly what these men are like, because I'm one of the bastards myself. But she wouldn't have known what I was talking about. She was all innocence, she thought it was all about raw fish and chicken on a stick and people appreciating you for doing a good job.

'Please, Cyd. Come with me.'

'No, Harry.'

'Then do what you want.'

'I will.'

So I left her at the party, left her feeding all those hard, empty faces, and went out to look for a cab. I left her there, all by herself, even though I knew she was too good for that place, and too good for those people.

When I got home Peggy had been in bed for hours. Sally was on the sofa, idly channel-surfing with one hand and soothing her baby in her carrycot with the other. Soothing Precious. That was the baby's name. Precious. Sally asked me how the evening had gone – she meant for Food Glorious Food, not the station – and I told her that everything was fine. Then I got her a minicab.

Luke Moore drove my wife home. By then I was pretending to be asleep, lying on my side, breathing easily, trying to fake the soft rhythms of sleep. I listened to my wife quietly undressing in the dark, heard her clothes slipping from her long, slim body, and inside my Marks & Spencer pyjamas, my heart ached for her. Then we lay in the darkness for a long time, trying hard not to disturb each other.

Back to back in the marital bed, and never quite touching.

'Your heart is a small miracle, Mr Silver,' said Dr Baggio. 'A small miracle.'

My wife is having an affair, I thought. She's fucking this guy. I just know it.

'The heart is a pump about the size of a fist,' said my doctor, inflating the strap she had wrapped around my arm. I could feel it tightening against my skin. 'We all have blood pressure. It's simply the pressure created by the constant pumping of blood around the body. In a healthy adult a normal blood pressure is 120 over 80. Yours is . . . goodness.'

It happens. You promise to love each other forever. You really mean it. You plan to sleep with no one else for the rest of your life. Then time wears away at your love, as the tide wears away a rock. And in the end your feelings – her feelings – are not what they were once upon a time. Other people are let in, like light in a darkened room. You can't get them out again. Not once you have let them in. What can you do once you have let them in?

'You can put your shirt back on,' my doctor said.

She didn't want sex any more. Not with me. Not even with one of my magic condoms. Oh, we still had our Saturday night shag, which was sometimes postponed to Sunday or Monday if the catering business was booming. But I felt as if she was just doing it to keep me quiet. That it was easier to lie back and think of nothing than argue about it. Too tired, she always said. Yeah, right. Tired of me. It wasn't even the sex I missed most.

It was all the other stuff. It was the being loved.

'There are lots of things you can do to control your blood pressure,' my doctor said. 'You can reduce your intake of alcohol. Lose weight. Increase physical activity. Most important of all, you can change your wife.'

Change my wife?

Things weren't that bad. I wanted my marriage to last. I wanted to get it right this time. Get it right once and forever.

'But I love my wife.'

'Not your wife. Your *life*. Don't let things get to you. Find time for yourself. Control your anxieties. You need to change your life, Mr Silver. You only get one of them.'

Life. Not wife.

You obviously get more than one of those.

The heart is a small miracle.

'I liked the way it made me feel,' Eamon said. 'Once upon a time. And I wanted to have that feeling again.'

We were walking in the grounds of a private hospital an hour's drive south of London. Eamon talked about cocaine as we kicked our way through the leaves. He was only halfway through a 28-day detox programme, but he was already looking fitter than I had seen him since he was fresh from the Edinburgh Festival. He was meant to be playing football this afternoon – substance abusers versus the manic depressives – but the match had been cancelled. The manic depressives were too depressed.

'We have these group sessions. Such stories, Harry. You'd love it. All these alcoholics and cokeheads and junkies telling you where it all went wrong. Every kind of addict under the sun. Some of them are very articulate. And do you know what I heard someone say this morning? *Alcohol gave me wings to fly – and then it took away the sky*. Isn't that great? That's exactly how I feel about coke.'

'But that still doesn't explain it. You've got this great life – money, fame, weather girls. And you screw it all up for a feeling. Not even a feeling – the memory of a feeling.'

'Come on, Harry. I know you're not a drinking man. And I know that drugs are not your thing. But it's the same for you.'

'How's that?'

'It's the same for you with women.'

And I saw that he was right. That's why I wanted Cyd to

be the woman I first met, that's why I had gone to Kazumi's door. I was hooked on a feeling too.

The remembrance of the greatest feeling in the world.

It wasn't the rush of cocaine or the fog of alcohol, it was the feeling I got when I was starting with a woman. Passion, sex, romance, feeling alive, feeling wanted – it was all of those things, wrapped up in a fleeting moment of time.

I liked the way it made me feel.

And I couldn't help it. I wanted that feeling again.

Even if it meant trouble galore.

fourteen

Jim Mason resembled a male model just starting to go to seed.

The chiselled features were beginning to show signs of a double chin, and under the leather jacket the beer paunch was developing like a promising marrow. But he still looked capable of causing trouble. Cyd's ex-husband arrived to pick up his daughter.

'Hello, Harry. How you doing, mate? Peggy ready to rock and roll?'

It was one of those scenes that I had never imagined playing, an event where I would love to have known the correct etiquette. This man had broken the heart of the woman I loved. But if he hadn't broken her heart, my wife and I wouldn't be together. Should I thank him or thump him? Or both?

Cyd was once crazy about this guy, and behind her back he had jumped on the bones of every Asian woman who would let him from Houston to Hoxton. My true love had done everything to make it work with this creep. She had followed him to London when it was clear that America was indifferent to his existence, she had supported him when he fell off his motorbike and mangled his stupid leg, and she even gave him a second chance after she had met me. And of course she had given birth to his child, and then raised her alone. I should have hated Jim Mason. But I found that I just couldn't quite manage hate. Only the dull ache of jealousy.

The real reason he made my flesh crawl wasn't because he had treated Cyd so badly. It was because he had won her heart without even trying, and shattered it so casually. But I couldn't loathe him, this man who was my wife's other husband.

He was always so nice to me.

'Cyd out working? A woman's work is never started, right? Only kidding, mate, only kidding. Give her my best. My little princess ready?'

'*Daddy!*'

Peggy threw aside her Lucy Doll Ballerina and charged her dad. Jim scooped her up and placed a loud kiss on the top of her dark hair as she wrapped her legs around his waist, her arms around his neck, hugging him with theatrical abandon. They saw each other so sporadically, this dad and daughter, that their reunions were always emotional affairs, resembling a prisoner of the Vietcong being reunited with his family. But I was never quite sure if the emotion was forced or not. Prolonged separation can sometimes make a parent and child act with the self-consciousness of strangers.

I saw them to the door. Their routine was always the same. A ride on Jim's motorbike to KFC or Pizza Express. At Peggy's age, I don't know if it was even legal. Jim wasn't the kind to care. Once Cyd had protested that Peggy was a bit too young for motorbikes, and Jim had stormed out, leaving his daughter in bitter tears. He didn't see her for three months. After that, the joy rides were never questioned.

Jim's visits traditionally involved the purchase of a large, inappropriate, stupendously useless toy. Stuffed bears that were bigger than Peggy herself were a favourite.

When Peggy had gone I realised with a jolt of alarm that she had forgotten her child-sized helmet. Cyd had laid down strict rules for motorbike riding.

Always wear a helmet.

Hold on tight to Daddy.

No riding in the rain.

No long journeys.

No motorways.

I dashed out to the street but the bike – a huge brute of a Norton – was already roaring away, Peggy clinging on to her dad's leather-clad back, the hair on her bare head flying.

I chased down the middle of the street, shouting their names, the kid's helmet in my hands. But they didn't hear me. It was a long straight road and I watched Jim's taillights receding, cursing him for being so thoughtless.

And then at the last moment they turned back.

I stood in the street as the bike barrelled towards me, my heart filling my chest with that boiling feeling you get when your child has been placed in unnecessary danger. The Norton skidded to a halt in front of me, Jim and Peggy grinning, their faces flushed with excitement. I jammed the helmet down on her head.

'You fucking idiot, Jim.'

He shook his handsome head in disbelief.

'What did you call me?'

'You heard. And what did your mum tell you, Peggy? What's the most important rule about the bike? What's rule number one?'

Neither of them was smiling now, and the way they were looking at me from under their helmets made their faces seem almost identical. I always thought that Peggy resembled Cyd. But I saw now that she was just as much Jim's child.

'Come on. What did Mummy say, Peggy? What did Mummy tell you again and again? What must you always remember?'

'Hold on tight to Daddy,' my stepdaughter said.

It's so difficult for the step-parent to strike a balance between caring too much and caring too little.

The horror step-parents – the ones who end up in court, or in newspapers, or in jail – don't think about it. They don't care. The child of their partner is a pain, a chore, and a living reminder of a dead relationship. But what about the rest of us? The ones who are desperate to do the right thing?

There's nothing special about us. We are not better human beings because we have taken on the parenting of a kid who is not our biological child. You get into these things without thinking about them, or if you think about it at all, you imagine that it will work itself out somehow. Love and the blended family will find a way. That's what you think.

But the blended family has all the problems of the old family, and problems that are all its own. You can't give your stepchild nothing but kindness and approval, because no parent can ever do that. And yet you do not have the right to reproach a stepchild the way a real parent does.

I had never raised a hand to Pat.

But I couldn't even raise my voice to Peggy.

Step-parents – the ones who are trying their best – want to be liked. Parents – real parents – don't need to be liked.

Because they know they are loved.

It is a love that is given unconditionally and without reservation. A parent has to do very bad things to squander the love of their child. A step-parent just doesn't get that kind of love.

And, increasingly, I believed that there was nothing you could do to earn it.

I was either too soft – desperate to be liked, starving for a few scraps of Peggy's approval – or I tried to pass myself off as the real thing. Passing, that was the step-parent's major crime. Pretending to be something I wasn't, and could never be.

I knew, in my calmer moments, that it was not easy for Richard. I knew that the things he wanted for my son – museums, Harry Potter, tofu, even the new life in another country – were not meant as punishments. I didn't hate Richard because of those things. I hated him because he had taken my son away from me. Who did he think he was? He wasn't Pat's father.

The step-parent has a thankless job. The step-parent can't win. You are either involved with this pint-sized stranger too much or not enough. But there's one thing that the step-parent should always remember. It is even worse for the child.

Grown-ups can always get a new husband or wife. But the children of divorce can't get a new father or mother, no more than they can get a new heart, new lungs, new eyes. For better for worse, for richer for poorer, you are trapped with the parents you are born with.

Peggy was lumbered with me, this man in her mother's bed who was neither fish nor fowl, friend nor father, just a male parent impersonator.

Uncle Dad.

A night that was just like the old days. That was the idea. There was a new print of *Annie Hall* showing at the Curzon Mayfair. Then we were going for Peking duck in Chinatown. And maybe we would end the evening with a shot of espresso in some small Soho dive before returning home for slow, lazy sex and a good night's sleep.

Film, duck, coffee, fuck.

Then making spoons, and sharing the same pillow for a good eight hours.

The perfect date.

Our night on the town wasn't exactly hanging out at the Met Bar with the Gallaghers, but I knew that it would make us happy. It had many times before. But maybe I tried a little too hard to make it like the old days.

The movie was good. And we walked through the narrow streets of Soho hand in hand, laughing about Alvy Singer and his Annie Hall, lost in the film and each other, just like it was in our once upon a time.

It only started to go wrong in Chinatown.

The Shenyang Tiger was crowded. There was an entire Chinese family at the next table – nan, granddad, a few young husbands and wives and their flock of beautiful kids, including a brand-new baby, a fat-faced Buddha with a startling shock of jet-black Elvis hair.

Cyd and I stared at the baby, then smiled at each other.

'Isn't he gorgeous?' she said. 'All that hair.'

'Would you like one? It's not too late to change your order. I can have the duck and you can have the baby.'

I was only kidding – wasn't I? – but her smile vanished instantly.

'Oh, come on. Not the baby thing again, Harry. You never shut up about it, do you?'

'What are you talking about? It wasn't the baby thing again. I'm just pulling your leg, darling. You used to have a sense of humour.'

'And you used to let me have a life.'

'What does that mean?'

'I know you want me to give up the business. It's true, isn't it? You want me pregnant and in the kitchen. I know you do.'

I said nothing. How could I deny that I would prefer her to make dinner for her family rather than half of fashionable London? How could I deny that I wanted a baby, a family, and all the old-fashioned dreams?

I wanted us to be the way we were. But it wasn't because I wanted to imprison her. It was because I loved her.

The waiter arrived with our Peking duck, and plates of cucumber, spring onion and plum sauce. I waited until he had shredded the duck and gone.

'I just want you to be happy, Cyd.'

'Then leave me alone, Harry. Let me run my business. Let me try to do something for myself for just once in my life. Stop trying to make me give it all up to be – I don't even know what it is you want. Doris Day, is it? Mary Tyler Moore? Your mother? Some fifties housewife who doesn't go out at night.'

My mother was actually out all the time. Doing the Four-Star Boogie and the Get In Line and the I Like It I Love It and the Walkin' Wazi. But I let it pass.

'I don't mind you going out at night. I'm happy your business is going so well. I just wish that there were more nights like this. When you were spending the night with me.'

But her blood was up now.

'You really want to be the sole breadwinner, don't you? The big man. Are you going to spend the rest of your life trying to be your father?'

'Probably. I can think of worse things to be than my old man.' I pushed my plate away. Suddenly I didn't have much of an appetite. 'And are you going to spend the rest of your life sucking up to creeps?'

'Luke Moore is not a creep. He's a brilliant businessman.'

'Who said anything about Luke bloody Moore? I'm talking about all those drunken City boys who think they can get into your thong because you give them a bit of chicken on a stick.'

A mobile phone began to ring from deep inside her handbag. She fished it out and immediately recognised the number calling. Because it was our number.

'Sally?' She was babysitting for us. Cyd didn't like anyone outside our little family looking after Peggy. 'Well, how long has she been vomiting?'

Oh great, I thought. Now the kid's puking all over the babysitter.

'Everything fine?' said the waiter.

'Wonderful, thanks.' I smiled.

'And is it solid or liquid?' Cyd said. 'Okay, okay. Well, can't you get her to be sick down the toilet? Right, right. Look, we'll be home in half an hour, Sally. What? Well, just change her pyjamas and stick the dirty ones in the washing machine. We're going to jump in a cab. See you.'

'Something wrong?'

'Peggy. You know she doesn't like it when we're both out at the same time. She gets an upset tummy.' She beckoned a passing waitress. 'Can we get the bill, please?' Then she looked at my stony face. 'Are you sulking because Peggy is sick?'

'We should stay. You should eat your lovely duck. There's nothing wrong with Peggy.'

'She's just brought up her Mister Milano pizza. How can you say there's nothing wrong with her?'

'This always happens.' It was true. Every time we had one of our rare nights out, it was as if Peggy was sticking her fingers down her throat. 'Look, if she was really sick, I'd be as worried as you.'

'Really? As worried as me? I don't think so, Harry.'

'Can't you see? It's a kind of blackmail. She only does it to get you to come home. Eat your dinner, Cyd.'

'I don't want my dinner. And you should understand how she feels, Harry. If anyone should understand, it's you. You know what it's like to be a single parent.'

'Is that what you think? That you're a single parent?' I shook my head. 'You're married, Cyd. You stopped being a single parent on our wedding day.'

'Then why do I still feel like a single parent? Why do I feel so alone?'

'It's not because there's something wrong with Peggy.' A waiter placed a bill and a quartered orange in front of us. 'It's because there's something wrong with us.'

Outside the night had soured.

The good-natured, slow-moving crowds of early evening had been replaced by mobs of noisy drunks. The tourists were coming out of *Mamma Mia!* and *Les Misérables*, desperately hailing cabs that were already occupied. The streets were full of yobs in from the suburbs and beggars in from faraway towns. A scrappy, half-hearted fight was starting outside a packed pub. You could hear the sound of broken glass and sirens.

Then I saw her.

Kazumi.

She was in the queue outside that church on Shaftesbury Avenue that they had turned into a club almost twenty years ago. Limelight. Gina and I had gone there a couple of times. I didn't even know that Limelight was still open.

Kazumi was with a bunch of men and women, slightly younger than herself, all locals by the look of them. She was at the centre of the crowd, the boys trying to impress her, the girls wanting to be her friend. She smiled patiently, caught my eye and stared straight through me, not recognising the man from her friend's past, or just not caring.

Kazumi was going dancing.

I was going home just as she was going out.

It wasn't a different kind of night out.

It was a different kind of life.

fifteen

Another postcard from America. On the front, under the words *Connecticut – the Nutmeg state, New England*, a rural wilderness ablaze with the colours of fall. On the back, in joined-up writing, a message from my son.

> *Dear Daddy. We have a dog. His name is Britney. We love him. Goodbye.*

'Britney's a funny old name for a dog,' said my mother. 'I suppose that was Gina's idea.'

My mum had once loved Gina. I always said that when they first met, my mum thought Gina was a Home Counties version of Grace Kelly, a perfect combination of blue-eyed beauty, old-fashioned decency and regal bearing. Since our divorce my mum had slowly revised her opinion. Now Gina was less the Princess of Monaco and more the Whore of Babylon.

'Maybe Britney is a bitch, Mum.'

'There's no need for talk like that,' said my mother.

We were at my dad's grave. It was the first time I had been here since Christmas Day after picking up my mum to take her to our place for the holiday. Three months ago now. It had been a surprisingly good Christmas – my mum and Cyd amusing each other greatly as they stuffed a giant turkey, Peggy on the phone to Pat for an hour comparing gifts, and the look on Peggy's face when she opened her surprise present – an Ibiza DJ Brucie Doll, including his own little turntables.

With Pat gone, I was expecting Christmas to be steeped in feelings of sadness and loss, and in fact it was more of a respite from those things. But time was grinding on, and I saw that my dad's headstone was no longer as white and pristine as it had seemed a few months ago. It was now stained by the winter, tilted by time. Things were wearing out without me even noticing.

'Is Pat all right?' my mum said. 'Does he like his school? Has he made friends? There was trouble here, wasn't there? You and Gina had to see his teacher, I remember. Is he all right now?'

'He's fine, Mum,' I said, although in truth I had no idea if Pat was a straight-A student or wandering his new classroom at will. It didn't feel like my son was thousands of miles away. It felt like light years.

'I miss him, you know.'

'I know you do, Mum. I miss him too.'

'Will he come back for the holidays?'

'The summer vacation. He'll be back for that.'

'That's a long time. Summer's a long way away. What about Easter? Couldn't he come over for Easter?'

'I'll talk about it with Gina, Mum.'

'I hope he comes back for his Easter holidays.'

'I'll try, Mum.'

'Because you never know what's going to happen, do you? You never know.'

'Mum, nothing is going to happen to him,' I said, trying to keep the exasperation out of my voice. 'Pat's fine.'

She looked up at me, briskly rubbing her hands together, wiping off the dirt from my father's grave.

'I'm not talking about Pat, Harry,' she said. 'I'm talking about me.'

And I just stared at her, as I felt the world turn and change.

I had always believed that my dad was the tough one. My mum didn't drive, she wouldn't open her front door after dark, and she hated confrontation of every kind. And because she didn't have a driving licence, because she was polite to rude waiters, because she slept with the light on, I was stupid enough to believe that my mother was a timid woman. Now I was about to learn that my mother had her own well of courage.

'What happened, Mum?'

She took another breath.

'Found a lump, Harry. When I was in the shower. In my breast.'

I could feel my heart.

'Oh God, Mum. Oh Jesus.'

'It's small. And very hard. I went to see the doctor. You know how much I hate seeing the doctor. A bit like your dad, really. Now I've got to go for tests. Graham's going to take me in his car.'

This is how it happens, I thought. You lose one parent, and then you lose the other. Selfishly, I thought – I went through all this with Dad, and I don't know if I can do it again. But I knew I would have to. It was the most natural thing in the world.

I could imagine her in the shower. I could see her washing herself with the Body Shop soap in the shape of a dolphin that her grandson had bought her for Christmas. I could see my mother's face, her kind and irreplaceable face, as she discovered something that had never been there before.

A small, hard lump.

That lump the size of a planet.

When I came home I found Peggy sitting cross-legged on the carpet, studying a book on Lucy Doll.

'Look what I've got, Harry.'

I sat on the floor with her and looked at the book. *I Love Lucy Doll: The World's Favourite Dolly* was a serious coffee-table job, full of social analysis and cultural deconstruction. First article – 'Where Is Lucy Doll From?' I skimmed the article, because I had always wondered that myself. It turned out that Lucy Doll was born in Paris of a part-Thai, part-Brazilian mother and an Anglo-Zulu father. The book revealed that Brucie Doll was from Ibiza.

There were more scholarly articles. Lucy Doll as modern icon. Lucy Doll as a feminist role model. Lucy Doll as a repository for traditional values. Lucy Doll as a radical of the sexual revolution. Lucy Doll was the perfect doll – you could get her to be anything you wanted her to be.

'Where did you get this, darling?'

'Uncle Luke gave it to me.'

'Uncle Luke?'

'He came home with Mummy in his racing car.'

'Did Uncle Luke come in?'

'No. But he gave Mummy this book for me. It's for big girls.'

I wondered why these creeps always gave this little girl the wrong presents. Her dad with those useless huge stuffed animals that were no good to man or beast. And now a coffee-table book from Uncle Luke. Peggy was at least a decade too young for *I Love Lucy Doll: The World's Favourite Dolly*. But what did I know? She loved poring over the pictures, and there were page after page of reproductions from all the Lucy Doll catalogues down the ages.

'All the different Lucy Dolls,' Peggy said.

There they were in all their glory. Office Lady Lucy Doll (Lucy Doll when she was working for a giant Japanese corporation before the bubble burst). Rio Dancer Lucy Doll (Carmen Miranda feathers and tails). And Working Girl Lucy Doll (the blonde locks dyed brunette to denote career-girl seriousness, Working Girl Lucy Doll carried a briefcase and wore spectacles with no lenses).

There was also Space Shuttle Lucy Doll. Funky Diva Lucy Doll. Left Bank Lucy Doll. Hippy Chick Lucy Doll. Chanteuse Lucy Doll. Bungee Jump Lucy Doll. Fighter Pilot Lucy Doll.

Lucy Doll as singer, shopper, housewife, commuter, cook, warrior, adventurer and tourist. Home and career, love and sex, domesticity and glamour, work and fun.

'Which Lucy Doll do you like best of all, Harry?'

I looked at Night-Night-Baby Lucy Doll, who wore a see-through white negligee that just about came down to her navel.

'I like Working Girl Lucy Doll,' I said.

'Why's that?'

'Reminds me of your mum.'

'Me too.'

Cyd was upstairs getting changed. She was sitting at the dressing table in her bra and pants, staring into the mirror. She looked up at me, already defensive, waiting for me to start complaining about the book, the lift home, Uncle Luke.

I shook my head, biting my lip.

'My mum,' I said.

'What happened?'

'She found a lump in her breast,' I said, my voice catching on those words and all they could mean. And my wife was across the room, taking me in her arms, and holding me in a way that she had only held me twice before.

When we knew my dad was dying.

And when my son went to live with his mother.

The really bad times, the worst times of all.

She held me. My wife held me. She put her arms around me and squeezed me tight, as if she would never let go, smoothing my hair, whispering words that were as soft as a prayer.

Gently rocking me as I cried, and cried, and cried.

My doctor had me swimming. Most mornings I went to the local public pool as soon as it opened, and joined the office workers doing their lengths.

I swam up and down, chanting my mantra: *my heart is a small miracle, my heart is a small miracle*. I swam until failure. That was a new expression I had recently learned. It meant doing something until you just couldn't do it any more. Until failure.

When I came out of the pool, the rush hour was in full booming flow. The people in the park were all hurrying to the tube station.

Apart from her.

Kazumi was crouching on the grass, peering into her camera, the office workers swarming either side of her. A squirrel and I stopped to watch her.

She was wearing a black parka, boots, and a short beige-coloured kilt. Even I could tell it was from Burberry. Black tights. Good legs. Hair falling in front of her face, getting pushed out again. She looked too good for the rush hour.

'What are you taking a picture of?'

She looked up at me. Recognised me this time. Smiled. 'The leaves. All the new leaves. They're beautiful but they just stay a moment. Like *sakura* in Japan. You know *sakura*?'

I nodded. 'Cherry blossom, right? The Japanese go to the park to look at the cherry blossom in full bloom for a few days every year. School kids, salary men, office ladies, old people. All watching the cherry blossom before it dies.'

She stood up, smoothed her Burberry kilt and pushed more hair out of her eyes. 'You know *sakura* because of Gina?'

'Yes, because of Gina.' All those years with my first wife had given me a crash course in Japanese culture. I knew my *sakura* traditions. 'I'm not sure a few leaves in north London are in quite the same league.'

She laughed. 'Beautiful colours. All the different greens. Not so obvious. You just have to look with different eyes. Are you interested in photography?'

'Me? Absolutely.'

'Really?'

'Sure. For me it's not just about getting the holiday snaps developed at the chemist. Photography is, you know, a twentieth-century art form. A, er, genuinely modern medium that hasn't been fully explored yet.'

What was I going on about? What was all this rubbish? She must have thought I was a complete jerk.

'*Plead the fleeting moment to remain*,' she said.

I must have looked baffled.

'Someone once said that about photography. A poet, I think. It's like watching *sakura*. The moment is interesting, because it is only a moment. *Plead the fleeting moment to remain*.' She smiled. 'I love that. It's so beautiful.'

Plead the fleeting moment to remain, I thought.

'I love it too,' I said. And I meant it.

She put the lens cap on her camera, smoothed her kilt again. She was getting ready to go. I scrambled to keep the conversation afloat.

'Everything okay with you, Kazumi? You working here?'

'Trying. Looking.'

'You found a place to live?'

She nodded. 'Still in Primrose Hill. A few blocks from Gina's old place.'

'That's nice. Primrose Hill is great.'

'Saw Jude Law in shop. With baby.'

'Lucky old you.' Although what I really thought was – lucky old Jude Law. 'I've been meaning to ask you – can I order some more of those pictures of Pat? If you're not too busy? I've marked the contact sheet. I know exactly what I want.'

She nodded. These small, encouraging nods. 'I post to you.'

'Or I could come to your place and collect them.'

'Or I post.'

'It's no trouble. Really.'

She stared at me for a moment, thinking about it.

'You want a cup of tea, Kazumi? There's a café over by the tennis courts.'

'Sure. British always want a cup of tea.'

'Just like the Japanese.'

We walked over to the small café by the tennis courts, moving against the scuttling tide of office workers. And as we ordered our drinks, I could picture myself in her flat in Primrose Hill, see her pulling off her boots and stepping out of her Burberry kilt. I could see it, and it felt like the best thing in the world. It was that old, dangerous feeling of something about to start.

'How's Pat?' she said, and I adored her for that. I would have adored anyone who cared enough to ask me about my boy.

'He's fine, I guess,' I said. 'Started school. Got a dog called Britney. He's coming over for his holidays. Soon, I hope. We have to work it out. What about you? Happy in London?'

'Happier than Tokyo. Happier than when I was married.'

I thought of the crying man in Gina's garden. Part of me didn't want to know. I hate it when they tell you about the old days. It just puts a crimp in everything for me. But she wanted me to hear. I was too curious to try stopping her.

'He's a photographer. Famous, sort of. At least in Tokyo. He loved lots of European photographers. Horst, Robert Doisneau, Alan Brooking. Magnum photographers. You know? Magnum agency? He was very brilliant. I was his assistant. First job after college. I – how to say? – looked up for him.'

'Looked up to him.'

'He was very encouraged. *Encouraging*. Then we got married and he changed. Wanted me to stay home. Have a baby.'

'What kind of man does a thing like that?'

'Didn't want me to work.' She sipped her tea. 'Like you and Gina.'

I couldn't let her get away with that.

'Nothing like me and Gina. She *wanted* to stay home and raise our son. At least at first.'

'Married men,' she said, as if that explained everything. She stood up, pulled out a little Prada purse. For all her talk about Magnum photographers, she was a classic Japanese girl. Prada and Burberry mad.

'Put your money away. I'll get these. You can get them next time.'

'No,' she said. 'No next time. I post those pictures of Pat.'

Then she was leaving, watched by our squirrel and me as she disappeared among the office workers. An Asian girl in a Burberry kilt. I called after her.

'But when will I see you again?'

She raised her left hand, without turning round. 'When your finger gets better.'

I looked down at my hand and saw the gold band glinting on my third finger. It felt like there was something wrong with it today.

It was cutting into me.

I knew that deep down inside Gina still had a soft spot for me.

'You bloody imbecile,' she said when I called. 'You dickhead.

You klutz. You 24-carat fool. Do you have any idea what time it is here? Gone one. Pat went to bed hours ago. You moron, Harry.'

'It's not Pat I want to talk to. It's you.'

'Make it snappy. I'm just about to floss and go to bed.'

'I want Pat to come back. For a week or so. Seven days. Anything. Easter. How's Easter?'

I could hear her putting her hand over the receiver, telling Richard that it was me. And I heard him sigh, slam a door, go into a sulk.

'That's not possible, Harry.'

'Why not?'

'Because it's too expensive to keep flying him back and forth across the Atlantic. It's too disruptive. And he's too young. Who do you think he is? Tony Blair? He's only seven.'

'He'll be fine. It will be an adventure. I have to see him. I can't wait until summer. And the money's not a problem.'

'Oh really?' She could be dead sarcastic. 'It might not be a problem for you. But Richard's job at Bridle-Worthington has not turned out too well.' A beat. 'He quit.'

'Jesus, he can't *keep* changing jobs. He's just going to have to buckle down and start remembering he has some responsibilities.'

A long silence in reply. And I guessed that my ex-wife had said almost those very words to fussy old Richard.

'So he's unemployed?'

'No – he's *looking round*. But we don't have money to go –'

'I'll pay. Don't worry about that, Gina. I just want to see my son. I just want him to remember he has a life here. He has holidays, doesn't he? Send him over at Easter. Send him any time.'

'I'll think about it.'

'Please.' Begging her to let me see my son. But for some reason I felt no anger. For some reason I couldn't quite fathom, it was something far closer to pity. 'How's it going over there?'

'Oh, the New England coast is beautiful. Very historic. Lots of little antique shops and fishing villages. And all these names that remind you of being a kid in England – Yarmouth, Portsmouth. I think there's even a Little Hampton. All these English names, Harry.'

'Sounds great. I'm happy for you, Gina.'

'But . . .'

'What?'

Her voice was just above a whisper. As if she was talking to herself, not me. 'Well, it's not really like that where we live. It's not so quaint and lovely in Hartford. See, Hartford is a big ugly town. There's crime. And I'm a bit – I don't know what you would call it. Lonely, I guess. I think I'm lonely. Richard's off to the city every day looking for a job. Pat's at school.'

'Doing well?'

'He's doing very well. He's not wandering around in the middle of lessons any more.'

'That's fantastic, Gina.'

'But I don't know anyone. Everybody's gone in the daytime, and locked up at home at night. It's not quite what I expected.' She recovered, remembered who she was talking to. 'But we'll be fine, we'll be fine.'

'Listen, let Pat come over for a week. He can spend some time with my mum. He'd love that. So would she.' I didn't tell Gina about my mum, about the lump the size of a planet. Those days were long gone. 'Because you never know what's going to happen in life, do you?'

'That's right,' said my ex-wife. 'You never know what's going to happen in life.'

sixteen

If you saw my mum walking down the street, you might think she was just another little old lady on her way to buy some cat food. But you would be wrong.

She can't stand cats for a start, because she claims they leave a terrible mess everywhere (although strangely she always stoops to pet and coo over even the most flea-bitten moggy she encounters on her travels). Looking at my mum, you might think you knew all about her. But you would not know her at all.

Some things I know about my mother.

She thinks Dolly Parton is the greatest singer in the world and that people shouldn't make fun of Dolly's figure all the time. She will watch any kind of sport on TV but prefers the more violent games (boxing, rugby, the NFL). She believes that her grandson was the most beautiful baby in the history of the world. She reckons that is a completely objective opinion, and she is not remotely biased.

Some more things I know about my mum. She gets unimaginably lonely since my dad died. It doesn't matter how many people are around her. She worshipped my father, and talks to his photographs when she thinks nobody is listening. A visit to his grave is my mum's idea of a good day out.

I know she inspires an incredible love in her family and friends – young neighbours repair her guttering for a cup of tea, her army of silver-haired friends are constantly asking her to hang out at the new shopping mall, and her brothers call her every day.

My mum is kind, funny and brave. Very brave. Although she doesn't open her front door after dark, she is always ready to stand up to any passing bully. When Pat was very small she threatened to punch out a gang of youths who were getting what she called *wild* in the local General Lee's Tasty Tennessee Kitchen.

I was angry with her at the time – I thought they might stab her, because even little old ladies are not safe in the lousy modern world – but now I am glad she did it. That's her. That's my mum. That's what she's like. I am proud of her.

She doesn't have the short fuse that my father had. She is tolerant of other ways of life, believing in the essential goodness of mankind. But when she loses her temper, she goes . . . well, *wild* is what she would call it.

Her favourite brother, the one who is closest to her in age, likes reminding her about the scar she put in the upright piano in the East End home they grew up in. My mum, enraged at some teasing from her brother, threw a knife at his head. It missed him by inches and stuck in the piano, quivering the way knives only do in cartoons. The attempted murder of her brother was out of character. She was a quiet, shy girl, bullied at school for a slight speech impediment (not bullied by her schoolmates, bullied by teachers, for that East End school was as brutal as a workhouse in Dickens). She always claimed the knife had slipped. Her brother insisted she had aimed the blade to perfection.

In a house full of boys, she was as distant and regal as a Virgin Queen. Doted on by her parents, encouraged to think of herself as special, she was as indulged as an only child.

I know my mum was always loved – as the only girl in a large family of boys, and as the only female in the small family that I grew up in – and I believe that is why she is so good at giving love. I know that Pat and I would be lost without her. I can't even imagine what the world would be like without my mum in it.

She is full of life. She has more life in her than anyone I've ever known. She likes to sing and dance. I know she likes a laugh, even at the worst of times, especially at the worst of times. We still smile about when she slammed her head against my father's coffin at his funeral.

Only someone who loves people as much as my mum could ever get so lonely. She carefully plans her evening viewing. She likes the news, real-people documentaries, but she raises an eyebrow at all the pierced tongues and nipples on *Six Pissed Students in a Flat*. I know she sneers at soap operas, although back in the eighties she liked JR in *Dallas*. Cartoon villainy amuses her.

What else? Oh yes.

I know my mother hates going to the doctor.

In the end Tex didn't take my mum to the hospital. Apparently his car was having trouble with its big end, although I suspected that the real problem was Tex having trouble with his nerve.

My mum told me she would get the bus. I said that I would come to the hospital with her. She said the bus was fine. She didn't want to make a fuss. That was always one of her big things – not making a fuss. If the Four Horsemen of the Apocalypse appeared in her back garden, rampaging through her rose bushes, my mum would try not to make a fuss.

Having a laugh and not making a fuss. That was her way. That was her philosophy. A kind of light-hearted stoicism that pulled at my heart, and made me feel like putting my arm around her.

But it was difficult to laugh today. It was difficult to grin and bear it on days like these.

When she came out from seeing the specialist I could tell the news was bad.

She was struggling to understand the diagnosis, trying to understand the language, trying to understand how a hardened piece of flesh could change your world so completely.

She didn't want to talk about it in the overcrowded waiting room. She didn't want to talk about it until we were back in my car.

We sat in the hospital's endless car park. Other cars circled like sharks, looking for a precious parking space. It was a busy day for the hospital. They were probably all busy days.

'Look – I've written it down.' She showed me a scrap of paper. She had written *invasive carcinoma* in her shaky hand.

'What does it mean?' I said, sort of knowing what it meant, but unable to believe it.

'Breast cancer,' said my mum.

Of course, I thought. First one parent and then the other. The most natural thing in the world, as natural as the birth of a child. Then why did it feel like the world was coming apart?

'The doctor at the breast unit says they don't know what they're going to do yet. How to treat it. Nice bloke. Some sort of Mediterranean. Spoke English better than me. They do, don't they? Gave it to me straight. Says there's something called *staging*. It means they have to assess the risk of it spreading. And, you know. How far it's spread already.'

I was speechless.

'I met the breast care nurse. She was nice. Lovely girl. Her nose was – what do you call it? Pierced. Specially trained to deal with my kind of case. I've got to go back, Harry. I can get the bus. Don't worry. I know you're busy.'

I stared at her profile as she looked across at the hospital, I watched that soft, kind face that I had known longer than any other, and saw all the emotions churning inside her.

Shock. Fear. Bewilderment. Anger. Even the darkest kind of amusement.

'Graham didn't stick around long, did he? Old Tex. Cowboy Joe from the Rio Southend. Soon buggered off when the music stopped. Your dad would have been here. Your dad would have been here for me, Harry. That man would have walked through fire for me. That's a marriage, Harry. That's what a marriage is all about.'

'There's lots they can do, isn't there?'

She was silent, lost in her own thoughts.

'Mum? I said, there's plenty they can do, isn't there?'

'Oh yes. Oh yes. Lots they can do. I'm going to beat this thing. I mean it, Harry. People live with breast cancer. They do. People *live*. It's not like your dad. Can't fight lung cancer. Can't fight that. Bloody lung cancer. Bloody cancer. Took your dad. It's not going to take me. Bloody, bloody cancer. It's a right . . . *bastard*.' She glanced at me. 'Excuse my language.'

'Mum?'

'What, love?'

'I'm really proud that you're my mum.'

She nodded, took my hand and held it. Held it so tight in her own small hand that I could feel that piece of precious metal pressing into my palm, that sliver of gold, burnished by a lifetime.

My mother's wedding ring.

It fit her perfectly.

My parents met through her brother. The one she threw the knife at and tried to kill. He was always her favourite.

My mum's brother and my dad went to the same boxing club for boys. This was back when boxing was as popular among schoolboys as football. That's all changed now, of course, and the only men in television I know who boxed at school all went to Eton.

But this was back when boxing was considered a healthy pastime for growing boys. And after sparring together – my uncle and my father were exactly the same weight and age, both one year older than my mum – my mum's brother brought my dad home to that house in an East End banjo, which was what they called their little dead-end street, a banjo, because that's exactly what it was shaped like. And growing up in that banjo, a house full of boys. And one girl.

At seventeen, my dad had already been at work for three years. He was cocky and wild, his pride primed with an explosive temper – after one of his army of cousins had sworn at him, he had tied her to a lamppost and washed her mouth out with soap. There was an anger in him. He would fight anyone. He seemed to enjoy it. Then he saw my mother, just sixteen years old, the spoilt princess of the banjo, and he found his reason to stop fighting and start living.

She taught him to be gentle – her and the unimaginable things he did and saw in the war. He taught her to be strong. Or maybe it was all there already – the roaring boy was more sensitive than he dared to let on. And perhaps she was always harder than she seemed. The reserved sixteen-year-old girl had been toughened up by poverty, life in the banjo and all those brothers.

But they had a deliriously happy marriage. Even up to the day my father died, they were mad about each other. For an entire lifetime, they never really stopped courting.

He sent her red roses, she brought him breakfast in bed. He stared at her, unable to believe his luck. She wrote him poems. Put them in his lunch box. I saw his cards to her – Mother's Day, birthday, Christmas. His angel, he called her. The love of his life. He seemed like the least romantic man in the world, and she inspired him to write sonnets.

The products of close-knit, crowded communities, they were content in the company of each other. The only real trauma in their union was all those years at the start when a baby just would not come. And later, after I finally arrived, when she suffered a heartbreaking string of miscarriages. One of my clearest memories of childhood is my mum sitting on the floor of our rented flat above a greengrocer's shop, inconsolable as my father tried to comfort her, his broken-hearted angel, his devastated true love, crying for another lost child.

My first look at married life.

When I became a parent, I found myself imitating them, trying to strike their balance between being strict and being gentle. They seemed like perfect parents to me. Loving and tough.

My father never lifted a finger to either of us – he reserved his violence for strangers who were dumb enough to cross him. My mum was not averse to aiming a shoe at me – at least it wasn't a knife – when I drove her to distraction with my daydreaming and solitary games, the comforts of the only child that frequently prevented me from coming when I was called. But she had waited too long for a baby to ever be mad at me for long.

'Wait until your father gets home,' she would tell me, and it was her ultimate threat.

It never frightened me, though. Because I knew they loved me, and I knew that it was a love that was unconditional and everlasting, a love that was built to last a lifetime and beyond.

No, what frightened me as a child was the thought of losing my mother. Small, curly-haired, five foot and a bit, she would disappear up to the row of shops near our home on black, blustery winter evenings, the kind of November and December nights that we no longer seem to get, off to buy something for our tea. Those were the years when it snowed in winter and, in my memory at least, the streets were shrouded in the fog of countless open fires. She would be on an errand for mince, pork chops or baked beans, or on Fridays fish and chips wrapped in newspaper – the menu of my childhood.

And I would be anxious, unbearably anxious for the return of this woman, my mum, who had just nipped down the shops. Still in my school uniform of grey flannel trousers, grey shirt and stripy tie, that old man's drag they made us wear, I would stand on the back of the sofa and press my face against a window streaming with condensation, scanning the dark, empty streets.

Searching for the irreplaceable sight of my mother, and tortured by the thought that she was never coming home again.

Cyd and I took my mum to a show.

My father had always taken my mother to shows. Every six months or so they would put on their best clothes and head for the bright lights of London. For two people who spent most evenings in front of the television set, they were connoisseurs of musical theatre.

When the film versions of *Oklahoma!*, *West Side Story* or *My Fair Lady* came on TV, they would both sing along, word perfect. My mum would also dance – she did a particularly good imitation of the cool-daddy-o ballet of the Sharks and the Jets in *West Side Story*. For my mum, musicals were not a passive experience. She had been going to the West End for fifty years, and there were few tunes being banged out nightly on Shaftesbury Avenue, the Strand and Haymarket that she didn't know better than the people singing them.

Now she decided she wanted to catch *Les Misérables* again.

'I love that one,' she told Cyd. 'I like the little girl. And I like the prostitutes. And I like it when all the students get shot. It's very sad and there are some lovely melodies in it.'

She wore a white two-piece suit from Bloomingdale's that I had brought her back from a trip to New York. She looked lovely but frail, and older, far older, than I had ever thought she would be.

Cyd took her hand when we picked her up, and never let it go as we made our way to the Palace Theatre in Cambridge Circus. Cyd held her hand on the drive into town, held it as we made our way through the teeming early-evening crowds, my mum looking too easily broken for the city, too delicate to be surrounded by all the traffic and bustle and hordes.

The audience inside the Palace was the usual mixture of foreign tourists, coach trips in from the suburbs and locals on a big night out. Directly in front of us there was a young man in a pinstripe suit, some well-scrubbed junior hotshot from the City, with what looked like his mother on one side and his grandmother on the other side. I didn't like him from the start.

He made a big deal about turning round and shaking his head just because my mum clipped him around the ear a few times with her coat as she was struggling to take it off. Then he tutted elaborately when she whistled through the overture. And then, when the show began, he kept on loudly clearing his throat when my mum sang along to Fantine's big dying number, 'I Dreamed a Dream'. Finally, as my mum joined in for the cast's stirring rendition of 'Do You Hear the People Sing?', he turned around angrily.

'Will you please shut up?' he hissed.

'Leave her alone, pal,' said Cyd, and I loved her for it. 'We've paid for our tickets too.'

'We can't enjoy the show if she acts like she's part of the chorus!'

'Who's *she?*' I demanded.

Behind us people started going, 'Ssssh!' Bald and permed heads were turning. Well-fed faces creased with irritation.

'*Do you hear the people sing, singing the song of angry men?*' sang my mum, happily oblivious. '*It is the music of a people who will not be slaves again!*'

The young suit's posh old granny stuck her oar in. 'We've paid for our seats, too, you know.'

'We can't concentrate on the performance,' whined her frumpy daughter.

'You don't need to concentrate, lady,' said Cyd. 'You just need to lie back and enjoy it. You know how to lie back and enjoy it, don't you?'

'Well, really!'

'I'm getting help,' said her son, and went off to find a young woman with a torch.

Then they threw us out.

They were very nice about it. Told us that if we couldn't silence my mum then the management reserved the right to ask us to leave. And there was no way of shutting up my mum when we still had the deaths of Valjean, Javert, Eponine and all those nice students to look forward to.

So we went. My wife and my mother and me. Laughing about it already, as though getting thrown out of a musical was actually much more fun than watching one. Making our way through the funky crowds to the Bar Italia where my mum was promised a lovely cup of tea.

The three of us, my wife and my mother and me, arm in arm in the streets of Soho.

Singing 'Empty Chairs at Empty Tables' at the top of our voices.

seventeen

I met my son at the airport.

He came through the arrival gate holding the hand of a young British Airways stewardess. There was some sort of identification tag around his neck, as worn by child evacuees in old black-and-white wars, or Paddington Bear.

Please look after this child.

'Pat! Over here! Pat!'

The stewardess spotted me before he did. He was chatting away to her, his face pale and serious, and then he saw me through the legs of all those arriving tourists and business types. He broke away from the BA girl and ran to my arms, and I was on my knees, holding him tight and kissing his mop of blond hair.

'Let me look at you, darling.'

He grinned and yawned, and I saw that the gummy gap that had existed at the front of his mouth had changed. There were now two uneven fragments of pure white bone pushing through. The teeth that would have to last him a lifetime.

There were other changes. He was taller, and his hair was maybe slightly darker, and I didn't recognise any of his clothes.

'Are you all right? How was the flight? It's so good to see you, darling!'

'You can't sleep on planes because they keep coming round making you try to eat things,' he reflected, blinking his tired blue eyes. 'You have to choose between fish and chicken.'

'He's a little bit jet-lagged, aren't you, Pat?' said the BA girl. Then she gave me a dazzling white smile. 'He's such a lovely boy.'

It was true. He was a lovely boy. Smart, funny and beautiful. And independent and brave – flying across the Atlantic all by himself. A terrific kid.

My son, when he was seven years old.

We thanked the girl from BA and caught a cab back into town. My heart felt lighter than it had in months.

'Everything okay in Connecticut?'

'Fine.'

'You like your new school? Making friends?'

'Good.'

'Mummy all right?'

'She's okay.' He paused, frowning at the slow-moving traffic heading for the motorway. 'But she argues with Richard. They had a little bit of a row about Britney.'

So that was the trouble with Gina. For a moment I wondered who Britney was – some hot little babysitter? Or some cute secretary looking for love? But Britney couldn't be a secretary. Richard didn't have a job. It had all fallen through at Bridle-Worthington. So who was this mystery woman?

'Britney was sick in the living room,' Pat said. 'Richard was very angry. Then Britney wet the Indian rug and had to have an operation and Richard said it was disgusting the way Britney kept biting at the stitches.'

I was thinking that Britney must be one hell of a babysitter, and then I remembered. Of course. My son had a dog now.

A slow smile spread across Pat's face.

'Guess what? At dinner he sits right by the table and licks his, you know, willie.'

I raised my eyebrows.

'Richard or Britney?'

My son thought about it for a moment.

'You must be joking,' he said.

'Come here, you.'

Then he slid across the seat and climbed on to my lap. I could smell that old Pat smell of sugar and dirt, sense his exhaustion. Within minutes he was fast asleep.

The cab driver had pictures of three small children on his dashboard. He looked at us in his rear-view mirror and smiled.

'You two boys come far?' he said.

I held my son close.

'Oh yes,' I said. 'We've come a very long way.'

Cyd had hung balloons on the front door, and it filled me with gratitude and love.

She was waiting for us as I paid the driver, wreathed in smiles. As I dragged Pat's suitcase up our garden path she crouched down and threw her arms around him and I felt like we were becoming a real family at last.

Peggy was in the living room watching a Lucy Doll video. It was a film that Peggy and I had watched before, an animated double bill featuring a cheapo cartoon version of Lucy Doll Rock and Roll and her blank-faced band getting stranded in a fifties time warp.

'Lucy Doll Rock and Roll and her friends can't wait to join the hep teens down at the soda shop for a bebopping, finger-licking good time,' said Peggy. 'Strap yourself in for action, because the countdown to fun has begun!'

Pat smiled shyly at his oldest friend.

'Hello, Pat,' Peggy said with the brisk formality of minor royalty. 'So how's America?'

'Good,' he said. 'I've got a dog. His name's Britney. He's not allowed in the house because he licks his willie right in front of everybody.'

'Sorry to disappoint you, Pat,' sniffed Peggy. 'But he can't be a boy dog if his name is Britney. Because Britney is a girl's name, *stupid*.'

Pat looked up at me for support. 'Britney is a boy dog, isn't he?'

I thought of Britney licking his enormous great penis at the dinner table.

'I would say so, darling.'

'Do you want to watch *Lucy Doll's American Graffiti* with me?' said Peggy. 'Lucy Doll Rock and Roll magically comes to life in this stunning adaptation of the much loved classic.'

Cyd and I smiled at each other. She gave my arm a little squeeze. She knew how much this meant to me.

Pat considered the vision in pink doing a Chuck Berry duck-walk across the TV screen.

'Lucy Doll sucks,' he said.

'Pat,' I said.

'Lucy Doll sucks big time.'

'*Pat.*'

'Lucy Doll can kiss my royal ass.'

'Pat, I'm warning you.'

'Lucy Doll can go fuck herself.'

And it sort of went downhill from there.

I had never seen my mother so happy in my life.

This was more than happiness. Seeing her grandson again provoked a kind of ecstasy, a kind of delirious abandon. My mum lost herself in her grandson.

Before I had the handbrake on she had picked him up and squeezed the air out of him. She held him at arm's length and stared with wonder at his gorgeous face. She shook her head, unable to believe that he was back.

If only for a week.

We went inside. Pink and purple leaflets were strewn across her coffee table. My mother quickly began to gather them up. But not before I caught sight of some of the titles.

Here for You. Coping with a Diagnosis. Breast Reconstruction. Friends of Breast Cancer Care. Going into Hospital. Zoladex. Taxol. Taxotere. Arimidex. Chemotherapy. Radiotherapy.

I didn't even understand half of the titles. But I knew what they all meant.

'You okay, Mum?' I asked, the most useless question of all, but one I couldn't stop myself asking. Because I wanted so much for her to tell me that everything was going to be all right, and that she would always be in this world.

'Oh, I'm fine,' she said, not wanting to make a fuss, seeking to avoid self-pity and melodrama at all costs. 'They sent me this stuff. I don't know how they expect me to read it all.'

She gathered up her cancer leaflets and stuffed them into a drawer.

Then she clapped her hands.

'I'm going to make a nice cup of tea for my two boys,' she said. 'How about that?'

'I can't have caffeine,' Pat said, picking up the television remote. 'Mummy said.'

'And I've already had a few cappuccinos,' I said. 'My doctor doesn't want me to have more than three shots of caffeine a day. Bad for blood pressure, you see.'

'Oh,' said my mum, bewildered. 'Oh, all right. I'll just make one for myself then, shall I?'

So Pat and I slumped on that sagging old sofa that seemed to know every last nook and curve in our bodies and my mum went off to the kitchen, humming Dolly Parton's 'Jolene', and contemplating this strange new world where her son and grandson were both forbidden from having a nice cup of tea.

Later we were in the park watching Pat tackle the upper regions of a rusty climbing frame. He wasn't the tentative small boy he had been only a couple of years earlier. Now he was as fearless as a mountain goat.

Two bigger boys were clambering around the very top like monkeys in Tommy Hilfiger. Every now and again Pat would pause, hold on tight, and gaze up at them with adoration. He still loved bigger boys. They ignored him completely.

'It's good to have him back,' I said. 'Feels more like a proper family again. Especially when we are out here with you. Just a regular family where you don't have to think too much about anything. Where it all seems – I don't know – normal. Like you and Dad.'

My father would have happily concurred with my yearning for normality. The old man would have bemoaned the death of the family, the rise in the divorce rate, the generation of children who were being brought up with one of their parents missing. He would have done all that while rolling himself a cigarette.

My dad was all for normality.

But my mum was made of different stuff.

'What's normal?' she said. 'Your dad and I were married for ten years before you came along. You call us normal? We felt like anything but normal. We felt like freaks.'

The two bigger boys jumped off the climbing frame and ran to the swings. Pat smiled at them with undiluted affection.

'All our friends were having children,' my mum said. 'Like a bunch of rabbits, they were. One of them always had a bun in the oven. Up the spout, in the club, knocked up. But it didn't happen for us.' She gave a smile. 'And you call us normal, Harry. Bless you. We didn't feel very normal, I can tell you.'

I watched my son laboriously edging his way up the climbing frame, his face stern with concentration, and rosy-cheeked from the cold.

'You know what I mean. We were normal. You, me and Dad.'

And I thought of Christmas with all the aunts and uncles, caravan holidays in Cornwall, the smell of the Sunday roast cooking while my old man washed his car in the little driveway. I remembered runs to Southend, not for the pier or the beach, but for the dog track. And I remembered lying on the back seat of the car, the yellow lights of the Essex A-roads streaming about my head, coming home from seeing my nan or, once a year, a pantomime at the London Palladium, telling my mum that I couldn't sleep, I wasn't tired, not tired at all. *Just rest your eyes*, she would tell me. *Just rest your eyes*. There was a simplicity and a goodness about my childhood, and already it seemed too late for my son to have the same thing. 'You couldn't get more normal than us,' I said.

'So we became normal when you came along? And if you hadn't come along, we would have stayed freaks?'

'I don't know. I just know it felt sort of easy. In a way that it doesn't feel easy any more. Pat and Peggy are not talking. Cyd's angry with me because she thinks I'm spoiling Pat. I'm mad at

Cyd because I think she resents Pat coming over for just one lousy week.'

'Why aren't Pat and Peggy talking?'

'They had a bit of a bust-up. He called Lucy Doll a two-dollar crack whore. You know how Peggy feels about Lucy Doll.'

'Brothers and sisters fight all the time. I nearly stabbed one of my brothers.'

'Yes, but they're not brother and sister, are they? That's the point. So it can never be normal. Not really. If it falls to pieces, then what happens? We never see each other again. You're telling me that's what you call normal? Come on, Mum. Not even you're that broad-minded.'

We watched Pat climb to the summit of the frame. He stood there silhouetted against the big blue sky, the smell of spring in the air despite the chill, grinning at us, all wrapped up in his padded anorak. He held on tight with both hands. Golden strands of hair stuck out from inside the bobble hat that his grandmother had knitted him.

'I just don't like all this talk about normal,' said my mum. 'Because for years I felt anything but normal. Ten years we tried for you. Every month was another heartbreak. Times that by ten, Harry. You're the smart one. You work it out.'

One of Pat's trainers seemed to slip and I watched the expression on his face change from pride to alarm as he suddenly lurched backwards into thin air. But then he recovered, found his footing and gripped the climbing frame with his tiny fists.

'There's no such thing as a normal family,' said my mum.

Gina called.

It was close to midnight. The kids had been asleep for hours – Peggy in her room, Pat on an old futon in the guest room – and Cyd was out catering for the launch of one of those trendy hotels that were springing up all over town. After the slurs on Lucy Doll's morality, we were all talking again, although it was with a strained politeness that sometimes seemed even worse than angry silence. I was glad that nobody was around when my ex-wife called.

'Is he okay, Harry?'

'He's fine.'

'You're not letting him have sugar, are you? Or caffeine? Or British beef?'

'He hasn't had a Happy Meal since he's been here.'

'I want you to take him to see my dad.'

'Your dad? Take him to see Glenn?'

'That's right. Pat's grandfather.'

It was always difficult for me to remember that Pat had two sets of grandparents. Gina's mother had died before our son was born, and although her old man was still out there and Pat had seen him sporadically down the years, he had never been a traditional grandfather figure.

Glenn was what he had always been – a mullet-haired musician who had never quite made it out of the minor leagues. There had been the odd appearance on *Top of the Pops* at the cusp of the sixties and seventies, but Glenn had spent almost three decades as a sales assistant in a guitar shop on Denmark Street, playing 'Stairway to Heaven' for teenage *NME* readers. The best part of his energies had gone into forming a new band every few years, not to mention a new family. Gina and her mother had been left behind a lifetime ago. Musical differences, probably.

'I want him to see my dad. I want him to know that he has another grandfather. It wasn't just your dad, Harry.'

'Okay. I'll take Pat to see Glenn.'

'Thank you.'

'How's everything over there? Britney still upsetting Richard? Pat's told me all about it. Is he still licking his penis at the dinner table? The dog, I mean. Not Richard.'

'That dog is the least of our troubles,' said my ex-wife.

My son cried out in the middle of the night. I slipped out of bed, feeling Cyd stir beside me, and I went to him, treading carefully as I was more asleep than awake.

And it was as if we had never been apart.

His long fair hair was stuck to his head with perspiration. I sat him up and gave him some water, rubbing his back the way I'd done when he was a baby and needed winding.

'You can't sleep on planes,' he said in the darkness, talking in a dream. 'It's very difficult, right, because you're moving and there's all this food all the time and a little telly too. Isn't it difficult, Daddy?'

'But it's okay now. Everything's okay now.'

I held my boy close and rocked him, feeling the warmth of him through the brushed-cotton pyjamas, sensing his little chest rise and fall with each passing breath, feeling all the love I had for him rise up inside me.

It was four in the morning. The house slept on. But now I was awake, and remembering some words from long ago.

'Just rest your eyes,' I told my boy.

eighteen

Peggy surveyed the crowds swarming around the giant Ferris wheel.

'There's lots of people,' she said, taking my hand.

I looked up at the London Eye towering above us, and down at her worried face. I smiled and gave her hand a squeeze.

'We'll be up there soon.'

She nodded, holding my hand tighter. Sometimes Peggy put her hand in mine and I thought that everything was going to be all right.

She was so small, so smart, so wise, so trusting and so beautiful that all she had to do was take my hand and I wanted to protect her for the rest of my life. I held that warm hand in mine and nothing else mattered. Not the sporadic visits from her useless father. Not the running battle she was currently having with Pat about their early-evening DVD entertainment. And not even the fact that her mother looked at her in a way she could never look at my son. Peggy took my hand and something chemical happened inside me. I felt like her father.

High above us the great wheel revolved in the clear April sky. It was turning so slowly that from where we were you could hardly tell that it was moving at all. But new people kept pouring in and out of the steel and glass capsules, so something was happening up there.

The crowd edged towards the departure gate. Pat was excitedly darting between the barriers, checking on our progress. Cyd was reading a brochure about the London Eye, occasionally saying, 'Now *this* is interesting . . .' before reading us some fact about the big wheel's architects, construction or size. But while Pat ran around and Cyd read aloud, Peggy just held my hand as we slowly moved forward.

She was far more self-possessed than Pat, but that was not the reason she was being quiet today. My son was giddy with the fairground excitement of the London Eye, but something about all these people unnerved Peggy.

'We'll be able to see where we live, Peg,' I told her. 'And we'll be able to see Parliament and all the parks and all the way to Docklands.'

'And Big Ben?' In a very small voice.

'And Big Ben too.' I gave her hand another squeeze. 'We'll be all right, Peg.'

She didn't look so certain. Pat dashed back, happy and breathless. Cyd tucked her brochure under her arm. She put her other arm around my waist and rested her head on my shoulder. When she lifted her face to look at me we smiled at each other, the kind of smiles that you can only really get after loving each other for a long time, smiles that somehow contained both a question and its answer.

Happy?

Thanks to you.

Then my wife slapped my arm with her London Eye brochure.

'Hey, don't forget,' she said. 'Peggy's school play is next week. It's really important that you guys are there. I'll slap your asses if you don't come.'

'We wouldn't miss it for the world.'

I really meant it. We felt like a family today. And I wanted this feeling to last.

We were so close to the giant wheel that now you had to crane your neck to see the top of it. You could see that it was definitely moving.

'Nearly there,' gasped Pat.

So I held Peggy's hand in mine as the big wheel kept turning and, everywhere she looked, the adult world towered above her.

* * *

'Hello, boys,' said Gina's dad. 'Cool. Sweet. How about a cup of tea? Herbal all right?'

Glenn. Pat's other grandfather. Easy to remember him as my ex-wife's useless bastard father, the sorry excuse for a man who made all men suspect, who made all men seem capable of terrible betrayal. Less easy to remember that he was my son's grandfather.

My parents had been such a large part of Pat's life, a source of stability and unconditional love during what sometimes seemed like unbroken years of domestic mayhem, that it was hard for me to think of Gina's wayward old man in quite the same way. Glenn wasn't my idea of a grandfather. He was more my idea of an ageing hippy who believed his withered old dick was the centre of the known universe. If Glenn wasn't there for his daughter, why should we expect any more for his grandson?

Yet it was difficult for me to hate him, despite all the sadness he had caused in his lifetime. On the odd occasions when we met, this elderly groover in his cracked leather trousers seemed like a lonely, pathetic figure. After all the big dreams and great loves and hysterical scenes in his life, he had ended up in a rented one-bedroom flat in Hadley Wood. Because he had mistaken hedonism for happiness.

And there was an undeniable sweetness about him. I knew that he was a selfish old git who had sacrificed everyone he had ever loved for his knob and his guitar, and I knew that Gina still carried the wounds that he had inflicted by walking out and casually starting again. But he appeared genuinely glad to see Pat and me, and there was something in the way that he looked at my son that seemed infinitely gentle. Given the chance, the pair of them got on very well. Maybe it was wishful thinking on my part, but when Glenn looked at Pat, I believed I saw love in his eyes.

While Glenn laboured with our drinks – the smallest act of domesticity was beyond him – I sat on a sofa that was made out of the same cracked leather material as his trousers. Pat wandered the flat. There wasn't a lot of space to stroll around, and everywhere you looked there was music.

Dad rock magazines on the coffee table. An acoustic and an electric guitar leaning back in their stands. A good sound system, although like Glenn himself, the material on the speakers was fraying with age. Shining towers of CDs. And fat stacks of old twelve-inch vinyl LPs. Pat picked one of them up.

'What's this then?' he said, brandishing a dark, twelve-inch cardboard square at me.

'That's a long-playing record, Pat.'

'What's it do then?'

'It plays music.'

Pat looked doubtful. 'It's too big,' he said.

On the cover of the album he was holding, a beautiful young man stared moodily out of the darkness. In the background three less lovely young men hovered like ugly sisters waiting to be invited to the ball.

Glenn came back into the room carrying our mugs of camomile.

'Good choice, man,' he said. 'That's the first Doors album. Considered by many to be the greatest debut album of all time.'

'Pat's not curious about Jim Morrison, Glenn,' I said. 'He's just never seen an LP before.'

Glenn almost dropped the herbal tea. 'You're kidding me!'

And then he was away. Sitting with Pat on the floor of his rented flat, sifting through half a century of music while the Doors belted out 'Break On Through (to the Other Side)'.

It was all there, from Elvis and Little Richard to the Beatles and the Stones, Hendrix and the Who, the Pistols and the Clash, the Smiths and the Stone Roses, Nirvana and the Strokes, and every side road, every detour, from country rock to glam to grunge to nu metal, the greats, the has-beens and – his speciality – the one-hit wonders. Glenn led his charmed, bewildered grandson on a guided tour through a rock and roll wonderland.

'Now *these* guys are interesting,' Glenn chuckled, producing a sleeve that showed five boys in psychedelic trousers frolicking in a children's park. 'Ah yes, the Trollies. Started out as a basic Mod covers band called the Trolley Boys. Got into the whole psychedelic thing as the Trollies. Wandering around the council flats having a bit of a cosmic vision – you know the sort of thing, Pat. And later recorded some rather interesting, hugely underrated concept albums as Maximum Troll.' Glenn handed the sleeve to Pat. 'See anyone you recognise?'

I peered over their shoulders. And I saw him immediately – the face of a drug-ravaged choirboy, the Robert Plant bubble cut tumbling over his velvet jacket, leering at the camera with his mates. The Glenn of thirty years ago, when Gina was a baby, the Glenn who was as close as he would ever be to having his dreams come true.

'That's your granddad, Pat,' I said, resisting the urge to say – your other granddad. 'He was on *Top of the Pops* once, isn't that right, Glenn?'

Pat's mouth dropped open. '*You* were on *Top Pops*?'

He had always called it *Top Pops*. I had given up trying to correct him. I sort of liked his mistake anyway.

'With this very line-up. Oh, apart from Chalky Brown on drums. By the time we did "Roundhouse Lady", we had Sniffer Penge on the skins.'

Pat was enchanted. He had never imagined his errant grandfather to be capable of such glory. And Glenn was humbled and happy, perhaps happier than I had ever seen him.

My father hated talking about his past – the poverty in the East End, the service with the Royal Naval Commandos, the death and destruction of the war, the nineteen-year-old friends who never came home. But Glenn didn't feel the same way about his past – playing the Scene as the Trolley Boys with Pete Townshend and Roger Daltry in the audience, getting a big hit as the Trollies with 'Roundhouse Lady', moving out to the country with Maximum Troll to record double concept albums. Glenn could hardly shut up about it.

And I saw for the first time that Glenn was as much a grandfather to Pat as my own dad.

It was certainly an alternative version of manhood that Gina's dad offered. Instead of the soldier, father and husband that my father had been, Glenn was musician, free man and artist.

If you can call a former member of Maximum Troll an artist.

We were late leaving Glenn's place.

The pair of them had been so wrapped up in talking about music – or rather Glenn talked about music while Pat stared in wonder, sometimes saying, '*You* were on *Top Pops*, Granddad?' – that by the time we got to the car, we were in the middle of the rush hour.

The car crawled south on the Finchley Road. In the end we decided to park, sit out the traffic for a while and get something to eat. We had an important date later that evening – Peggy's school play was tonight – but we had plenty of time.

At least that's the way it seemed.

There was a little Japanese place in Camden Town. Thanks to his mother, Pat was an expert on Japanese food, adept with chopsticks and capable of putting away sashimi and tempura the way most seven-year-olds polish off a Big Mac. It was only when we went inside that we discovered we were in a tepenyaki restaurant. This place wasn't about food so much as theatre.

All the seating was at big tables arranged around large metal grills with a space for a chef to do his stuff. These cooks strutted the restaurant like culinary gunslingers, bandy-legged as if they had just done ten days in the saddle, big white hats perched on the back of their heads, and huge knives in low-slung holsters hanging by the side of their aprons.

These chefs didn't just cook for you, they put on a show. All over the restaurant they were dealing prawns and slivers of meat or vegetables on to the sizzling grills, slicing them up, mixing them with rice, then flamboyantly throwing jars of spices and herbs in the air and catching them behind their back. And all of it executed in a lightning blur of speed, just like Tom Cruise in *Cocktail*, but done with an extremely large chopper.

But it took ages to even get started. We had to wait for our table to fill up with other customers before the show could begin. I looked at my watch, calculating how late we could leave this place and still make it to Peggy's play. Finally, when our table was fully occupied, a young Filipino chef greeted us, melodramatically whipped out his knife and started tossing foodstuffs into the air. He must have been new because he kept dropping things – a wayward prawn nearly took out the eye of a German tourist – but Pat smiled encouragement. The time ebbed away, and Pat kept ordering more food to be thrown, sliced and sizzled.

'We really should make a move, Pat,' I said, knowing that I didn't have the heart to stop his fun.

The young tepenyaki chef threw a jar of cinnamon into the air and came really, really close to catching it. I half-heartedly joined in the sympathetic applause.

'I'm very hungry,' Pat said, his eyes sparkling with wonder.

What was it with my family and the theatre?

Pat was green around the gills by the time we reached the school.

'I told you not to have that third helping of squid,' I said.

The play had already begun. All around the assembly hall, proud parents were filming a multicultural celebration of diversity called *The Egg*. What did it have to do with Easter? As little as possible.

Children representing the religions of the world were in a stable where a papier-mâché dove of peace had just been born. On the tiny stage, there was a little boy in a white sheet and a black beret, possibly representing a Shinto priest, a little girl in an orange beach towel with a pink swimming cap on her head, denoting baldness, who was definitely meant to be a Buddhist monk, and a child of indeterminate sex with a cotton-wool beard and sandals meant to represent either Islam or Judaism or both.

And then there was Peggy, her arms and legs sticking out of an old *Pocahontas* duvet, with a Habitat scarf around her head, probably representing the Virgin Mary.

I could see Cyd in the middle of a row, two empty seats

beside her. I grabbed Pat's hand and we began inching our way towards her. Proud parents with digicams cried out in pain and tutted disapprovingly as we trod on their toes and banged against their knees.

'Sorry, sorry,' I whispered, as Pat moaned and groaned and clutched his stomach. On stage the play was reaching its climax.

'What-is-this-strange-creature?' said the Shinto priest.

'Where-has-it-come-from?' said the Buddhist monk.

'What-does-it-mean-for-the-people-of-the-world?' said the child with the cotton-wool beard.

'Where the hell have you two been?' demanded my wife.

'Sssh!' One of the parents with a camera.

'Sorry. I couldn't get him away from Glenn.'

'Glenn? That disgusting old punk?'

'And then we got stuck in a tepenyaki restaurant.'

'SSSH!'

We turned our attention to the stage.

Cyd hissed at me out of the corner of her mouth. 'You knew this was Peggy's special night. You knew it.'

'WILL YOU PLEASE STOP TALKING, PLEASE?' Some old granny in the row directly behind us.

Pat opened his mouth, leaned forward and quietly began to retch.

Everyone on stage was looking at Peggy. The Buddhist monk in the orange beach towel and swimming cap. The Shinto priest in the white sheet and black beret. The bearded elder with cotton-wool facial hair and sandals. All waiting for Peggy to say her line.

'*What-does-it-mean-for-the-people-of-the-world?*' repeated the elder.

'You're so selfish,' Cyd told me, hardly bothering to keep her voice down. 'All you care about is your son. Nobody else means a thing to you.'

'WILL YOU PLEASE –'

Cyd swivelled in her seat. 'Oh, change the record, Granny.'

Peggy was staring out into the crowd, as if waiting for a prompt. Her mouth opened but nothing came out. Unlike

Pat, who chose this moment to vomit elaborately over my lap.

The voice of a kindly teacher came from the wings.

'This bird means that all persons must live as one and . . .'

'And-love-one-another,' mumbled the actors on the stage, gathering around their cardboard dove. Apart from Peggy, who was looking imploringly at her mother. As I cleaned up Pat and myself with a lone Kleenex, Peggy moved towards the edge of the stage, the scarf around her head starting to unravel.

I called out to her but it was too late. She raised her hand to shield her eyes from the footlights and, to the gasps of the audience, promptly fell off the stage.

'I'll never forgive you for this,' said Cyd.

Nobody was seriously hurt.

Peggy's fall was broken by a group of first years sitting cross-legged in the front row. Pat immediately felt better after throwing up his tepenyaki squid. Proud, happy parents and grandparents enjoyed tea, biscuits and after-show analysis. But Cyd and I decided that we didn't need to stick around for the social stuff.

As soon as Pat had been cleaned up a bit and Peggy's tears had dried, we apologised once again to the first years, their parents and the teachers and headed for the car park, my wife and I almost dragging our children out of there.

'You just don't care, do you?' said Cyd. 'If it's nothing to do with you and Pat, you don't give a damn.'

'That's not true.'

'It was the squid what did it,' said Pat, like a hopeless drunk blaming it all on a bad pint.

'Let's just go home,' I said, although the thought of another night in my blended home filled me with despair.

'It would have been all right if you had been here,' Cyd said, her eyes all wet. 'If only you had cared enough to be here.'

'Harry?' A little voice at my side.

'Yes, Peggy?'

I bent down beside her.

She whispered in my ear.
'I fucking hate you, Harry.'
An old lady with a camera around her neck smiled at us.
'What a lovely little family,' she said.

nineteen

We lay in the darkness, not touching, waiting for sleep to come, although it was a very long way off.

'You spoil him,' she said. She didn't say it in a spiteful way. It was almost gentle, the way she said it. 'If you didn't spoil him so much, these things wouldn't happen.'

'Someone's got to spoil him. Who else is going to do it? You?'

'There was no need to stay so long with his granddad.'

'They haven't seen each other for ages. I don't know when they'll see each other again. They were having a good time.'

'I really wanted the pair of you to be there tonight. For Peggy. And me.'

'You don't want him around. One lousy week he's with us. And it's too much for you.'

'That's not true. And it's not fair.'

'Do you know why I got married? Do you have any idea, Cyd? I got married so that my son could have a family. Isn't that a laugh? Isn't that the funniest thing in the world? Some family this turned out to be.'

She didn't say anything. As though she was thinking it over.

'I thought you got married because you wanted a family, Harry. You. A family for yourself. Not a family for Pat.'

'One rotten week, that's all. And it's too much for you.'

We lay there for a while in silence. We had already said too much. After a bit I thought she was asleep.

But she wasn't sleeping at all.

'We used to be crazy about each other. It wasn't long ago. We were going to give each other so much. Remember all that, Harry? I don't know what's happening to us. We used to be happy together.'

I thought she was going to reach out and touch me. But she didn't. And I didn't reach out for her. We just lay there in the darkness, my wife and I, wondering how it ever had come to this.

'Sometimes I wonder why you married me,' I said.

It was true. I knew that the sex was good, and we could talk to each other, and that on most days she was a joy to be around. But so what? She could have picked almost anyone. Out of all the guys in the world, why did she choose me?

'I fell in love with you,' she said.

'But why? That's the bit I don't get, Cyd. I mean it. Falling in love doesn't explain it. If you had looked around a bit, you could have found someone with more money, a bigger dick and a much nicer personality.'

'I didn't want anyone else. I wanted you.'

'But why?'

'Because you're a good father.'

In the garden of the old house, there was an air of real excitement.

We were excited because Pat was flying back to America in the morning, and my mother and I were desperate to make every hour special.

And we were excited because it was the first really hot day of the year, and I had stretched a long piece of plastic sheeting down the length of the garden, which my mum hosed down until it was as slippery as an ice rink.

But mostly the excitement was because of our very special guest.

Bernie Cooper was with us.

As I heard the pair of them happily jabbering upstairs as they changed into their swimming trunks, I realised that I should have arranged this earlier in the week. Bernie Cooper and Pat should have spent more than one day together. But I was so anxious for Pat to see my mum, and Cyd, and Peggy, and even old Glenn, that I almost forgot to schedule time for the person he wanted to see most of all. So on the night before the last day, I called Bernie's parents, and got permission to take him out to my mum's place. We were going to see a movie, have a kickabout in the park, and go for a pizza. But the sun shone as if it was already summer, and the two boys never left my mum's back garden.

They spent the long hot afternoon skidding across a water-soaked piece of plastic. Bernie as dark as Pat was fair, fearless where Pat was careful – Bernie sliding on his stomach, hurtling down the strip of plastic and into the rose bushes – and loud where Pat was quiet. So different, and yet somehow perfect together.

My mother and I watched them for hours, their thin, wet limbs skidding across the garden, my mum occasionally hosing down the sheet of plastic, telling them to be careful when they clattered to the ground while running across the wet grass to do it all over again, smiling to herself as the boys almost exploded with laughter. Bernie Cooper and Pat, seven years old, and a day that they wished could last for the rest of their lives.

And I knew that my son would make other friends. In Connecticut. In the new neighbourhood. At big school. At college. He was a likeable boy, and he would always make new friends. Maybe never quite as good as this one, maybe never quite as good as Bernie Cooper, but they would still be real friends. No matter how much it hurt, Bernie would have to let him go.

And so would I.

My mum came with us to the airport.

Pat took her hand when we got off the Heathrow Express, the tourists and businessmen swarming all around us, and it was almost as if he was taking care of her, rather than the other way around. When had that changed? When had my mum become old?

We found the British Airways desk and handed Pat over to a smiling stewardess. She seemed genuinely happy to see him. People were like that with Pat. They were always happy to see him. An easy child to love.

I crouched by his side at the departure gate and kissed his face, telling him we would see each other again soon. He nodded curtly. He wasn't afraid, he wasn't sad. But he seemed a long way away, as if he was already back in his other life.

My mum gave him a hug that squeezed the breath out of him. The young woman from British Airways took his hand. It was only then that my son seemed concerned.

'It's a long way to go,' he said. 'It will take me all night to get there.'

'Just rest your eyes,' said my mum.

I remembered the day that I took Pat to see his grandfather in the hospital, when it was near the end and the breath wouldn't come any more and I thought that my father and my son should see each other one last time. The loss of our grandparents, I thought, that's usually the first time we understand that life is a series of goodbyes.

And as my son took the hand of the girl from British Airways, I wondered if my mum and Pat would ever see each other again.

'As you know, the station has the highest regard for Eamon Fish,' Barry Twist told me in the snug of the Merry Leper.

That sounded like trouble.

'He's funky. He's spunky. He's cutting edge,' gushed Barry. 'He's hot. He's cool. Research shows that, among ABC males in the eighteen to thirty club, he's the comedian of choice.'

'You wait until Eamon's back in Ireland to tell me all this?'

Eamon was resting. I thought of him on a farm in County Kerry. He had been there for weeks now, where the mountains met the sea, and where there was no chance of Eamon meeting his cocaine dealer.

The waiter came.

'Glass of champagne. Two, Harry? Two. And some nibbles. Peanuts, rice crackers, crisps.'

'Not for me.'

Too much salt in those things. Poison for your blood pressure. I had to worry about all that old-man stuff these days. And losing my job. I had to worry about that, too.

'We want to come back,' I said, switching into producer mode. 'Eamon Fish is the most important comic of his generation. Keeping him off air is a crime against broadcasting.'

'It's not quite that simple,' said Barry Twist.

'Why not?'

'Well, our research shows us also that a majority of AB males between twenty and forty in the south-east quite like the fact that Eamon has been – you know – resting. The advertisers are not quite so keen. The Big Six – beer, cars, soft drinks, sporting equipment, personal grooming and finance – don't want to be associated with someone who was so recently . . . exhausted.'

'Speak English, damn you.'

'The Colombian marching powder. The Charlie. The hokey-cokey. It's changed Eamon's image, kid. He used to be this loveable Irish rogue with a taste for weather girls. Now he's not quite so loveable. And not quite so hot.'

He tossed a paper on the table between us. 'You seen this thing in the *Trumpet*? Evelyn Blunt on Eamon Fish. Actually it's a piece about the death of the new comedy.'

'Evelyn Blunt's a wanker. A bitter, twisted hack who hates the world because he never quite made it as a – what was it he wanted to be? A novelist? A human being?'

'I quite like Evelyn Blunt. He's waspish, he's irreverent, he's controversial.'

He foraged around in a bowl of nibbles.

'Any tosspot with a PC can make a minor splash and six figures by being waspish, irreverent and controversial.'

'Six figures? Really? That's not bad. I mean, his column can't take him very long, can it?'

'He's always had it in for Eamon. Jealous twat. What did the fat, oily bastard write this time?'

Barry Twist wiped the crumbs from his fingers and put on his reading glasses.

'*For a generation of comedians whose careers are receding faster than their hairlines –*'

'That's rich. Evelyn Blunt is no oil painting. It's always the ugliest fuckers who are always going on about someone's physical appearance.'

'*– Eamon Fish was the poster-boy of cutting-edge, stand-up comedy. But now Fish is "resting". The edge is dull. And the roaring boys of open-mike night just can't make it stand up the way they did way back in the nineties*. Then he starts getting personal. Headline – *Waiter, There's a Fish in a Stew*.'

'Those that can, do,' I said. 'Those that can't, become irreverent critics.'

'How is the lad? Doing well? Chilling out?'

'He's anxious to get back to work. To get back to his show.'

'The show.' Barry's eyes roamed the Merry Leper. He waved half-heartedly at someone he knew. 'Of course, of course.'

'Is there a problem?'

'No problem. Just a slight change of plan.'

He let the words hang between us.

'You're dropping *Fish on Friday*?'

Barry laughed at the very idea. 'No, no, no, no, no,' he said. Then he looked sheepish. 'Yes.'

'Christ, Barry. That show is Eamon's life.'

I also thought – and my livelihood. I thought of the money I sent to Gina, the money for Pat, the bills at home, and wondered what I would do if our show went down the pan. Perhaps Marty Mann had been right. I was stupid to trust so much in just one person. When it all goes wrong, what have you got left? Monogamy breaks your fucking heart.

'We remain committed to Eamon. But after recent events, all to do with his ravenous little nose, we no longer see Eamon as talk-show material. We see him as something a bit more . . . street. Slightly more . . . youth. Bringing the drama, as it were. Busting a cap and so on. We want him to host *Wicked World*.'

'What's *Wicked World* when it's at home?'

'Well, co-host, actually. With Hermione Gates.'

'That airhead with the tattoos who's always at some launch party showing her drawers?'

Barry nodded enthusiastically. 'That's Hermione. Isn't she great? Very hip. Spunky. With a post-girl power sort of vibe.' He stroked his chin thoughtfully. 'She does show her drawers a lot, doesn't she?'

'And *Wicked World*? What is it? Some harebrained mix of inane chat and bad music for pissed students who are just back from the uni bar and want to gorge themselves on borderline obscenity for an hour before they collapse in a stupor?'

'That's the general idea,' said Barry. 'It's made by Mad Mann Productions. Your old pal, Marty Mann. Their star is in the ascendant, Harry. Marty's got a whole raft of programmes on air this season. The reality TV thing, *Six Pissed Students in a Flat*, is back with a bang. And he's got that new dating game, *Dude, Where's My Trousers?* And that quiz show, *Sorry, I'm a Complete Git*. Marty's also doing our new late-night cultural review – *Art? My Arse!*'

'Up my arse? What kind of a title is that?'

'Not *up* my arse. *Art? My Arse!* Harry. *Art? My Arse!* It's irreverent, topical, cutting edge.'

He saw the look on my face.

'Just run it past him, will you? The *Wicked World* thing. Time moves on. I know young men like Eamon – and you, Harry – imagine that TV is always going to be there for them. But it doesn't work like that. The world keeps turning. New faces are coming up all the time. Television is a good mistress but a bad wife.'

I was about to launch into my defence of Eamon – he had cleaned up his act, he was far too good to present late-night rubbish designed to ingratiate itself to drunken thickos – when over Barry's shoulder I saw Cyd come into the Merry Leper. She was not alone.

Luke Moore had a proprietorial arm around my wife's waist as he steered her through the bar and into the restaurant at the back. There was something different about her, I thought. And then I realised.

She looked happy.

I felt a stab of pain when I remembered she used to look like that when she was by my side. The mixture of pride and happiness you feel when you have found the one you have been looking for. And suddenly I knew that I didn't marry her just for the sake of my son. I married Cyd because I was crazy about her. Because I loved her.

The man from the TV station stifled a yawn.

'That's the thing about the modern world,' he told me. 'Sooner or later, we all get dropped.'

When I got home Sally was sleeping on the sofa.

A mop of dyed blonde hair, baggy jeans, and a discreet navel ring just visible under her cropped T-shirt. The girl next door. What made Sally slightly different from the average babysitter was that her own baby was sleeping on the rug in front of the fire.

Precious was on her back, wearing Gap Kid pyjamas, her arms raised level with her ears, like a pint-sized weightlifter. She looked a lot bigger than I remembered, but then she must have been two years old already. And I realised that soon I would be exactly like one of those old wrinklies who got on my nerves all the time when I was growing up, saying *aren't you getting big?* And the kid will think – stupid old git, that Uncle Harry.

Sally woke up, rubbing her eyes and smiling.

'Peggy went down well,' she said. 'It's very quiet without Pat.'

'How do you do it, Sally?'

She scooped up her sleeping daughter, started fussing with her wispy hair. 'How do I do what?'

'Precious. Bringing her up on your own. How do you manage it?'

'Well, my parents are great. Like your mum with Pat. And you know what it's like. You looked after Pat by yourself for a bit, didn't you? It's not so bad.'

'I did it for a while. You're doing it for life. It must be hard without – what's his name? Steve? – pulling his weight.'

'I'd rather be on my own than with some useless bastard of a man,' said Sally, rocking Precious in her arms. 'Like her fat-arsed father. No arguments. No bitching about who does what. Just me and my girl. The single parent answers to no one. Tell you what I like about it, Harry.' She kissed the fluff on Precious's head. 'It's uncomplicated.'

I remembered the time Pat and I had been on our own, after Gina had gone to Japan to find herself, to get her life back, but before Cyd and I had begun. For all the support I had received from my parents, I had often felt like the last line of defence between my son and all the dark stuff in the world. Sometimes I felt lonely and afraid. And yet I remembered it as a happy time in my life. Pat and me together, just the two of us – I sort of missed those days.

Because Sally was right.

It was uncomplicated.

I was taking a shower when Cyd came home.

She stuck her head around the shower curtain and gave me her goofy grin.

'Room for one more inside?'

She looked as though she'd had a drink or two. I thought of my wife with Luke Moore at the back of the Merry Leper. Why hadn't she told me that she was meeting that creep? What was she trying to hide?

I could hear her humming to herself as she slipped out of her clothes. She seemed happy and playful, a slightly drunk woman coming home to her husband with a clear conscience. I turned my face to the shower head and let the hot water beat against my face.

Cyd stepped into the shower with me, her long, slim body pressing against me. I felt myself respond immediately. I couldn't deny it to myself. I still fancied her like mad.

'Ho ho ho,' she said. Boy, she was really tipsy. 'Are you just pleased to see me or is that a large erection? Come on, give me that soap.'

She worked up some suds and started lathering her limbs. Then she turned her attention to me, soaping my back. It was diligent rather than sexy – the work of a woman used to cleaning a child – but I was soon bone hard. I turned to face her, her wide-set eyes squinting in the spray, black hair plastered to her shoulders.

'In the shower,' she laughed. 'We haven't done this for ages, have we?'

'How was your evening?'

'Fine.'

'Sorry, who did you say you were seeing?'

'Oh, just these two women who do the catering for some of the blue-chip corporations in the City. We had a couple of drinks and grabbed some supper in the Merry Leper. Pat get off okay?'

'A couple of women, you say?'

She closed her eyes and moaned, gripping me like a handbrake about to be released.

I broke away from her, pushing the shower curtain aside and grabbing the nearest towel.

'What's wrong? Harry?'

I furiously dried myself, soap all over my back, my wife's face all wet and confused. I wished I didn't want her so badly. I wanted it to be over, so that all this feeling would stop.

'There's not enough room in there for me,' I told her, tossing the towel at the laundry basket and leaving her to shower alone.

And I saw that our marriage was a lot like the London Eye, that giant Ferris wheel on the south bank of the Thames.

Even when everything appeared to be perfectly still, even when nothing at all seemed to be happening, it was up there in the darkness, turning, turning, in motion all the time.

twenty

'Keep it simple,' Eamon said. 'That's the first thing they tell you in AA. All the lying and the running around will never do you any good. If you're ever going to get well, you have to keep it simple, Harry.'

Before us the land stretched out like a postcard of County Kerry. A still silver lake was the only break in miles of moorland that ran all the way to where the rocks of the mountains finally met the sea. That sea looked enormous, as though it went on not to America, but to the end of the world.

Eamon had warned me that the tourists were trampling all over his homeland, seeking the craic in every pub, a bit of Celtic mysticism around every corner, and girls who looked like the Corrs at every bed and breakfast. But the only sign of life I saw in all of this wild, rugged landscape was a comedian who had put on a few pounds since the last time I saw him.

'They want to drop the show, Eamon. I know this isn't the best time to tell you, but I can't help it. The drugs scared them. If you had just been pissed out of your skull it would be another matter. They could have passed that off as jack-the-lad antics. They think that alcohol abuse is cute. It would have gone down well with all the booze advertisers. But drugs are something else.'

'I'm out? Just like that?'

'They're not going to recommission *Fish on Friday*. They want you to co-present some late-night zoo. *Wicked World*, it's called. You and Hermione Gates.'

'Her who's always showing her drawers?'

'That's the one.'

He thought about it for a while. The sweet-smelling grass scrunched under my brand-new Timberland boots.

'And what about you, Harry? Are you coming with me? I'm not doing it if they don't want you.'

I was touched that Eamon would think of me. But it hadn't crossed my mind that the makers of a funky, spunky show like *Wicked World* would want an unfunky, unspunky producer like me. I assumed that they would want some young hotshot with jeans so low that you could see his pierced scrotum.

'Don't worry about me.' I thought of the money that I sent to Gina for Pat, the money that Cyd and I relied on for our mortgage. 'I'll be fine.'

We walked down into a shadowy dip in the land and came up into sunlight on a small rise. In the distance, just before the bracken gave way to the rocks by the sea, there was a small farmhouse. It hadn't been anyone's home since the potato famine, but it had been an authentically rustic holiday home ever since Ireland had become a place that people came to rather than left. This had been Eamon's home the last month. And now a taxi was approaching it on the winding peninsula road.

'That'll be him,' Eamon said. 'Evelyn Blunt.'

We watched the taxi.

'Are you sure you want to do this, Eamon? You don't have to talk to this guy.'

'I trust Blunt about as far as I can ejaculate.'

'That far?'

'But he's already called me every dirty name under the sun. What else can he do to me?'

The interview had been Barry Twist's brainwave.

Twist believed that the public loved the idea of a sinner eventually seeing the error of his ways. The folks out there would forgive you anything, Barry reckoned, as long as you didn't look as though you had actually enjoyed any of it in the first place. It was no longer enough for someone to dry out, they had to be seen to have dried out. The world had a taste for public repentance.

Evelyn Blunt, the poison pen in Eamon's side for so long, had been invited to do the interview because his paper was thought to have an influential circulation – that is, people in the media read it, the opinion formers who would decide if this comeback was a success – while Blunt himself was writing longer, more thoughtful features these days, as he attempted to make the transition from his spiteful little hatchet jobs to something more like real writing. Blunt had failed as a TV presenter, novelist and talk-radio jock. It was inevitable that sooner or later he would have a go at being a journalist.

We came down the hill to the farmhouse as the taxi deposited its passengers next to my hire car. Blunt got out and looked at all that wild grandeur with his sour, crumpled face. There was something sweaty about him, as though he was still recovering from the dipso he had been in his debauched youth. He wasn't alone. There was a young woman with him. The photographer.

I couldn't see her face as the taxi driver helped her haul out black nylon bags full of lights, film and tripod from the boot of his cab. Then she straightened up, looking at the land as she pushed a veil of black hair out of her face. And I saw her.

Kazumi.

We were at the farmhouse now. Blunt took Eamon's hand and pumped it as though he hadn't really been using my friend as a punch bag for the last two years. Kazumi and I stared at each other. Then she nodded at the Atlantic.

'Look.'

Many miles out to sea, a storm was coming in. Huge black rolling clouds were sweeping towards the coast, but they seemed so far away that it felt like weather seen in a dream.

'Ah, that's a long ways out,' said Eamon. His Kerry accent was always a lot thicker once you got him out of Soho. 'We don't run for cover round here. We have a nap and then we run for cover.'

But Kazumi had already gone, clambering over the jagged rocks with a camera swinging around her neck. We watched her crouch on the rocks and start taking pictures of the coming storm.

'Sweet little Kazumi,' said Evelyn Blunt. 'I'm in there tonight.'

It wasn't until Eamon had been cornered in the toilets by a gang of English tourists in Manchester United shirts and Evelyn Blunt had climbed on the table to show us his Riverdance routine that Kazumi and I had a chance to be alone.

'So did London work out for you?' I shouted over the pub band's spirited version of Van Morrison's 'Real Real Gone'.

She tapped her ears. I liked the way they stuck out a bit. I liked it quite a lot.

'Can't hear,' she said, sipping her Guinness.

'Are you getting much freelance work? Have you worked for the *Trumpet* before?'

She smiled, shook her head, and touched those sticky-out ears. It was true. The noise in here was deafening. I realised I could say what I liked to her.

'I said – I'm so happy to see you. You look gorgeous. I think you're lovely. I am so glad you walked into my life. I think I'm losing my mind.'

She smiled politely.

A laughing German tourist in a Glasgow Celtic shirt smashed into our table. He was clapping his hands and stamping his feet as Blunt jigged around with his arms so stiff by his side that they could have been tied there.

'These crazy Irish,' said the German. 'They have such a good time, no?'

'He lives in Hampstead,' I said. '*Hampstead in London.*'

'Crazy, crazy Irish.'

A cheer went up as the band, a bunch of crusty-looking hippies who resembled extras from *Braveheart*, tore into Van Morrison's 'One Irish Rover'.

Blunt went up a gear.

A coach party of Italians arrived, swelling the pub to overload. They placed their orders for Guinness with the red-haired student behind the bar. Blunt stubbed his toe on a large glass ashtray and began hopping around on one leg, grimacing in agony. The tourists applauded excitedly, mistaking his injury for part of the official floorshow.

The German tourist nodded knowledgably. 'Music is very important to the Irish. Boomtown Rats. Thin Lizzy. U2. It's in their soul.'

He climbed on to the table with Blunt.

Eamon came back. He looked up at Blunt and the German, shaking his head. 'Will you look what happens when they watch *Titanic* one time too many?'

A tray of pints was placed on the table and, trying to upstage the German, who was doing a basic acid house dance – arms waving, feet planted, the antithesis of the common or garden Riverdance – Blunt attempted to execute an advanced *Lord of the Dance* leap across the stout. That's when he fell off the table and landed face first in an Australian tourist's cheese and tomato toastie.

Eamon sipped his mineral water and smiled at Kazumi. My spirits dipped. Eamon wasn't going to try to sleep with her, was he? The drugs had replaced the girls in his life. But now the drugs were gone.

Then the band got stuck into 'Brown-Eyed Girl' and the whole place was up on its feet. A handsome young Italian approached Kazumi and asked her if she wanted to dance. Suddenly Evelyn Blunt was between them, his red face scowling, and a slice of tomato hanging from one sweaty eyebrow.

'She's taken, mate.'

They eventually threw us out.

The visitors were willing to go right through till dawn, but the young red-haired bartender had to get up for his IT course at college in the morning.

So the four of us walked back along a rutted country road where the only light was the twinkling canopy of stars and the only sound was the roaring boom of the sea.

That and the tourists throwing up in the coach car park.

It was hard to sleep in that farmhouse by the bay.

The night winds whipped off the Atlantic and made the

ancient timbers of the farmhouse creak and groan like a ship tossed on a stormy sea. And it was freezing – my M&S pyjamas were supplemented with an old *Fish on Friday* T-shirt and thermal socks, and I still shivered under the wafer-thin duvet that was there for the summer trade.

But tonight it wasn't the cold or the noise that kept me awake. It was the thought of Kazumi huddled beneath the sheets of the room at the top of the house. That's what truly kept me from sleeping. And that's why I was awake when she knocked on my door at three in the morning.

She was wearing tartan pyjamas. That girl liked her tartan more than any Scot I ever knew. She was also wearing chunky socks and a woollen hat. It must have been even colder at the top of the building. I blinked at her, uncertain if this was a dream. Then she spoke. In a whisper, as if afraid of waking the house.

'Sorry,' she said.

'It's okay. What's wrong?'

'Problem in room.'

I followed her across the darkened living room and, carefully, up a short ladder to the top of the farmhouse. Evelyn Blunt was lying on his stomach across her bed, mouth agape and drooling, snoring loudly.

'Said he went to toilet and got the wrong room coming back,' she said.

We looked from the drunken hack to the rickety ladder that you needed to climb to enter this room. Nobody gets as drunk as that, I thought.

'Big fat liar,' Kazumi said.

'Did he – did he hurt you at all?'

She shook her pretty head. 'Grabbed my hot-water bottle and then fell asleep. I can't wake him up.'

'I'll try.' I shook his shoulder. 'Wake up, Blunt, you're in the wrong room. Wake up, you sweaty fat bastard.'

He moaned a bit and held my hand to his cheek, a look of inebriated ecstasy passing across his bloated features. It was no use. I couldn't stir him.

'You can have my room,' I told her. 'I'll sleep on the couch.'

'No, no, no.'

'It's not a problem. Really. Go on. You take my room.'

She looked at me for a moment. 'Or we could – you know – share your room.'

In the silence you could hear the sea smashing against the shore.

'Yes,' I said. 'We could always do that.'

As shy as two five-year-olds on our first day at school, we made our way back to my room. Then we quickly jumped into opposite sides of the bed, and my hopeful heart soared, although I knew that she was driven not by passion, but by the possibility of hypothermia.

I lay on my back, with Kazumi turned away from me. I could hear my breathing, feel her body warmth, and when I couldn't stand it any more I reached out and lightly touched her ribs, feeling the brushed cotton of her tartan pyjamas on the palm of my hand.

'No, Harry,' she said, a bit sad, but not moving.

I took my hand away. I didn't want to be like Blunt. Whatever else I was, I didn't want to be that kind of man.

'Why not?'

'You've got a wife and son.'

'It's a bit more complicated than that.'

'And other reasons.'

'Like what?' I tried out a little laugh. 'Because you're not that kind of girl? I know you're not that kind of girl. That's why I like you so much.'

'I like you too. You're nice.'

'You do?'

'Yes. You're funny and kind. And lonely.'

'Lonely? Am I?'

'I think so, yes.'

'Then what's wrong?'

'You're not that kind of man.' She rolled on to her back and looked at me, her brown eyes shining in the moonlight, like a girl in a song by Van Morrison.

I rolled on to my side, loving the way her black hair fell across her face. I touched her foot with mine, woolly sock against woolly sock. She placed the palm of her hand against my chest and it made me catch my breath. Our voices in the dark were as soft as prayers.

'I want to sleep with you,' I said.

'Then close your eyes and go to sleep.' Unsmiling.

'You know what I mean. I want to make love to you.'

She shook her head. 'You're not free.'

'The world wouldn't care. It's just you and me. We're not hurting anyone. Nobody would know, Kazumi.'

'We would know.'

She had me there.

'I don't want to be the kind of woman who sleeps with a married man. And you don't want to be that kind of married man.'

'I do.'

'No, Harry. You're better than that.' She stroked my face. 'Just hold me,' she said, rolling on to her side. I pushed up against her, two layers of pyjamas between her bottom and my erection. I put my free arm around her waist and pulled her close. She lifted my arm, placed a chaste kiss on my wrist, and squeezed my hand. We stopped talking, and for a long time I listened to the winds whipping off the Atlantic, the old farmhouse creaking in the night and the soft sound of her breathing.

And as Kazumi slept in my arms, I wondered how you keep a life simple. Do you keep it simple by staying where you are?

Or by starting all over again?

twenty-one

She was gone when I awoke.

I could hear voices down on the rocky beach. From the window I saw Kazumi already up and taking her pictures of Eamon.

Huddled up inside a red fleece, he struck his carefully casual poses – staring moodily out to sea, staring moodily straight at the camera, staring moodily at nothing in particular – while she moved around him, briskly click-clicking her way through another roll, changing film, murmuring instructions and encouragement.

A Japanese person with a camera, I thought. One of the clichés of the modern world. The snapping hordes mindlessly documenting every tourist site, and then getting back on the bus. But as I watched Kazumi taking her photographs of Eamon on the wind-lashed beach by Dingle Bay, it seemed to me that this young woman with her camera was possessed by an insatiable curiosity for this world and everything in it, and I felt an enormous surge of tenderness for her and her camera. *Plead the fleeting moment to remain*, she had told me some poet said of photography. And that's what she was doing. Pleading the fleeting moment to remain.

By the time I was washed and dressed, Eamon and Kazumi had moved further down the beach. She must have thought that she had the images she needed, because now they were working more slowly, trying things out. She crouched on the kelp-strewn rocks while Eamon slowly strolled towards her, hands stuffed inside his pockets, staring – I guess you would call it moodily – at a point just above her head.

And although it filled me with regret to admit it, I thought that perhaps she was right after all. Sex last night would not have been wise. A one-night stand with Kazumi would have been a big mistake. Because one night with this woman would never be enough.

And what did that mean? What did it mean when one night was not enough?

It meant an affair.

I had worked with enough married men who were conducting affairs to know that they were hard work.

The one-way telephone communications, the constant fear of discovery, the guilt, the anxiety, the tears at Christmas and New Year when home and hearth were calling, the feeling of being constantly and forever torn. And the lying. It couldn't be done without the lying.

I wasn't the man for all of that. I didn't have the heart. I couldn't do it to Cyd. Or myself. Or Kazumi. At least that's how I felt in the light of day with Kazumi fifty metres away, not wrapped up in tartan pyjamas and my arms.

I had been true to my wife.

I had done the right thing.

So why did I feel so miserable?

There was a low, mournful mooing by my side. It was Blunt, green around the gills and still buttoning his shirt. A muted belch escaped his lips. His face was covered in a thin film of sweat.

'Must have got a bad pint,' he said, wandering off down to the beach where Kazumi was taking a final few shots of Eamon.

And I didn't want to be so stuck on this young woman I hardly knew. Cyd was more than my wife and my lover. She was my best friend. At least until the other man came into our lives.

I remembered the moments that measured out our love. Cyd and I had had our share of good times. Looking at the lights by the Thames, the first night we ever spent together, last Christmas Day when everything struck us as hilarious, from Ibiza DJ Brucie Doll's tiny turntables to my mum's appalled expression as she inserted the stuffing up the turkey's rear end.

But what had really forged the bond between us were the other times, the bad times. My son in the hospital, his head split open from a fall in the park. The wrenching sadness of my divorce from Gina. Cyd was there for me through all of that, and I knew she cared about me in a way that nobody else in the world did.

But now it felt like I was losing my wife, and finding a gap in my life that Kazumi was filling, even if she didn't want to.

That gap the size of a family, and the shape of a heart.

One night I had cooked dinner for the four of us. Cyd and me, Peggy and Pat. Since I married Cyd, my cooking skills had atrophied. But I thought I would do it one night. Do it for the family.

The four of us were sitting around the table's points of the compass. At the start Cyd and Pat had made a good job of feigning enthusiasm for my cooking, even if what Peggy said sounded spiced with sarcasm.

'Spaghetti Bolognese, Harry. Mmmm, I can't wait!'

'Hah! You might have to, Peg!'

There was sometimes a sickening jollity in the exchanges between my stepdaughter and myself.

'Make sure the pasta is *al dente*, will you?' she advised imperiously. 'I don't like it too soft. You *do* know what I mean by *al dente*, don't you?'

I stirred my bubbling meat and tomato sauce at the stove, my smile stiff with tension.

'You know you have to essentially treat it like a stew, don't you?' Cyd said gently. 'It takes a long, long time simmering that amount of meat.'

'Please,' I said, trying to keep it friendly. 'My turn to cook tonight, okay?'

I cooked spaghetti Bolognese. Spag Bog. Can't go wrong. I used to cook this stuff all the time when Pat and I were living alone. But for some reason I had it in my head that spaghetti Bolognese was a quick dish to prepare. I thought it took as long as – I don't know. As long as it takes them to bring it to you in a restaurant. But I was wrong about spaghetti Bolognese, just as I have been wrong about so many things.

After an hour or so, Peggy was impatiently tapping Lucy Doll Secret Agent against the table. Pat was gawping at the remote control in his fist, as if waiting for a sign. And Cyd – after asking me really nicely if I minded – was doing her tax return. And still I stood at the stove, stirring the sauce that was taking inexplicably longer than any restaurant. I thought that maybe it wasn't spaghetti Bolognese that I cooked so quickly and so easily for Pat and myself. Maybe it was spaghetti pesto. Yes, that was it. Spaghetti pesto was the one that was done in minutes. You just opened the can and chucked it on the pasta. It was simple and tasty. Green spaghetti, my son had called it.

Now, two years on from the days of green spaghetti, he dropped the remote control. It clattered against the wooden floor. 'Whoops,' he said, smirking around the table, looking for supportive laughter. Peggy and Cyd ignored him.

I picked up the remote and angrily stuffed it inside my apron pocket.

'Stop thinking about TV for five minutes of your life, will you?'

My son's chin began to tremble, a sure sign that he was fighting back tears. Peggy sighed elaborately.

'*Please* may I leave the table now?' she said. 'I am *very* busy tonight.'

'Wait a little while longer,' Cyd said, not looking up from her accounts. 'You can go and get Brucie Doll Secret Agent if you want. He can talk to Lucy Doll about their mission while we're waiting for Harry.'

'Yeah, everybody just wait a little while longer,' I said, furiously stirring my meat sauce. 'Lucy Doll's costume change can wait until after dinner.'

'Well!' said Peggy. '*Someone* got out of bed the wrong day.'

Cyd looked up from her accounts. 'It's okay, Harry. I've

spoken to her. You don't have to put your five cents in, darling.'

'If you did it more often, I wouldn't have to, *darling*.'

My wife put down her calculator and sighed. 'How much longer anyway?'

'I don't know. It's this minced beef. It's taking ages.'

'Beef?' Peggy said. 'Did you say – beef? I can't eat *beef*.'

'Why not?'

'Because meat is murder.' She paused dramatically. 'Didn't I tell you? I am not eating meat any more. I've decided to become a vegetarian.'

'Me too,' said Pat. 'I'm a vegetable, too. Can I watch TV now? *Dude, Where's My Trousers?* is on soon.'

I wanted a meal that would make us feel like a real family. That's all. Not much to ask for. And maybe that's exactly what I achieved.

Because by the time my spaghetti Bolognese was ready, none of us were talking to each other.

Eamon was walking towards me. Blunt and Kazumi were still down on the beach. He was saying something to her while scratching his distended belly. She was shaking her head and packing away her equipment. They began making their way back to the farmhouse, Blunt making no attempt to help Kazumi carry her gear.

'Good night last night?' Eamon said.

'Nothing happened.'

'Hey, who am I to cast the first stone? What you get up to on a business trip is none of my business.'

'I mean it, Eamon. Nothing happened.'

'Sort of like Tantric sex, you mean?'

'Nothing happened.'

Nothing happened and everything happened. Because for the first time it had occurred to me that, if I couldn't have a family with my wife, then perhaps I could have one with someone else.

'I love a bit of the old Tantric sex, me,' Eamon said. 'Lasts for hours, doesn't it? You know my favourite position in Tantric sex? The plumber. You stay in all day and nobody comes.'

If we had slept together – or rather, if we had not just slept together – there would have been a shyness between us now. Or, far worse, a false intimacy that we hadn't really earned. But we walked on the beach, away from the farmhouse where Blunt was interviewing Eamon, and there was no postcoital awkwardness between us. We had spent the night in each other's arms, but that was all we had done. Walking on that rocky beach, the clouds whipping in off the sea, the first of the day's tourist coaches creeping around Dingle Bay, felt like the most natural thing in the world.

'I hope the pictures are okay,' Kazumi said. 'This is my first job for them. The photo editor is – how to say? – a tough old bitch. She doesn't give you second chances.'

'The pictures will be fine. You're a brilliant photographer.'

She gave me a smile. 'Smooth talk.'

'No, not smooth talk. I've seen your photographs. You took pictures of my son.'

'Of course,' she said. 'Pat.'

I liked it that she could see my boy's spark. That she could tell he was special. I really liked it quite a lot.

'Will I see you in London?'

She stopped and stared out to sea. Another storm was coming in, the clouds bigger and blacker than they had been yesterday, rolling and tumbling low above the surf-skimmed Atlantic towards the shore. It was coming in quickly. Eamon's folk wisdom – that you could have a pint of Guinness and listen to the Corrs' greatest hits before a storm arrived – looked increasingly like a load of old bollocks.

'Kazumi?'

'What's the point?'

'The point?'

'If we each other in London, what's the point?' She abruptly took my left hand and pulled at my wedding ring. 'Doesn't come off. You see? Not so easy.'

'We haven't done anything wrong.'

'Not yet.'

'I'll meet you on Primrose Hill. Right on the top where you can see the entire city. Sunday morning. About ten?'

The rain started to fall. We were a long way down the beach now. The farmhouse was disappearing in a sudden shroud of sea mist.

'This way,' she said, breaking into a run.

I followed her to a broken-down shed with a rotting rowing boat outside. The door was unlocked. Inside it was dark. It smelled of tobacco and kelp. It was some kind of abandoned fisherman's hut. Either that, or a holiday home for a family of affluent Bavarians.

We were both soaked through to the skin. I thought perhaps that this was the bit where we would take off our sodden clothes and fall into each other's arms. But she just sat shivering on the kitchen table and fussed over the camera that she had slung around her neck, examining it for damage.

I stood at the window, watching the fog come in, hearing but no longer seeing the waves crash against the rocks. I was cold inside my damp clothes but then a pair of arms were wrapping around me from behind, hugging me hard, bringing the warmth that I needed.

This is what it is, I thought. Nothing more. Just two animals, huddling together on the west coast of Ireland. Looking for a little comfort. Doing nothing wrong.

'I'm not going to Primrose Hill.'

'Okay.'

'Not on Sunday morning.'

'Fine.'

'Not ever.'

'All right then.'

Somehow I had turned around and faced her, and she was tilting her head, lifting it towards me. Then I kissed her, and I saw her brown eyes close, and open, shining in the misty twilight, the rattle of the rain on the roof, and I felt the heat of her body through the dampness of her clothes, and I tasted the sea on her lips.

This is what it is, I thought. Two cold, wet creatures shivering in the fog. That's all. Don't turn it into something that it's not, Harry.

And I thought of Gina, and also of Cyd. I had lost the two best friends I ever had by having sex with them, by marrying them, by trying to make it last forever. Kazumi and I were never going to get that far, and it was probably just as well.

But I knew that I would keep this moment. I would lock it away and take it out when the world was hard and lonely. This was enough.

Primrose Hill was too much to hope for.

twenty-two

When I arrived home there was an airmail envelope on the welcome mat. My name and address in Gina's neat, elegant handwriting.

And inside, a photograph – a man, woman and child, standing by a white picket fence in dazzling sunshine. Pat was at the front of the picture, in faded *Phantom Menace* T-shirt and shorts, squinting in the light, that half-filled gap in the middle of his smile. Gina was right behind him, one hand raised against the sun, the other lightly resting on our son's shoulder. She was thinner than I had ever seen her, wearing some worn sweatshirt with the sleeves pulled up. But for all the years and whatever her troubles in her new life, she still had that radiant beauty that I had fallen in love with, she still had those looks that she didn't really like you to talk about.

Then there was Richard, this man my ex-wife had married, standing to one side, unsmiling, half lost in the shadows of a white clapboard house. He didn't look happy. He had the look of an expatriate who had returned home, but not in triumph. But what did I know? He had married my former wife, he lived with my only son. I couldn't think of him as a loser. There was a piece of paper still in the envelope.

A note from Gina.

Harry –

We are coming back to London for a few weeks. Just the two of us. Pat and me. My dad has something wrong with his leg. He

needs some help around the house. We are not staying with him – I have a flat. Will call you when we get in. Pat seems to have had a good time with you. But you know Pat – he doesn't say much. Please thank Cyd. I hope your mum is okay. Got to go.
Gina

'Hello, Harry.'

Peggy was at the top of the stairs. She was dressed in a long white lacy dress with short puffed-up sleeves. She looked like a bride. Or an angel.

'You look lovely, Peg.'

'My daddy's getting married. To his girlfriend Liberty. She's a nurse. From Manila. I'm going to be their bridesmaid.'

'Come on,' Cyd said, appearing on the landing next to her. 'You go and take off that dress. Watch the pins on the hem, okay? I'll be right in.'

My wife came down the stairs.

'Good trip? How's Eamon? Is he all right?'

I didn't reply. I left my bags in the hall and went into the kitchen. The work surfaces were covered with dishes of guacamole, chilli sauce and Tabasco, bottles of Cantonese plum sauce and Caribbean banana ketchup. Sweet and sharp.

'Experimenting with my dips,' Cyd said. 'I spoke to your mum. She's not feeling so good.'

My wife held out her arms to me but I just stared at her.

'You lied to me,' I said.

'What?'

'Before I went away. You told me some story about going out with two women. Two women, you said. But I saw you with him. Luke Moore. In the Merry Leper. I saw you, Cyd.'

'Harry.'

'I saw the pair of you.'

'Harry?'

'What?'

'It's not what it seems. He wants to buy the company. That's why I met him. I couldn't tell you because I knew you would – do this.'

For the first time since I had come home, I looked my wife in the eye.

'And what did you tell him?'

'I told him what I have told him all along, Harry.' We stared at each other. 'I told him no.'

'What else did he try to buy? Don't tell me. I can fucking guess.'

I tried to brush past her but she grabbed my arm. 'I don't want anyone else, okay? That's it. You should know that already. I don't want anyone else, Harry. Never have done. But you can wear out someone's love, Harry, just like you can wear out anything else. So you either stop all this or . . .'

'Or what?'

'Or I don't know what's going to happen to us.'

She touched my face, and then saw the photograph I was holding. She took my hand and held it.

'Is that a picture of Pat?'

'What do you care?'

'Oh Harry.' She released my hand. 'That's not fair. If I don't love your son in exactly the same way as you, that's not some kind of betrayal.'

She had me there, of course.

Eamon cracked.

Perhaps it was Evelyn Blunt's hatchet job. The journalist had pulled off the oldest party trick known to hacks – acting as Eamon's best friend in the flesh, and then his public executioner in print. Under the headline *No Laughing Matter*, Blunt devoted 3,000 words to explaining why Eamon Fish was unimportant and the readers of his newspaper should take absolutely no interest in him. The photos were good, though – Eamon wild-eyed and windswept, his dark good looks almost a part of the Kerry landscape. And very, very moody.

Or perhaps it was the celebrity chef that made him crack. Eamon's first chore on *Wicked World* was interviewing Wee Willie Hiscock, the loveable Geordie cook. All through the big English breakfast Hiscock blatantly plugged his new book, *Right in Your Gobhole, Too, Bonnie Lad*, the sequel to his bestseller, *Right in Your Gobhole, Bonnie Lad*. Eamon had always been averse to such blatant promotion, but where he had happily slapped it down on *Fish on Friday*, now he seemed unable to stem the flow of plugs.

Or perhaps it was the boy group that pushed him over the edge. Hermione Gates made no secret of the fact that she was a huge fan of Lads Unlimited, five young, handsome, hairless men who could carry a tune, but not very far, and who performed a series of dance steps that looked like gentle exercises for sufferers of arthritis.

The studio monitor clearly showed Hermione flashing her drawers in excitement during Lads Unlimited's rendition of 'Our Funky Love Will Live Forever'. The monitor also clearly showed Eamon (favourite albums: *Nevermind* by Nirvana, *Physical Graffiti* by Led Zeppelin and *Is This It?* by the Strokes) looking at his watch.

But probably Eamon would still be presenting *Wicked World* to this very day if he hadn't been asked to interview the winner of *Six Pissed Students in a Flat*.

The winner was Warren, a tanned, pierced, pumped-up plumber with a fashionably shaven head who was hoping that the success of *Six Pissed Students in a Flat* would allow him to put down his tool box and become something really useful, like a game-show host or a DJ in Ibiza.

Warren sat between Hermione and a dazed-looking Eamon. The retired plumber idly lifted up his pastel-blue vest, revealing his rippling six-pack and a diamond stud in his navel.

'For me the, like, turning point? Was in week six? When I discovered Darren had taken me milk out of the fridge. Without asking, innit?'

Hermione frowned at the memory. 'You were very angry, weren't you, babes?'

Eamon's head was hanging.

'Well, for me, asking before you use someone's milk is what it's all about.'

'Absolutely, babes. I'm, like – have a word with yourself, Darren, you muppet.'

Eamon had buried his face in his hands.

'Chloe and Zoë, right, they wanted to stop me confronting, Darren, innit? Who I could always relate to because we both have issues because of not being properly parented?'

Suddenly Eamon was on his feet, addressing camera two with its little red light shining above it. I felt a surge of pride. Even at moments of supreme stress, he never looked into the wrong camera.

'Turn it off,' he said. 'Turn it off right now!'

'Babes?' said Hermione Gates.

'You're poisoning your mind with this rubbish. We all are. What's wrong with us? We used to fill our screens with heroes. Now we want people we can look down on. *People we can look down on.*' He looked with real sadness at Hermione and Warren. 'I want no part of it.' He tore off his microphone, pulled out the clear wax earplug that linked him to the gallery, threw them at the feet of the stunned floor manager. 'I'm going outside now. I may be a while.'

Then he was gone. In the gloaming of the studio wings, Barry Twist and I watched him go.

'You know he'll never read an autocue in this town again, don't you?' said Barry.

'Sometimes you have to start again,' I said. 'It's painful and it's messy. But sometimes you just have to make the break and start again.'

My mother was going into hospital in the morning.

I would pick her up first thing, and I knew already she would be wearing what she called her Sunday best, and then I would drive her to the hospital in the next town. And that's where a surgeon would perform what they called a simple mastectomy.

One of her breasts, the one with the tumour, would be lost so that her life could be saved. That breast – one of the curves my father had fallen in love with when she was a young girl, and never stopped loving as they grew old together, the breast that had sustained me as a baby – would be gone, cut off to separate my mother from the tumour that wanted to kill her.

This thing that had given me life, that had made my father gasp with wonder and gratitude, would be cut off and – what? – thrown away? Burned? Preserved for medical science?

I couldn't think about these things, and none of the brochures – not *Talking with Your Children about Breast Cancer*, or *Living with Lymphoedema*, or *Exercises after Breast Surgery* – gave any hint as to the fate of the amputated breast. They didn't want you to think about it.

I sat in the living room of the old house, drinking cup after cup of strong sweet tea, feeling that my mother had been thrust into some kind of war. Everything suddenly seemed uncertain, unbalanced, in opposition. The breast and the tumour, love and sickness, life and death.

My mother was happy. She was happy because the old house was full of people, and this woman – one of seven children, mother of an only child who took years to arrive, widow of two years – seemed to feel that she was fulfilling her destiny again. The tea and biscuits, the sandwiches in the kitchen, the occasional beer produced for one of her brothers. It didn't feel like the house was full because of cancer surgery. It felt more like Christmas.

The family is dying off now, that old family I knew as a child. All the aunts and uncles, the brothers of my parents, and the matches they made, beloved wives found in the same few streets, and then kept for a lifetime.

I knew these people better than I knew anyone. I knew their generosity, their resilience and their loyalty.

I was thankful that they fussed around my mother now – 'Anything we can do, love, anything at all, let us know,' I was told, time after time – but I wasn't surprised.

My uncles and my aunts. Retired now, for the most part, or getting there. But I remembered them from the years when I was a child. Their aches and pains, the pills that now had to be taken, the unsettling visits to the doctor – they couldn't cloud my memory of lean, hard men and their small, pretty wives, the men all factory workers and printers and shopkeepers at first, and later the shops being replaced by supermarkets, back when supermarkets were modern and new, and the women homemakers decades before the term was invented, homemakers the lot of them, even the ones who worked. And how they worked.

These women, my aunts, would never have thought of themselves as career women, but they worked in school kitchens, on the buses, doing the books in a wholesale warehouse, in shops and supermarkets. They worked because they had to.

They didn't work to be fulfilled or to discover themselves. They worked to pay the rent, they worked because there were always children – my army of cousins – and never much money.

That old family rallied around my mother the night before she had a date with the surgeon. And even though their numbers were diminishing – my old man had been the first to go, but my mother had already lost two of her brothers since then, their hearts giving out on them just when they were ready to enjoy their gardens and their grandchildren – there was still something indomitable about these old Londoners who moved out to the suburbs a lifetime ago.

The house was full of cowboy music and laughter. I was sent to the local shop for more milk and sugar. The cancer leaflets with their terrible drawings of women who had had a breast surgically removed were ignored, lying on the coffee table next to the TV listings and a biography of Shirley Bassey.

When I was growing up, dreaming of escape, plotting a career in television, I believed that my family had lived small lives – never thinking of what was out there beyond their few suburban towns, never caring, never dreaming. But now I saw that they had lived better lives than me – fuller, happier lives, lives with more meaning, where loyalty and decency were taken for granted, where you reacted to cancer by putting on the kettle and a Dolly Parton record. How I envied them now, now that I saw that old dying family as my mother fought for her life, now that it was all too late.

My Aunt Doll talked softly with my mother in the kitchen. Sometimes this old family seemed as segregated as Muslims.

There were things that my mother would never dream of discussing with me, or with her brothers. Things that I only read about in the cancer literature.

Total mastectomy can be the better option when – the tumour is in the centre of the breast or directly behind the nipple; the breast is small and would be distorted by a partial mastectomy; there are several cancerous or precancerous areas in the breast; the woman would rather have the whole breast removed.

I had to read about these things. Perhaps I was glad my mother would not talk to me about them.

In the garden my Uncle Jack, my dad's brother, Aunt Doll's small, dark, nattily dressed husband, was smoking a roll-up. Smoking outside the house. A new thing. A small concession to the new century, or perhaps my father's lung cancer. Cigarettes, once consumed as freely as tea and chocolate digestives in this house, now had to be smoked in the garden. I watched my Uncle Jack smoke, and I saw the ghost of my father's face in his face.

Uncle Jack's big black Merc was parked outside the house, a superior set of wheels on a street full of light vans and old Fords. Uncle Jack was a driver – taking businessmen to the airport, waiting for them with his sign at arrivals, smoking his roll-ups outside the car so that the air inside was daisy fresh. Uncle Jack came with me when I went to see my father's body at the undertaker's. I wondered if we would have to look at my mother's body soon.

When the family had all gone, my Aunt Doll and Uncle Jack the last ones to leave, my mum made some tea for the two of us. The light was failing and there would be no more visitors tonight. No more visitors before the operation. Somehow the years had slipped away, and aunts and uncles who once stayed up playing poker until dawn – smoking their cigarettes, drinking their beer and sherry, their laughter ringing all night long – now liked to be home behind locked doors before it was too dark.

'How are you, Mum?'

'I'm all right, love. Don't worry about me. How are you?'

'Me?'

'You and Cyd.'

'Things are not so good right now, Mum.' I didn't want to upset her, tonight of all nights. Yet I felt her bravery deserved some of my own. 'I've met someone else. Someone I like a lot. And I think Cyd has too.'

I expected my mother – half of that great double act, my parents, the first husband-and-wife team I knew, the pair who cast their giant shadow on every relationship I'd ever had with a woman – to give me a lecture about the sanctity of the wedding vows, the importance of marriage, the horror of divorce.

But she didn't do any of these things.

'Life is very short,' my mum said. 'You have to take your pleasures where you can.'

My mum stood at the window, watching the street, as if waiting for someone. But everyone had been. There was nobody left to visit. And then I realised.

My dad.

She was waiting for my dad.

My mother stood at the window of the house that I had grown up in, the house that she had grown old in, and when I saw her waiting for a husband who would never come home, I loved her more than I could bear.

Waiting. The night before going into hospital for her simple mastectomy, although there was nothing simple about it, nothing simple at all, my mother standing at the window of the old house, looking out at the empty street beyond the net curtains, waiting for my old man.

Waiting to see him come around that bend in the road in his company car, and take her in his hard old tattooed arms one more time, my father come home to tell her she is beautiful – her face, her body, all of her – and that he loves her as he has always done, and that everything is going to be all right.

Or maybe just to take her in his arms.

I saw Tex.

I had left my mother at the hospital, left her unpacking her small suitcase in a ward where no bed was empty, a ward full of mostly elderly women in their prim nightdresses, with orange squash, boxes of Quality Street and romantic novels on their bedside tables. My father had died in this hospital and I was surprised how familiar it all was to me – the rank smell of hospital cooking in the corridors, the queues everywhere, the defiant crowds of smokers sucking their cigarettes outside the main doors. The smell of food, disease and medicine seemed to have seeped into every brick. What was different now was that I was visiting a ward full of women – women who laughed, women who talked and complained and commiserated in a way that didn't happen in the ward full of men.

There was a lot to do. A nurse to take my mum's blood pressure. A chat with the anaesthetist. The surgeon was on his way. And my mum had to change, from her Sunday best two-piece suit into her own Marks & Spencer nightdress. My mum acted as if she was on a day trip to the seaside. She was being too breezy, too jokey, overdoing the jollity, always her defence in the face of crisis.

I kissed her, much too hard, and left. And when I was filling up my car at the local petrol station, that's when I saw Tex.

Or rather Graham the insurance salesman from Southend, dressed up for his weekly line dancing, drawing amused glances from pale Essex teenagers in their souped-up Escorts as he filled his battered old estate with diesel. And he wasn't alone. In the passenger seat, there was an elderly cowgirl – some game old dear in rhinestone and buckskin, a ten-gallon hat sitting on top of her Maggie Thatcher perm. My mother's line-dancing replacement. Or maybe there had been a few since Tex dumped my mum because he found out that she was ill.

I watched him cross the forecourt and enter the garage. When he came out he was carrying a box of After Eight mints and a cheap bouquet of flowers, the kind you can only buy in petrol stations. Maggie Thatcher saw him coming with his gifts and smiled shyly. What a guy. And I moved to go over to him, to take his arm and make him listen while I told him about what was happening to my mum in the hospital down the road that morning, to tell him about the surgery, and to use words like mastectomy, chemotherapy, radiotherapy, lymphoedema, until I saw him squirm with shame at his cowardice.

But I didn't do it. I finished filling my tank as he was making a great play of giving Maggie Thatcher the chocolates and flowers, and that's when I caught a glimpse of myself in my car window, and the image held me. By the time I had recovered, Tex and his dancing partner had gone.

And I knew I could not approach him because I was afraid that I was that kind of man too – a pretender, conning a woman out of her love by appearing to be nice, terminating all emotion when the first bill arrived. What Tex did to my mum – was it really so different from what I was doing to Cyd?

With all my heart, I wanted to be the other sort of man, a man like my father. Loyal, true, a keeper of promises. A forever and ever man. But I suspected that I was much more like this toy cowboy than I was ever like my dad.

All smooth talk and empty promises, all milk chocolates and flowers, then running a country mile as soon as the going got rough.

Gina called me on the day she arrived in London, but it wasn't the call I'd been expecting – cursory, formal, and anxious to get me off the line and out of her life.

Instead, the call, when it came, was at midnight, with Gina in tears, a hard-core soundtrack booming in the background.

'Harry?'

One word and I could tell it was her, even if the word was all choked up with emotion.

'Gina, what's wrong?'

Cyd stirred beside me as I sat up in bed. She'd had a late night, catering for some launch, and she had fallen asleep as soon as her head touched the pillow.

'Harry, it's awful.'

'You're in London? Speak up, I can't hear you.'

'We're in our flat. Pat and me. In Belsize Park. I thought it would be nice around here. But the people next door – they've got So Solid Crew going at full blast.'

'You want me – what? You want me to come around?'

I felt my wife – my current wife, that is – pick up her alarm clock and slam it back down.

'Do you know what time it is, Harry?' Cyd said.

'Could you, Harry?' Gina said. 'It's driving me nuts and it sounds like there are a lot of them. Some sort of party. I'm afraid to knock on the door.'

I put my hand over the mouthpiece. 'Gina's in town. There's a problem with the flat. Noisy neighbours.'

'Tell her to call the police.' Cyd sat up in bed. She was wearing this old Tom Petty T-shirt. When we first started, even when we were first married, she used to wear the kind of nightdresses that drove me wild. Short, silky, see-through. Pants like dental floss at the top of her dancer's legs. Now it was Tom Petty T-shirts. 'Give me the phone, and I'll tell her myself.'

'Pat can't sleep either,' Gina said.

That was enough for me.

'Give me the address,' I said. 'I'll be there as soon as I can.'

As I was pulling on my clothes in the darkness, Cyd turned on her bedside light.

'She's not your problem any more, Harry. You're divorced. That relationship is *over*. Let her husband sort it out. Let the cops.'

I didn't reply. I didn't want to fight. But I knew that I couldn't just ignore Gina's call and go back to sleep. The old saying was right.

Our marriage had lasted for seven years.

But our divorce would last forever.

It was a big white house in Belsize Park. A good house, in an affluent neighbourhood. Lots of trees and builders' skips, and the two kinds of cars that you always saw in neighbourhoods like this, the cars that were serious – Mercedes-Benz SLKs, Audi TTs, 3-series BMWs – and the cars that were just for fun – original Beetles and Minis, and the new nostalgia versions, rusty Morris Minors, prehistoric Citroëns. I paid the minicab, already looking up at the house that contained my son and my former wife. I didn't need to look at the numbers. I could hear the music coming from the second floor.

I pressed the button for the top floor and Gina buzzed me through the front door. The music thundered above my head. Once you got inside, the big white house reeked of rented property. Stacks of mail addressed to former tenants were piled on the worn carpet like autumn leaves. This place would not be cheap, probably two grand a month, but it didn't feel like anyone's home. The owners of the flats inside the big white house all lived somewhere else.

I walked up past the party on the second floor, hearing their laughter and screams, a smashing glass. The music they were playing sounded like a never-ending burglar alarm.

Getting old, Harry.

Gina opened her door, pale and tearful, wrapped up in some kimono-style dressing gown that looked a few sizes too big. Or maybe it was meant to be like that. Underneath she had her pyjamas on, and I thought how unfair it was of Cyd to expect Gina to break up a drunken party in her pyjamas.

'I'll go and have a word with them, okay?'

'Thanks, Harry.'

'Pat?'

'He's all right. Sleeping, the last time I looked. Although God knows how.'

I felt my heart beating as I went down a flight of stairs and knocked on the door. No response. I knocked harder. Finally a gawky white kid with a retro Beatle cut opened the door. Students, I thought. Unlikely to knife me. But what was I expecting in Belsize Park? The Bloods and the Crips?

'You should have four American Hots, two Garlic Love-ins, and a Capricciosa,' the gawky kid said. 'And a Vesuvio with extra pepperoni. Plus, you know, some coleslaw, garlic bread and stuff.'

'Actually I'm not delivering pizza. I'm from upstairs. Your music is keeping my son and my . . . wife awake.'

Over his high, bony shoulder I could see a flat full of young people laughing and dancing and trying to convince themselves that they were in a vodka commercial. A shorter, fatter youth appeared by his side.

'Has he got the Belgian chocolate ice cream?'

I could smell the sickly-sweet aroma of puff. Would that affect my son one flight up? Could my boy get passively stoned?

'He's not from Mister Milano,' said the gawky kid. 'He's from upstairs.'

'Upstairs?' said fatty.

'Wants us to keep the noise down.'

'Disturbing him, is it?'

'Apparently.'

They were laughing at me. I had been expecting threats to my person. I hadn't expected them to laugh at me.

'No problem, mate,' the fat one said. 'We'll be quiet as a rat.'

'You won't hear us – what is it rats do? – squeak,' said the gawky one.

They held on to each other, rocking with laughter.

'Appreciate it,' I said. 'Because my son, he's seven, he –'

'No problem, mate.'

They closed the door in my face. And as I climbed the stairs to Gina's place, the music miraculously decreased to a level that didn't rattle the fillings in my teeth.

'Well done, Harry.'

I gave my ex-wife an it-was-nothing smile. And immediately the music was turned up to a volume that was louder than ever.

'Little bastards,' I said, making for the door.

'Don't go.'

I looked at her. She pulled the kimono thing tighter, as if trying to hide inside it.

'Gina? It's not just those idiots downstairs, is it?'

'No.'

I put my arm around her and we went inside her flat. It was clearly expensive, but clearly on a lease. The heavy olde-English furniture, the blood-red leather sofa, the Gustav Klimt prints on the wall – none of these things could have been chosen by

Gina, who loved all that was light and modern and Japanese. This place looked as though it had been decorated by Queen Victoria.

We sat on the blood-red leather sofa.

'Is it your dad?' I hadn't asked what was actually wrong with him. Since my own father had died, I fatalistically assumed that any illness an old person contracted was terminal.

'My dad's okay.' She smiled for the first time, wiping her nose with the back of her hand. 'He's a silly old bugger. He put his hip out snowboarding.'

'Snowboarding? I thought there was something wrong with him.'

'Only the thing that's been wrong with him all his life. He can't grow up.'

I had slipped my shoes off at the door – even in these rented rooms, I didn't need to be told that Gina liked you to take your shoes off at the door, Japanese style – and now I could feel my feet quivering with the vibrations coming through the floor.

'I'm going to go and talk to those morons.'

'Don't, Harry.'

'Don't worry, they're not going to hurt me. They're all middle-class kiddies from safe, rich homes.'

'Not like us, then.'

'No, nothing like us.'

I looked at her. Despite her tiredness and the tears, and all the years, she had the same glow about her that had left me breathless and speechless the first time I ever saw her. But something had happened to Gina, something terrible.

'Go and look in on Pat, will you? I'll make us some tea. Is jasmine okay? It's all I've got.'

'Jasmine's fine.'

Gina went into the small kitchen and I tried a few doors until I saw the familiar tousle-haired figure sleeping flat on his back.

My son, at seven years of age, sleeping in the second bedroom of a rented flat in Belsize Park. While I lived a few miles away with another woman, another child. As always, I was shocked by the love I felt for my boy. The hip-hop from below was shaking his windows. He didn't seem to care. I pulled his *Phantom Menace* duvet up over his shoulders and closed his door as quietly as I could.

Gina was placing two cups of pale-green tea on the coffee table.

'Sleeping,' I said.

'He could sleep through anything, that kid. You should have seen him on the plane. Turbulence all the way across the Atlantic. Didn't even stir.'

'What is it, Gina? What's really wrong?'

'It's Richard. I've left him.'

It took a moment for this to sink in. 'You've left Richard? So this trip to London –'

'Permanent. We're not going back.'

'So when you said it was for a few weeks . . .'

'That was the original plan. But there's no point in going back. Oh fuck, Harry, my life is such a mess. What am I doing in this bloody flat with these stupid students and their awful music? I'm going to end up on *Jerry Springer*, I swear I am.'

'You're not going to end up on *Jerry Springer*. What happened?'

'Children.'

I thought she meant Pat. I thought she meant that her life didn't fit with both Richard and Pat. But that wasn't it.

'We couldn't have any,' she said. 'We tried and tried. I couldn't get pregnant. And it broke us up, Harry. It just broke us up.'

I sipped my tea. Even though it was scalding hot. I didn't know if I should be hearing this. I didn't know if I wanted to.

'I think a marriage needs children, Harry. It's hard enough to keep together even if you have a kid. Without them – I don't know if it's possible. We had all the tests. Richard and me. It was okay at first. We even laughed about it – him masturbating into a little plastic container, me with my legs up in the air getting prodded and probed. They couldn't find anything. But there's something wrong somewhere. In the end, it was too much of a strain. Maybe it would have been easier, maybe we could have stood it, if Pat wasn't there. But it was hard for Richard. It's hard loving someone else's child when you can't have one of your own.'

'So Richard blamed Pat?'

'I didn't say that, Harry. But it's such a thankless task, being a step-parent. I think in the end Richard felt he couldn't win.' She sighed. 'Then I saw his credit card bill. Flowers, hotel rooms, restaurants.' She looked at me. 'Flowers I didn't receive. Hotel rooms I had never stayed in. Restaurants I had only read about.'

'Who was she?'

'A neighbour. Some bored housewife with three kids, funnily enough. No doubt it would have been some woman at work if he'd had a job. Because he's still unemployed, he had to find what he was looking for in Safeway. She probably thought she was missing out on something too.'

'He must be crazy. Cheating on you.'

That gave her a laugh. 'You did, Harry. You did.'

'I'm sorry, Gina. Sorry about you and Richard. About you and me. About the students downstairs. About everything.'

'What happened to us, Harry? What happened to the boy and girl who were going to stay together forever?'

'I don't know what happened. Time, I guess. Just time, Gina.'

'Don't you ever wish that it could be like that again? That innocent? That straightforward?'

I finished my Japanese tea and stood up. I was ready to face the music.

'Now and then,' I said.

My mother slept.

White with exhaustion and pumped full of painkillers and medicine to kill the sickness, oblivious to the echoing, malodorous life of the hospital going on all around her, she was tucked into bed in her own little post-operation room, an

IV drip attached to a pale-blue vein in her hand, and she lay on her back and slept.

Sleeping at noon on a Sunday. Something she had never done in her life. If you could call it sleep, that drugged unconsciousness that was the aftermath of her operation.

I sat by her side, afraid to touch her.

Her kind face, her smallness, and the thought of the dressing on her wound under that hospital nightdress – these things tore at my heart, and made me hold my head and almost choke on all that was inside me.

There were no visitors, not yet, and the doctors and nurses had all gone away. They had cut off the breast with the tumour and they were confident that the operation had been a success.

They talked me through what happened next. Chemotherapy. Then radiotherapy. The chemotherapy would most likely cause my mother's hair to fall out and make her sick to her stomach. The radiotherapy would feel itchy, sore, like bad sunburn. Before all of that, when she awoke, she would feel a pain in her arm, and pins and needles, and sickness, the sickness would never be far away now. The wound, the cut that had been made to remove the thing that was killing her, that would be sore and tender and tight for months.

The doctors told me something that my mother would never tell me. That she wouldn't be able to wear a bra. Not yet. The wound was too fresh. It seemed as if everything about this illness was painstakingly designed to make my mother feel less like a woman.

When they had all gone, the optimistic doctors and the cheerful nurses, the affable oncologist and the genial surgeon and the easy-going anaesthetist, I cried for what my mother had gone through, and all that she still had to go through.

Even if she beat this thing, even if she lived.

'I love you so much,' I whispered, telling her things that we would both have been too shy and embarrassed to hear if she was awake. 'You don't deserve this, Mum. Not you. Not anyone.'

I sat there for hours. All that Sunday she didn't wake up. It felt like the kind of sleep that would last for decades, like something from a fairy tale. By the time I left, the spring afternoon was fading behind the drawn curtains of that tiny room. It was only when I was looking for my car in the hospital's vast parking lot that I remembered the appointment I had missed.

I liked the lights on Primrose Hill.

They were, and still are, those old kind of Victorian street-lamps. Tall and black with a chunky glass casing at the top. Those lamps look like throwbacks to some older, lost city, the London of Sherlock Holmes and Watson, peasouper fogs and tugs on the Thames.

The lamps had not been illuminated when I arrived at Primrose Hill. The days were getting longer. But night was falling at last and they would be turned on soon.

The crowds were thinning. It was becoming too dark for ball games, the pampered dogs of the neighbourhood were almost exhausted, and the young lovers were strolling off arm-in-arm to dinner in Camden Town or Hampstead or Swiss Cottage. I decided to take a quick walk to the top, and then go home.

The park on Primrose Hill is built upon one high, grassy peak. From up there you can see for miles. Down to London Zoo and the lush expanse of Regent's Park. The West End and the City and Docklands in the distance. And, on the hill behind you, the wild woods of Hampstead Heath. I watched my city as day turned to night. The stars came out. The great metropolis was starting to twinkle.

And that's when I saw her walking up the hill towards me. Her pretty face was flushed with exertion. She looked as though she had been walking all day. Ever since we had been supposed to meet, in fact.

'Sorry I'm a bit late, Kazumi.'

She reached the top of the hill, breathing heavily. She shook her head, and I didn't know if she was telling me that she didn't care or that she was speechless with rage. Then she sort of looked at me in a way that I understood completely.

Because it said – kiss me, stupid.

So I did.

And just at that moment, from Prince Albert Road in the south, to King Henry's Road in the north, from St John's Wood in the west, to Grand Union Canal in the east, all over the length and breadth of Primrose Hill, the lights came on.

part three: *the greatest girl in the history of the world*

twenty-three

'Viagra,' Eamon suggested, without me even asking him. 'Just the thing for a man with both a wife and a girlfriend. That's what you need, Harry. Viagra. Amazing stuff. Although of course you know you're getting a bit old when you can't get it down.'

But it wasn't Viagra that I needed. Because for a man with both a wife and a girlfriend, it was amazing how little sex I was getting.

You might think that my seed would have been spread thin and wide as I bounced from the marital bed to the girlfriend's futon and back again. But Cyd had moved into the spare bedroom. The world my parents knew had finally turned inside out. For them there was no sex before marriage. For me there was none after.

We had separate rooms because I usually went to bed long after midnight, while suddenly Cyd was tucked up with a camomile tea just after the ten o'clock news. Cyd and I were both blaming work, because it was just too sad to admit that our problems went far deeper than mere scheduling.

Now she had turned down the offer to sell him Food Glorious Food, Cyd's freelance work with Luke Moore was really taking off. She suddenly had a spate of early-morning breakfast meetings to cater, all these jobs in the City and the West End where businessmen ate croissants, pains au raisin and six kinds of bagel. And while my wife got her early nights, I was often out into the early hours, supervising Eamon's return to stand-up.

Now that the TV was over, Eamon was going back to his roots, doing stand-up for the first time in years, even some open-mike stuff, and thinking about taking his act on the road. There was no money in it at this stage, and my savings account was steadily shrinking, but we both felt it was the only way back. He performed in small clubs, not much more than basements, where all we had to do was turn up. And I saw that the comedian dreams of stand-up the way the clown yearns to play Hamlet.

This was the heart of his craft, this was where he was truly tested. By nerves, by drunks, by all his limitations. So we spent our nights in sweaty cellars, where he was sometimes good and sometimes not so good but he was always funnier than his hecklers – 'Don't I remember you from medical school? You were the one in the jar' – and I wondered if he could really still do it without re-takes, an autocue, a full production crew and the Dutch courage of cocaine.

Eamon's comeback took up a lot of my time, but in truth not all of it. Sometimes I told Cyd I was seeing Eamon when the person I was really seeing was Kazumi. And when I told her nothing at all, she didn't seem to care.

I was out late and my wife was out early. And we both knew it was more than work. There were now long calls to her sisters and her mother in the States, as – I was guessing here, but I believed it was a good guess – the possibility of moving back home finally took shape in her mind. Our problem, this problem my wife and I had, was that we just couldn't imagine our future together. We still loved each other, but there was a politeness and formality to our dealings that broke my heart. And we just couldn't see how this thing between us was ever going to work out.

'Let's see how it goes, shall we?' Cyd said, making up her bed in the guest room.

So we see how it goes. Just another man and wife having trouble. But it seemed like the saddest thing in the world, this feeling that what we had right now was not good enough to stay for, and not bad enough to leave.

And although there was no sex after marriage, there was none in Primrose Hill in the flat that Kazumi shared with a Swedish woman who was a second-year student at the Royal Academy of Music. It felt like our kiss in the dusk above London had opened a door for me, but now I was faced by a locked gate.

As Kazumi and I lay on her single bed, our clothes on and the curtains drawn, we heard the flatmate practising her cello in the next room. She was so good that the music, just the other side of the wall, was never intrusive. It was strangely soothing to have Chopin and Elgar and Haydn seeping through the thin wall, great swirling sounds of romance, all the passion that felt just out of reach. The flatmate played music that I somehow knew, although I couldn't say where from, and also things that I had never heard before in my life. One piece that she played again and again – an exam was coming up – turned out to be 'Song Without Words' by Mendelssohn.

The flatmate could have been studying accountancy or tree surgery, but romance is a series of happy accidents, and the fact that she played the most beautiful music ever written as Kazumi lay chastely in my arms seemed predestined, written in the stars, and made me certain that I was in the right place.

That music would have been the perfect accompaniment to a few hours of passion. But that was not what Kazumi wanted. Kazumi didn't want to sleep with me. Just like my wife, in fact.

'I don't want to be your dirty little secret,' Kazumi said. 'It never works. Afraid to be seen together. Afraid of bumping against someone you know. What kind of life is that? You can call me but I can't call you. And all the questions I would have to ask you. Such as, do you still have sex with your wife?'

'I can tell you the answer to that now.'

'No.' She pressed a finger to my lips. 'Because I don't want you to start lying to me. And even if they leave their wife, it never works. I don't know why. Price too high, maybe.'

And I was torn. I wanted to look after both of them. To love both of them. Kazumi and Cyd. In the way that they both deserved. And already I knew that was impossible.

You can love two women at once, but not in the way they deserve.

So I was constantly looking for the exit sign, trying doors, seeking a way out of this chaos. And I did it with Kazumi as well as Cyd. In my mad moments, when it all became too much, and the music stopped, I wanted someone – Cyd, Kazumi, one of them, either of them – to reveal something so painful that it would drive me away, that it would settle things once and forever.

'You seem to know a lot about sex with a married man, Kazumi. How come you're such an expert?'

'Doesn't matter.'

'I want to know.'

'Not me. Friend.'

'A friend. Sure.'

'Really.'

'So who was this secret friend? Someone here?'

'No. Japan. A close friend in Japan.'

And then the yen finally dropped.

'What was her name, this friend with the married man?'

On the other side of the wall, the sound of a cello pouring out a kind of stately melancholy. 'Song Without Words' again. The exam must be soon.

'Gina,' Kazumi said. 'My friend's name was Gina.'

My doctor thought that I had something called White Coat Syndrome.

'You see a doctor' – she smiled, her adorable Italian accent adding unexpected vowels to the ends of nouns – 'and your blood pressure goes through the *roof-a*.'

She was sort of right. When I first entered her surgery, my systolic pressure was usually around 180 and my diastolic pressure around 95. My doctor made me lie down for ten or fifteen minutes, then took another reading. This was always a vast improvement – around 150 over 90. That was not great, but it meant I was unlikely to have a stroke any time soon.

White Coat Syndrome. Well, maybe. I knew it had something

to do with my heart. But what my doctor never factored into her diagnosis was that I came to her surgery from home. So when she took my blood pressure, at least part of it was a judgement on my life with my wife – that bleak, stagnated life of separate beds, blended families and an ex-husband who was getting married next week. Of course my blood pressure was sky high. Where else would it be?

When I lay there on the couch for a while, listening to the distant traffic rumble down Harley Street, my mind drifted away to the happier part of my life. The first reading was my life with Cyd. And the second reading was my other life, my secret life, my life with Kazumi.

I knew her now. She was not just a pretty young woman who had caught my eye. I knew about her childhood, the salary man father who drank himself senseless after work, the mother who gave up her dreams of travelling the world for a man who didn't love her. I knew about Kazumi's broken marriage, and the courage it took to come to London to start again, and I knew how her face, often seriously dreaming, lost in her thoughts, could suddenly light up with happiness, light up totally without warning, like the old-fashioned lamps on Primrose Hill.

I knew it wasn't the same as building a real life with someone. It wasn't the same as dealing with the grind of all the things that can break down – washing machines, boilers, cars, families, marriages – but she was still the sweetest thing in my world, and that was real too, more real than anything. We talked to each other, Kazumi and I. We talked about everything. Apart from my wife, of course. We never talked about her.

'We need to be more aggressive in treating you,' said my doctor.

She adjusted my prescription. Instead of taking 40 mg of Zestril once a day, I would now take 20 mg of Zestril and 20 mg of Zestoretic.

But in my heart – my mad, pumping, lovesick heart – I felt that for what ailed me now, pills would never be enough.

* * *

How many girls and women had I taken home to meet my mum?

It was not every girl I ever took to the pictures, and not every woman I ever took to bed. But, what with the teenage girlfriends and the two wives, we must have been in double figures by now. And as Kazumi and I drove deeper into the suburbs, the urban sprawl finally giving way to the fields of summer, I realised the criteria for bringing a woman to meet my mum had always been the same – this one, this special one, would be the last girl that I ever brought home. Why do we place so much importance on the first? It's the last one that counts.

At this time in her life, I would like to have spared my mum my latest domestic upheaval. But there was no point in telling her that Kazumi was just a friend.

My mum knew that for a man whose marriage was in trouble, there was no such thing.

The old house on a Sunday afternoon.

Pat let us in, smiling at Kazumi, not quite able to work out what she was doing here. In the living room my mum was sitting on the carpet, rotating her shoulders with a look of quiet concentration on her face. She got up, a little embarrassed to be discovered like this, but kissed Kazumi as if she had known her forever.

'Hello, love, just doing my exercises.'

My mother had been through hell, and she acted as if it had been a stroll in the park.

After surgery and radiotherapy, the muscles in her right arm were stiff and tight. She had exercises to control the pain, and different exercises to regain the use of her right arm. She did these exercises with a good grace, never complaining, and I knew now that she was actually tougher than all of us men in her life.

'Two years I have to do them for, sweetheart,' she told Kazumi. My mum only needed to know you for five seconds before she started calling you *love*, *darling* and *sweetheart*. 'That's what they told me.'

Kazumi, Pat and I watched my mum run through her exercise programme for our benefit. She demonstrated Shoulder Circling. Hair Brushing. Assisted Lift. Back Scratching. Bent Arm. Proudly tossing out the names of her exercises the way she had once mentioned the Walkin' Wazi, the Lost in Austin and the Four-Star Boogie.

And I knew that these exercises were the least of it. She would not put this thing behind her with a bit of stretching. Even after the monstrous surgery that was necessary to save her life, she would never really be over this thing. The monitoring, the exercises, the drugs, fear that the cancer would come back – it was all measured in years.

My mum got pins and needles in her arm, an agonising pain in her chest. And as we had our tea and biscuits, I noticed that she had developed this habit of examining her hand.

Some of the lymph nodes under her arm had been removed, and my mum had been told that this could cause lymphoedema – a build-up of fluid in the tissues of her arm. She had been told to watch out for swelling on the affected side, her right side, and she watched all the time. Perhaps she would always watch now. Every few minutes or so, she examined her hand, looking for signs of the beginning of the end.

Chemotherapy had left her feeling as though she had the worst hangover in the world, a hangover that would not get better. Mercifully her hair did not fall out. Radiotherapy left her tired and sore, feeling like she had fallen asleep in a burning sun. She laughed about things that would have grown men – me, for example – weeping in a darkened room.

'I was looking forward to my hair falling out,' she said, smiling mischievously. 'I could have worn my Dolly Parton wig.'

Pat laughed appreciatively. He didn't understand too much of this, even though my mum and I had both pored over every word in the leaflet *Talking with Your Children about Breast Cancer*. (*If you are able to talk honestly and openly with your family at each step, you will hopefully find that families can be a great source of love and support*.) But he knew the signals that indicated a joke was being made – the breezy tilt in the voice, the raised eyebrows, the rolled eyes – and he was always delighted to respond enthusiastically.

I found it much harder to smile, because I knew my son would be fully grown before we could say this thing inside my mother was truly beaten. Years and years, it would all take years. The best that could happen would take years. The worst that could happen would be there in a moment.

There were 20 mg of Tamoxifen, a hormone treatment, every day, which made my mum feel like she was having another menopause. She would take it for five years. After two years, perhaps she would no longer have to do exercises. Perhaps. See what the doctors say. Have to wait and see.

And there were still many things she would not talk to me about, things that I had to guess at, to wheedle out of surgeons and her female friends and all those pink and purple leaflets. What my mum would call – *women things*.

She still couldn't wear a bra because of the scar, because it was still so raw and sore. This seemed insultingly cruel. Again I was reminded that this cancer seemed sadistically committed to making my mum feel like less of a woman than she was before.

But she dealt with all the indignity, pain and terror without complaint, with the kind of good-natured, mocking pragmatism that she had shown all her life. She went to make more tea, and she smiled at me over Kazumi's shoulder, raising her eyebrows while giving a little nod. I knew that look. I had seen it when I brought Gina home for the first time. And Cyd, too. That look meant – *she's a smasher*.

Kazumi was on the living-room floor with Pat. They had met before, of course, when she took his photograph in Gina's garden, and I was both happy and worried that my son remembered her so clearly.

Would he mention Kazumi to Gina? Or, worse still, to Cyd? How would I get out of that one? Kazumi was patient and kind, playing with one of his video games, while he regarded her with a kind of delighted curiosity. I feared that my son understood more than I would wish. Not yet eight years old, he was already wise to the ways of the world. Or at least the ways of his old man.

Is this what it would be like for Pat and me at the other end of our lives? In thirty years or so, would I be old and fighting illness, with my son all grown-up and divorced and ready to try again? And when I was fighting for my life, would my adult son still be bringing home some young woman for my approval, acting like he'd never been in love before?

Kazumi was good with Pat. They laughed together, they played together, and although I knew it was unfair to compare her to Cyd, who had the permanently thankless role of step-parent, I couldn't help it. This just felt easier.

Maybe it would have been different if we were living together. No, definitely it would have been different. But as Kazumi and Pat played Nuke Universe Two I dreamed of running off with the pair of them. To Paris or County Kerry or anywhere far from here. I looked at my son with Kazumi and I believed that it was not too late to start again. And as I thought of the infinite kindness in my mother's face, I also desperately wanted to travel with her, to see some other things while we still could and before it was too late. I wanted to get us all away from this place.

My mum returned with tea and biscuits and I showed her the brochures that I had brought with me. She handled them carefully, as if she had to give them back to their rightful owner.

'Nashville, Mum. The home of country. Listen to this, Mum. We can go together. Pat, too. In one of the holidays. Kazumi, if she's not busy with her work. A real holiday for you. Listen, Mum: *Six million people a year travel to Nashville, Tennessee, the home of country music. Enjoy the rhinestone glitter of the Grand Ole Opry, Music Row and the Country Music Hall of Fame. Experience the Nashville Sound of Hank Williams, Patsy Cline, Jim Reeves, Kenny Rogers and Shania Twain.* Sounds great, doesn't it? Mum?'

But my mum was different from me. She didn't dream of escape. She wanted to stay here.

'Sounds lovely, darling, but I'm happy in my own home.'

She put the brochure down. And I saw that my mum was

never going to make it to Nashville. This is where we were so different. Unlike me, my mother didn't believe that happiness was always somewhere else.

'I like holidays,' she said to Kazumi. 'My husband and I, we used to go somewhere every year. Cornwall and Dorset when Harry was young. We even went to Norway a few times – I've got a brother who settled there after the war, met a lovely girl. I had six brothers, did Harry tell you that?'

Kazumi made suitably impressed noises. She was getting the hang of this very quickly.

'Then Spain later, when Harry didn't want to come with us any more,' continued my mum. 'But I like it here. Do you know what I mean? I like that feeling you get, that feeling you don't get on holiday, when you're away from everything familiar. You know, that feeling you get when you're part of a family.'

Then my mum looked at her hands, as if admiring her bright-red nail polish, or searching for signs of lymphoedema, or maybe just looking at her wedding ring, a modest band of burnished gold that somehow contained an entire world.

twenty-four

You never saw anyone so happy to be having a baby.

When I came back from running in the park, she was on the stairs, laughing and crying at the same time.

'I'm *pregnant*,' she said, like it was the best thing in the world. Then she was in my arms and later, when we had untangled our limbs, and stared at each other, laughing out loud, unable to believe our luck, after all of that she showed me the blue line on the pregnancy test – that thin, blue, indisputable line.

And in the days and weeks ahead, she kept taking more pregnancy tests, looking for that blue line again and again, as if it was too good to be true. Maybe there are other pregnant women whose favourite pastime is taking pregnancy tests, even though they already know the answer, even though they have already had the happy result confirmed dozens of times.

But Gina was the first woman that I ever really knew.

The first woman I lived with, the first woman I married. She found a source of endless wonder in her daily pregnancy tests, and I found a source of wonder in her.

That was almost nine years ago now. The world turned, and kept turning, and not only was my wife now my ex-wife, but she was about to become the ex-wife of another man. They talk about the divorce statistics, and the fluctuating failure rate of the modern marriage, but for my ex-wife and me the rate seemed to be 100 per cent.

That thin blue line represented a little heartbeat inside her, and that glimmer of life was now a boy, almost eight years old, changing every week, growing teeth that would have to last him until his dying day, and this life he was leading – bouncing from one home to another, one school to another, one country to another, seeing marriages crumble, learning that the adult world was fragile and weak and fallible – seemed to be robbing him of his – well, I don't know what you would call it.

Robbing him of his halo of innocence. The aura of light that was all around him as a little boy, the light that made strangers stop and smile at him in the street.

Pat is still a boy in a million. He still shines. To me he still looks like the most beautiful child in the world. But this life has robbed him of that angel glow. It has gone, and it will never come back, and while it is possible that we all lose that angel glow in the end, I can't help feeling that Gina and I – who held that very first pregnancy test as if it was as precious as our baby himself – share most of the blame. We could have done better for our boy. But Gina's mood was such that right now she blamed her latest ex-husband for everything.

'Easter, right? Shouldn't be a problem, should it? You would think that Easter doesn't present too many possibilities for domestic strife.'

We were in the tiny kitchen of her flat, drinking some jasmine tea. This love of Japan, this yearning for the life she had given up for marriage and me and Pat – she was never going to grow out of it now, she was never going to stop missing that life she had never known.

'But Richard objected to the Easter egg that I bought Pat. Can you believe it?'

Pat appeared in the doorway.

'Can I watch *The Phantom Menace* on DVD?' This to Gina.

'No, you're going out with your father.'

'Just some of the special features. A few of the deleted scenes. The interview with the director. Production notes.'

'Go on then.' Pat disappeared. Stirring orchestral music swelled from the living room. 'This Easter egg I bought – it was bloody lovely, Harry. Milk chocolate and covered with little hearts in red icing. A big purple bow around it. And

Richard – get this – said it was the kind of egg you buy for a *lover*, not a child. For a lover! An Easter egg for a lover! That's what he said! He said it was the kind of egg you buy for your husband or wife. I mean, can you believe the pettiness of the man? As if I can't buy my son whatever Easter egg I bloody well like . . .'

'Are you talking to him?'

She smiled. 'You've heard of the old cow syndrome?'

'Don't think so.'

'When a bull has mated with a cow once, he's not interested any more. Doesn't matter if the cow is really cute. The bull couldn't care less. It's called the old cow syndrome.'

'Is that true?'

She nodded. 'Once is enough for the bull. No matter how attractive the cow is, he's just not interested. Well, it works the other way around for this old cow. When I've finished with them, I've finished with them.'

She made me laugh. I could hear the bitterness in her voice, and I knew that this new life was hard for her too. Because it was hard for any single parent. And – incredibly, it seemed to me – that's what Gina was now. She was angry, sour and sad. But I felt an enormous affection for this woman who had once been closer to me than anyone in the world. A woman who would almost certainly be my best friend if we hadn't ruined it by getting married.

And for the first time I started to think that our marriage hadn't been a failure. Not really. We could have done better for Pat. We could have been kinder to each other. All this was true. But we were together for seven years, we produced a sweet, caring kid whose existence will make this world a better place, and we could still talk to each other. Most of the time. When she was not being an old cow and I was not full of too much old bull. So who is to say that our marriage failed? A few good years and a great kid – maybe that's the best anyone can hope for.

Gina and I had been through the mill, and we could still sit in a room together, drinking jasmine tea while she bitched about her future ex-husband. Deep in our history, Gina and I had something that Cyd and I lacked.

It went back to that blue line.

It went back to that day I came home from running in the park and, through laughter and tears, Gina told me that she was having our baby.

We had missed that, Cyd and I, the hope and joy and optimism that Gina saw in that blue line, that thin blue line leading to all our tomorrows, and our stake in the future.

'Ah, sure, there's nothing like it,' Eamon said. 'To love pure and chaste from afar. Nothing like it – except, perhaps, wild unprotected sex as you take her roughly from behind. Sure, that's even slightly better.'

I was beginning to wish that I had lied. I was beginning to wish that I had never told him that Kazumi and I hadn't consummated our relationship.

'She understands me.' It was true. Kazumi knew what I was going through with my mum. And my son. Even, although we didn't like to put it into so many words, with my wife.

'She understands you too well, Harry.' Eamon took a slug of his mineral water, ran a hand through his thick black locks. 'She's playing you, man. Don't be fooled by that sweet act. All that hello-flowers, hello-sky stuff.'

'Hello-flowers, hello-sky?'

'Kazumi understands that when a man gets what he wants, he never wants it again.'

We were in Eamon's dressing room in a comedy club in the East End. The dressing room was more of a broom cupboard compared with what we were used to in television, and the club was actually an old-fashioned, pints-and-pork-scratchings, tobacco-stained pub that had belatedly tried to hitch a ride on the comedy bandwagon.

It was not a million miles away from the kind of place that Eamon had appeared in before TV came calling. What had changed was his attitude to women. The cavalier shag merchant of old was now urging caution, doing everything he could to get me to go back to my wife and stop the madness. Addiction had done to Eamon what it does to a lot of people.

It had made him long for stability.

'You're messed up, Harry. You've screwed too many of the wrong women and screwed over too many of the right women. Like your wife.'

He had always had a soft spot for Cyd.

'You're on in five minutes.'

But he would not let it go. Eamon – the only one who knew anything about us, apart from the cello-playing flatmate – thought that it would be different if I could sleep with Kazumi. Get it out of my system. If Kazumi and I had sex, Eamon told me, then I would see her as just another girl. Because right now that was the one thing Kazumi was not – just another girl. But I didn't think that sex, when it finally happened, would make any difference. Except to make it impossible to live without her.

'Can't you see what you're doing, Harry? You're making the best bit go on and on.'

'The best bit?'

'The chase. The pursuit. The fever of anticipation. It's the best bit, isn't it? If we own up, it's much better than anything that comes later.'

'Remind me never to have sex with you.'

'You don't want the good stuff to die, Harry. Like it died with Gina. And with Cyd. Your wife. And every other woman you ever knew. You want the best to last. So what do you do? You get this platonic thing going. You make the chase, the pursuit, the delay of pleasure last forever.'

'Is that what I am doing? I don't think so. I've slept with plenty of women that I didn't love. Why can't I love a woman that I haven't slept with?'

Slept with – I couldn't stop using that inaccurate euphemism. Everything else just sounded too mechanical.

'Look at it this way. What is it all about? The whole thing – sex and romance, men and women? It's about delaying the moment of release. It's about postponing pleasure. It's about putting ecstasy on hold. Relax, don't do it. Frankie Goes to

Hollywood knew what they were talking about, Harry. And what are you doing with this woman you haven't slept with?'

'Tell me.'

'It's obvious. By falling so hard for someone you haven't shagged, you're delaying the moment of release – permanently. Of course you're mad about her. Why wouldn't you be? You'll be mad about her until you see that she's flesh and blood. Just like your wife.'

'You think I'd stop caring about Kazumi if we had sex?'

'No. I think you would be able to think more clearly. At the moment you're falling in love with a fantasy, and that's the most dangerous thing in the world.'

'You really think you can't care about someone until you've exchanged bodily fluids?'

'Hey, don't knock it, Harry. It breaks the ice.'

I looked at my watch. 'You're on in one minute.'

'No man can think clearly until he's been despunked, Harry.'

Maybe. I could see that a platonic relationship made everything seem hopelessly romantic. A mid-afternoon cappuccino with Kazumi in some sun-dappled little café became something I'd remember forever. A Polaroid we took of ourselves on Primrose Hill – Kazumi laughing as we banged our heads together, trying to get in shot – became the highlight of my week. She squeezed my hand in the back row of the Swiss Cottage Odeon and it was more exciting than most of the blow jobs I'd had in my brief career as a boy about town. She just did it for me.

And, yes, I could see that this thing was getting out of control. But it was more than a fantasy. I was starting to measure the practicalities of a life with Kazumi. Dismantling one home, setting up another home, giving Kazumi and me the chance to get to that point that all couples, even the ones that are crazy about each other, have to reach eventually. That point where you don't even feel the need to talk to each other.

It could work. I knew it could work. And maybe she was the one that I had needed all along. And perhaps it would make

Cyd happier if she was with someone else. She certainly didn't seem too thrilled by her life with me right now. So maybe it would be better all round. One harsh, painful tearing asunder – of a marriage, a house, a home – and then everybody would get a chance to have their happy ending.

'You don't even *know* her,' Eamon said, interrupting my plans for a new life. 'You've spent – what? – a hundred hours around each other? If that.'

'How long do you think it takes? How long before you know?'

He shook his head, exasperated. Outside, surprisingly close, we could hear hecklers shouting down the female comedian on stage.

'You fucking idiot, Harry. You're really going to leave your wife, your terrific wife, who you do not fucking deserve, for some slip of a girl you hardly know?'

He was genuinely angry with me.

'I didn't say that.'

'Well, where do you think this thing is heading?'

'I don't know.'

'You better start knowing, pal. You have started it now, and sooner or later – probably sooner – it will all end in tears.'

'Why should it end in tears?'

'Because you have to choose, you dumb bastard. Once you get into one of these things, you always have to choose.'

'And what if I make my choice, and I choose Kazumi? How do you know it would be a disaster? How can you be so sure?'

He held up his hands, a mocking surrender.

'I don't know, Harry. Neither do you. But have sex with Kazumi. Have lots of sex. Then see how you feel the first time she says something negative about your son.'

'What if she never does? What if she's great with him?'

'Then pack your bags and go.'

He pressed a silver key in my hand. I stared at it. He didn't have to tell me that it was the key to his flat.

'Kazumi's great,' Eamon said. 'But the world is full of great women. That's what romantic fools like you never admit. There are a million great women out there. Ten million. You could be in love with any one of them. Given the right circumstances, given timing. Sooner or later you have to stop tormenting yourself with the thought that there's just one out there with your name on. You have to be happy with what you've got. You have to love the one you're with. You have to say – this is my home now, this is my wife, and this is where I'm staying. Stop looking, Harry. Just stop looking, will you?'

From long ago, I heard the voices of my parents. *Just rest your eyes*, my mum and dad would tell me. *Just rest your eyes.*

But Eamon held out the silver key.

And I took it.

'I started using these sensitive condoms,' Eamon said, prowling across the tiny stage. 'Sensitive condoms – yeah, they're great. What they do is, after you have had sex and fallen asleep, the sensitive condom cuddles the girl and talks to her about her feelings. Sensitive condoms send flowers the next day. Never forget to call . . .'

A swell of laughter in the audience, mixed with a few groans. There wasn't the easy willingness to laugh that you found in a TV audience. There was a kind of punter who came to these things for the pleasure of baiting the poor sap on stage. Out in the smoky darkness, some of them were restless.

'Got any coke, Eamon?'

'Ah, I don't do that any more,' Eamon said mildly. 'The doctor gave me suppositories for my addiction. I told him they weren't working. He said, "Well, have you been taking them regularly?" I said, "What do you think I've been doing, doc? Shoving them up my arse?"'

More laughter. And some boos.

'Yeah, sensitive condoms. People say wearing a condom during sex is like wearing a raincoat in the shower. They've got to be kidding. With all these new diseases, *not* wearing a condom during sex is like wearing a live fuse box in the bath . . .'

Laughter and a smattering of increasingly vitriolic abuse.

'You loser, Eamon, you has-been!'

'Fuck off back to the detox clinic!'

'Waiter, this fish is off!'

'Condoms, yeah.' The little Woody Allen cough. 'These days you get packs of condoms for all different nationalities. You get the six-pack for Italians. That's Monday to Saturday with a day of rest on Sunday. And you get the eight-pack for the French. That's Monday to Saturday, and twice on Sunday. And you get the twelve-pack for the British.' A pause. His timing was always good. 'January, February, March . . .'

A belligerent voice from the back, hoarse with cigarettes and loathing.

'Come in, Eamon Fish – your fifteen minutes is up!'

'My parents didn't have to worry about condoms. Buy me and stop one – no, they didn't have to worry about any of that. Not that their sex life was very happy. One night I heard them through the bedroom wall. They were trying to have sex and it just wasn't working. My mother said, "What's the matter? Can't you think of anyone either?"'

'You're not funny!' the voice shouted.

'It's not that kind of comedy,' Eamon said.

It was a big city but a small world. Sooner or later we were going to be seen together.

Naturally we avoided the danger zones of north and central London, that surprisingly large swathe of the city where Cyd could be working, or Gina could be lurking. But eventually we would be spotted. I knew it.

When it happened it was worse than I had imagined – and it was not my wife, or even my ex-wife, but someone from the outer suburbs of my life. He saw me as soon as he walked into the club, and took it all in.

The married man, the girl by his side who wasn't his wife. In a quiet corner of the pub above the comedy club, having a drink, holding hands like they had done it before.

And I felt a sickening guilt that this man knew, this stranger, and my wife didn't. I was ashamed of myself. It seemed like the worst betrayal imaginable.

'Harry,' Richard said, looking at Kazumi.

What the hell was he doing here? What possible reason could this man have to be in a comedy club in Hackney?

'Richard. I thought you were still in the States.'

'Came over to see Gina.' He finally took his eyes off Kazumi. 'To be honest, I want her to come back.'

'This is Kazumi,' I said, for a cowardly moment thinking about passing her off as a work colleague, or a business associate.

But the truth is that Richard didn't care. He was in a state that was beyond caring about the romantic tangles of others – no job, no wife, and a life that had reached a point that he had never imagined. I knew the feeling.

'I'm staying with some friends,' he said. 'They've got a house around here. It's becoming quite popular with the City people, isn't it?'

'Them and the crack dealers. Listen, Richard, we have to go. Good luck with . . . everything.'

I watched Kazumi and Richard smiling and shaking hands and I thought of Gina's old bull theory, knowing he didn't have a chance in hell of getting her back.

Then we left him, our drinks abruptly abandoned, my guilt herding us out of the door.

And that's when I remembered the key in my pocket.

We let ourselves into Eamon's flat.

It had been bought during the boom years of *Fish on Friday*, lucrative personal appearances and beer endorsements – a waterfront loft overlooking Tower Bridge, the Thames and the colonised docks, all lit up like a tourist postcard of London at night. Kazumi went to the wall-high windows and stared out at the inky-black river, the illuminated bridge, the glittering city.

Then she faced me.

'Kazumi –'

'No more talk.'

Lit only by the moonlight and the lights of the waterfront, we struggled to undress while kissing each other at the same time. We were half dressed and grappling on the sofa like teenagers in heat when Eamon came home.

Kazumi heard the key in the door before I did, and she was off the sofa and into the bathroom before Eamon and his companion were even in the living room.

I recognised the woman – a TV producer who had once worked as a runner on *The Marty Mann Show*. Eamon waved from the doorway, and then they disappeared into his bedroom. I heard laughter and music from behind the closed door. It shouldn't have mattered, but the spell had been broken. Kazumi came back from the bathroom fully dressed and ready to go.

'Ah, not yet,' I said. 'Please, Kazumi. Come here. Nobody's going to disturb us again. Look at the view.'

She shook her head. 'It's not my view.'

I didn't try to argue with her. I wearily did up the buttons of my shirt. We quietly let ourselves out of the flat.

'It can't go on like this,' she said as I flagged down a taxi. 'I mean it, Harry. It can't go on.'

And it didn't.

Because after dropping Kazumi off I went home, where my wife told me that she was leaving me.

twenty-five

I had been left before, of course.

But this time was different.

When Gina left me, she went in a fury – not caring what she took and what she left behind, just wanting to be out of our home, just wanting to be away from me and our life.

I remembered a half-shut suitcase spilling Pat's socks, betrayed tears smudging her mascara and a throbbing pain just above my heart, where she had thrown my mobile phone at me.

Despite all of that, when Gina left there still felt like the faint chance that she would one day change her mind, that she would come back home, and that the rage would eventually pass.

It wasn't like that with Cyd.

Cyd's leaving was calm and methodical.

No tears, no raised voices, nothing done in haste. A grown-up, rational leaving, that somehow felt even worse. She wasn't leaving tonight. She wasn't leaving tomorrow. But she was leaving soon.

In our little guest room my wife had suitcases and overnight bags open on the single bed, and covering what looked like every spare square inch of the parquet floor. Some of the cases were almost empty. Others were already filling up with books, toys, CDs and winter clothes belonging to both her and Peggy. By the time the season changed, Cyd planned to be somewhere else.

With Gina I had felt that I still had a chance.

With Cyd there was no doubt at all.

She was never coming back.

'Going somewhere?'

She turned to face me. 'Sorry. I didn't hear you come in.' She turned back to the suitcase she was packing, stacking a pile of Peggy's thick woollen sweaters, shaking her head. 'Sorry.'

'What is this?' I said, coming slowly into the room.

'What does it look like?'

'Looks like you're moving out.'

She nodded. 'Like I said – sorry.'

'Why?'

She turned and faced me, and I saw the hurt and anger under the calm. 'Because you've left me already. I can feel it. I don't know why you stay, Harry. And you know the sad thing? Neither do you. You can't work out what you are doing with me. You can't remember.'

I shook my head, although I knew every word was true. Somewhere along the line I had forgotten why we were together, and that's why it had been so easy to fall for someone else.

'I can't mess around, Harry. I told you that from the start. It's not just me. I've got a daughter. I have to think about her. And I know that, with things the way they are between us, sooner or later you're going to meet some little fuck buddy.'

'A fucky buddy?'

'Fuck buddy. Someone you can have uncomplicated sex with – you'll meet her sooner or later. Maybe you already have, I don't know. I don't think I want to know. Come on, Harry – we don't even sleep in the same bed any more. There's a fuck buddy out there with your name on.'

Blended families and fuck buddies. It was a whole new world out there. My father wouldn't have recognised it. I didn't recognise it myself.

'Cyd, the last thing I'm looking for is a fuck buddy.'

She studied me for a bit. And perhaps she could see that this was true too.

'Then you'll find somebody you love, and that will be even messier. Not messier for you. But for me and my daughter. Remember her? And that's who I have to worry about now. You'll meet some young woman, and you'll do what you always do, Harry – tell her that she is the greatest girl in the history of the world.'

'Is that what I do?'

My wife nodded. 'And you will believe every word of it, Harry. And so will she. Or maybe it's happened already. Has it, Harry? Have you met the greatest girl in the history of the world? Or just the latest in a long line of them?'

I looked from Cyd to her open cases and back again. She had packed her photo albums. The ones of Peggy growing up. The one of our wedding day. The ones that recorded our holidays over the years. She had stored them all away.

'Please don't leave.' I didn't want it to end this way. Not any way. Something inside me recoiled from making the final, necessary break.

'Why not? This isn't working, Harry. Not for you. And not for me.'

'Please . . .'

I made a move towards her, but she held up her hand like a traffic cop.

'You're not a bad guy, Harry. You've got a good heart. I really believe that. But we could waste our lives being kind to each other. Twenty years could go by, and we still wouldn't know why we were together. I know you want what your parents had, Harry. I know you want a marriage like that. Well, guess what? You're not the only one.'

'It's been a tough time. With my mum, with our kids, with work.'

'The tough times should bring us closer together. I wasn't expecting nothing but fun-packed adventure. This is a marriage, not Club Med. Sticking together through the bad times, growing stronger and closer through them – that's what it's all about. But not our marriage, Harry. And not us.'

I knew I had no right to feel as bad as I felt. But I couldn't help it. Seeing Cyd packing her bags seemed like the greatest failure of my life. And what pulled at the wound was that I knew she was right. She deserved more than she was getting in this marriage.

'I'm leaving because you can't, Harry. Because you're not cruel enough to go. But don't do me any favours, okay? Don't stay because you pity me. Don't stay because you feel guilty. Don't stay just because you're not strong enough to go.'

'I stay because I care about you.'

She smiled gently, placing her hand on my face. 'If you really care about me, you'll help me get out of this thing.'

'But where will you go?'

'Back home. To Houston. To my mother and my sisters. There's nothing for me here any more.'

'When?'

'After Jim's wedding. Peggy is looking forward to being his bridesmaid. I'm not going to take that away from her.'

I picked up a leather photo album from the suitcase on the bed, opening it at a picture that felt like it was taken a lifetime ago. Pat's fifth birthday party, in the back garden of my parents' house. Pat fresh-faced and gorgeous. Peggy, that crucial bit older, grave and serious as she examined the strawberry jelly in front of her. And my mum and dad, healthy and grinning for the camera and relieved that the day was going well. And Cyd – smiling, waving a fish-paste sandwich at me as I took the picture. A tall, slim, beautiful woman, a single mother who had just realised that she was not only going to get through this ordeal – meeting her boyfriend's parents for the first time – but she was actually going to enjoy it. How young we all seemed.

'Remember this? Remember Pat's fifth birthday party?'

She laughed.

'What I remember is your dad choking on a sausage roll when I told him my ex-husband was going out with a Thai stripper.'

I smiled at the memory. '*A bit went down the wrong hole*. That was one of my old man's favourite expressions.'

I closed the photo album and placed it back in the suitcase. 'I'm sorry too, Cyd. I'm sorry I didn't make you happy.'

I meant it.

'Come here,' she said, and I went to her, and we held each other for the longest time.

'Still friends then?' I said.

'Always friends, Harry.' She gently released me and turned back to her packing. 'But I'd rather get out while there's still a little love left.'

My mum had taken to wearing her Dolly Parton wig.

Losing her hair during chemo was about the only indignity that she had been spared, but the big, golden wig was now seeing active service. It framed her still-pretty face as she let Pat and me into her home, and it glinted and glistened in the sunlight like a knight's suit of armour.

'But what happened to your head?' Pat asked.

'This is my Dolly Parton hair, darling.'

'You're okay, are you?' I asked. 'Your hair hasn't started – you know.'

'Not at all. Fifty pounds this was in Harrods. Shame to waste it. Besides, blondes have more fun. As Rod Stewart said.'

She actually looked terrific in her wig. But as Pat busied himself with the DVD player, I sat in the back garden with my mum while she told me that wearing it had nothing to do with wanting to be blonde.

'I'm different now,' she said. 'People think you're over it. But you're never over it. Every ache, every pain – you wonder if it's coming back, if this is it. You get a cold and you wonder if it's the cancer. Listen to me. I sound so sorry for myself.'

'No, you don't, Mum.'

'My Dolly Parton wig,' she said, touching the spun-gold locks. 'It's a way of showing the world I'm not the same. I'm different now, okay? People say to me – *back to normal, Liz?*' My mum shook her head. 'I get so mad. I can't pretend that this thing hasn't happened to me. How can you tell them? How can you make them understand? Life will never be normal again. Normal has changed.'

I knew what she meant. At least, I think I did. Getting sick again was always going to be a possibility. And now it was going to be like this forever.

'But I'm stronger too,' my mum said. 'Look at me in my big

hair – I go down the shops and I don't care who looks at me. What people say – that's the least of our problems, isn't it? I'm living for now. Trying to live life to the full. In my own quiet way. I don't plan ten years ahead. If you want a guarantee, buy a toaster. Now I try to appreciate what I've got.' She took my hand. 'And appreciate how much I'm loved.'

'You're going to be around for years, Mum. You've beaten this thing. You'll see Pat grow up.'

I really wanted to believe it.

'It's hard for people,' she said, as if she hadn't heard a word I had said. 'I think your dad felt this way. When he came back from the war. Who could he talk to – really talk to – about what he'd been through? Only men who had been through the same thing. The ones who knew.'

She showed me a leaflet. It was one of those pink and purple breast cancer leaflets. But this was a new one.

'You can get training,' my mum said, opening the leaflet. 'They train you to be a counsellor. So you can talk to women who are going through the same thing you went through. And I know now that's what I want to do. I want to help women who are fighting breast cancer. See, Harry? I can actually say it now. I couldn't even say it before. *Cancer*. As if I had something to be ashamed of, as if it was my fault. Do you remember a young blonde girl at the hospital? A pretty thing? A bit younger than you. Two little boys, she had. Little smashers. About Pat's age.'

I had a vague memory of a pale young woman who was in my mother's ward.

'Well, she died,' my mum said, her eyes suddenly welling up.

'You're not going to die.'

'I want to talk to girls like that. Women, I mean. You have to call them women now, don't you? Well, she was just a girl to me.'

Pat came into the garden, bored with the DVD. He hadn't wanted to come to his grandmother's house today. Bernie Cooper had asked him over to play. I felt guilty doing it, but I had persuaded my son that we had to be with his grandmother now. Because my mum was right. Normal had changed. And I had no way of knowing how long we had left.

'My two beautiful boys,' she said, throwing open her arms. 'Hug me. The pair of you. Come on, I'm not going to break.'

So we hugged her, and we laughed as we buried our faces in that Dolly Parton wig, and we knew that at that moment we loved her more than anyone on the face of the earth.

Pat wandered back to the living room, and my mum smiled with sadness and happiness all at once, patting my shoulder.

'Your dad would be proud of you.'

I laughed. 'I don't know why.'

'Because you've taken good care of me through all this. Because you love your son. Because you're a good man. You always compare yourself to your dad and find yourself lacking. And you're wrong, Harry. No matter how tall your father is, you still have to do your own growing.'

'But how did you and Dad *do* it, Mum? How do you love someone for a lifetime? How do you make a marriage work for all that time?'

My mum didn't even have to think about it.

'You have to keep falling in love,' she said. 'You just have to keep falling in love with the same person.'

You always took your shoes off at Gina's, so the moment Pat let us in with his own personal key, I saw them immediately – great big size tens forcing everything else off the WELCOME mat, a bit down at heel and in need of a good polish, more like landing craft than shoes.

A new boyfriend, I guessed. No surprise there. She was never going to be alone for very long. Not looking like that. Still.

And as I helped Pat out of his coat, I thought what I so often thought when I was around my ex-wife.

What about my boy?

If Gina starts seeing someone new, then what does that mean

for Pat? Will the guy like my son? Or will he see him as an irritation?

Gina appeared by our side, looking red-faced and flustered. I felt a flash of irritation at my ex-wife. What the hell was she doing in there with that big-foot guy?

'Granny's got new hair,' Pat told her.

'That's nice, darling,' she said, not listening to him, looking at me looking at the landing craft.

'It's yellow,' Pat said.

'Lovely.'

Pat was out of his coat and kicking off his shoes.

'You go inside. Someone in there wants to see you. I want to talk to your daddy.'

Pat ran up the stairs to the living area of the flat. I could hear a man's baritone talking to him, and Pat responding with his sweet, high voice.

'Richard,' Gina said.

'Richard?'

'Looks like we're going to have another crack at it.'

Upstairs I could hear Richard and Pat exchanging stilted small talk.

What about my boy?

'You surprise me, Gina.'

'Do I?'

'Yes. What about the old cow theory?'

'The old bull theory.'

'Whatever it was. I thought that when you were finished with them, you were really finished with them.'

She laughed. 'Maybe I was thinking of you, Harry.'

I took a breath, let it pass.

'What happened?'

She shrugged. 'I guess I felt isolated. And a little bit scared, maybe. You know what it's like when you're living on your own with a child.'

'Yes, I know what it's like.'

'You get lonesome. You do. No matter how much you love them, you get lonesome. And it's hard to meet new people. It's really hard, Harry. And I'm not even sure I want to go through all that crap. Dates – God, spare me from dates. Who's got the energy for all that crap at our age?'

'I bumped into Richard. Did he tell you?'

She nodded, but there was nothing in her eyes to indicate that she knew about Kazumi and me. So Richard had kept my secret. Or perhaps he truly didn't care.

All he wanted was his wife back.

'It wasn't so bad between us,' Gina said. 'The move was tough. And trying for a baby and not getting one – that was even tougher. But we're going to have a crack at IVF.'

'Fertility treatment?'

She nodded. 'They give me drugs to produce a large number of eggs. Richard has to – you know – masturbate.'

Shouldn't be too much of a stretch for Richard.

I stared at her. One minute she was finished with this guy, and the next minute her ovaries were working overtime to have his baby. I didn't understand her at all. Is who we share our life with really so random? Is it so easily torn down, and then put back together?

Gina mistook my silence for doubts about fertility treatment.

'It's all the rage these days, Harry. In some fertility clinics, the really good ones, you have a better chance of conception with IVF than you have with regular old-fashioned shagging. It's true.'

'I don't know, Gina. I heard IVF treatment is expensive. And doesn't always work.'

'Maybe going through it will make us stronger. Make us a real husband and wife. Isn't that what we all want?'

'But you don't love him any more, Gina. You can't just be with someone – be married to them, have a baby with them – because you're feeling a bit lonesome.'

'Can't you? What am I supposed to do? Wait for Mr Right to come along? Not enough time, Harry, not enough energy. Sometimes this is what I think – the person you're with is just the person you're with. That's all. End of story. It's no more than that.'

'You old romantic.'

'It's not so bad. You're partners. You stick together. You support each other. So it's not like one of the old songs – so what? A grown-up can't go around falling in love all the time like some dumb-ass teenager. What kind of mess would that make of your life?'

'You don't choose who you fall in love with.'

'How naïve you sound. Of course you choose, Harry. Of course you do.'

I liked to think that we were friends. And I liked to think that I still cared about her. That I would always care about her. But this caring for my ex-wife, it only went so far. In the end, my thoughts always came back to the same place.

'What about my boy?'

'Your boy?' she said. 'Your boy, Harry? You should have thought of your boy before you banged some little slut from your office, shouldn't you?'

And all at once I saw that there's no one on this planet more distant than someone you were once married to.

twenty-six

'Man gets on a crowded flight,' said Eamon, roaming through the smoky gloaming. 'Plane's totally full. But the seat next to him, the seat next to him is empty.' Hand to mouth, little Woody Allen cough. 'Thinks – wonder who I'm going to be sitting next to? As you do, right? Then the most beautiful woman he ever saw in his life comes down the aisle. The face of an angel and legs up to her neck. Sure enough, she sits right down in the seat next to our man.' Hunched in the spotlight. The crowd paying attention. 'The guy finally works up the courage to talk to her. "Excuse me? Excuse me? Where are you headed?" "Oh," says she, "I'm off to the Kilcarney Sex Convention. I lecture on the subject. Dispel some of the myths surrounding sex." "Like what?" "Well, for example," says she, "many people believe that black men are more generously endowed than other men. And in fact it is Native American men who are more likely to reveal that physiological trait. And then popular wisdom has it that French men make the best lovers. Whereas statistics show that Greek men are far more likely to give sexual pleasure to their partners." Then she blushed. "But I'm telling you all this, and I don't even know your name." The guy reached out his hand. "Tonto," he said. "Tonto Papadopolous."'

And as the crowd laughed, I could see myself in that man, and in that punch line.

It had never been in my plans to become the kind of man who lies without even having to think about it. That had never been the kind of man I wanted to be. My father had never been that kind of man.

But by now I found I needed to lie just to balance the demands on my time. It was madness.

Just call me Tonto. Tonto Papadopolous.

As Cyd helped Peggy into her bridesmaid's dress upstairs, and Pat sat on the carpet watching the horse racing on Channel 4 – that kid would watch anything, I swear – I sneaked down to the bottom of the garden to call Kazumi on my mobile.

We were meeting for dinner. That was the schedule. And this simple thing – a man having dinner with a woman – had to be planned in utmost secrecy, as though we were doing something illegal, or incredibly dangerous. And I was sick of it, to tell the truth. I would be glad when all the sneaking around was over. Not long now.

When I went back into the house Peggy was standing at the top of the stairs, grinning from ear to ear, wearing her bridesmaid's dress.

'How do I look, Harry?'

'Like an angel.'

And she did. Just like a little angel. And I felt a stab of regret that this child who I had watched grow up would soon be out of my life forever.

She ran back into the bedroom with some instructions for her mother about the flowers she was wearing in her hair while I went into the living room and sat next to my son. He was still staring blankly at the race meeting on the box. Sometimes I worried about this kid.

'You want to see what else is on, Pat?'

He grunted a negative, not looking at me.

Pat had come home with me because his mother had things to discuss with his – what was Richard these days? His ex-stepfather? His future stepdad? The designated sperm donor to his half-siblings? I was finding it increasingly difficult to keep up with my ex-wife's soap opera. But then who was I to feel superior?

At least everything that Gina did was out in the open.

'I didn't know you were a gambling man, Pat,' Cyd said, coming into the room.

'Horses,' Pat said, turning his face to look up at Cyd. 'Horses are so beautiful.'

I felt a stab of guilt. So he wasn't gawping mindlessly at the box. The horses enchanted him. Why hadn't he told me that? Why had he saved this revelation for Cyd? Was it perhaps because I hadn't asked him?

She smiled and sat down on the floor with him. 'Horses *are* beautiful, aren't they?' she said. 'There's a – what would you call it? – nobility, I guess. Yes, there's a nobility about horses.'

'A what?'

'Nobility.' She turned to look at me. 'How would you define *nobility*, Harry?'

'Dignity,' I said. 'Decency. Goodness.'

Like you, I thought, looking at the woman I had married. Dignity, decency and goodness. Just like you.

Not that Cyd resembled a horse.

She put her arm around my boy's shoulder and watched the horses with him and I realised that she had always been good with him – kind, patient, loving even. So what had been the problem? The problem had been me, and not being satisfied with her kindness, patience and love.

The problem had been me all along, and wanting Cyd to be something that she could never ever be.

His mother.

I had never seen Peggy so excited.

She was in her bridesmaid's outfit for hours before she was due to be picked up, posing and preening in front of every available reflecting surface in the house, then running to the window to check the street for her father.

Finally we heard the sound of a bike revving its engine in the street.

'He's here!' Peggy shouted, tearing herself away from the mirror in the hall.

'Don't forget your crash helmet,' her mother called from upstairs.

It was a themed wedding. The bride and groom were arriving at the registrar's office on motorbikes. Even the priest who was giving their union a blessing at a nearby church was turning up on his Honda and conducting the service in his leathers. The reception was at the historic Ton Up Café on the M1.

Peggy was at the door waving to Jim when Cyd came down the stairs.

And the sight of her stunned me.

She was wearing a dress I hadn't seen for years. Her old green silk cheongsam. The dress she had been wearing the night I fell in love with her.

She saw me looking at her, but ignored me, as if it was perfectly natural to walk around in this special dress. She helped Peggy into her crash helmet. 'Hold Daddy tight, okay?'

Together we escorted Peggy to the kerb. There were two bikes, Jim on his Norton with Liberty, the happy bride, perched on the back in her wedding dress, and the best man on an ancient Triumph with a sidecar. Jim and his best man were both wearing leathers over their wedding tails. Liberty's only concession to road safety was a snow-white helmet. I stiffly congratulated Jim. It was not an easy situation. His ex-wife's estranged husband wishing her first husband well on his most recent wedding day. So we did what adults always do at a time like this – we concentrated on the child. Cyd fussed with Peggy's frills as she placed her in the sidecar, and I made sure her crash helmet was secure.

Then they were gone, roaring off down the street, wedding tails and bride's dress flying.

'You going out somewhere?' I said.

Cyd replied without looking at me. 'Just doing some packing,' she said. 'Deciding what I want to take and what I want to throw away.'

'And are you taking that dress with you?'

'No. I just wanted to see if it still fits.' The bikes were gone now. She looked at me. 'Before I throw it away.'

She had worn that dress on what was probably the happiest night of my life. That happiness just came upon me, the way true happiness does, and it was caused by the joy of simply standing by her side. We were at an awards ceremony at one of the big hotels on Park Lane, the kind of long, drunken, back-slapping shindig that I usually despised.

But that night I was so glad to be alive as the soft blue light faded over Hyde Park, and I was so grateful to be with this incredible woman in her green silk dress that I honestly believed I would never be sad again.

'It still fits,' I told her.

Cyd took herself upstairs to pack.

I went into the living room and sat next to my son on the carpet. The beautiful horses had gone and he was channel-surfing through the mind-numbing doldrums of mid-afternoon television. The snatched images flashed before his blue eyes. *Dude, Where's My Trousers?*, snowboarding, *Six Pissed Students in a Flat*, old music videos, *Wicked World*, Russian fashion models, *Art? My Arse!*, the baking channel, *Sorry, I'm a Complete Git*. I gently took the remote from his hot little hand, and switched off the TV.

'Are you okay, Pat?'

He nodded, noncommittal.

'Didn't Peggy look lovely in her bridesmaid's dress?'

He thought about it. 'She looked like a lady.'

'Didn't she?' I put my arm around him. He snuggled close to me. 'And what about you? How are you feeling?'

'I'm a little bit worried.'

'What about, darling?'

'Bernie Cooper,' he said. 'Bernie Cooper says that dogs need a passport.'

'Well, I guess that's true. If a dog is going to be moved from one country to another, it needs some form of ID. Bernie's right there.'

'Well, then, this is what I want to know – does Britney have a passport?'

'Britney?'

'My dog Britney. Because, if Britney doesn't have a passport, then how is Richard going to get him into London, where we all live now?'

'I'm sure Richard can work that one out. And what about Richard? How do you feel about seeing him again?'

He shrugged. I believe he was genuinely more concerned about his dog than his stepfather. Britney meant infinitely more to Pat than Richard ever could. And of course a dog is for life, whereas a step-parent could be for any length of time.

'Mummy and Richard – they might live together again.'

My son nodded, biting his bottom lip thoughtfully as he eyed the remote control in my hand.

'Are you happy about that, darling? It doesn't just affect Mummy and Richard. It affects you too. I want you to – I don't know – tell me if anything worries you. That's what I'm here for, okay? You can always talk to me. Did Mummy talk to you about any of this stuff? About what she's planning to do with Richard?'

Another nod.

'They're going to try to make it work, Daddy.'

They're going to try to make it work.

When I was a kid, a seven-year-old talking about trying to make it work meant a wonky train set on your birthday or a new Scalextric on Christmas Day. We put the TV back on in silence.

Now when a kid talked about making it work, he meant a marriage.

There was a howl of motorbikes in the street.

Peggy was back from her wedding.

Cyd came downstairs, still in her green dress. I felt a surge of something that might have been hope, or maybe only nostalgia. But I was glad she hadn't thrown the dress out yet.

We went out to the street where a dozen bikes were idling. All these men in tails and women in party dresses, leathers and helmets on top of their wedding kit, sitting proudly astride their big BMWs and Nortons and Harleys and Triumphs. The bride was riding pillion on Jim's bike while Peggy was sitting primly in the only sidecar in the convoy. Her mother fished her out.

'Good wedding?' Cyd said.

Peggy began to babble with excitement. 'I held the flowers and walked right behind Liberty as she walked up the aisle of the registration office.'

Jim laughed. 'That's my girl. Come here, princess, give your daddy a big kiss.'

Cyd and I watched awkwardly while father and daughter embraced. Peggy's part in the celebrations was over. She wasn't joining the happy couple for their wedding reception at the Ton Up Café. Then they would be off to Manila for their honeymoon. Jim placed his daughter on his lap, facing him, both of them wreathed in smiles.

Pat had joined us on the pavement. He covered his ears against the noise of the bikes.

'Well,' Cyd said. 'Congratulations.'

'Yes,' I said. 'Congratulations.'

Jim just grinned and then they were gone. I couldn't believe it. Jim's bike roaring off down the street with his bride behind him and his daughter in front. You could hear the bride and the bridesmaid shrieking with delight. I thought it was a kidnapping. I thought he was stealing her.

'She should have her helmet,' Cyd said. 'I know it's just a bit of fun, but I don't like this.'

Jim turned at the end of the street and headed back towards us, his daughter laughing in his arms, his bride's wedding dress streaming behind them. The bike flared up on its back wheel, and all three of them cried out with that sound of appalled pleasure you hear on a roller-coaster ride. Jim's bike squealed to a halt. The other wedding guests applauded and revved their engines.

'More,' said Peggy.

'Just once more,' said Jim.

'No more,' said Cyd, lifting Peggy from the bike.

'Oh, *Mum*!'

Jim sighed elaborately. 'Same old Cyd.'

'Enough,' I told him.

The groom looked at me, his smile all gone, and I realised that it was the first time that day he had actually looked me in the eye.

'Enough?' he said. 'Enough, did you say? Who are you to tell me enough, pal? She's my daughter.'

'I live with her,' I said.

He sneered at me. 'Yeah, but not for much longer, right?'

I looked at Cyd and she looked away. So she had told her ex-husband about us. And I suspected that this show of happiness – the themed wedding, the crowd of friends on our doorstep, the Evel Knievel routine with Peggy – had less to do with his daughter than with his first wife.

We can resist every temptation with our old partners, apart from telling them how happy we are now.

'I know about you, Harry,' Jim said. 'You're no parent to Peggy. You're not even a father to your own son, are you?'

I looked at Pat. He was covering his ears. I didn't know if it was because of the bikes or Jim.

First Luke Moore, now Jim. The world was full of people who thought they had a better claim on my wife than me. And maybe what made me so angry was that I knew it was my own fault they felt that way.

'You're a jerk, Jim. You've always been a jerk and you always will be. You love your daughter, do you? You're a good dad, are you? It takes more than inviting her to your latest wedding.'

'Stop it, you two!' Cyd shouted, putting Peggy on the ground. She began shoving Jim away. 'Just go, will you? Just go. Liberty, tell him to go.'

But Jim wouldn't budge. He was acting all indignant, as if he had restrained himself with me for years, but was finally going to tell me what was on his mind.

'I'll be glad when you're out of Peggy's life,' he told me.

I pushed my face close to his. I could smell cheap champagne and Calvin Klein. 'You think you're in her life, do you? Coming round when you feel like it and then not a word for weeks? You call that being in a child's life?'

Cyd was screaming now. 'Go! Go!'

Out of the corner of my eye I saw Peggy and Pat backing away. They were holding hands. Both of them were crying. A couple of the wedding guests were dismounting their bikes and giving me meaningful looks. It was getting nasty.

And that was when Peggy stumbled from the pavement, let go of Pat's hand and fell into the road.

She was immediately hit by a car.

The impact spun her around and dumped her back on the pavement, her legs still sprawling in the road. There was dirt all over the top of her bridesmaid's dress. Christ no, not again, I thought, remembering Pat with his head split open at four years old, sprawled at the bottom of an empty swimming pool. I stood there stunned as Cyd rushed to her daughter. Somebody was screaming. Then Liberty was on her knees, pushing Cyd aside. A nurse, I thought. She's a nurse.

I looked at the white-faced driver of the car. He was about my age, but in a suit and tie, driving a brand-new BMW. He hadn't been going fast – just crawling past the unbroken lines of cars, looking for a precious parking space – but he must have been doing something with his mobile phone, because it was still in his hand, playing a speeded-up version of 'Waltzing Matilda'. Not watching the road well enough to avoid hitting a little girl who fell right in front of him without warning. There was a slight dent in his nearside bumper.

Cyd was screaming and crying, trying to hold her daughter while Liberty pushed her away with one hand, and cradled Peggy with the other. Jim was pulling at me – trying to get me out of the way, trying to hit me, I couldn't tell. And Liberty was shouting at someone, but I couldn't work out who, and then I got it. It seemed strange to me that, out of all the people she could be addressing, Liberty was talking to the BMW driver with the mobile playing 'Waltzing Matilda'.

'Ambulance,' she said. 'Call an ambulance!'

I wondered what had been so important. A text message from his girlfriend, I thought. He's just like me.

In his own little dream world, hurting everyone around him.

Peggy fractured her leg.

That was it. That was all. And that was bad enough – I hope I never see a child in that much pain again – but we sat in the back of the ambulance knowing that she could have been killed.

A greenstick fracture, the doctor at the hospital called it, meaning an incomplete break of the bone. The outer shell of the bone was intact, and the fracture was inside. The doctor said that a greenstick fracture is what children get, because their bones are so flexible. The bones of adults just break in two. Give them a hard enough knock, and adults just fall to pieces.

They gave her a CT scan even though her head wasn't bruised, and it was clear. They gave her junior painkillers, put her in plaster and hiked up her leg in a kind of hammock that sat on top of her hospital bed. She was soon sitting up and gazing imperiously at the other residents of the children's ward.

It wasn't like Pat's accident. She was never in any life-threatening danger. But I still glimpsed a vision of a world where something unspeakable had happened, and it made my blood run cold.

There were five of us sitting by her bed. Jim and Liberty. Cyd and Pat. And me. Drinking bad tea from Styrofoam cups, not talking much, still numb with shock. After screaming at each other in the street, we might have felt embarrassed to be here together, if relief had not overwhelmed every other emotion. When the doctor came to the bedside, we all jumped to our feet.

'We'll keep her with us for a while,' he said. 'What we've done is reduce the fracture, meaning the broken ends have been restored to their natural position, and now we just have to hold the reduced fracture in place while it heals.' He patted Peggy on the head. 'Do you like dancing, little lady?'

'I dance very well, actually,' Peggy said.

'Well, you'll soon be dancing as well as ever.'

Out of the corner of my eye, I saw Jim glance at his watch. He and Liberty had a plane to catch. When the doctor had gone, the bride and groom said their goodbyes and rushed off to the airport. Then there were just the three of us.

We stayed by Peggy's bed until night had fallen and she had slipped into sleep. Cyd put her arms around Pat and me, and that somehow seemed to be the signal to release all the pent-up tension of the day.

Keeping the noise down so we wouldn't disturb Peggy and her sleeping neighbours, Cyd and Pat and I held on to each other as we all cried with relief.

And for the very first time in my entire life, I couldn't tell where my family ended, and where it began.

twenty-seven

I still went to see Kazumi.

Despite everything that had happened.

And as she buzzed me through the front door, I wondered – how can you do it? How can you come to see this girl when Peggy is in the hospital? And, not for the first time, I wondered what my father would have thought of me.

But I knew I was there simply because it was easier than not being there. I had taken Pat to my mum's, wanting to spare him from Gina and Richard's latest reconciliation, and cancelling Kazumi would have been harder – more excuses, more lies – than just turning up late for this appointment with my secret life.

There was nothing I could do at the hospital. Once the initial shock had passed, Cyd even seemed a little embarrassed to have me touching her – holding her, cuddling her, trying to comfort her. Inappropriate, she seemed to feel, what with all those half-packed suitcases waiting for her in the guest room. We had come too far apart for all that. What good would I have done at the hospital? I couldn't even hold my wife's hand.

So I went to see Kazumi. I came up the stairs, still sick to my stomach from the trauma of the accident and the rush to the hospital, still numb from the hours of waiting around and then more hours crawling on the motorway out to my mum's place. I had spent the day watching a child in trouble and I couldn't do a damn thing about it. The worst feeling in the world.

Kazumi looked down over the banisters. And when I saw her, the long black hair pulled back from her smiling, lovely face, it occurred to me that this was meant to be our special night. And when she kissed me I was certain. She was ready to take that final step. All my old wedding vows had been declared null and void. We were going to cross the line, and make promises of our own.

Inside the flat the sound of a cello running through its scales came from the second bedroom. The flatmate was home, but Kazumi smiled conspiratorially.

'Staying in room,' she said. 'Has to practise. Don't worry.'

The table was set for two, a special dinner for two – champagne flutes, linen napkins, a single white candle in a silver candlestick, already lit, the flame dancing in the twilight. And my heart throbbed like an old, fading bruise when I saw all the trouble she had gone to.

'Pat okay? Mum okay?'

'They're fine.'

She was in my life. She knew my son and my mother. She cared about them, they liked her. In time, if you gave it years to grow, they could love her. And she could love them. I knew it. This was all true. She was in my blood now. She was part of it all. Well, not quite all of it. For just as she was locked away from Cyd, so Cyd was locked away from her. And I couldn't tell Kazumi about Peggy, I wouldn't know where to start.

In the middle of the table was a large pan sitting on top of some kind of small gas cooker. Like something you would use for camping, if you were a gourmet chef with a taste for the great outdoors. There were plates of thinly sliced beef, white chunks of tofu and piles of uncooked vegetables, some of which I recognised.

'Sukiyaki,' I said. 'Lovely.'

She was delighted. 'All westerner love sukiyaki. Began in Japan when Meiji Emperor started eating meat. Start of twentieth century. Until then – fish only.'

'I didn't know that,' I said, sinking into a chair. 'I didn't know any of that.'

A champagne cork popped, and she filled our glasses.

'*Kampai*,' I said.

'Cheers,' she said.

She came around the table, placed a quick kiss on my lips and then, smiling, threw some thin slices of beef and some raw vegetables into the sizzling pan, covering them with some kind of sauce. In the bedroom the flatmate had stopped practising her scales and started playing 'Song Without Words'. And with all its sadness and stillness and sense of things being lost forever, that music was like a fist around my throat.

'Sauce called *warashita*. Made of soy sauce, sweet rice wine and sugar. You know what happens next?'

There were two eggs on the table next to a pair of lacquered bowls.

'We whip up the raw eggs, and then dip in the beef and vegetables,' I said, struggling against the fist around my throat.

'Hah!' she said. 'Big sukiyaki expert, I can see.'

And I saw something too. All at once I saw that the dream I'd had would never come true, not in a million years. I had dreamed of starting again – running away with Kazumi, taking my son with us. That's what I wanted. Not merely a new woman. Not just that. But a world made whole and a family restored. A new wife. A new life.

I don't know where I honestly thought we were going to go. The west of Ireland. Paris. Maybe some other corner of north London would have been enough. Maybe Primrose Hill would have been far enough. Anywhere. But we were going, and in my dream we were already on our way.

Now I saw that the dream would never come true. It wasn't Kazumi's fault. It was because the price was too high to pay. Too much that was precious would have to be discarded, too much life thrown away, before I could start again.

I thought that my feeling for her – love, romance, you can call it what you like – was the only thing that mattered.

And that just wasn't true.

Other things mattered too.

I know I could have done the traditional thing. I could have tried to keep Cyd halfway happy, while stringing Kazumi along, keeping her halfway happy too. Screwing the pair of them, in every way possible. And I could have got away with it by lying to everyone, to Cyd, to Kazumi, but mostly myself – telling myself that I genuinely loved both of them. In my own sweet way.

But try loving two women and you end up loving nobody at all, not in the way they warrant.

Try loving two of them and this is what it does – it breaks you in half.

You need a heart of stone to lead one of those double lives. And so does she. The other woman. I knew Kazumi wasn't built for that kind of life. I knew that Kazumi wasn't cut out to be my mistress. She wasn't cold enough, old enough, tough enough. All the reasons that I loved her were all the reasons she could never be a bit on the side. She had the sweetest, gentlest heart in the world. I still believe that. Even now.

In the end, I knew her so well. And I could see glimpses of myself in her, or at least the best of me. She believed, really believed, that she could find a love that would transform her world. And perhaps she was right. But I knew now she was never going to find it with me.

It was all or nothing with this woman. That's why I loved her – and I can say that now. I loved her. But she wasn't cut out for an affair. The right girl in so many ways, she was the wrong girl to play that role. She was a romantic. Say what you like about those starry-eyed souls, about the upheaval and destruction they always leave in their wake, but there is one thing about romantics that nobody can deny. They never settle for second best.

'Kazumi,' I said, standing up.

Her face fell. 'Problem – with egg? You don't like raw egg?'

I carefully placed my champagne flute on the table.

'Raw egg is fine. It's just that . . . I can't do this. I am so, so sorry. I have to go.'

She nodded, taking it all in, the anger flaring.

'Go on, then. Go back to your wife.'

'I'm so sorry.'

She picked up the silver candlestick and threw it at me, a

wild throw that made it fly past my head and left a splash of white candle wax on the tablecloth. She lashed out at our special meal with furious fists, and it all went crashing. Glasses and vegetables, silver cutlery and chopsticks, pretty napkins splashed with soy sauce. Across the table, to the floor, fragments of our special meal smashing against my legs. Just ruined, the lot of it.

Kazumi with her head hanging. Hair like a long, black veil.

'Kazumi.'

'Go back to your home.'

I left her then, with the smell of burning beef in the air and the flatmate's cello coming through the walls and the unwanted champagne in my gut. It was not easy to leave her. But in the end, Cyd's claim on me was stronger. Cyd had home advantage.

Whatever happened next, I had to be with my wife.

Even if the only thing left to say was goodbye.

Cyd was still at the hospital.

Peggy looked tiny in the hospital bed, a kind of protective tent above her plastered leg, her sleeping face grave and frowning. She was sitting up in bed, her head tilted to one side, as if she had only just nodded off.

At first I didn't see Cyd. Then I noticed her on the far side of the bed, sleeping on the floor, between a couple of blue hospital blankets. It was after midnight now. I crouched by her side and she stirred.

'She woke up. In a lot of pain. They gave her a shot of something and it's knocked her out. The nurse says she should be all right until morning.' We both watched the sleeping child. She didn't move. 'Not much is going to happen until then. Apart from, you know. All this. The waiting.'

'Come home for a bit, Cyd.'

'No, I couldn't leave her.'

'Come home. Shower. Get some sleep. In your own bed. Some tea and toast, maybe. Come on. You'll be stronger for tomorrow.'

She smiled wearily, and touched my arm.

'Thanks for sticking by me, Harry,' she said, and I felt my face flush with shame.

'You were there for me,' I said. 'When Pat was hurt. Remember?'

It was almost three years ago now. I could still see my son falling into that empty swimming pool, the dark halo of blood growing around his dirty-blond hair. That's when I learned. That's when I discovered that this world could take your children away from you. And Cyd was there for me. With Gina in Japan, getting her life back or discovering her true self or looking for love or whatever the fuck she was doing, there was nobody for me here. Apart from my parents, who would always be there. And Cyd, who could have been somewhere else. Somewhere a lot easier.

'Seems like a long time ago now,' she said.

'Let's go home, Cyd. Just for a few hours. Come on, you're out on your feet.'

But there was something she wanted to say to me.

'I know you want to be free, Harry.'

'Not now. Not all this talk now. Please.'

'No, listen. I know you want to be free. Because all men want to be free, but you more than most. Maybe because you were such a young dad, such a young husband. And it all went wrong for you so young. I don't know exactly why you want it so bad. But I know you dream of freedom – you wonder what it would be like with no wife, no kids, no responsibility. But what would happen if you were free, Harry? Do you know?'

'Let's go home now.'

She smiled triumphantly. 'Because I know, Harry. I do. I know what would happen if you were free.'

'Cyd –'

'Listen to me. This is what would happen if you were free, Harry. You'd meet some girl, some sweet young thing, and you'd fall for her. You'd be crazy about her. And you'd end up somewhere not so different from where you are with me, where you were with Gina, where you were with every woman you ever loved. Can't you see, Harry? If you're capable of loving someone, then there's *never* total freedom. There can't be. You give it up. You give up your freedom. For something that's better.'

I picked up her coat and helped her into it. We both stared at the sleeping child, reluctant to leave her. White on white, Peggy's face almost seemed to disappear into the pillow.

'It wasn't meant to trap you, Harry,' Cyd said. 'The marriage, the wedding ring, me and Peggy. I know that's how it made you feel, but it wasn't meant to be like that. You and me – it wasn't meant to make you feel trapped, Harry.'

'Let's go home now, okay?'

'It was meant to set you free.'

I lay in my bed in the darkness, listening to the sound of the shower, then later her footsteps leading to the guest room. I didn't notice she had come into our bedroom until she was standing by the bed. Her black hair wet and shining, her long legs bare, shivering a little in the chill of the night. And still wearing her green dress.

'It still fits, Harry,' she said, and then she was in my arms. And then, as so often happens when illness and death are at the door, the urge for life never greater than when the alternative makes itself known, we made love as if we were an endangered species.

There are really only two kinds of sex in the world. Unmarried and married. Desire and duty. Passionate and compassionate. Hot and lukewarm. Fucking and making love.

Usually, in time, you lose one kind for the other. It happens. But you can always get the other kind back.

It's like my mum said.

You just have to fall in love again.

twenty-eight

On Primrose Hill we said goodbye.

I would hardly have been surprised if she had never wanted to talk to me again. But there was something in her, a kind of generous formality – perhaps it was something Japanese – which let her come back just this once.

It was one of those clear bright summer days when London goes on forever. From Primrose Hill you could see the entire city, and yet the soft boom of the traffic seemed very distant. The real world felt a long way away. But I knew it was getting closer.

It was still very early. There were dogs and joggers everywhere, people rushing to work with a cappuccino in their hand, and the lights, those old-fashioned lamps that recalled some other lost city, another London, still shining weakly in the morning light all over Primrose Hill.

'Will you stay here or go back to Japan?'

'You can't ask me that. You don't have the right to ask me that.'

'I'm sorry.'

'Stop saying that. Don't say that again. Please.'

She held something out to me. It was the Polaroid we had taken ourselves, holding the camera at arm's length, laughing as though none of this would ever have to end.

'I used to think that if you took someone's photograph, then you could never lose them,' Kazumi said. 'But now I see it's the other way round. That our pictures show us all that we have lost.'

'We're not losing each other,' I said. 'When two people care for each other, they don't lose each other.'

'That's a bollock,' she said, her temper flaring. I couldn't help smiling. She always mangled the language just enough to make it special. 'That's a complete bollock.'

I shook my head. 'You'll always matter to me, Kazumi. I'll always care about you. I won't stop caring about you if you're with some other man. How can two people who have loved each other ever really lose each other?'

'I don't know,' she said. 'I can't explain it, but that's what happens.'

'I don't want you out of my life.'

'Me neither.'

'Four billion people in the world, and I care about a handful of them. Including you. Especially you. So don't talk as though we are throwing each other away.'

'Okay, Harry.'

'Together forever?'

She smiled. 'Together forever, Harry.'

'See you, Kazumi.'

'See you.'

I watched her walking down Primrose Hill, on one of those strange little paths that abruptly crisscross the park, pointing off in completely different directions, just like the impossible choices you are forced to make as you move through your life.

I watched her until she was gone, knowing that I would never stop wondering how it would have been if we were together, never stop caring about her, and never stop meeting her in dreams.

And just as she walked from the park and I finally lost sight of her, something happened, although I might have imagined it. It felt like the lights went out all over Primrose Hill.

I never saw her again.

My mum put on her Dolly Parton wig and went shopping.

The little neighbourhood store where she had bought her food for decades had recently closed down after the owner retired, and now she had to go to a huge hypermarket miles away. My mum actually preferred the hypermarket – 'Much more choice, love' – but the bus service out there was almost non-existent, so once a week Pat and I would go with her in the car.

We were steering our trolley to the fresh meat counter when an old man with a solitary tin of cat food in his wonky wire basket collided with us. He had grey, three-day-old stubble on his sagging old-geezer chin and a cardigan that looked as though it had been feeding a good-sized family of moths. As I dusted down the shabby old man, I realised we had met before.

'Elizabeth!' he cried.

It was Tex, although he definitely looked more like Graham today.

My mum nonchalantly tossed some organic bacon into her sleek bulging trolley. 'Oh, hello,' she said, not deigning to call him by his cowboy name, or indeed any name at all. 'How's the line dancing going?'

Tex exhaled with a grimace on his wrinkled face, rubbing his hip. 'Cracked me femur, Liz. Doing the Hardwood Stomp in Wickford. Had to lay off the old line dancing for a bit.'

He was staring at my mum as if she was Joan Collins on a good day. And it was true – she looked great.

It wasn't just the big blonde country and western hair, or the weight she had lost. There was a confidence about my mum now, a hard-earned inner force that put a glint in her eye that had never been there before. Being unceremoniously dumped by this little old man was the least of it. She had survived far bigger blows than that.

'Well, you look . . . lovely,' Tex said.

'Thanks.' My mum smiled politely, looking at the wizened old man before her as if she couldn't quite place him. 'Nice seeing you.' My mum turned to Pat and me. 'Let's roll, boys.'

'Maybe, maybe we could have a cup of tea some time,' Tex stammered. 'If you're not too busy.'

My mum affected not to have heard. So we left Graham and his lonely can of cat food by the frozen meat counter.

'You could have a cup of tea with him,' I told my mum,

although secretly I was proud of the way she had cut him down to size. 'He's a harmless old man.'

'But he's not *my* man, Harry. I forgot that for a while. Then I remembered. There's only one man for me. And that's the way it has always been.'

Pat and I struggled to keep up with her as her blonde head bobbed towards the checkout desk. And I thought – Dolly Parton would be proud of my mum. No matter what horrific surgery she had undergone, there was something inside her that was untouchable.

And as my car was pulling out of the parking lot, we saw Tex waiting for a bus in the drizzling rain. I knew better than to suggest we give him a lift.

My mum stared straight at him without expression, and for just a moment I thought she was going to stick up a finger or two. I knew in my heart she was far too polite for that. But if she had given Graham also-known-as-Tex the finger, I knew it wouldn't have been the middle one.

It would have been the one right next to it, the third finger left hand, the one where she had never stopped wearing her wedding ring.

There were already three women waiting outside my mum's house. One of them was in her forties, but the other two were younger than me. They all looked as though they had a world pressing down on them.

My mum let us all into the house. She didn't have to tell me that these were some of the women that she counselled about breast cancer. They went into the living room with Pat while my mum and I made tea. I could hear the sound of the women laughing at something my boy had said. It felt as though they hadn't laughed for quite a while.

'See that young one, Harry? She had the same operation as me. Same breast removed too. Scared to look at herself now. Imagine that. Afraid of the mirror. You can't let that happen. You can't be scared to look at yourself. They can talk to me. Because their family – the husband, the daughters, the sons – they want to be reassured. They don't want the truth – they want reassurance. And they don't have to reassure me. And they don't have to be ashamed in front of me. Because I'm the same. And what have we got to be ashamed of? It's not so bad. They're shy. I'm older than they are, Harry, and I'm stronger than I've ever been. It's made me stronger. It's given me a funny kind of power. I'm not scared of this world any more. These girls – and I know I'm meant to say women, but they're girls to me – they can't tell their husbands how they feel. That's okay. There's no such thing as an uncomplicated life. I see that now. I loved your dad more than life itself. But we don't need to tell everything to the person we're married to. There's no shame in that.'

'But maybe their husbands would understand,' I said. 'You should try to understand each other, shouldn't you? And if they really love them, then maybe they would understand.'

'Maybe,' said my mum. 'If they really love them.'

'Can I ask you something? About you and Dad?'

'Go ahead.'

'Does it change? As the years go by, I mean. Should I expect my marriage to be something different from what it was at the start?'

My mother smiled.

'It changes all the time, it never stops changing. When you're young you say – *I love you because I need you*. When you're old it's – *I need you because I love you*. Big difference. And I'm not saying that one is better than the other, although the second one tends to last a bit longer. But you never stop loving each other, Harry. Not if it's real.' She took my hands. 'Look, Harry. Talk to her if you want to. Talk to Cyd. Tell her what's been happening. Talk to your wife if you think it will help.'

'But I don't know if I can. See, I want her to be proud of me, Mum. The way you were proud of Dad.' I squeezed her hands. 'And I want you to be proud of me, too.'

'I'm proud of you already,' said my mum.

Peggy came home, her plaster cast signed by every child on her ward. There was a way to go before she would be well enough to go back to school. But the fracture was mending and we went to bed that night weak with relief. Peggy was healing. And in a way that I couldn't quite explain, so was I.

'I've got something to tell you, Cyd.'

'You don't have to tell me anything. Just as I don't have to tell you anything about Luke. Because there's nothing to tell.'

'But I want to say something. It's about what happened. How we lost each other for a while.'

'You don't have to tell me a thing. Just rest your eyes.' I felt my wife touch my arm in the darkness. 'You're home now,' she said.

twenty-nine

Life holds hostage all those we love.

That's why it was so tough for my wife after Peggy came back home. Once you have seen your child in a hospital, you are never truly free again. Never really free the way you were in the past, not once you know how it feels to love a sick child, not once you realise how hard it is out there. Because you are never free from the fear that it could happen again, and next time be even worse.

And it was not just her daughter. There were late-night calls from Texas, where her sisters were worried about their mother, who had been found wandering around a parking lot in downtown Houston with a DVD of *Gone With the Wind* in her hand, no money in her purse and no memory of how she got there. 'Sounds like the start of old-timer's disease,' my mum said, and it was terrifying, one more thing for my wife to worry about.

So when we turned out the light one night and Cyd idly mentioned that she had missed her period, I thought to myself – stress.

It does strange things to your body.

And when my wife woke up the next morning, running to the bathroom and retching although nothing came up, I thought to myself – poor kid. Worried sick about her daughter, and now worried sick about her mother.

And even then, standing outside the bathroom door, listening to my wife trying to throw up, even then I still didn't get it. I still didn't understand that it was happening all over again.

The best thing in the world.

I had seen one of these things before.

In fact, when Gina first found out about Pat, I saw dozens of them. There was nothing much to it. Just a white plastic handle. It looked as though it had something missing, like a toothbrush without the bristles.

I picked up the pregnancy test. It felt surprisingly light. And so did my head.

There were two tiny windows on the thing. In one of them, the little round window, there was a thin blue line. And in the other one, the little square window – which I somehow understood was the important one, the crucial one, the window that would change everything – there was another thin blue line.

And finally I understood. Not just the missed period and the sickness, but everything. I finally got it. I understood why I had to stay, and why I would always stay.

That's when I sensed rather than heard Cyd in the doorway of the bathroom. She was laughing and crying all at once – I guess that must be standard procedure – wiping her eyes on the sleeve of her Gap T-shirt.

'Is this okay with you?' she asked me.

I took her in my arms. 'It's more than okay. This is great. This is the very best.'

Then my wife looked at me and smiled and, for perhaps the second time in my life, I knew why I was alive.

'Wait a minute,' Eamon said. 'You're staying with your wife because of some stupid wanker in a BMW? Is that what you're saying?'

'I didn't say that.'

'You said the accident changed everything. That she was packing her bags before that happened. She was leaving you, Harry, and you were ready to begin again with someone else.'

Would Cyd and I have split up if Peggy hadn't had her accident? In my heart, I didn't see what could have stopped us.

That's how fragile all this is, as gossamer thin as a spider's web, as intricate and fragile as that, meticulously built but easily torn apart by a few cruel, casual blows. My parents' marriage looked like it was made of sterner stuff. My mum and dad genuinely believed that they couldn't be happy with anyone else. And I knew that wasn't true for me. I could have been happy with Kazumi. Just as Kazumi could find the human bond we all seek with some other man. And just as Cyd could have found someone else to love her. That didn't make what I had with my wife feel like nothing. In some ways the knowledge that either of us could survive without the other made what we had seem even more precious. We stayed together because we chose to stay together.

In a world full of choices, we chose each other.

'There's the baby,' I told Eamon. 'That's the thing that really brought us back together. This baby we're bringing into the world. We are going to be a real family. Maybe we were already.'

He didn't look convinced. I knew he wanted certainty from me, cast-iron guarantees that love would last and marriage would endure.

But like my mum says – if you want guarantees, kid, buy a toaster.

'Listen, Eamon, the reason I'm still with my wife is not complicated. I'm with her because I love her.'

'Like you loved Kazumi? Or in a different way? A different kind of love, or exactly the same kind of love? I need to know. What if it had been the other way round, Harry? What if you had actually slept with Kazumi in Ireland? And you hadn't slept with your wife back in London? What – and this is the big one – what if the other woman was the woman carrying your baby?'

'Well, then –'

But I can't answer.

The chaos that lurks just beyond all of our front doors is sometimes best ignored.

All the other women I could love, all the other lives I could lead, all the babies waiting to be born – I just can't think about all of that today.

After all, I'm a married man.

The blood pressure was down. The hypertension was easing. The blood supply to my brain was not going to be cut off any time soon.

Good news, I thought. I want to see this baby grow up. I want to be around for long enough for this coming child to think that I am an old fool who doesn't know anything about life. I want to live long enough to see my youngest child become an adult. That was the plan now. That was my new ambition.

Increasingly, it felt like the only ambition really worth having.

'It's 135 over 75,' my doctor said. 'Not bad. Not bad at all. You're keeping your weight down . . . you don't smoke . . . Getting plenty of exercise?'

'Thirty minutes of cardiovascular, three times a week.'

'That's just about right. You don't want to overdo it. These days the gym is killing as many middle-aged men as cancer and heart disease. How's your salt intake?'

'Never touch the stuff.'

'Caffeine?'

'Well. Difficult to give up those cappuccinos. But I've cut right back.'

'Sometimes we have to stay away from the things we love, and learn to appreciate the things we need.'

And I saw my wife's face before me. The black hair cut in a China chop, the wide-set brown eyes, and the toothy smile, the little nicks of laughter lines that were starting to appear around her small, sweet mouth. That face so familiar, that face so loved.

'But what if they're the same thing? What if we realise that the things we love are the same as the things we need?'

My doctor grinned, packing her blood pressure kit away.

'Then you don't need me any more,' she said.

* * *

Peggy and I came through the gilded doors of the department store and were immediately assaulted by the perfume of a thousand different scents. The store was crowded, and we instinctively reached out and took each other's hand.

'Look, Harry – free manicure! They do your nails and you don't even pay nothing at all!'

'Maybe later, darling.'

We caught an escalator up to the department for children and babies.

So much had changed since the last time I became a father. Or perhaps Gina and I didn't have the money to go shopping for every baby aid on the market. But a lot of this stuff was completely new to me.

A baby bouncer – okay, I recognised that, and vividly recalled Pat bouncing up and down like a little toothless Buddha, baring his gums with delight. But a cot-rail teether to stop a baby gnawing its crib – when did they start selling that? And a car toy tidy – surely toys were still just chucked all over the back seat? And look at all this other gear – a Nature's Lullaby Baby Soother (plays four relaxing sounds to soothe baby to sleep), a Baby Bath Float (a soft cocoon shape to keep baby's head out of the water and its body floating safely near the surface).

And shampoo eye shields – protective glasses for hair washing. Now *that's* clever, now that's a brilliant idea. Pat could have done with some of those. And look at this – a suction bowl. A strong suction base to prevent spillage at mealtime. The twenty-first century baby doesn't even get to throw its food around.

'What will they think of next, Peg? Peggy?'

And that's when I realised she was gone.

The fear ran through me like a fever.

I searched all over the children's department, but she wasn't there. And I thought of her father, who had gone on honeymoon and never come back, who had broken Peggy's heart by going to live in Manila, to try his luck again on some other foreign shore, abandoning his child like she was nothing more than a bad debt.

Jim had deserted his daughter once and for all, and although it made life easier for me with him not around, his leaving had inflicted a wound on Peggy that she would carry for the rest of her life, a wound that would never heal, this beautiful child who deserved only to be loved.

And I wondered if I was really any different from him, any better than Jim, who always put his child way down on his list of priorities. Was I really a better man than that? Or so wrapped up in dreams of the new baby that I had forgotten about the reality of the living child by my side.

I searched the entire floor, doing frantic deals with God, praying for a second chance, desperately asking staff and shoppers if they had seen a small girl with a pink Lucy Doll backpack.

Then all at once I knew where I would find her.

She was on the ground floor, near those gilded doors, among the perfume of a thousand scents, patiently having her nails done for free in the make-up department.

'Hello, Harry,' she said. 'Did you find what you were looking for?'

'Hello, gorgeous. Yes, I think we've got everything now.'

The white-coated sales assistant beamed at the pair of us.

'What a beautiful daughter you have,' she said.

Peggy and I just smiled at each other.

There was a problem.

After eight weeks of the pregnancy, Cyd had some bleeding in the morning. And suddenly we didn't know if our stake in the future was going to be taken away from us.

When Cyd went for her scan, there was a silver bowl of condoms by the door, as delicately arranged as potpourri. Seeing the question mark hovering above my head, Cyd said that the condoms were for the instrument the obstetrician put inside her, so we could see the baby. To see if it was okay. To see if our baby was still alive.

'My word, you've had some strange things inside you, girl,' I said to my wife, taking her hand.

'But nothing quite as strange as your penis, Harry,' my wife said to me.

Later, when the obstetrician arrived, Cyd sat in this complicated chair, like something British Airways might have in First Class, and on the TV screen by her side the doctor showed us the small pulsating light that was the heartbeat of our unborn child. The baby was fine. The baby was still there. The baby was going to live. Nothing could stop this baby being born.

Cyd squeezed my hand without looking at me – we couldn't take our eyes from the screen – as the obstetrician showed us the head, comically large, like a light bulb made in heaven, and the tiny arms and legs, which the baby seemed to be crossing and uncrossing.

We laughed out loud, laughed with the purest joy at this miracle, this tiny miracle, the greatest miracle of all.

And I knew that this child would be loved like every child deserves to be loved, this baby who was our connection to the great unspoilt future, and our bond, our unbreakable bond, to what it means to be alive in this world, and – above and beyond it all – to each other.

thirty

When the weather was good and the sky was clear, my son and I lay on our backs in the garden of the old house, side by side, staring straight up, watching the stars come out.

Pat loved the stars now. Children change, they change so fast, they change even when you are looking at them. After watching a documentary that held him spellbound every Wednesday night for six weeks, Luke Skywalker and Darth Vader and Han Solo finally had to make some room in his expanding imagination for the Pole Star and Sirius and Vega.

'Dad?'

'What is it, darling?'

'Bernie Cooper says that the stars are all dead people looking down on us. And guess what? One of them, right? One of them is Bernie Cooper's granddad.' A pause. We kept staring up at infinity. Inside the house I could hear soft, female voices – my mother and one of the women who came to visit, wanting to talk, looking for their future. 'Is that true, Dad?'

'I'd like to think so, Pat.'

'Then what I'd like to know is – which one is *my* granddad?'

And I knew that my father would have loved this boy.

My dad would have loved watching Pat's new teeth coming through, loved his obsession with the stars, loved his devotion to his grandmother and Bernie Cooper and Britney the dog – newly arrived in the country, and settling in very nicely, amiably roaming around all those big London parks – loved the curious, open-hearted kid that my son was growing to be. Horses and stars. My son was enchanted by horses and stars, and my father would have been enchanted by that.

A hard man for as long as I could remember, the hardest man in the world, my dad had never seemed quite so hard after Pat was born. Perhaps that's what grandchildren are for – to allow you to give unconditional, unchanging love one last time. Something frozen deep inside my father began to thaw on the morning that Pat was born, and I knew that my dad would have continued to soften with the passing of the years, and with the coming of the new baby.

We just ran out of time, that's all.

'Pick the biggest star you can see,' I told Pat. 'Pick the brightest one. And that's your grandfather watching over you. And that's how you will always know.'

The stars are like photographs. You can read into them what you will. You can believe that they measure all you have lost, or you can believe that they represent all you have loved, and continue to love.

I guess I'm with young Bernie Cooper on that one.

As we watched the stars I thought of the twin babies that Gina had lost at ten weeks, the unborn children who would be with her always, the poor, tiny ghosts of her marriage.

And I thought of my own ghosts.

'Do you remember my friend Kazu?' Gina said one morning when I went to pick up Pat, Britney enthusiastically sniffing at my crutch, Gina still pale and drawn from her loss, and finally ready to tell me that she had known all along. 'She got married, Harry. Back in Japan. Kazu met the man of her dreams. She got stuck in an elevator with him in the Ginza. Just going for dinner, and there he was. Never can tell, can you? Never can tell when it's going to strike.'

It was a postcard from another life, a map of a road not taken. And I knew that I wanted for Kazumi exactly what my ex-wife wanted for me, what we all want for our former partners.

Happiness, but maybe not too much of it.

As I heard my son breathing by my side, watching the stars above, I thought of my three children.

The boy, the girl, the baby.

The two born, the one unborn.

I looked at the stars and thought of Peggy and Pat forming an orderly queue to feel Cyd's gently expanding belly, Peggy open-mouthed with awe as she tried to feel the baby's tiny, miraculous movements, and then, when it was his turn, Pat smiling secretly and murmuring to himself, 'Oh, the Force is strong in *this* one.'

Soon this modern family would be even more complicated, full of half-brothers and stepsisters and stepbrothers and half-sisters and step-parents and blood parents.

But now I finally saw that it was up to us if we felt like a real family or not. Nobody else mattered. The labels they stuck on us meant nothing at all.

There was a real family here if we wanted it. Anything else, well – as an old friend of mine used to say, it's all a bollock.

'Look at you two layabouts,' laughed my mum, padding into the garden, her last visitor gone home to her family. My mum swung a pink carpet slipper at a plastic football and sent it flying into my dad's rose bushes.

Our cosmic reverie broken, Pat and I got up to play three-goals-and-you're-in with my mum. It was getting quite dark now, one of the last days of an Indian summer, but the suburban night was soft and warm and starry, so we were reluctant to go inside.

And so we stayed out in the garden of the old house until we couldn't see to kick a ball, laughing in the gathering twilight, making the most of the good weather and all the days that were left, our little game watched only by next door's cat, and every star in the heavens.

Inside:

Our New Family:
Q & A with Tony Parsons

Exclusive extract from *My Favourite Wife*

Don't miss Tony's other books

Our new family: Q & A with Tony Parsons

***Man and Wife* is the sequel to *Man and Boy* – why did you feel the need to write a sequel?**

TP: I thought that the end of *Man and Boy* set up some interesting themes that were worth exploring. Harry is divorced and his son is living with his mother and her new partner. Harry's mum has lost her husband and has to face the future alone. And Harry is moving in with Cyd and her small daughter. I thought this looked like fertile ground, and I felt that these themes would make it quite a modern book because the idea of blended families would be at the heart of it. Harry's son is living with his mum and her new husband, Harry is living with his girlfriend and her daughter. The book would be about the post-nuclear family, the blended family. And also, when *Man and Boy* was clawing its way up the bestseller list, I noticed that a lot of the other books around were sequels – the second Bridget Jones book, a new Hannibal Lecter novel. So that encouraged me with the idea of a follow-up to *Man and Boy*, because I knew that the public were receptive to the idea of sequels. I guess you know what you're getting with a sequel. Or you think you do.

So there were commercial pressures to write a sequel to *Man and Boy*?

TP: Only the commercial pressures on following up any kind of major success. My agents and publishers were not encouraging me to write a sequel. It doesn't really work like that, which is strange in a way – publishing is a hard, competitive business, but at the heart of it are people who love books and who know that a novel has to come from the heart. That's not a hopelessly idealistic way to think, because anything that's done cynically or for the bottom line inevitably fails.

So what is the essential difference between *Man and Boy* and *Man and Wife*?

TP: I think that *Man and Wife* is a much more modern book, in that it reflects a society that's decimated by divorce, and full of all these blended families that are made up of what were originally other families. My parents never lived in a family like that, where they were living with a child who was not their own, or with a partner who was not the parent of their child, but I have. I was a single parent at an early age and any woman who came into my life had to deal with the fact that I had a small son. He wasn't going away. He was part of the package. And my son was a very sweet and cute little boy who was very easy to love. If anything, having him around was a bonus when it came to attracting the opposite sex. Much better than having a dog.

So being a single father or part of a blended family wasn't a painful experience for you?

TP: Ultimately it's always tough for a single parent because you feel like you are the last line of defence; that you are the only thing standing between your child and the world. That's quite a burden to carry around with you, and I think that single parents are heroes. All of them. I have nothing but love and respect and empathy for any single parent, whether they are a single father or a single mother. I had it easy as a single dad because my parents were still alive back then, and they were an enormous help. I am not sure how I could have coped without them because I didn't have the money to hire any help. So I never like to whine too loudly about being a single dad, because I know that I had it a lot easier than most single parents. My parents loved my son, and so did my girlfriends. In fact, they usually preferred him to me.

What about being part of a blended family?

TP: That's hard. And I think that it's hard for everyone. It's hard for the new person who comes in, it's hard for the child who has certainly not chosen this new person, and has no biological or emotional connection to them, and it's hard for the parent of the child because he or she loves both their child and their partner, and desperately wants them to get along. And sometimes they don't. There's not that easy, unthinking relationship that you get with your own children, and your own parents. The new addition in a blended family – didn't we used to call them step-parents? – have it hard because they can never really win. If they do not try to give the kid some sort of guidance, then they are called uncaring. But if they try to discipline a child who is not their child, then it can cause enormous resentment – from the child, and the child's parent. What a nightmare! Today I am back in a nuclear family with my wife and my daughter and it's just so easy when you don't have to think too much about how you treat each other. If you're living with a child who is not yours, then you constantly worry and wonder if you are being too soft, or too strict, or getting too involved, or not getting involved enough. Good step-parents are heroes too.

Is it easier to write a sequel than inventing the whole thing from scratch?

TP: It is easier in the sense that the characters already exist. But it can be restrictive because you are stuck in a world that you have already invented. I only attempted it because I felt there was a very different book waiting to be written. I just felt in my bones that *Man and Wife* could be sufficiently different from *Man and Boy* to be of interest to the reader and myself.

So what are the essential differences between *Man and Boy* and *Man and Wife*?

TP: *Man and Boy* was published in the twentieth century; *Man and Wife* was published in the twenty-first century. *Man and Boy* is about a man who lives with his wife and son, who has two living parents; a man who has never experienced loss – the loss of a loved one, the end of a marriage. The guy in *Man and Wife* is very different – his father is dead and he has an ageing mother. His marriage is over and he is struggling to maintain some sort of relationship with his ex-wife and to be a good dad to a son he doesn't live with. And he is in a relationship with a woman who already has a child, a broken marriage behind her, and wounds of her own. Nothing is simple any more. *Man and Boy* is a book about youth; *Man and Wife* is a book about experience. At the start of *Man and Boy*, Harry has that sense of immortality that we have when we are young – as though nothing can ever go wrong. It doesn't cross his mind that his marriage will end; he doesn't believe he will ever lose his parents. By the end of *Man and Wife*, he has learned about the fragility of all things, and how nothing is certain. And I think he has really learned to love by the end of the second book, and learned how to be loved. Both books are about Harry becoming a better father, a better husband, a better son. They are books about becoming a man.

How do you feel about the use of autobiography in fiction?

TP: I think you use it when you have to. The true story can be incredibly powerful – more powerful than anything. One of the reasons I love J.G. Ballard's *Empire of the Sun* is because I know he was very much like that little boy in Shanghai and the Japanese internment camp. Would that book have such power if he had made it all up? I don't see how it could have. But you have to make the personal into something universal – you don't use something simply because it is true. Everything has to be a slave to the story, a slave to the book. You use the truth when you need it, and you invent when that works better, and most of the time you are using elements of both. Ballard left his parents out of the second half of *Empire of the Sun* – in real life his mother and father were actually with him in the camp, but he felt it was somehow more psychologically true to leave them out, and to have the boy alone. I can understand that. In the end you use whatever it takes to tell your story. There are the facts, and then there's the truth, and they are not always the same thing.

Exclusive extract from *My Favourite Wife* – out now in paperback

He was ready for home.

The trip to Yangdong had left him with dirt on his shoes and stains on his suit and the urgent need to crawl into bed next to Becca and just hold her for a while. Or perhaps she could come to his bed and then they would not have to worry about waking Holly and they could do more than just cuddle.

But Jurgen and Wolfgang were in Shane's office when Bill was leaving, clearly agitated, expressing some concern in streams of German to each other, and broken English to their lawyer. Shane came out of his office and took Bill to one side.

'They're getting their lederhosen in a twist,' Shane sighed. 'Worried about what the hacks might write after today. Let's buy them a couple of drinks and calm their nerves, mate. Tell them we're all going to live happily ever after.'

'I've really got to get home,' Bill said. 'I don't see my wife. I don't see my kid.'

'One drink,' Shane said. 'They're your Germans too, mate.'

'All right,' Bill said. 'But just the one.'

There was an Irish bar on Tongren Lu called BB's – Bejeebers-Bejaybers – run by a large Swede with absolutely no Irish blood whatsoever.

BB's was always mobbed because you could get English football with Cantonese commentators from Star TV, Guinness on tap and live music by a band from Manila.

'You see them all over Asia,' Shane said, recovered from his hangover and ready for the night. 'These Filippino bands with singers who can really sing and musicians who can really play. Maybe in the West they would have a record deal, or at least appear on some television talent show. Out here they play dives for the likes of us.' He chugged down his Guinness and called for another. 'You see it all the time.'

Bill stared at him. Because what you didn't see all the time was Shane looking at a woman the way he was looking at the tiny Filippina singer who was leaning against her keyboard player's back and giving a pitch-perfect rendition of 'We've Only Just Begun' by the Carpenters. She tossed back her waist-length hair, jet black but shot through with blonde highlights, and when she smiled it seemed to light up every dark corner of Bejeebers-Bejaybers. A little further down the bar, Wolfgang and Jurgen sipped their Guinnesses and stared up at her, the press forgotten.

'Who is she?' Bill said.

'Rosalita,' Shane said with real tenderness. 'Rosalita and the Roxas Boulevard Boys.'

'You know her?' Bill asked. Shane looked as though he had thought about her a lot.

Shane looked at him. 'I see you with your wife,' he said, taking Bill by surprise. 'I see you with Becca. Saw you together at that dinner. And I envy you, Bill.' He turned his gaze back to the stage. 'It can't go on forever, can it? This life.'

Rosalita was doing an upbeat number now. She shook her hair, she flashed her luminous teeth, and she jiggled her tiny rump. The top of a lemon thong peeked above the waistband of her trousers, which were as tight as a wet suit. The Germans licked their lips.

'She's got a tattoo,' Shane confessed, watching Bill warily to see how he would react to this news.

Bill shrugged. 'Well, a lot of women have tattoos these days.'

'Yeah, but her tattoo says Tom.'

Bill thought about it. 'Who's Tom?'

'Some asshole,' Shane said, and a cloud of depression seemed to pass across his face. 'She says Tom was just some asshole.'

The Roxas Boulevard Boys brought it back to a more romantic gear – Lionel Ritchie's 'Penny Lover' – and Rosalita tipped forward as if with an unendurable melancholy, her hair falling over her face. Shane sighed. And then, over the mournful minor chords, Bill heard the sound of expatriate whooping and jeering, the sound of men urging a woman on. He turned to look.

There were five of them, white boys in suits, surrounding her, the one, the tall girl he had seen with the orchid in her hair outside Paradise Mansions, although the flower was gone now, and they were all out on the tiny BB's dance floor.

She seemed to be in a daze, dancing alone to some song in her head, her eyes closed and her arms held high above her head, and their hands were all over her: the tall girl, with a scrape high on one cheekbone, as if she had been struck.

'Come on, darling,' one of the men said, tugging at the button of her trousers. 'Show us what you got.'

Another one was behind her. A young man, but already run to fat. His hands on her buttocks, her breasts, biting his bottom lip as he mimed taking her from behind, to the huge amusement of his laughing friends.

They moved in closer, getting bolder now, one of them pulling down the zip of his trousers, and then the zip of her trousers, another yanking up her cut-off top so that you saw a glimpse of a black bra. The girl didn't notice or she was too far gone to care. Then Bill was wading among them, shoving off the fat boy behind her, and then getting between the girl and the suit who had pulled down her zip, and their expressions changed from leering delight to bewilderment, then apoplectic rage.

As Bill took the tall girl by the arm and led her from the dance floor, one of them threw a punch at the back of his head. He caught it just below the base of the skull, turned and took another one on his ear. He threw a couple of punches but they were all over him, pushing each other out of the way for the chance to lash out at him.

But then Shane was there, meaty fists flying, and then there were Wolfgang and Jurgen doing these surprisingly authentic-looking side-kicks, and then the Swedish owner and a lad from Belfast who worked behind the bar were joining in, putting themselves between Bill and the girl and the five drunken suits. A full-scale brawl broke out for about five seconds and then it was over as quickly as it had begun and the suits were running to the back of BB's, throwing around a few bar stools as they retreated.

Bill held the tall girl's hand as Shane got them out of the club and into the back of a Santana taxi. 'Just go,' he said. The cab pulled away and she still hadn't opened her eyes. He saw that the wound on her cheekbone was livid and fresh.

'Did they do that to you?' he said. 'The mark on your face. Did those bastards do that to you?'

She leaned forward, touching her face. Then she sat back up, fighting back the sickness. Bill realised he had never seen anyone so hopelessly drunk.

'Airbag,' she said. 'The airbag from my Mini.'

Then they had to stop by the side of the road so that she could be sick. She bent double out of the open back door, dry heaving because there was nothing left to bring up. The driver watched Bill in his rear-view mirror with barely concealed contempt.

Fucking Westerners, his eyes seemed to say. Ruining our lovely girls.

'Can't stop throwing out,' she said when they were on the road again. 'Please excuse me. I am throwing out all the time.'

Her English was almost perfect. Too clearly learned in a classroom, perhaps. Too painfully formal. But she got almost everything right, he realised, and when she did get something wrong, he still had no trouble understanding her. Didn't throwing out make more sense than throwing up? It was an improvement on the original.

'You had an accident,' Bill said. 'What happened?'

She exhaled, shivering with grief.

'My husband is very angry with me,' she said. 'Very angry with me for breaking the new car.'

He took off his jacket and wrapped it around her thin shoulders. She burrowed down inside it, trying to hide from the world, and he patted her gently, the way he might try to reassure Holly if she had a bad dream. And then she fell asleep. Leaning against him. He patted her again.

He looked at her asleep in his jacket and he saw that it was the one that still bore the ghost of a handprint.

That's never going to come out now, he thought.

Don't miss Tony's other books ➔